DAVVD ONG

OF THE

GALACTIC SPACE FLEET

BY

LEO STURMAN

Strategic Book Group

Strategic Book Group
P.O. Box 333
Durham CT 06422
www.StrategicBookClub.com

ISBN: 978-1-60976-704-4

The Fleet cruiser *Lotus Breath* hung a curve around the planet Leonardo and then settled into an orbit of the moon Beebop. Beebop was an unlovely moon both in appearance and temperament, and it was named because of its variations in spin. To say that it wobbled would be close to describing its journey round the planet. It had a green atmosphere with dark, swirling clouds of noxious gases; it was unpleasant to look at from a distance and worse from closer up.

The armed force, crammed into the shuttle that would drop them onto the surface, were unable to see anything much except each other, bathed as they were in the red glow of the lighting in the hold. They were encased in battle armor and held in their metal seats by electromagnets. The last thing anyone wanted was to become a missile while armed with a photon cannon and a handgun. They had a grenade at each breast, which added to their strange and bizarre appearance. Their helmets were already closed and sealed against mishap.

Captain Ong was listening to the voices. Most of them were muttering about "shit." Everything was shit. The service was shit; this assignment was shit; and the result would be shit. He let them carry on. It was merely nerves, and he felt the same. Beside him, Sergeant Kruft was making deep breathing noises, and he heard her say something about "Linda," but he ignored that. Kruft was a hard-nosed combat soldier, and she could hold her own anywhere. She was Ong's buddy on this trip, and he trusted her to do what she had to do. She had a reputation for being hard and efficient, and he was pleased to know she would be there.

The shuttle did a turn that made the bile rise; atmosphere screeched on the hull; the lights turned green; the magnetic straps were gone; the floor opened up; and they fell out onto the surface of the moon. It was a surface that had little surface. It was mud and rotting vegetation, and visibility was short. The landscape bubbled from the gases within, and strange growths reared up like grasping fingers. Even with the totally enclosed suit, there was a smell like a sewer in heat.

"Right, you mules, get together and take a line from me and Kruft. Straight ahead. You can see the light of the beacon. That's where we are going, so let's go!"

Kruft was slightly ahead of him when something reared out of the dung. It was huge and had a white underbelly, and it had a mouth big enough to swallow a cow. Ong had one thought: How the hell did a Valderian slime worm get to Beebop? Then it went pear shaped. Kruft had the cannon raised but didn't fire it, and he heard her make a noise like a primeval wail as the worm reared over her and sucked her into its maw. To the left of him he was aware of cannon fire and worms blowing apart, but he was suddenly very much alone. He raised the cannon and then hesitated. If he blew the worm apart, he would blow Kruft apart with it. He dropped the cannon down beside his leg, and the worm leant over and sucked him up. His head hit boots. He was being squeezed by the gullet of the worm, and the boots were kicking. Inside the helmet, he grinned and then fired the cannon down between his boots. The charge blew the worm's head apart, and the percussion stunned him, but he and Kruft were spewed out of the mangled corpse and were wallowing in the deep slime and shit of lovely Beebop. He was aware that she was swearing and sobbing, so he knew she was alive. He tried to raise contact with the rest of the platoon, but there was noise and confusion. He just hoped they had done what they were supposed to do.

He woke up in the sick bay of the *Lotus Breath* feeling sick and disorientated. He wondered what had happened to Kruft.

The admiral paced slowly about the office and watched his assistant sort paper and make notes. She was a young captain, very smart and slim, and had been chosen for her looks and figure. She knew exactly why she had been chosen; to make life easier for the "old man," and she didn't mind. He wasn't exactly demanding sexually and was very discreet, and she quite liked his wife. This job was a step up to higher rank; she knew it and he knew it, and they played the game as if it had rules like standing orders. She bent over the desk and put the recorders on, and he couldn't resist running his hand over the tight skirt that covered her backside. She let him stroke her curve for a few seconds, and then she slipped away.

"Everything is here and ready, sir."

"I can see it is, Captain, but we have a meeting, don't we?"

"We may have time later for what you have in mind, but you have Davvd Ong outside, and it would be better if you didn't keep him waiting, sir."

He grumbled but knew that Davvd Ong wasn't someone to fool with. His family owned half the wealth of this side of the galaxy, had influence in high places because they were the influence in high places. The Ong Dynasty was bigger than anything Fleet could poke a stick at, and the admiral knew it. His one thought was that Davvd Ong had better things to do than play soldier boy. All right, the man had won more medals than an Olympic champion, was the pinup boy in all the girly media, so what was he doing soldiering with Fleet?

Captain Sonna had let him in and was smiling. The admiral had to admit that Davvd Ong was personable. He was tall and had the build that suggested hard workouts and fast sprints. He had a scar above his left eyebrow just large enough to look like it was a war wound but just small enough to not appear too nasty, and his voice had a hint of culture that went way back. He was a man who inspired respect regardless of rank, and the admiral knew he had to be cautious. They all sat. Davvd refused a drink. Captain Sonna gave the admiral a file, and the wheels began to roll. It was about the slime worms on the Beebop moon and the implications of that. Fleet had found out that the slime worms had been transported to Beebop. The beacon that directed the battlewagons of Fleet was going to be made a pile of wreckage. The Valderians were denying all knowledge of an attack. The worms had eaten half the staff and had undermined the tower, but they hadn't put the worms on there. The admiral had his doubts, but as the Valderians had pointed out, all it took to start

3

a colony of worms was to drop a bucket of spawn in the right environment, and away they went. Ong's party had eliminated the worms, poisoned anything that looked like spawn, and had set up a monitor to warn of anything like a worm in the future. As the admiral pointed out, if the Valderians had succeeded in knocking out the beacon, any number of its ships could pass through that portal without detection and could be anywhere this side of Fleet-controlled space.

The admiral, having set that part of the record straight, now led on to the debriefing. He wanted to know what had gone wrong when Kruft was swallowed by the worm, closely followed by Ong. It was hard to say. They had the infrared and the ultraviolet and the sonic scans and the holograms from the shuttle, and it was all there. Kruft saw the worm. Kruft froze. Kruft was a highly trained combat officer. She was a weapons expert. She was a decorated soldier. She knew her stuff. They watched again as she froze, and the scenario of Davvd Ong going in after her ran through. The admiral knew a lot of brave men and women. He was no slouch himself, but he wondered just what it took to stand and allow oneself to be swallowed by something out of a pit of vomit without going mad. He shuddered when he saw it happen, but Sonna was moist-eyed.

"Captain Ong, I know I shouldn't say this in this meeting, but that was one hell of a thing to do, to go in there after Sergeant Kruft, not knowing if she was alive or not and not knowing if you were going to get out either."

Davvd coughed and huffed a bit. "Well, it wasn't all gung ho, really. Slime worms have no teeth, and they have a huge throat. They toss down prey, and then they squeeze it together with internal muscles. We had on battle armor, which will withstand a lot, and I mean a lot of stress. I gambled that Kruft wasn't dead, and that if I acted pretty sharply I could get her out. The only way to do that was to follow her in. The worm obliged. I had the cannon pointing back and down, and when Kruft started kicking me in the head I figured it was time to get out of there."

The admiral coughed. "Better you than me, Captain Ong! I throw up just seeing those things here on the screen."

"Where is Sergeant Kruft now, Captain?" said Sonna.

Ong looked a little shy. "Well, she is in base hospital with cracked ribs and mild concussion, thanks to me. The cannon has one heck of a sonic boom, as you know, and the worm had got her far enough down to put the squeeze on her more than me. I am going in to see her when you have finished with me, sir."

They waved him away. The admiral just knew that Davvd Ong was going to collect another decoration after the top brass had seen what he had seen today. Captain Sonna was thinking that maybe she could get a posting closer to the wonder boy if she played her cards right, but the admiral could read her like a book.

"Stay away from Davvd Ong, sweetheart. You may not have all the excitement you want here, but it's a heck of a lot safer than his side of the street."

Kruft was sedated. Her ribs hurt, but she was tough physically and would heal quickly. The mental side of her was being twisted. The medication was making her dream, and she was going back to her childhood. The med psychs had her wired up. Lights were chasing each other across screens. Records were being kept. A nurse came in.

"You will feel better soon."

"What are you doing to my head?"

"It's called a regression probe. We look back at your past, that's all."

"So you can find an excuse to court-martial me for freezing up on Beebop, right?"

"Who said you were dumb, Kruft."

"Why don't you ask me?"

"People lie about things like that, and we have to go back and forth. This way is quicker. When we come across something, and the professionals have analyzed it, you will be off the hook, maybe"

"Sweet dreams, Sergeant." She went out and closed the

curtains. Kruft felt as if she was sliding down a steep slope into a black pit.

The sun was shining, and the lake was blue and reflected the even bluer mountains in the distance. She was with Rory, her younger brother. She was fourteen and wearing the new polka-dot bikini her mother had bought her for her birthday. Rory wanted to go fishing. They found a couple of rods and dug worms for bait. When it became too hot to just fish, they swam in the shallow water and then lay on the big towels to dry off. Her stepbrothers, Morgan and Hunt, were diving off the limb of the ancient oak near the water's edge, making splashes and roaring at each other. She had never liked them, and when her mother had re-married Carl, she had felt lost and alone. Rory was too young to feel it the way she did, but she was afraid of their aggression, masculinity and lack of sensitivity. When she could, she chose to stay clear of them. Morgan was sixteen and Hunt fourteen. Strong and hard, they were like her stepfather, sports all over.

Rory was shivering. "I'm going up to the house. Are you coming?"

She waved him away. "I'm working on my tan."

He laughed and ran off up the path. She closed her eyes and let the sun warm her face. Her closed eyes registered a shadow. Morgan was standing very close.

"Hey sister, what are you doing?"

"Getting a tan." She sat up. There was a feeling in the air she couldn't quite identify. Morgan was looking at her in a way she didn't like.

"Well, if you really want a tan you need to get that top off, sister. Get your tits brown too."

She put her arms across her chest.

"Get away from me, Morgan."

"Hey, just being friendly. You got nice tits, you know that? Show me your tits, Mary. No one to see us here. Hunt is up at the house."

She started to stand up to run away, but he grabbed her and pulled her down and tore the top off her breasts.

"See how nice they are. Oh yes, very nice." He was lying across her and feeling her breasts, and she was suddenly very afraid. She had to fight back, but he was very strong and had her head in the crook of his

6

left arm, while his right hand was between her legs. She screamed, but he choked it off. She hit out at his face with her fists, groped for dirt beside the towel, and flung it in his eyes. He hit her with the flat of his hand across her face, twice, very hard and her head rang with the force of the blow. He threw her down hard on her back, winding her.

"Stupid bitch."

The can of worms had toppled in the struggle. He scooped the worms up with one hand and sat hard on her stomach, and then as she tried to scream once more he pushed them into her open mouth, forcing them down her throat. She vomited, and he stood over her.

"You should be nice to me, Mary; like, I am your brother. We could have real fun together, you know that?"

Davvd Ong sat beside the bed. The nurse had fussed around him, brought him coffee. Kruft was coming out of the deep probe hypnotic state. She was free of wires and sensors, and her face was pale under the outdoor tan that all Fleeters had. There were flowers in a vase and a card he couldn't read. She knew he was there. Had seen him coming in but had closed her eyes like a child who pretends to be invisible. He made appropriate noises and then felt for her hand. It startled her to feel his warm hand on hers, and she jerked her eyes open.

"Sorry, Captain, my head isn't straight yet."

"You are looking pretty good. How're the cracked ribs?"

"You just want to make me laugh and see me cry, right Captain?"

"Something like that."

She grimaced. "You didn't have to come in after me, did you?"

"Well, I didn't have time to ask it to open wide so I could pull you out, Kruft. I had to make a quick decision, that's all."

"Yeah, they'll give you another medal and me a court-martial, right?"

"What makes you say that?"

"They'll have the scans from the dim Kruft past, Captain, and they'll find something to hang on me for sure. You'll see it; the brass will see it; and I'll be declared a coward. So don't tell me I'm wrong."

"Whoa, I haven't seen anything yet, but it wasn't just you, Kruft, feeling like you had just run into your worst nightmare. I nearly wet myself when that thing came out of the mud, but I had you in front of me, remember? Okay, so we didn't do it by the manual, but we got rid of it. We achieved the mission. We lost seven; you know that? They were either crunched or drowned. We saved the beacon; we got back home; and we survived another mission."

"That sounds a lot like Fleet, sir."

"Sorry, I didn't mean it to. That's what comes of doing reports that have to sound that way; you know that."

"Yeah, I know Fleet." The silence was a little too long.

"Look, I know you. You are the last person who would freeze. There had to be a reason."

"I like and respect you, Captain, so if you don't mind, whatever you think did or didn't happen, I don't want to talk about it, all right? You and me are going to be sitting in a hearing or courts-martial or whatever they dream up, and you are going to give evidence, and if I open my big mouth you are going to be forced to tell them about it. So, however much I trust you, let's leave it there, sir."

He shook his head. "Boy, did I hit the wrong note!"

"Can you do me a favor, sir?"

He recognized the change of subject and welcomed it. "Sure, if I can."

"My partner, Linda Costa, Sergeant Costa, she is on Mars in the Fleet hospital, Dome three, you know; she is a nurse. She got transferred just before we hit Beebop. They won't let me make a call from here. Okay. Don't look at me that way. Linda and I have been together for three years. It just isn't the news you spread around base; you know what I mean? Are you shocked, Captain?"

He laughed.

"Mary Kruft, is there anything that goes on around the base

that everyone doesn't know? I have guys telling me what color the admiral's underpants are and what his ADC wears underneath that tight skirt. Sorry, but your romance was way down the priority list, and if I can say so, if you are happy, then that's fine with me! Let's face it; there are a lot of hard men on this base with cuddle bunny boys, so you are not alone."

"How about you, Captain?"

"Well, since we are into show and tell, you would know I was married and that she died. All the holos and tri-dees made a meal of it. No, I ain't got nobody. I don't get much chance of meeting anyone without the media sticking a 3-D camera in my face. Now you know why I like Fleet. I can go off somewhere with a bunch of uniforms front and back, and no one asks for my autograph. He gestured over his shoulder. Outside the glass there were a dozen lenses pointing at them. "See you on the news, Kruft. Just get well and don't worry. We'll work something out."

There was no inquiry. Kruft was transferred to Mars as an instructor, and Linda did much to ease her recovery.

They gave Ong another medal that he threw in the drawer with the others. There was no one to appreciate it other than himself. His father often said, "Rank can enslave you. Rise too high and someone will say he used his family influence to get there. Be your own man, be proud of the family name, and be content with that. You know that we are proud of you."

Maggda Styxx was in her boss's office on the thirty-fourth floor of the Media Tower on Mars, Dome Eight.

Dome Eight was the center of culture on Mars. It was haute couture, art, music, and theatre. The Martian Symphony Orchestra played across the galaxy. The Media Tower was Maggda's world. She stood with her back to the airlock door, and when she heard the hiss of air balancing pressure, she turned and saw Simon, her boss. He was young by executive standards. She guessed at forty-five ESYs, but it was hard to tell. Interplanetary travel played hell with time zones, so ESY was the only constant. An Earth Standard

Year had a basic solidity to it. Age wasn't something one spoke about much. The slim, vibrant girl on the tri-dee show might well be seventy ESYs, but with enough credits . . .

"You get younger, Maggda?"

"Beware of the man dishing out compliments."

"I meant to say that you are as beautiful as the day we first met."

She sat and crossed her legs, giving him ample opportunity to look at them. "All right, I like that. Now what is it I have to do?" She was hoping this meeting was going to lead to something better than her interviewing a sand jockey or the latest Old Earth chef at the Epicurean complex.

"What do you know about Davvd Ong, Maggs?"

She hated that nickname but said nothing. "Career soldier with Fleet. Much medaled, much admired. Starred on Beebop recently. Very brave, resourceful. Ong family dynasty. Doesn't have to stick his neck out. Was married to Su Lin Wu, who was killed along with his father and mother in a shuttle accident on Minerva? Yeah, Minerva. He wasn't there but was supposed to be going with them. Ong family, almost a secret society as far as the press goes, but it's all there. Just press a button, Simon. So why all this?"

"What will you say if I could get you an interview with Davvd Ong.?"

She laughed. "Now, Simon, you and I know that Davvd Ong doesn't give interviews. Fleet won't allow him to do that because he is a serving officer, apart from the constraints that are put on him from the family lawyers. He hasn't spoken to the press since his family was wiped out. How could you swing that?"

He smiled again. "How would you like a first-class return trip to Alpha Six on the *Double Happiness*, Maggs?"

"Look, Simon, you know I like and trust you, but this has to be bullshit. Any cabin on that starliner would cost more than three years of my paychecks, including bonuses. So where does Captain Ong fit into this?"

"Have a drink. It makes the eyes water."

She sipped her drink, and it made her eyes water in an interesting way.

"I have it on the best authority that Davvd Ong is going out to Alpha Six on the *Double Happiness*. It picks up passengers here. Davvd Ong will be on it. He will be travelling as one 'David Essex,' businessman from Fleet Metals. Both of those exist. There is a David Essex and Fleet Metals. I have this information on the best authority."

"Did this come off the back of a buckwheat packet or what? If this stuff is that secret, no one would be handing it out."

"We pay for information. Say we had a clerk working in Fleet who hacked into the coded messages and sold that to us and takes the risk."

"Of losing his life, Simon. Anyone who crosses Fleet is a dead man or going to spend a very long time on a penal colony on a very bad planet. I'll bet that bit of gossip doesn't even mention Ong, does it?"

"No, but it mentions David Essex. Essex is on Old Earth trying to pull off a deal over bauxite. It doesn't take much to make David Essex into Davvd Ong, does it?"

"This is madness, Simon. Why doesn't Ong just take off on a Fleet cruiser and zip off into hyperspace? Who would know?"

"We think that he is going incognito to avoid publicity. Right now he is hot after Beebop, and we also think that Fleet is sending him off undercover somewhere."

"He could just be slipping off on family business or on leave, couldn't he?"

"Maybe, but this is a golden opportunity for you to corner him so he can't run off. Where would he hide on a starliner?"

"So what next? I am still underwhelmed, Simon."

He slid across a rectangle of gold and blue plasticard with the Ong crest on it. "First-class return on the *Double Happiness* to Alpha Six."

"All right, so you are serious. Now what, and if you say, 'sleep with me', the deal is off."

"As if I would, Maggda. Right, you go first class, and you take all the nano stuff and the recorders, and then you get pictures, and you get him to talk. You get a first-class trip; we get a very exclusive story. We all make lots of credits, and everyone is happy."

"How am I going to get close to the hero of the hour, Simon? Knowing Fleet, he will have a couple of very hard men trying to look like potted palms, just waiting to crunch anyone who gets too near."

"That's why we are sending a very beautiful woman to tempt him to talk. We don't think he will have security with him because it would attract too much attention, and if he is going as Essex, he would be alone anyway."

"Clothes?"

"We can give you an open order at Maxxi's. You love that stuff. Get us the exclusive story, and we'll pay the bills. Come back without it, and we'll be docking your pay for the next ten ESYs."

"Credits?"

"You can have the usual expenses, so don't go overboard."

"Simon, I am the little rich girl on a cruise, and I will have to spend. Double the allowance; starliners aren't cheap."

"Get the story, and you can have a big bonus. Double allowance and keep the receipts. I have a business to run."

Customs asked a lot of questions about the recording equipment, the mini holos stuff, and the nanotech equipment, and she was pleased she had her Galactic staff ID. She was on assignment and felt good. Being seated on the shuttle made her feel nervous again. She hated that take-off, the almost vertical climb, and the high g-forces that were all over in no time but which made her feel green. Then it was a clang and bang docking and she staggered down the chute into *Double Happiness* along with the other pale-faced passengers. The starship was an older Ong liner. It reeked of a stylistic yesterday, but wealth and good taste had been preserved in the real wood, the gilded furniture, the deep pile carpets, the opulent bathroom in her suite, and the huge bed. She climbed upon it like a drowning man onto a raft and slept.

Double Happiness cleared the planetary influence and boosted, then located the beacon and made the first jump towards Alpha Six. Maggda lay awake, thinking of where she was and what had been, childhood on Mars—dome life, and lava tubes. Her father the gold miner and her mother, the doctor at the mining company hospital, mending broken bones and injuries from cave-ins. She was a leggy, willowy teenager, and smart. They sent her to a good school and expected a life in metallurgy or medicine. Her parents paid for a course in modeling in Paris on Old Earth, and her career took off.

She was the face and the figure that made anything she modeled a best seller. She was asked to model a revolutionary underwear collection, and she signed up and made a fortune but suddenly had the thought that showing her all to anyone and everyone wasn't really what she wanted to do.

She came back home, walked into the Galactic Media offices, and they gave her a bad contract, but they trained her, and Simon Brent was an honest broker. She worked and learned.

Now she was on *Double Happiness* and wondering what to do next.

Davvd Ong had boarded the starship via the back door the night before it left for Alpha Six. A small Fleet shuttle had shipped him aboard with his gear, and he had slipped onto the vessel without fuss. Only the captain and the first officer knew he was there.

The admiral had called him in, offered him a drink, and he had refused.

"You are officially on leave after the Beebop fiasco, but we need a man to go to E5 to just find out what, if anything, is going on down there. You'll be bound to get some R & R on the ship, but you will get dropped off as it stops for a 're-alignment' by E5. Do you know much about E5?"

"A naturalist moon, no humans in residence. Monitored by robots and serviced by them. Data uploaded with an occasional scientist dropping by with permission from Ong Wu Foundation. Devoted to the preservation and breeding of a whole gang of endangered species, including flora. Lots of them now off the lists and being returned to their home planets. Some exotic species."

"Didn't someone introduce giant cave bears and mammoths?"

"And even the odd dinosaur or two. I think they had a period when it was scientifically fashionable to just show it could be done."

"I am supposed to be going fishing with my uncle, you know that?"

"Plenty of fishing down on E5, if you can get a permit."

"So what's so important that you send me, when there are a thousand scientists who would love to get there?"

"The robots discovered an animal that had been killed and slaughtered. Not another predator kill but one that involved very sharp knives. The thought is that there are humans on the moon hunting the game."

"So?"

"What are they doing there? Slipped onto the moon and not been observed and no permission from the Foundation, which, I might add, has asked us to send someone to sniff the dung and find out."

"First I get Beebop, and now I get dung on E5?"

"Shouldn't take you long. It is close to the research center complex. Go and tell us what you find, report back here, go on leave. Simple and we don't raise a media dust storm or wild speculation."

"What is really behind this?"

"Off the record, we think that these may be another planetary expedition, testing to see what's down there worth taking over, or maybe someone planted these, whatever they are, down there on purpose. You go find the purpose; Ong and Wu will be happy; Fleet will be happy; and we keep everything quiet."

"About a couple of weeks?"

"Maybe a week. Get smart and get back."

"So I get what to back me up? Laser rifle, or sonic cannon, or missiles?"

"You get a couple of stun guns, and that's it. It's a non-weapon moon. Kill anything and you get into trouble, you know that."

"What if it tries to kill me?"

"You should be used to that. That's what you got all those medals for, remember?"

"This had better be easy, sir, or I quit."

"C'mon, Davvd. Do some fishing and some fishing for Fleet, get a tan, come back here, and then go on real leave."

Maggda circulated like a shark around a reef looking for her prey. She had a small holo of David Essex. Davvd Ong everyone could recognize. First class was a bare board. No Ong there. She spoke to one of the few human stewards.

He consulted his pod.

"We have a passenger called David Essex listed as being on 'C' class. I have no cabin listed. You would have to ask the purser for that."

She gave him twenty credits and watched him leave. Ask the purser and stir up curiosity? Better just prowl C class, Maggda. Her search paid off in a C-class restaurant where she found him hiding behind a palm tree that had ancestors in the Jurassic and in a booth that had ever changing holos on the panels of Old Earth, dust storms on Mars, and the planets that *Double Happiness* visited. She sat at the bar for a while until she was sure she had the right man and then drifted over to his table. She was wearing a Maxxi dress that revealed enough of her breasts to leave little to the imagination and was almost transparent from mid-thigh level. If that didn't get his attention, nothing would.

She held out a hand. "David Essex?"

He looked up at her and smiled. It made his moustache slip a little, and he fixed it with a finger.

She held out her ID card. "Maggda Styxx."

"Yes. The face and the form for Second Skin underwear. It made how many millions in ten days? So what's this journalist angle? You want to talk to me?"

"May I sit?" He waved her to a chair.

"Can I be frank? Now you and I know that David Essex is somewhere on Old Earth playing games with the Chinese who want more zinc or whatever, and he can supply it if the Martian Conglomerate gets its backside into gear."

He smiled and had to adjust the moustache again. "So?"

"We had a tip-off that you would be on this ship. I am supposed to track you down and get an interview. My boss has promised me a huge bonus if I can do it."

"Sorry, but it wouldn't do you any good, Maggda. Anything you record on here will get wiped when you go through the departure gates. I really would like to say yes, but I can't."

"Davvd Ong pleads helplessness because Fleet has him by the short and curlies. Am I right?"

"Right."

"They have you that close?"

"You'd better believe it."

"Buy me a drink?"

The android waiter came over.

"What are you drinking?"

She sat back in the chair. "I don't know what it is called, but it makes the eyes water, so make it a large one."

"Two of whatever it is."

She told him her story, and he told her nothing.

"That scar on your forehead, if I was a scar designer for heroes that would have to be the one I'd pick."

The drink was very strong, and she began to feel it taking effect.

"You want to hear how I got this scar? You want all the gory details of how I got this in a hand to hand with the rebel leader on Backpakk Four? How I fended off a star blade and knocked the teeth in of the guy who nearly killed me?"

"You got that on Backpakk Four?"

"Nah. I was a kid trying to jump ten steps and a garbage bin on my hover board, and I missed."

She laughed."Boy, your reputation would suffer if that came out."

"Now you know why I don't give interviews."

The drink was getting to her, and she felt warm. He could see her feeling the effects.

"You want to dance with me, Maggda?"

There was a dance band playing ancient music that included Latin American smoochiness, and she was led out onto the floor, where she clung to him. "Just hold me and don't let me fall over and none of the wild spinning about stuff, all right?"

"I promise."

They danced, and she felt his warmth. He just couldn't ignore her body next to his, and he led her off the floor. "Was it something I said?" she asked.

"I haven't had a beautiful woman in my arms for Aton knows how long, Maggda, and you are beautiful, and you do things to me I might regret. I am going to walk you to your room and put you inside and close the door, and I suggest you lock it. I might get the urge to come knocking, and you might let me in."

"At least kiss me goodnight, Ong. I think I'm worth that."

With Maggda safely out of his hair he headed for the bowels of the liner. He had much to do, but the tiny bug she had slipped under his collar as they danced was a beacon for her to follow. His supplies had come aboard with him but were down on the escape pod level. He dodged the robot loader that was filling the hold of pod twenty-five and climbed the ladder to the bunkroom above. His scanner informed him there were only work clothes and boots to come aboard. He looked at his time band and saw there wasn't going to be much time. *Double Happiness* would rendezvous with E5 that night, and he wanted nothing left undone. He made his way back to his cabin and packed a duffel bag.

Maggda had traced him to C-deck escape pod level and watched him go in and out of pod twenty-five. She saw that there were two number twenty-fives and wondered. Then it occurred to her that to have one missing wasn't a good thing if one were trying to evade the curious. A loader appeared with a bundle of what looked like clothing, but it was dimly lit in the pod level, and she couldn't be sure. She waited until it backed out and then squeezed past the packages and into the hold. Then she heard boots on the plating and went into a mild panic. There was only one way to go, and that was up. She climbed the ladder into the bunkroom. Four bunks in two tiers and there was just enough room on the uncluttered one to squeeze under and pull a couple of boxes under with her. The boots advanced; then a body sat on the bunk and pinned her down. The boots were taken off and tidily put together at the end of the bed, and the body lay down on the bunk. She knew she wasn't going anywhere right then. The light was turned off, and she dared not move. She felt him get comfortable, and she pulled a heavy overall from the bed end and tucked it quietly as she could around her. It wasn't spider-silk sheets, but it would have to do. She waited and hoped she didn't snore or sneeze.

The captain watched the charts and said to the first officer, "Make a tight orbit around E5. When we reach the coordinates, I want a gentle stop; we'll drop our bundle and gently move back on course."

The pod slid down the rails, dropped into the chute, and fell. The maneuver completed, "pod away" came and went. Maggda was feeling very sick as it veered and the landing thrusters came into play. Through a vicious jet stream, another violent plunge, and then a savage braking as the pod settled in the long grasses of a beautiful meadow. The sun was hidden by clouds, but the air was pristine, birds sang, and Aton smiled. Maggda was cheerfully sick under the bunk. Ong had left at touchdown. He had put on his boots when the pod left the starliner, and as soon as the ramp came down he had grabbed his duffle and was gone.

She felt weary and sore and had a mouth like the dung pits on New Babylon. She wanted water. She staggered down a slope to a stream coursing down between high banks, and she virtually fell into it. She scooped water into her mouth with two hands and felt better. Her expensive Maxxi boots just had to suffer. She went back and grabbed her bag with the recording devices of all shapes and tiny sizes, and launched the little dragonfly probe, which picked up the bent and crushed grass and heat spots left by Ong's footsteps. They led down the bank and onto the gravel of a "beach." She followed the probe down, and then it lost contact, which made her swear. Her feet were wet, and she was hungry, and now she had lost him. Behind her she heard the clatter of machinery, and a battered loader appeared above the meadow and came down close to the pod. A robot sled began to ferry goods out of the pod and stack them neatly. She continued down the side of the stream and looked for footprints, and there they were, on the other side leading to a fissure in the rocks. The sky had become darker. The loader clattered away and then came back. It was clearing the contents of the pod quickly.

Lightning flashed beyond the tree line behind her, and thunder followed. It began to rain, quite heavily. She crossed the stream and peered into the fissure. It appeared to be larger than she first thought. She hesitated, and the rain pelted down, soaking her. She went into the fissure, dragging her bag, and called her drone back. It was dark, but the gap became wider; she felt a violent zap and let out a scream. Light flooded the area. She was aware of two neon-like eye cells attached to a large robot made of polished plas-steel, and it was extending a hand. She backed away, but the voice was calm. "Forgive me, miss, but it would be better if you took my hand and came inside. The rocks here are quite slippery, and the mud is caused by Master Davvd not wiping his feet. We have the entrance guarded by a simple electronic fence because animals find the cavern attractive, and we have to deter them as best we can without injury. Do come inside."

She felt a little hysterical. Above her was darkness, but the rest of the cavern was bathed in blue light. It was larger and more complex than she imagined.

"Captain Ong. Where is Captain Ong, please?" She felt that this was the kind of robot one said please and thank you to.

"Master Davvd is supervising the unloading of the stores, miss. Does he expect you to come in this entrance?"

It wasn't a question she was prepared for, so she ducked. "My name is Maggda Styxx, and I am a friend of Captain Ong. And what is your name?"

"Don, miss, my name is Don. You arrived just in time. When we get storms, the river rises very swiftly and carries everything away with it. How long have you known Captain Ong?"

"Well, Don, not really that long."

"The reason I ask, miss, is because I have no memory of you in my database, and all his friends and acquaintances are stored there." She realized she was shivering.

"If you follow me, miss, I will show you the showers, and you can change your wet clothes. I will show you your room."

"Well, Don, I don't know if I will be here overnight. I might just jump back into the pod and go back up, if you follow me."

"That would be impossible, miss. The pod has returned to orbit. There is no authority for it to stay on E5. This is the only place to stay."

She was resigned. She had a hot shower and was drying her hair when Don appeared. He had found her some denims that were shapeless but were dry and warm.

"The master has returned, miss. He is not in a very good frame of mind."

Outside, the river was doing its best to smash everything in its path.

"What in Aton's name were you thinking, Styxx? I am going

to look like an idiot. Fleet will scalp me. This was supposed to be a little secret mission with no dust, no publicity. How do I explain you to them?"

"Davvd, I really am sorry. I had no idea you were going to fly the coop and take me with you. I just wanted a story, and you hijacked me. Put yourself in my place. I was just trying to follow orders like you."

"Do you want something to eat?"

"Who's doing the cooking, Ong? Don't look at me; I am not checked out on strange kitchens."

"Relax. Joe, can you do breakfast for both of us? Scrambled eggs, bacon, toast, the usual menu? Thank you, Joe."

He was a different model from Don but obviously of the same vintage with the same strong body and head.

She laughed.

"My pleasure, Master Davvd."

"You don't stint yourself, do you, Ong?"

"Not if I can help it."

"What are you going to do now?"

"Well, what can I do? How do I explain you under my bunk? How do I explain your sudden disappearance off *Double Happiness* in the middle of nowhere? Think of the story, Maggda. Boy meets girl on luxury starliner. Boy goes off on a secret mission for Fleet. Girl smuggles herself onboard his ship. Can't bear to be parted. Boy gets slung out of the service as a stupid romantic. Girl loses her job and career as star reporter for Galactic. Media has a field day, and we have to restart our lives."

"Hey, I was just trying to get an interview with the great Captain Ong, hero and Ong heir. I had no idea you were going to jump ship and take me with you."

They ate and then sat in the battered but comfortable chairs. "What now, Master of the Universe?"

"Looks like we are stuck with each other for a while. Don't worry, you get your own bedroom and bathroom, and Joe does the household chores and does those well."

"What about clothes? I left a whole wardrobe up there on the ship. All I have is what I stand up in."

"Talk to Joe. He is tinker, tailor, candlestick maker, and chef, apart from being a number-one good guy."

"Does he do underwear?"

"Tell him what you want, go look at what is in stores, but don't get too surprised if it turns out to be basic cotton denim."

"Where did he come from, Ong?"

"I grew up with him and Don. We lived on a vast and often lonely estate. Didn't have too many friends my age, so my father gave me Don and Joe. They were teachers, friends, and playmates. They know more about anything than I ever will. When my family went, these two were sent out here to run this station, so coming here is a lot like coming home. These guys are like brothers. They can do just about anything, so if you want frilly denim undies, talk to Joe. He does things with a sewing machine and a laser seam-stitcher that will amaze you."

She laughed. "That's a side to you I would never have seen, would I?"

The captain of the *Double Happiness* was relieved to hear that the pod had been gone, been retrieved, and was now back in orbit above E5.

"Any problems?"

"Robot cleaner reported vomit under a bunk, that's all."

"Are you sure?"

"And just to make you really interested, sir, we seem to have mislaid a first class passenger by the name of Maggda Styxx."

"By Aton's breath, how the! . . . Get a search going but just be discreet. She might be shacked up with someone and is having a love-in somewhere."

"Well, sir, Ong goes and so does Ms. Styxx. How's that for a love-in?"

"Be discreet. We just stay quiet, and we wait until we get asked questions. Meantime, if Fleet starts asking questions, you stick to the truth. We don't start sending out distress calls until we are sure Styxx isn't here and that there have been no airlocks opened."

"We only opened up for the pod."

"And I thought I was going to have a sweet trip! Check the sludge tanks; she may have been murdered . . .

The storm subsided, and the river went down at the rear entrance to the complex.

"There is an entrance on the other side under the overhanging rock face. We bring equipment in and out there, and we have an access to the valley. This whole complex was designed to be as unobtrusive as possible and to be as environmentally friendly as technology could make it. The whole moon is like that. There are other stations."

"What is the basic purpose for all this?"

"Environmental research. Ong Foundation pays for most of it. You can get to play god out here if you get the permission. You get a nice, clean environment, and you can put any kind of flora and fauna out here so it doesn't have human pollution or interference. Like the Agitarian antelope. What killed it off on Agitar? So you put some out here and let them breed up numbers, and you keep an eye on them and if they die off . . .

"They probably died from boredom, Davvd."

"You think so?"

"Have you ever been to Agitar, Davvd?"

He laughed. "I have to work. Don and I are doing a lot of checking, so if you and Joe want to play dressmakers, go for it. We will be back early evening. So make yourself at home."

She used her and Joe's time very effectively. She had never had a working experience with a robot before, but after an hour or so she forgot his plas-steel body and treated him like a friend. She realized that he and Don were exceptional. She asked him to cut her hair and showed him a picture from an ancient magazine she found in a drawer, and he worked wonders. Her clothes were the best fit outside of Maxxi's, and he made her some underwear to change into from her Second Skins. It was the most stylish cotton denim lingerie she had ever seen, and she laughed. "Joe, you are wasted here, you know that?"

"Yes, miss. I try to please."

She looked in the mirror and felt pleased. She had decided to make some changes to the starkness and had gone out and found some fresh wildflowers and put those in a specimen jar on the table. She nearly forgot to ask Joe to cook dinner and settled for fish and salad, and he even produced fresh bread rolls.

The "boys" appeared; Davvd had taken off his boots and disappeared, and she heard a shower. Then there was the intense noise of high-pressure water, and Don appeared, shining and polished. Out the back there was singing, and it was bad, and she smiled.

"Don, you look like someone just made you."

"Thank you, Miss Maggda. The master has a shower; we have to have a high-pressure hose-down, or we might bring in contamination from out there. Has Joe changed your appearance? You are not the same as my memory recorded this morning."

She said, "Joe works in mysterious ways, Don."

Davvd Ong appeared in clean denims and gave her a hard look. "Hey, you look good! Joe did a great job with the hair and the outfit."

"Yeah, I'm thinking of taking him back with me. I hate cooking and housework."

"Nah! If they go anywhere, they go with me. I was first in line."

It seemed appropriate to ask if he had had a good day. "We flew; we slogged; we looked to see if there was anyone human out there, but we didn't see a soul. Don's records show that whatever killed the deer wasn't using tooth or claw, and it was cut up using a very sharp blade."

Joe appeared "Dinner is ready, sir."

"Thank you, Joe. Did you dress up the table?"

"No sir, Miss Maggda did. She said she felt in a domesticated mood." Ong gave her a quizzical look.

"He is being a bit loose with the truth, Captain."

He laughed. "Now you know that they can't lie, Maggda." They ate fish with vegetables and some kind of grain. She couldn't identify it and didn't ask.

They relaxed in the old, comfortable chairs. Ong found a drink that didn't make her eyes water. "What now, ruler of the world?"

"I guess I have to let Fleet know I am officially here. I guess I have to tell them about you, so wait for flack."

"Wouldn't Fleet know you were here anyway?"

"Yes, but I have to send the identification code." He went off to the communication center, and she heard the musical tones of the code going out. Joe hovered near her shoulder. "Would you like dessert, miss?"

It seemed totally incongruous to have half a ton of plas-steel asking if she wanted ice cream.

She reflected that she was on a moon she had never really heard much about, with a man whom she had been sent to scalp, and was probably listed as "lost in space" right now.

"Can I talk to you right now, Maggda? We need to do some serious talking. You may not appreciate it, but we are in serious trouble. You see, I *can* disappear off the starship because I was never there, never listed on the passenger list, so that isn't the problem. The whole of that starliner is going to get searched for you. I mean you aren't just anybody. The captain will guess you went with me, so he can tell Fleet, which gets him off the hook, but your boss isn't going to be too enthralled when you don't land on Alpha Six, is he? Lose a well-known, good-looking gal somewhere in space, and people start talking, right?"

"Can you reach *Double Happiness* and tell them I am alive and well and then get in touch with Simon on Mars and say 'mission accomplished'?"

"Can do, if you think Simon will understand. As for Fleet, they don't have to know just yet that you are here, do they? If your spacewalk doesn't get publicized, we can keep it dark. So we stay cool, Styxx, and make ice cubes in our undies. I can reach *Double Happiness* so they can relax."

"When do I get to see what is outside there, Davvd?"

"We'll talk about it in the morning. Get an early night. I have a lot of serious thinking to do."

Food, drink, and a comfortable bed helped a lot. The air that circulated was redolent with meadow grass and wildflowers. She slept well.

He went back through the scans and looked for hot spots and anomalies. There was something there that didn't fit quite right, but it wasn't anything he could capture on the screens. It was an animal, but what kind he had no idea. There was always tomorrow. Don and Joe had gone into recharge mode. He wondered what he could do with Maggda Styxx. She was both a nuisance and a pleasure. "Make no waves, Ong, make no waves."

Maggda was prowling like a caged lion.

She wanted to get outside, smell the breeze and see the sky. Finally, she braved the control room and Davvd Ong. "Davvd, can I get out of here for a while? I am going stir-crazy when just out there is sun and flowers and birds and breeze."

He broke off from screen-gazing at what looked like a close-up of broken grass stems.

"Sorry, of course you can. If Joe isn't busy take him but don't go too far out. Everything here is classified as 'feral,' you know that." She found Joe, and they went out into the meadow. It was wonderful to smell the breeze. She had taken off her Maxxi lizard-skin boots in favor of a rough pair of work boots she had found in a woman's locker and felt free. They walked through the tall grasses and flowers towards the edge of the woods.

"Are there really cave bears here, Joe?"

"Yes, miss, but if you really want to see bears then I suggest I take you in a vehicle, which the bears will not associate with food."

26

She sighed and went to walk closer to the woods, but a dark shape suddenly appeared. "Joe, is that what I think it is?" He tilted his head a little and focused his telescopic eyes. "Yes, miss."

The huge bear had come out of the woods and was into the meadow. It reared up and sniffed the breeze.

"It is using its olfactory senses to test the strange scent, miss."

"That thing is huge, Joe."

"Yes, miss, it can break an antelope's neck with a bite or good blow. It is not an animal to trifle with."

"I feel like running, Joe."

"It would be unwise, miss. It has weak eyes compared with its scent organs but can detect sudden movement, and it is conditioned to chase other running animals. You could not outrun a bear, miss."

"Thank you Joe, you are a comfort."

"There is no need to fear it, Miss Maggda. It is digging up the animals that live in burrows under the soil. There are many of them that live in the grasses close to the edge of the forest. We can walk slowly back, and it will ignore us."

"Help me pick some flowers for the table, please, Joe. If I am going to be accused of domestication I had better live the part." They picked red and blue flowers and took then back, and it took three specimen flasks to display them. "Now, Mister Joe, we need a decent tablecloth. Any ideas? No, don't tell me, just come up with something."

She had been on the run with Galactic, so this interlude was peaceful. She wandered about and checked the Med Robot, and it was up to date. She felt that Ong and his "boys" could handle anything. She went in search of him, and he was at the console and looking bleary eyed. "How now, Master of the Universe?"

"Making mistakes, working the problem from the wrong end. Whatever it is out there it is hard to find because the heat signal just wasn't strong enough. Could be humanoid but could also be a couple of animals away from a herd . . . who knows?"

"So?"

"We backtrack on anything that came here just before Don discovered the meat, and what it was here for. Don is looking for a ship that came to upload data or stayed for a few hours or had humans aboard. Everything that comes and goes is monitored in one way or the other, either by its coded log or via the Research Foundation records."

"You think a ship came here and made some illegal move?"

"Have to wait and see what Don comes up with."

"And I thought you said this place was tight."

"Hey! This place is a research moon, not a Fleet military arms dump! Security isn't like a duck's backside, Maggda. It's as tight as any research planet can be. We aren't a hostile world; we are a registered research facility. The people who come and go here are re-scientists engaged in environmental research of some kind or the other."

"So what do we do now?"

"Nothing much I can do until Joe or Don gives me the list of names. Once we get a list we narrow it down to a few ships that fit the time frame . . ."

"Then we tell Fleet, and they send a cruiser and blow the home planet to rubble, right?"

"You know something; I get the feeling you're getting a bit stir-crazy. Right?"

"Look at it from my point of view. I got hijacked. I get to be here with you because that is where I am supposed to be, but you are so tied up with work I can't talk to you. You don't give interviews, right, but I'm going crazy because I have no human to talk to. Now don't tell me that Don isn't worth talking to, or Joe, because they both are, but they don't feel like a human does now do they?"

"Sorry."

"Would you do me a favor, Master of the Universe?"

"Anything."

"Would you just come over here and give me a hug. Just a hug, a nice, soft, gentle hug, because I need one right now."

He hugged her, and he felt her warmth and she felt his, and they broke apart slowly. "I'm sorry, Davvd. I just needed that."

"I did too, Maggda."

"Can I talk to you? Like person to person?"

"Can we get a drink first, find a comfortable chair?"

"I thought you'd never ask."

The drink was something made from fermented honey and herbs, and it was sweet as a kiss but had a kick like a mule. They sat and sipped.

"Can I ask about your wife? Or is it still too painful?"

"No, not too painful. She was beautiful, very quiet but had a steel resolve, I guess. She was Su Lin Wu, you know that?"

"The daughter of Solomon Wu? You mean the man who owns the other half of the galaxy almost?"

"My father's partner, really. The descendant of the ancestors who developed the Ong Wu drive that gets everyone from star to star; that's the one. Now I have to tell you that it was an arranged marriage . . ."

"Davvd Ong! You were in an arranged marriage?"

"No, because although the families wanted us to marry because it was a nice, neat business arrangement, the plans went wrong, but they went right, if you can follow that."

"Tell me."

"Well, we had to meet, so they arranged for us to meet at a dinner that Solomon was giving at his estate on Little Lotus. Huge dinner, a thousand guests, everyone looking like a fashion plate, everyone spread through the gardens. Can you imagine those gardens? Solomon had two-hundred human gardeners, not to mention the robotic staff. My father kept saying to me, 'You know the Wu motto, don't you? Nothing succeeds like excess.' It was his joke, of course."

"Well, what happened?"

"We sat opposite each other at dinner. Huge table about a mile long. We didn't actually get to speak to each other at all. After dinner she was formally introduced to me. It was the custom, you see. She held out her hand, and when I held hers it was like getting a hundred volts up my arm."

"And did she feel the same?"

"She dropped my hand like a hot potato."

"Well, tell me!"

"I guess she did; it was uncanny. Then she went to bed."

"Just like that?"

"Well, yes, but she was going back to Belvedere the next morning to the university."

"Just like that?"

"And I was going back to Fleet."

"That must have been terrible. So when did you actually meet?"

"Are you going to laugh at me, Styxx?"

"Tell me, and I'll let you know."

"I sent her a holo of me in uniform at my graduation and told her 'I would defend her always.'"

She sat and looked at him in silence.

"Well, I didn't know what else to do."

"Can I give you a hug, you big, soft man. Did you never think of telling her you loved her?"

"No, because I didn't know right then. It was later when she met me off the shuttle to Old Earth and we kissed, and, well that was that. We had been sending each other messages and holos and tri-dees and everything, but it was all very secret. I think the families thought we hated each other. So we just went and got married and told no one, and they got angry because it was very sneaky, but we did what they wanted anyway."

"And you're not being sneaky here on E5?"

"This is Fleet business; you know that."

"Do you have a holo of her? I want to see her."

"May be able to do better than that. Don, can you come in here please?"

The robot slid across the polished rock floor and came to a halt beside the chair.

"Don, could you run the holo of Su Lin, please."

The holo showed Su Lin dancing. Great beauty is hard to describe. Maggda was beautiful in an immediate here and now way, but Su Lin was ethereal, spiritual, and esoteric. Her hair was polished ebony, her flawless skin a pale gold. Her grace was that of a willow, pliant in a breeze. She was dancing with a lantern of spider silk that was lit from within; she made it float and fall, and she spun gently, catching it just before it touched the ground. It was a demonstration of skill and supreme grace. "She wasn't a professional dancer. She was a doctor who danced. Can you turn it off please, Don?"

"I am sorry, Davvd. I had no right to ask you to do that."

"Well, I get to see her do that, and she lives. Oh, I know she is gone, and the pain gets a little less each time. She died so young we never knew a long happiness, but we did have each other, even though it was such a short time."

She went over and kissed him on the mouth.

"I am sorry, Davvd, but I have to go to my room. I can't take anymore. Sorry."

She went to bed and felt guilty. She had no right to be such an invasive and insensitive bitch.

When the sickness came it was winter. People die in the winter, especially the old and the very young. Sometimes it is the cold, or because there is not enough to eat. We have dried the fish and the meat for the winter. But if the winter is too long, we go hungry.

The sickness made even the strong weaken and die. Old Agarth, the wise man, called to me and told me to take the strongest of the men and the women and the children who were not sick and find somewhere away from the tribe. He said that if we stayed, we would all die.

So I spoke to the men who could hunt and had no women, and we took the strongest children, and packed our belongings onto a travois and dragged it away to the caves alongside the hills that we knew, and we slept there. The next night, when the second moon rose, there was great light in the sky, and it hid the lights of the dead hunters in the heavens. Then strange beings came into the cave. They were shining bright; they came close, and we felt some pain, and then we were suddenly asleep.

We awoke in a large silver cave and Olan, son of Agarth, said that we were all dead, but my woman Annrath said, "If we are dead, why are we breathing?"

Then the side of the cave opened. A silver man came in with a large silver bowl, and he put it down and gave us small bowls. We ate the meat from the large bowl and drank water. Then we were left in the darkness, and we slept again.

When we awoke the side of the cave opened, and we could see a large meadow full of flowers and tall grasses. There were mountains and a blue sky, but they were not our mountains. The two moons had vanished, and there was one great swirling ball in the sky.

So we left the shining cave, and the silver man gave us knives. These knives were silver and very sharp and long. Then the silver man waved us away, and the great cave roared and went up into the skies and was gone.

So then we began to look for a shelter, and Olan went into the woods and cried out, and when we found him, he had killed a great deer, and we had food. We cut the meat up, and it was easy to do with the new knives, and we laughed.

That night we slept under our skins, and the next day we went across a plain to the hills where we found a wide and deep cave that faced the morning sun, and we made a home there. Annrath has told me she is carrying a child, so I must keep her safe.

We watch for the fires of other tribes, but there are none, and we think we are alone.

There is a river close by that runs into a lake where there are fish, so we speared some and cooked them and are well fed.

At night the sky hunters shine, but they are not our hunters. Everything is strange, but we are strong hunters and will survive. We have escaped the sickness.

When Maggda had showered and dressed and breakfasted alone, she was feeling better. It had been a bitchy thing to do to ask to see the images of Su Lin when she knew that Davvd was still grieving.

Joe was doing something with a very complex machine.

"Do you know where Captain Ong is, Joe?"

"He is with Don, miss, checking lists."

"Thank you, Joe." It seemed totally natural to thank a hunk of plas-steel for some reason.

She found them at the consoles.

"Tell me the news, Master of the Universe."

"We are down to three. They all arrived at about the right time. Two were oceanographic, robot piloted, and they went out to New Atlantic. They do a regular survey of blue whale numbers and other large sea life."

"What is bigger than a blue whale, or daren't I ask?"

"Stuff that comes straight from the prehistoric ichthyosaurs, I think, and some other stuff."

"Next thing you will be telling me is there are dinosaurs here too."

"Well, why not? We have herds of woolly mammoths out on the plains. They began as an Old Earth research project, and then it was taken over by another group on Alpha Six."

"Don't overload me, Ong. Some things I don't want to know. Can Joe help me for five minutes, please?"

"Providing it's constructive. He has a lot of work to do getting some trace elements off the bones that were cut. We should know the weapon when he has that sorted out."

"So what was the third on the list?"

"Will tell you at lunch. I have a feeling we are not going to like what we have found."

She and Joe went out of the fissure and onto the now wider beach after rain and flood had done their work. There were some substantial logs swept down, and she selected two of the longer and stronger ones and asked Joe to help.

"Can you make me a simple footbridge across the stream, Joe, so I can sit out on the beach in the sun?"

"Yes, miss."

He lifted the logs into place and jacked them up with rocks until they were level, and they made a secure footbridge.

"Thank you, Joe."

"Will that be all, miss?"

"If you weren't so cool, Joe, I might give you a kiss."

"Thank you, miss."

It went back to its work, and she collected a folding chair and a solid lab stool as a small table and sat in the sun to read "Listed Species on E5." She read and became aware that she felt at peace here. When Davvd Ong appeared she was finding out more than she wanted to know.

"This whole moon is like some crazy museum, right?"

"Well, yes and no."

"Stuff gets started here, and some species just get left to breed while others die out, and there are all kinds of genetic mutations listed here."

"Right."

"So who or what is in control?"

"What do you want to control?"

"Well, doesn't it get a bit messy? For example, the bears eat the deer that were put here for research into herds that were going to supply the tribes on Venturi, right?"

"Right, but they don't eat that many. If you read 'Volume Four, Specific Projections,' you will see how it all pans out."

"How come you know so much, Ong?"

"Because I am supposed to know what did come here that isn't supposed to be here."

"Can we eat, and you can tell me what *did* come here?"

Joe had laid the table using an old Ong flag as a tablecloth, deep blue with the faded Ong crest, and it took away the starkness of the old plas-steel table. He had replaced the flowers with others that were long stemmed and pink and ones she couldn't recognize.

The food came in a steaming casserole, with fresh salad and

34

boiled vegetables and an iced drink that looked and tasted like spring water because it was spring water. The meat was delicate and had lots of small bones, but it was a wonderful meal when she thought that a robot had been slaving in the kitchen, not her.

They pushed the chairs away and retired to the larger chairs in the rec room.

"What did you think of that, Maggda?"

"Wonderful taste. What was it?"

"Rats legs. Now before you get excited, rodents, to be precise, they are what the bears like to eat. There are lots of them around the forest edge. Joe cooks them in a sauce made from red berries and mushrooms with a dash of honey and his own stock. The salad comes from along the water's edge and is much loved by the little antelopes. It is one of his best meals, I think."

"I came all this way to eat rats?"

"Well, here you take what you can get."

"What did you find out, lord of the universe?"

"The one ship that fits the bill is a Wu vessel."

"Are you sure?"

"Perfectly, but it gets complicated after that. It is a registered Wu research vessel but rented to a company called 'Galactic Biotics' on Valderia."

"Hey, aren't they the enemy?"

"Perfectly legal company, registered and approved, and with research credentials."

"Didn't they try to wipe out everyone on Beebop?"

"Can't be proven, and you would be treading on very dangerous ground to accuse anyone. No, all we can do is to trace the crew, if any, and find out what they did here. They don't have to tell us, by the way. It would be hard to find out, but I could try through the Wu network, and they are a tight-lipped lot. Old Solomon doesn't like anyone meddling in his affairs. They keep everything 'in-house,' if they can."

"But you are the son-in-law, aren't you? Isn't that in-house enough?"

35

He laughed. "Not even his wife knows what goes on if Solomon doesn't want her to know."

She went out into the sunlight, and he followed her.

"What do we do next, Captain Ong?"

"Tomorrow, as a special treat for my honored guest, I shall take you out to the research station at Bare Head, out in the New Atlantic. That way we can kill two birds with one stone. There was a research probe out there at the same time as the Wu vessel, so we can backtrack on both and find out a bit more. Apart from that, Aton smiles, and we can view the scenery, smell the fresh salt air. Go for a swim on a white sand beach and just play for a while."

Dinner was simple. A thick soup with fresh bread, crusty and with something that tasted almost like butter. She didn't ask. Joe brought the wine, which was red, and smooth, and satisfying.

She raised her glass and her eyebrows.

"Made from red berries that are everywhere in the autumn. Joe ferments them and racks the bottles up, and what you have is, how old, Joe?"

"Three seasons, sir."

"I think it gets better after ten, but three is pretty well matured."

"You like it here, Ong, don't you?"

"What's not to like? I am not being told what to do; I don't have to go and kill things or take a platoon into places where things can kill me. I'm doing my job, and I have a beautiful and famous woman sitting beside me. Hey, how much better can it get?"

"Less of the famous, Captain."

"Well, it could have been 'infamous,' I suppose, in the nicest possible way."

"And what does *that* mean, Ong?"

"You don't know? Don, can you come in here, please? Okay, Don, can you run the holos of the Second Skin promotion from how far back? From Old Earth, Don, the Paris ones.

She cringed and sunk down into her chair.

She was wearing the Second Skin lingerie that had caused a sensation even in those parts of the galaxy known for their liberated thinking. She watched herself display her breasts and her backside in ways she hadn't thought of as provocative, until now. The underwear was sensuous, and so was she. Her body made it live. She became aware that her nipples had stiffened up and were literally trying to poke through the synthetic spider-silk fabric; she saw herself acting like a high-priced whore to sell the stuff, and it had worked so well that the company had made millions, and she had never been so well-off.

She was blushing, and she never blushed, and she said nothing.

"Turn it off, please, Don," he said, "before I get too excited."

"I was under contract to sell that stuff, Davvd."

"No blame intended, Maggda. I thought I had never seen such an exciting woman in years. I saw you do that, and I couldn't take my eyes off you. I was stunned. I never thought that I would have the real Maggda Styxx sitting here beside me, ever!"

"I feel like a fool; do you know that?"

"Well, don't. Whatever it was you were selling there isn't the Maggda I am getting to know. Can I tell you this? I think you are a bright, sensitive girl with a big heart, and even in those damn denims you still look good to me."

"I am going to keep away from you, Ong. You are getting to be too nice, you know that?"

"Sorry."

"On the *Double Happiness* when we danced, you know I was feeling a little drunk, but I felt good. I forgot what I was there for. I just felt good.

"Want to try it again? And I promise I will take you to your room, and I want you to lock the door, same as last time."

"Okay. Do I have to lock the door?"

"Sorry, but you do. I would love to creep into a warm bed with you, but we can't right now. There is still a lot of crap out there ready to hit a fan, and we don't want complications just now."

"Dance with me then."

Don provided a holo and the musicians. He held her close, and they danced, a little too slow, and they became aware of each other's bodies moving together until she said, "Stop! I am off to my room, Ong. You do things to me my mother warned me about, but you know that I love it."

"Good night, Maggda."

"Good night, Davvd. See you bright and early." Then she went to bed.

He briefed Don and Joe and went off to his room, and he could feel her moving with him. He thought of Su Lin, and he said, "Sorry."

Maggda had had an uneasy night. The images of Su Lin kept coming and going, and when she did sleep, she dreamt she was making love with Davvd Ong and that Su Lin was watching them.

Outside at the rear of the ridge, on the flat rock platform in front of the overhanging cavern entrance was a machine that at first glance appeared to be a real, giant insect, a dragonfly.

She had dressed for the real outdoors in the drab denims and had grabbed a bush hat at the last minute and slung some essentials into a small backpack. He was there checking the machine with Don and Joe, and he smiled as she appeared.

"Well, what do you think of this?"

"Is it real or just a toy?"

"Put it this way, it is a lot of fun, but it is a vital research vehicle. It doesn't fly that high, no pressurization, but it is quieter than a rotor, and it can glide for kilometer after kilometer or soar, if we can find the right thermals."

"Is there room for the two of us?"

"For what we are going to do, plenty. Here, come and sit."

He went to the front of the giant fly and opened a door which was part of the great eye and windscreen combined. In the pale green light there was a very comfortable seat, not unlike the contoured seats of the sand racers on Mars. She sank into it, and he came round and joined her in the other seat.

"How does it fly?"

"Flaps its wings like a real fly. Hydrogen engine in the 'thorax' behind us. Solar panels provide the energy to suck hydrogen out of the air, but we do have a big tank to kick off with, in the body. Give me your bag, and I'll put it in the hold behind us. Are you ready, by the way?"

"I think so. Are we going overnight or what?"

"Should be back before dark. Just have to check the records there, and our time is our own. Joe and Don can handle anything here. I don't see any problems unless we hit a storm, and the weather is good. Belt up and we can get out of here."

The engine was strangely quiet and hummed. He engaged the wings, and there was a drumming as the large wings began to beat, and they were off the ground and climbing up and into a clear blue sky. He angled the craft into a nose-down attitude, and they began to make speed. Every now and then, the wings stopped, and they glided for long distances until they needed to make height again.

"I am going to find a thermal above the plains if I can. That will lift us up over a thousand meters or more, and we can then virtually idle our way over that range and out to the ocean shore."

She watched as the craft slipped across the landscape. Animals she did and didn't recognize came and went. Things that flew appeared and gave them a close-up look and then veered off. There were birds and something else.

"What the heck is *that*?" She pointed to a large dark shape making circles in the sky to the north of them.

"Pterodactyl."

"Is it dangerous?"

"Not as a rule. They leave most other big flying stuff alone. Size rules and we are a bit big."

They found a thermal and rocketed upwards. It was exhilarating stuff, and she loved it.

"Look over there. What do you see?"

"Something shining through the haze. The sea?"

"Won't be long, and we can land on Bare Head Island, but I want a swim first, so we'll put down on the beach at back of it. The beach is white. The sea is blue. The waves are kind--well until there is a storm."

He banked the craft and engaged the wings, and they fluttered down towards a beach that was almost white in the sun and wide enough for them to just drop gently onto it with barely a swirl of sand.

"Where is Bare Head?"

"Out there, see that lump out there in the haze from the spray? It looks just like any other rocky island, but it is a hollow shell. Much the same setup as we have back there but geared to marine research. The nice thing is you can go down inside the base, and they have a huge clear plast-glass window so you can see the wildlife. A couple of robots there too but not like our 'boys,' I am afraid."

"What do you mean?"

"Well, just standard Wu Industries models. They do what they are told, but you won't find the personality circuits our boys have."

"I like our boys a lot."

"You should. They are as human as they could make them, you know that. Let's swim, and then we can go out there."

She climbed out, felt the warm sand under her feet, and kicked off her boots. He stripped off his shirt, dropped his denim pants, and she could see he had brief, royal blue trunks under them.

"All Ong, I see."

"Well, come on. Are you going to stand there all day?"

"I don't have a suit. When you hijacked me, you didn't tell me we were going swimming."

"After the display you put on last night in that holo, Miss Styxx, am I going to be amazed at what you have?"

40

She dropped her denims, took off her Joe-tailored top, and stood in her underwear.

"This is what I was wearing when we dropped out of *Double Happiness*."

Her Second Skins were red and lacy, and her skin showed through them. He looked at her and shook his head.

"And I thought that holo was inspirational!"

He turned and jogged into the surf. It wasn't much of a sea, and he swam out a bit and watched her as she plunged into the surf. She swam well. The underwear clung to her just like Second Skins should. The surf hid her, and she was glad about that. Her real swimsuit was nearly as scanty, but it was strange how different it felt knowing she was in her underwear instead.

They trod water together, her hair plastered over her face.

"Is there anything in here that might eat us, Ong?"

"Just about everything. Out there, in deeper water, I have seen things that attack blue whales."

She tried to look through the water around and beneath her. Something flashed by, then another, and then a lot more sped past her.

"I am getting cold, Davvd; I am going in. Sorry, but I feel terribly vulnerable all of a sudden."

She made a hasty exit to the beach, and he followed and pulled two big towels out of the Fly.

She wrapped herself tight in the large towel and looked out to sea.

"Something swam under us when were out there; did you see that?"

"A lot of big fish, all harmless. More frightened of us than the other way round."

"Speak for yourself, Ong. I am not too familiar with all this wet stuff. I was born and bred on Mars, remember, where the water doesn't come in oceans or waves except in the swimming pools."

"You swim really well."

"Yeah, well, I had a crush on the young guy who taught us, so I had to perform or get ignored."

He laughed.

"Are you dry enough to dress, or are you going to stay like that? It's only a minute or two to the island.

They climbed into the machine. He powered up, and they lifted off. The beach fell away beneath them, and he countered the sudden snatch of a wind gust. They flew low over the water, and there was the flat top of the island. He dropped lower and was about to lift up and onto the pad in the lee of the mass when something hit them.

It had a large body and a snake-like head and neck, and it leaped out of the ocean like a seal. It grabbed the body of the Fly just behind their seats and fell back into the water with them, shaking its huge head and scattering debris into the waves that broke on the rocky outcrop.

She was aware that she was underwater. The small cabin had filled with seawater. Davvd was on top of her and fighting to get the door open. She was aware that she was going to drown. The whole front end of the Fly was sinking, and she was trapped against the cabin roof when suddenly the door opened, and she felt his hand grasp her wrist. He gripped her so tightly she wanted to scream, there was a great wall of white water, and a large wave broke over them, hurling them against the weed-covered rock. She managed to get a breath, and he grabbed her again.

"With me! Stay with me!" he managed to roar before another wave picked them up again and forced them against the rocks. He grabbed her arm.

"Follow me . . . steps! Follow me!" he sputtered just before another wave roared over them. She was weakening and struggled after him as he swam round the island to the lee of the rock mass. When she was sure she was going to drown, he grabbed her again and hauled her up beside him against the rocks. She was dimly aware that he was hanging onto something, and then she saw it was a chain, a weed and shellfish-encrusted chain and that his hand was bleeding. He hauled her up again; she hit her knees against an edge covered in weed, then another; he was hauling her out of the sea and onto steps, and she was crying hysterically and gasping for breath. Another big sea roared past, divided by the rocks, and he grabbed her again, up another three steps, out of the water. She had just enough strength left to sit up a little and saw that he was vomiting seawater.

They crawled up the steps and struggled onto the flat of the landing pad. On one side was a projecting rock, and he crawled towards it. A wave suddenly shot spray up and into the air, and the wind blew across the pad. Davvd reached the rock, found the flat surface that contained the palm lock, and pressed. She had stumbled after him, and wondered what he was doing. He pressed again after wiping the blood off his palm on his trunks, and the door opened up to reveal stairs going down into the rock. It wasn't a large door, barely big enough for them to scramble through, but suddenly, once inside, it felt like the most secure place on earth.

The door closed behind them, wiping out the roar of the sea, and they sat in almost silence on the steps to catch their breath. He was cut by the shellfish, and she was too, and what remained of her underwear were red scraps, and then he suddenly laughed. For one moment, she thought he had been pushed to the edge of sanity, but he calmed down and grinned at her. He had a scratch down the side of his face that was weeping watery blood, and he grinned at her again. Then he pulled her into his arms and held her very tightly.

"Welcome to Bare Head Island, you bare-assed girl!"

Bare Head Island was similar to their research labs but not so large; he found them clothes, the familiar, ubiquitous denims. Down another level were bedrooms, bunks, blankets, and bathrooms. Bare Head had never had a large staff of humans at any time, and the facilities were basic, but she felt like she had felt in the luxury suite on *Double Happiness*. He turned on the robots and they stood ready for orders. Don and Joe were huge compared to these two bots, but they were almost company. He sat down on the battered old lounge, and she sat beside him and clung to him and kissed him on the mouth, then just clung until he gently pushed her away.

"We have to do some serious thinking now. We have to get back to base, and there isn't a Flyer here, just subs, small and one-man, apart from the crew boat."

"What the heck was it that jumped us, Davvd?"

"Off hand, and don't quote me, a plesiosaur . . . hunting that big shoal of fish that went past us. They have bred them here. Got them from the Old Earth Jurassic period for some reason."

"Why?"

"I think it was scientific enthusiasm, a case of 'because we can do it.' Someone found a way to extract DNA from a fossil; someone found a way to put that into something that could replicate it; someone got some money, and we got plesiosaurs."

"That bastard nearly got us."

"It just thought we might be edible."

"I am working you out, Ong. You don't back down, do you? You saved me out there in the same way you saved Kruft. Just wouldn't let her or me die because you can't do it. You have to act, to stick your neck out. I mean, you could have let Kruft die, couldn't you, and who would be the wiser? You, that's who! I know how you got all those damn medals. You knew what to do; you just did. You don't freeze up, do you? You just do what has to be done, right?"

"What are you trying to pin on me, Maggda?"

"Oh I don't know. I just think you're natural hero material."

"Listen. I just happened to be in the right place at the right time to do things."

"But you, and only you, knew what to do at the right time. I rest my case, my hero!"

"Why don't you do something really useful and find food. These bots know where everything is, and they may even cook, but I doubt that. I am going to contact Don or Joe and get them to come out here and take us off this lump of rock. To do that I need Research Foundation permission, so it may take a couple of days. Can you stand the excitement of that?"

She went on an exploration tour of the complex. She found the kitchens and the food stores, all deep-frozen stuff. Some of it looked interesting. She went down another level and found the glass wall that looked out into the ocean. The big swells were surging, and the seaweeds were waving, and things were swimming out there. When they saw her in the window, large fish came to kiss the glass. Something very long and sleek swam by, just out of focus. It looked like something she had seen in a book. It didn't look like it belonged there, but then what did on a moon where all wildlife had been imported or created in a test tube. She went into the crew quarters and found the women's rooms. She foraged through drawers and bingo! Panties that looked like they had come out of the ark, but who cared? She found some almost dried-up makeup sticks and a pot of something that might have been to put on a face or on toast. She found a kind of jacket top that almost fitted her and in a bottom drawer a pair of brightly colored sandals. Too big but she wore them anyway. She was determined to get dressy. Wasn't she the face and the body of the year at one stage of her career? She went back up with her spoils and found the bots standing, almost dead looking, in the kitchen.

"What are you named, please?"

"My name is Robert, miss."

"My name is Randolph, miss."

She just knew that someone with an IQ over two hundred had chosen those names.

"Okay, Robert, are you a cooking robot?"

"Yes, miss."

"Randolph, are you a cooking robot?"

"Yes, miss."

"Now for the big one, I would like you to cook a meal for Captain Ong and myself, starting in five minutes. It has to feed two adults. It has to be a known recipe from your memories, it has to be edible, and it has to be, how the heck do I say this?

"It has to be presented correctly, miss," said Robert.

"You have done this before, haven't you, boys?"

They replied in unison, "Yes, miss."

She left them to it. She had a little bet with herself that it would be a fish dish.

Davvd Ong was tapping a pencil on a yellow pad when she found him at the com desk.

"Any luck?"

"Don has responded. Joe has responded."

"That sounds, well, a bit negative, doesn't it?"

"Yes and no."

"What does that mean?"

"Research gave permission but not for three days. Don can come and get us with the loader. Rough ride but better than walking. Joe has found trace elements on the bones of the kill."

"So?"

"Modern knife, plas-steel, carbon, made by Wu industries."

"So is just about everything these days."

"What and who is wandering about out there with a carving knife?"

"Hadn't we better get back in a hurry?"

"I don't think that whatever or whoever it is, will do much harm in three days. Now we have established it is human, we can go from there."

"Guess what we are having for dinner, lord of the universe?"

"Oysters followed by duck in an orange sauce, with noodles, fresh green salad, and stuffed avocado. Dessert? I think a simple treacle tart with piped cream. Then, maybe coffee, with a honey syrup to sweeten."

"How can you guess all that, Ong?"

"I didn't. I asked Randolph."

She gave a strangled groan and went to her room.

During the night a storm rose out at sea, and she woke to the sound of the great waves thumping on the rocks, but she was safe and warm, and the sounds became just a background noise to her thoughts. They contained a sense of helplessness. She was somewhere with a man she admired a lot, doing bizarre things on a strange and dangerous world and for what real reason? Why would Fleet send one of its top soldier boys to a place to play games when there were a thousand highly qualified experts who could get down here and sort the whole thing out in a few days? There had to be other reasons. Fleet was doing this on the hush-hush basis. There were hidden agendas. Then there was her hidden agenda, no longer hidden because she had tracked down her quarry, but it had captured her, not the other way round. The Galactic Media employee wanted to spill the beans about all this, but the Maggda who was daily bonding with Davvd Ong knew she couldn't, even if he had given her an open channel to Simon's desk. What was that slick bastard doing about her, anyway? Was he worried about her or just about getting the story?

Her mind roved around, and she thought that she was here because someone in Fleet had sold out to Galactic. Simon had told her that. Who the heck was that? You didn't sell out to a conglomerate media empire unless you were pretty desperate. That was a military crime punishable by death, no less, if you got caught. Who would risk that? She wished she could talk to Simon. Then she let her thoughts go to Su Lin and the shuttle and the deaths of Davvd's parents. Davvd was supposed to have been on that shuttle but wasn't for reasons beyond his control. Was that accident not an "accident"? Or was Davvd Ong the target of an assassination? Who was going to benefit if he and his family ceased to exist and lost control of Ong empire?

She got out of bed, put on a white lab coat as a dressing gown and went out into the kitchen to make a drink. She still had those thoughts in her head. Why did Davvd Ong go nowhere without a couple of very large minders hovering nearby? Why couldn't he talk to the media, *any* media, not even the Fleet journals? They wrote his exploits up, but he never gave them anything from the horse's mouth.

Randolph was standing in the corner, but he registered her presence by the green LED on his forehead.

"Yes, miss."

"Can you make me a hot chocolate and find me a pill to help me sleep? Something mild, I don't want to get knocked out."

"Yes, miss, shall I bring those to your room?"

"Yes, please."

She went back to her room and thought that she could get to like the lifestyle where one just ordered the bots about and got waited on hand and foot. She drank her chocolate, took her little white pill and went into a deep sleep.

She woke late but felt better after a dreamless night. She showered and dressed but kept the lab coat on and wandered into the kitchen expecting to find Davvd eating, but there was only Robert.

"Has Captain Ong had breakfast, Robert?"

"No, miss, he said he was waiting for you to join him."

"Can you tell me where he is, please?"

"He is checking satellite images, miss."

She went into the control room, and he turned from the screens as she came in.

"Hey, you look like 'staff' in that coat."

"If we get marooned here long enough, I might end up doing that. What are you doing now?

"Playing. The tide was coming in when we got trashed, so—"

"How did you find that out?"

"Checked the tide charts on this thing. This is a place where tides are vital, so they have all that stuff right here."

"Okay, so I am simpleminded."

"Never. It's just that you haven't had to do this stuff much."

"So what are we looking for?"

"Tide comes in as we get trashed. Debris gets taken in by tide. Waves wash stuff up on beach. We had bags in the Fly. Bags tend to float a long time before they sink, and even then, the tide was coming in, right?"

"Any luck?"

"Working at it, come and look."

The screen wavered about, focused, and swept along the beach. She could even see the marks where they had landed. He worked the focus along the edge of the surf.

There was nothing except pieces of wreckage from the body of the Fly.

"Keep going, maybe the current sweeps round that headland, maybe our stuff is still floating."

He worked along the surf towards the headland and out to the rocks, and there was nothing.

"Go back, we may have missed something."

The image swept slowly along the breaking waves.

"There. There is something there. Go back a bit!"

He slowly backtracked.

"There, the waves just broke over it. See it?" Can you close up on it?"

The image grew, and he sharpened it up. It was a bag, his duffel bag, slopping in the waves.

"Wonderful, Master of the Universe, but how do we get it? I am *not* going swimming again."

"We can solve that in a minute. How heavy was your bag. Did you have stuff in there that would sink it, hair dryers, female stuff?"

"I will ignore that sexist comment, Ong. Do another scan. Can we see down through the water, or not?"

"Have to find the right controls. I haven't been checked out on this thing."

The screen became a jumble of images before it settled down. They could suddenly see the bottom of the bay.

"Too close, Davvd, pull back a bit so we get a wider image."

"Well, we found the seats and the motor and . . . what is that, close to that seat, just there?"

"My bag! Hooked up on the bits of that seat! So, Ong, now we go back to my first question. Like, how do we get them back? Do we have a trained lobster or a codfish we send out?"

"You need your breakfast. Don't be negative. Robert, can you get in here please?"

"He is going for a walk underwater, right? He just strolls down there and picks up the bags, and he walks back here. Hello crab, hello fish, nice morning!"

He stood up and put his arms around her and laughed.

"Let's eat. I will get the bags back. You seem to forget, Styxx, this is a marine research establishment. They have things that they put into the sea, and those things can come and go and pick up things and take samples, and they have robotic controls, and guess who is going to control them while we get a cup of coffee?"

"Robert the robot, right?"

"Genius thinking, Styxx. With a brain like yours, you could become a fashion model." He ducked and went out with Robert.

After an hour, Robert came into the room where their meal had been prepared by Randolph.

"Your bags are back, sir, miss, but I have left them to drain the water out on the grill in the recovery deck."

"Thank you, Robert."

"It is a pleasure to be appreciated, sir."

She gave Davvd a look. "That robot is getting just like Don, you know that? They never, well, responded like *that* before, did they?"

"Well, they do have circuitry that allows for a certain level of sympathetic human responses, and that is part of their 'learning' program. They learn as they experience; that's why they are so expensive to own. This station is lucky to have two of them."

"When you fall in love with me, Ong, and you marry me and buy me an estate of half a million hectares of gardens, I want a couple of Dons and Joes, to look after me while you go around solving all the riddles in the galaxy."

"How about when we get out of this mess, I hire you a 'Donna' and 'Josephine', and you can have them in your apartment and order them about and have them wait on you hand and foot."

"I quite liked the first option."

"I'll let you know about that, but I am serious about the second one. Uncle Wu would let me have a very good deal. Of course, they may be a couple of rejects off the assembly line . . ."

"I am going to sort out our bags, cheapskate."

Joe had finalized his results and sent them to Davvd. The analysis showed quite clearly that the tool was a modern knife. The blade was made of plas-steel, reinforced with a high carbon content and other durable metal traces. It was very sharp. It had cut into bone. The remains showed the cuts. It had a clean, smooth edge, not serrated like a primitive tool. What was a chef's knife doing on E5 unless it came out of the base kitchens? Well, there was a thought—maybe it had. Make a note, Ong, and check. Stranger things can happen, but who was out there, and how did they, whoever they were, steal the thing? When all was said and done, it wasn't the knife that was important but the creature at the other end of it.

"We are happy. None of us have the sickness. Our blades are strong and sharp. Olann has found good flints to make the long spear tips. There are trees here like those from home where the bark can be made to give up the glue to hold the spearhead tight within the thongs. The children are strong and are good at catching the fish. There are many good fish and water birds. The traps that the women have made are good. The men went to the edge of the forest where the trees have long straight stems that can be bent around each other, and they have brought so many back that the women and the boys worked all day, making them into a wall to put up at the entrance to the cave to shield us from the winter wind. We wonder when it will come.

We have gone hunting across the plain and found great herds of deer, and we have enough good meat for many days. The women have found trees that they say will give fruit, but we will have to wait for that. Manta saw a great bear, but it was a long way off. It did not pursue him. We have seen no sign of men. We have seen strange and fearful animals, but they have not attacked us. Manta says he wants to go over the mountain to see what the world is like there, but I have asked him to stay until the winter has come and gone, because we need every hunter now. We saw a great dragonfly in the sky that sang as it flew above us, but it went towards the mountains and did not return.

Vesta, one of the girls, found clay beside the stream, and she made a bowl like the one the shining creature fed us from but not so big. She dried it in the sun, but it fell apart as she put water in it. She threw it into the fire to dry again, and the next morning, that part which was not broken had turned to stone and was as hard as the rocks. My woman Annrath has found the clay and is making a bigger bowl. She has found a round, smooth rock and beaten the clay over it into a shape, and she has dried it in the sun. She is making more and wants to make enough for every woman. I think she is mad because of the child she carries, but she just laughs at me and tells me to go hunting and to leave her in peace. So we went and hunted, and we killed an animal that had tusks that stood out each side of its mouth and rooted in the ground. It was not very large, but it was very fierce. We found some little ones, and we caught three and brought them back with us. The children play with them and feed them, and they stay within the caves or play in the grass. They are just babies.

We wonder if the shining creatures will come back.

Annrath has been collecting a great heap of branches and bark and has told me to collect more when I come back from the woods. She is mad, but I care for her so will help her make her pile of wood. I think she will burn it, but I don't know why."

Simon Brent was watching the sunset. It was quite an experience being so high in the dome that the building very nearly didn't fit it, but the view across the red Martian landscape never failed to grab him. He had earned his position, and he cherished it. He was in many ways pleased to be known as a "hard bastard," but he did have scruples. He never ever let a story go out without checking its credentials.

"Don't do your homework, Brent, and you end up getting your ass sued off," his previous boss had told him, and because he knew that that boss *had* been sued very nearly into total penury and made almost unemployable, he covered his tracks. That was why he liked Maggda. Maggda checked and rewrote until she got it right. She had never let him down, from saying that I hate doing this shit interview with a dumb sand racer to a polished piece about the subtle politics of mining rights. She was good. He wondered where the heck she was right now. He looked at her holo on the wall with the other top staffers and thought about Ong. If she was with Ong, where the heck were they? Both of them had just got lost in space, and it made him angry that there was a huge story gone down the tubes of hyperspace, and he couldn't get a sniff of it.

Maggda was sitting down in the observation deck, watching the underwater life and having a drink that Davvd had told her was made from fermented seaweed pods. Since it tasted fine and had the desired effect, she didn't care if it was the truth or not. She had focused on something that looked like an octopus that lived outside the glass. It had found a large shell and had backed into it so that only its tentacles protruded. One hung onto a stalk of red weed, which anchored it against the surge, and it waited until an unsuspecting fish came to investigate; then, like lightning, it grabbed it and ate it, folding it into its tentacles in a final deadly embrace. That had made her think about the intelligence of the creature. How did it know that if it hid and lay in ambush, it could eat better? Was it really an adaptation to the environment, a good old Darwinian solution, or just chance? She was finishing her drink when Robert approached.

"The master would like to speak to you, miss."

She hurried up the ramp. What had happened now? She thought of all the things she could have done and hadn't as sins of omission, then discarded that. Something was going on out there.

She found him, as usual, at the console, the nerve center of the place, and pulled up a chair beside him.

"Tell me, Master of the Universe, what is going on?"

"Don has found our killers, Lady of the Lace Knickers. We flew over them in the Fly, would you believe? Don did a close-up ground search by satellite, early in the morning when the shadows reveal a lot. They look like Neanderthals, an early humanoid. They got away from our normal visuals search because they wear animal skins, and they passed for a small herd" . . .

"What do you call a small herd?"

"Four."

"Just four so-called cavemen?"

"Numbers don't matter, Maggda. Just their being there does."

"And if Don found four, then there could be more, right?"

"Evidence of a cave dwelling and fires in the cliff face close to the lake."

"So how long can they have been there?"

"I suspect that they killed that deer just after they arrived. Don picked that up while it was very fresh, remember? Another problem is that they have modern weapons, well, knives at least."

"Where did they come from?"

"If I knew that, I really would be master of the universe, wouldn't I?"

"What are we going to do?"

"I love the way you say 'we'."

"Sorry, I just have this team spirit thing, and I can't help it."

"With you on the team, how can we fail?"

"You are being nice again."

She turned his head and looked at the deep graze down his face.

"If that scars up, you are going to look like a real pirate, you know that?"

"Randolph insisted on putting on Nu-Skin, so it will heal without trace. I shall retain my classic good looks, whether you like it or not. By the way, are you going to show me your scars?"

"If you think I am going to drop my pants just so you can leer at me, Ong, you can forget it,"

"That bad, huh?"

"No. While the lovely Robert was making *you* pretty, the rugged Randolph worked on my butt, and for a tin man, he has a lovely touch."

"You are just trying to make me jealous."

"Pity it doesn't work."

There was a chime from the console, and Don had more news.

There were more kills, and the tiny probe that he had sent out to examine the cave had revealed more men, women, and children. He ran the holo, and they could see that the tribe had set up house, and it looked like they were there for the long haul. They appeared to be building walls and weatherizing the place. They were there to survive.

Maggda felt immediate sympathy for them. She had been flung down here too, but her cave was a little bit more refined.

"All right, what is the next move?"

"If you had the choice, what would you do?"

"Are you really asking me?"

"Tell me, I am tired from just thinking about this."

"Well, they didn't ask to be here, did they? They came from somewhere they knew was safe and home, and they got dumped here. Someone wanted them to survive because they gave them good sharp tools right from the start. They are damned adaptable. They have not only got over the shock of the strangeness, but they have found shelter and protection, and they are making it tight. If I had the choice . . ."

"No, go on."

"I would just leave them alone for a while and even, well,

look out for them. They aren't 'enemies,' are they? Look at it this way; they are 'displaced persons' just like us in here."

"How would you feel if I said, 'Well, that's fine, but they have brought the Minnagra virus with them, and in three months all life on this moon will be gone.' Ashes to ashes, dust to dust."

She stared at him.

"Could that happen, Davvd? Seriously, could that happen?"

"Maybe."

"Look, we can check on that, can't we? We can send Don or Joe and get a blood sample, can't we?

He put his head down on the console.

"I feel so tired, Maggda. I feel so damn tired."

She kissed the back of his neck.

"Go and have a rest, but if you trust me enough, I can monitor the stuff from Don, or why not get Robert to record it all? We are not going to physically do anything until we get off this rock, are we?"

He crawled out of the chair, and she could see that the wreck and her rescue had finally caught up with him.

"Wake me if the place catches fire, but not before."

"Will do."

He went to his bedroom, and she just sat there. What could he do? He might be the Davvd Ong of fame and fortune, but he was as helpless as an octopus without a seashell on its back.

Horatio Winston Wu, Captain. Com Division, degrees in communication from Fleet Academy, with honors, was staring at the views from the space station that was in a fixed polar orbit above Alpha Six. The station was very large and it appeared to those on Alpha Six as a small moon, albeit a flattish disc of one. It received a constant flow of information from anywhere that Fleet had vessels, from robot observation stations strung out in space, from planets where Fleet had bases that housed a couple of thousand trained men, to bare and biting moons that were frozen, with swirls of methane outside the window slit.

Captain Wu had no real cause to be bitter. He had been promoted because of his ability, but he had a limited imagination and had gravitated to the communications sector where all he had to do was translate, pass on, or encrypt.

Space Station A6 was a very easy place to be. He had access to Alpha Six, where he could enjoy the high life whenever he felt the need, but he had a niggling resentment against a Captain Ong, who kept getting into the media as some kind of hero and was well-liked by his father, although Solomon would never admit that.

Ong had gone missing, which Horatio had noted with some small pleasure. Had absented himself from Fleet, and there had been no traffic to or from him since he had come back from Beebop, and the media had made a meal of it. Horatio knew that he had been slipped on board *Double Happiness*, but after that? Ong had not spoken to the media. There had been a few holos of him at the bedside of the stupid sergeant he had rescued from "a fate worse than death," though what that meant, he had no idea.

Horatio had an idea that the media would love to know more about Ong. He also had the idea that if the media did reveal stuff that Ong didn't want them to know, he would get angry, and that, in some way, would be a kind of irritation that Horatio felt that damn Davvd Ong deserved. Davvd Ong had married his sister, Su Lin, and for some reason he had resented that too. Another Ong getting a share of Wu companies interests-- and his legacy. The one real regret was that Davvd Ong hadn't been obliterated with the rest of them in the shuttle accident. A pity about his sister, but she was a dreamer. Wanted to be a doctor to go off and help some backward tribe on some backward planet out in the back blocks of backwardness and had married Ong behind everyone's back.

Solomon, he knew, had plans for the Wu and Ong empires but had kept a very tight lip about whatever it was. He knew that Davvd Ong's father was part of that secret deal, but he was gone, so maybe Captain Ong knew about it. Had his father passed that on? Was that why Fleet kept him under such a tight security net? Why had they assigned him some of their top heavies whenever he went out in public? Why did they forbid interviews, make him keep his mouth shut about everything and keep as low a profile as they could devise?

He was deep in thought when a message came through for the admiral at Fleet HQ. He observed that it was in the admiral's very secret code that even he and half his staff would take weeks to decipher. He had once cracked a coded message written in an obscure language used by a tribe of mountain shepherds on a planet that had such a low population that it was still listed as "uninhabited."

He looked for the source, but even that was hidden. He shrugged, handed over to his second in command and went to the mess. It was time for a drink even though it wasn't even near lunchtime. He would make a point of sitting with his back to the portrait holo of damn Captain Ong.

Maggda was looking at the manual for the console controls, which was thick and sectioned into all kinds of things that had never occurred to her, might be interesting, but to her sudden realization, were. She had reached the part where climatic conditions could be revealed with direct weather information from the satellites and sensors on the ocean floor, and she brought up the research station and its unlovely rocky islet. The tide was changing, and the wind was increasing a bit, so the records told her, and she was about to close things down when the console rang a very pleasant little chime, and the screens changed. "Ding-dong," she thought, "what are you trying to tell me now?"

She didn't make sense of the barometric whorls, but it looked a bit wild.

Robert came to her side, and she looked up.

"Tell me, Robert, what does this mean?"

"We have secured the station, miss. The remotes have been brought in off the ocean floor. The wave-recording buoys have been hauled down to the seabed and secured. We have sealed the top entrance and pressurized the lock. We have tied down the submarine vessels. We have sealed the outlet drains against surges, we have--"

"Robert!"

"Yes, miss."

"Does this mean we are in terrible trouble?"

"No, miss, we have secured--"

"Robert, just tell me what the heck is going to happen, please!"

"A very violent, low-pressure system is moving very rapidly up from the pole. It will bring very high winds, and wave heights will increase by forty-three percent."

"What do we do, Robert?"

"We have secured all--"

"Robert!"

"There is no danger to life, miss. The storm will be very violent, but we have secured--"

"Robert, I think you and Randolph have done all you can. The place is secure, and we are in no danger inside here, right?"

"No danger, miss, but it will get very noisy. There will be quite violent buffeting. There will be no means of going outside, and no craft will be able to land on the island for--"

"Yes, Robert?"

"My records and new calculations give an estimate of eight days, using ESY timescales."

"Should I alert Captain Ong?"

"May I suggest, miss, that even Captain Ong would be unable to quiet this storm."

She looked at his expressionless face and blinked.

"Will that be all, miss?"

"Yes, Robert, and thank you."

"It is a pleasure to be of service, miss."

She went back to the console and now understood what all

that damn swirling isobar activity meant. This storm was going to be a lulu. She had to admit that even her hero, Davvd Ong, was pretty helpless against this. Robert had been right. She wondered if it would affect the base over the ranges that she now almost considered home. How would the new arrivals fare, or would they just batten down and be safe in their deep caves? She toyed with waking Davvd, but thought better of it. He obviously needed a break. Let him sleep. The storm would wake him up soon enough. She should have asked Robert when it would hit. Ask the console, stupid, if you can find the right controls!

It was moving very fast. She went out into the kitchen and made herself a hot drink, took the station manual with her, sat in the most comfortable chair and waited. There was no way now for Don or Joe to play guardian angels and come clattering out of the blue to fly them home. She got into the section on "Larger Marine Species" and became absorbed. The noise of the winds and waves began to increase. For some reason, she went and put on her "dressing gown." There was a chill in the air.

Don had sent out a probe, no larger than a small bat, which had entered the cave and was, bat like, hanging from the ceiling. If it had had feelings, it would have felt at home; there were other small bats there. The tribe, such as it was, was eating fish, cooked in leaves in the hot coals of the hearth. They ate pretty much in silence. When the fire was raked back, one of the women brought a bowl, which looked like it had been made of red clay, and stood it near to catch the heat; then she brought another one, then another. They were crude. She brought more small branches and made up the fire, taking care not to disturb her creations. The cave was a warm haven. There were beds made from branches over which were laid skins, and the small rocks had been taken off the floor and piled to make a base for the plaited wood and rush wall that shielded the entrance. There was an overlapping gap where the tribe could come and go. Larger poles had been raised to support the woven portions. Don recorded the speech, the tool making, and faces that glowed from the light of the flames. He left it taking notes and awaited the instructions from Captain Ong.

Davvd Ong woke and was disoriented. It was dark. He had turned off all the lights in his room. He switched on the bedside lamp, pulled on his denims and went out to find Maggda and a drink. There was a great roaring from the ocean and grumbling thumps as the seas pounded their hideaway. The noise had steadily increased as he had slept. He headed for the kitchen and found Maggda with Randolph. She was eating. It looked like soup and rolls.

"Did you order all this mayhem, Styxx?"

"Just to make you grumpy, yes!"

"Is everything battened down and—"

"Tell him, Randolph. No! I will, you'll take all week. Category four storm from the pole. Force ten to twelve gale. Very high seas. Yes, Lord of the Universe, we are battened down. Robert and Randolph have done all there can be done with machines and hatches and anything else. Duration? Did you say about a week? Don and Joe will not be able to fly us out until this wind drops in maybe three, four, or five days, but who knows? We are not in danger, just yet. Come and have a drink and some of this. I don't know what is in it, and I am not going to ask, but it tastes fine."

"I should try to contact Fleet to report the finding."

"They can wait."

"You obviously don't know what 'orders' are, do you?"

"I can tell you now that there ain't *nothing* going in or out of here until this whirligig blows itself out. Ask Randolph!"

"All communications are shut down, sir, to avoid surge damage. It would be unwise to risk the satellite links or the communication frequency to Fleet, sir."

"You have talked me out of it. Could you get me a drink, please, Randolph?" What are you drinking, Maggda?"

"Don't know and don't care. This is my third."

"Please, Randolph, a large one of those."

He ate and drank, and they listened to the increasing fury all around them.

"Are we really safe down here, Davvd?"

"I would guess this rock has withstood much worse. It has been here a long time, that's why everything is a bit dated. Most of the research is done by the bots and machines and simply uploaded when it's asked for. They used to have crews here, but I don't think they have been here for . . . how long, Robert?"

"Three cycles, sir."

"What's that in ESYs?"

"About two years. They send a service shuttle down to keep the base supplied; that's why we can eat pretty well, but as you can see, it isn't five-star, but it works all right."

There was a huge, roaring crash, and they could feel the whole rock shake.

"A big one."

"What happens to all the wildlife out there?"

"Like us. Dive deep and cover the backside. It is their environment, after all."

"What about our so called Neanderthals, Davvd?"

"Well, I did ask Don to keep an eye on them. My guess is they will be pretty sheltered where they are, and this storm won't have half the force if it does get over the range. Are you worried about that little tribe, Styxx?"

"I just feel sorry for them and angry that someone dumped them here like a dog and left them to fend for themselves."

"Someone with enough sympathy or plan or just cunning to give them knives, way ahead of their technology. I'm not really clever enough to know much about the research stuff here, but when you take a group like these away from their technology, and you give them stuff way ahead of their normal stage of development, you are going to make changes."

"Could be exactly what was intended, huh?"

"Bit of a half-assed way to do it, I would have thought. I would have thought you would have needed a bigger 'sample' somehow.

I have a nagging feeling that this wasn't planned as in any good research program, but an act of desperation, almost."

"Are we back to the Minnagra virus?"

"I don't think so. They would have been dead or dying if it were. The admiral told me to go out and smell the dung if I had to. It could come to that, except that we can get samples from a probe rather than me doing it. Then we can analyze the bugs in it."

Another huge wave crashed over the island.

"How is the tide, Robert?"

"It will be full tide very soon, sir."

"Good, that means we shall be pretty well underwater, and this bashing will get a bit quieter."

She stood up and went down to the recreation room and found a couple of larger chairs.

"No one knows you are here, do they?"

"Admiral accepted of course, and a few crew who barely saw me on *Double Happiness*, and that's not taking into account my million-dollar disguise."

She spluttered into her drink.

"That moustache was wonderful. What did you do with it?"

"I think it fell in the soup, and I ate it."

"Can we be serious for a minute? No one knew that there would be a human observer here on E5 when they dropped those people off here, did they?"

"Unless there was a serious security breach."

"You know that I knew you would be on *Double Happiness*, don't you? My boss had a tipoff from someone in Fleet. No names were mentioned, but he knew that the David Essex who was on board was actually you. Knew it and told me. Gave me the ticket, told me to prowl first class, knew you would be there."

His expression was one of anger and disbelief.

"My boss has this contact somewhere in Fleet who passes on stuff to him. He pays for information, but you know something, those credits never get banked. Never ever. Simon hasn't had to pay out. The Galactic account never gets debited. I think you have someone inside Fleet, very undercover, spying on your communications."

"It would have to be someone with access to the high-level coded stuff. The admiral has special codes, and very few officers or staff can access those."

"Who hates you most, Davvd?"

"Just about everyone, I think."

"But why?"

"The Ongs and the Wu's represent a huge empire of just about any commercial venture you care to name in the galaxy. We have corporations and industries on every livable planet or rock. We collectively own five or more moons or mini planets devoted to scientific research. We endow universities. We influence governments who want our finance or expertise. We have research teams looking at everything and anything that will benefit the whole human race in medicine or drug research, and we pass most of that over free. On the other hand, Wu and Ong are hardheaded businessmen. Since my father and mother and Su Lin passed away, I carry the name of Ong. I inherit control of all Ong enterprises. No, I don't mean I sit at every board table and say yes or no, but the boards my father set up would have to get my signature if they strayed away from strict company policy. Now you know why I hide behind Fleet and play soldier boy. I don't need to be a planetary delegate. I have more clout than they have. No, I stay low and duck every now and then, and Fleet makes sure that I don't have too many attempts on my life by madmen who would love to wipe out an Ong."

"How do you cope with it all?"

"Stay low, never speak to the media, never do anything damaging to Wu or Ong or Fleet, if I can help it."

"Fleet got you out of the heat by sending you here, right?"

"I was supposed to be alone. Get down here, rummage about, report findings to Fleet, go back and go on leave to my uncle's place and go fishing. Nice and easy, then you dropped in."

She was very quiet.

"But Maggda, having you here has made my life a lot more interesting than having to sit and talk to Joe or Don about old times."

"I didn't know I was going to be such a wrench in the works, and that is the truth."

"I know that. Tell me more about Simon and his information sources."

"Well, I don't know much. All I know is that he knew you were going to be on *Double Happiness* posing as David Essex. He knew that for sure. Someone tipped him off, and he specifically mentioned Fleet. Something about a clerk somewhere."

He sat and closed his eyes. A huge wave pounded the island, and the rocks reverberated like a large drum.

"I can't think a mere clerk would have access to that level of stuff, but what is curious is that he doesn't spend the loot. He doesn't need the money."

"Or she."

"How can you tell your boss?"

"Let's lay low for a while. Nothing is going in or out of here for at least a couple of days. I have to think about whom I could talk to about this without creating a full blown security scare. If we give this to the admiral, he is going to press the panic button. Let's face it, it isn't as if this leak gave away vital information to an enemy. All he or she did was tip off the media."

"As far as we know."

"Don't let's jump to conclusions just yet. What else has this leak passed on to Mr. Brent?"

"I don't know. Simon just waved that in my face. 'We have an informant in Fleet.' Who knows what else Simon has had?"

"Right, but we are stuck inside a rock with a force ten or twelve or whatever gale outside, and we ain't goin' nowhere, babe, not *nowhere!*"

"I found some home movies."

"What?"

"There is a drawer full of holo cubes in the women's quarters. Hi Mom, Hi Dad, you know. Want to take a look?"

"Isn't that a bit like spying?"

"These are just stuff sent from home to here and back again. 'Look at this fish I caught' stuff."

They passed an hour or so watching mothers and fathers and young and old, new puppies, and messages of 'see you soon' until Maggda had had enough.

"That kind of stuff makes me homesick. How about you?"

"What is it there at home to make you emotional, Ms. Styxx?"

"I have a really beautiful apartment in Dome Six, thanks to Second Skin. Made enough to make myself comfortable. I come home, and, I think, I really am at home, how about you?"

"Well, Su Lin and I made a home for a little while, then the bottom dropped out of the world, and I went back to Fleet apartment number 15. It is bare-assed and totally functional, and let's face it, I am never there very long, so I haven't, what's the word, well, 'personalized' it. The strange thing is, when we get back to 'base,' and Joe and Don, I think *that* is pretty much 'home' right now.

"Well, it grows on you. What next then, Ong?"

"Probably get sent off to some isolated rock where I get shot at, or blown up, or flattened by something."

"Tell me about your folks. If we ever get out of here, I promise not to use it."

"You really want to know?"

"Why not? What made Davvd Ong what he is today?"

"My father and mother were a pair. My mother was a real mother when she had the time and a lovely woman, kind and a hugger. Know what I mean? I'd get home, and she just hugged me to death. My father was quite brilliant, you know that? He had a research laboratory devoted to nothing but mental disease on Alpha Six. A huge place, he had the best people he could get working there. He was a doctor of medicine and a biologist, and he made a pretty good stab at engineering. What he didn't know he would hire people who did know to tell him.

"He was concerned with what he called 'reputation.' He was very big on reputation. He would talk about that as if it had a body and mind. He said to me once, 'Beware of reputation, Davvd. A good, honest reputation is just like a young woman's virginity. You can't get it back once you've lost it. People only respect those with a good reputation. If you respect your doctor or your planetary delegates or even your wife or your cook, you can trust them, however high or low they are. Trust comes from a good reputation, and Ong tries so hard to keep that clean and honest. We are impartial. We are cruelly impartial. We will give to both sides provided there is real need. Ong will build schools and hospitals wherever there is need, and you know that we never ever allow a plaque or a sign telling anyone that we put the place there. That was an early decision of the family. If you are doing good, you don't need a big sign to say so. Build on your reputation, Davvd, not on your publicity.'

"So I made some comment about Uncle Wu, and he laughed and said, 'Solomon wants to be an emperor.' Solomon and the Wu's are the other side of the philanthropist coin. Solomon wants the galaxy to know that it was Wu who built the largest dome on Old Earth moon, cut the deepest mines, gave the most credits to the 'backward' planets. I keep telling you that the Wu family motto, even though it isn't written down, is that 'Nothing succeeds like excess.' It is a poor joke, but even he would agree with me. And Solomon isn't a bad man. He just wants to be appreciated. Understand Solomon and don't judge him too harshly."

She looked at him and thought that the father had shaped the man without the man knowing it.

"Your father sounds like a real good man, Ong."

"I think he was."

There was silence between them while the sea did its best to destroy the rocks.

"What now, Master of the Universe?"

"You tell me, Mistress of the Wonder Undies."

"Do you have to go running to Fleet about the little tribe back

67

there? Can't we just turn our backs for a while and work on who is selling Fleet to Galactic and who knows who else. I mean, isn't the spy inside Fleet worse than a few hunters with knives?"

Another huge sea roared against and over the island. They could hear boulders crashing across the landing pad.

"Right now, all we can do is wait. The electrical mayhem from this little disturbance is going to disrupt any kind of communication we want to use."

"Can we see anything from our local scanners, holos, or sensors. I want to see what is happening outside. Can we do that?"

"Robert, can we access some visuals of what is going on out there, please?"

The robot activated a screen above the main console, and for a moment all that could be seen was a whiteout. Then the wave passed, and they were looking out to sea from the edge of the landing pad. The horizon showed as blue black, lightning flashed across the sky, and huge breakers were roaring in towards their sanctuary. Enormous mountains of water reared up and flung themselves at them, and rain, blinding rain, was blown in sheets over all. The noise was deafening, the chaos was frightening to watch, and Maggda turned away.

"What can live in that, Davvd?"

"They go deep, Maggda, they go deep. Get deep enough and all this is just surface noise. Like us watching the clouds go by way up above."

The camera changed as Robert switched from sea to shore.

"Scan the beach, please, Robert, what there is left of it."

The camera on the headland swept along the long beach. The waves were piling up and breaking in great roaring surges up the sloping sands, almost totally obscuring it. Along the edge of the beachfront, trees were being washed away. A few had already toppled and were being ravaged by the waves.

Maggda watched the violence and suddenly shouted, "Stop, Robert, stop! Can you freeze it just there? No, back a bit, among those tree limbs . . ."

The camera stopped and scanned slowly. A big surge turned the vegetation over, and there appeared a huge head, a long neck.

"Close-up on that, Robert, please."

"Well, he didn't get far, did he?" said Ong. "There is our plesiosaur, washed up on the beach."

"Can you make it tighter, please, Robert?"

They could see the huge head and the open mouth and, piercing the upper and lower jaws, a distorted strut from the frame of the Fly.

"Bit off more than he could chew," she said. "I can't say I am sorry, Davvd,"

"Look at it this way, how many live plesiosaurs are there these days? Now there's one less to study and one less to wonder over, but I know how you feel."

"You feel sorry for something that damn near ate us, Ong?"

"It was just doing what it was designed to naturally do. It wasn't feeling vindictive."

"Not like the person selling Fleet stuff to anyone who wants it?"

"Maybe."

"Do you think it is something personal?"

"In what way?"

"Maybe it is someone who wants to get at you personally."

"I thought you meant it could be someone with a personal grudge against Fleet."

"Either way."

"Won't know until we have some evidence that he or she has been slipping other stuff out of Fleet that isn't related to me. So far all we have is a cryptic hint that it wasn't Essex but me. Simon had to fill in the dots."

"My mother said to me once, "If you get too well-liked, you get disliked.""

"She could be right."

"Now you, Ong, Captain of the Universe, have a huge following. All right, I know you don't go out of your way to get that, but people just think of you as being likeable."

"I can't think why. I just try to be a good little soldier boy. Yes sir, no sir, do as I am told and hope I can duck fast enough when things get hot. Don't talk to the media, smile at the holos and the tri-dees and keep quiet. Don't go out and party with wild women, or men for that matter, keep things clean and act like butter wouldn't melt in my jocks. What more do I have to do?"

"Your trouble is that you are so clean you squeak. You are very attractive. Young women want to get into your jocks. Men envy you getting all the attention because of the hero and medal thing, you know that? When you got your first medal as a lieutenant on Virdana—"

"It was an accident, Maggda.

"Davvd, I have seen the holos!"

"All right, but they don't tell the whole story. I was there as an Ong because my father couldn't be there. Fleet sent me out there to stand next to the planetary delegate and the government party just to show the flag, all right?"

"Then what happened?"

"Well, as far as anyone could work out, the northern tribes were put out because Ong Foundation had built a hospital that was in southern tribal territory."

"But from what I remember, Wu Foundation was going to build them one in their largest city, so what went wrong?"

"The northern tribal chiefs got their tribes people all stirred up and told them this wasn't going to happen. The government had cut them out, and they were being treated as second-class. There wasn't going to be a hospital; instead, there was going to be an army barracks staffed by all southern tribes' people."

"Sounds just like Virdana."

"Well, we were all there lined up like shop window dummies on the steps of the hospital, and they had a typical army salute. The trucks were driving past and all that stuff, and this truck came down the hill, and instead of going past, it suddenly swerved into the forecourt, the driver rolled out, and everyone who could run, ran like chickens."

"Except you!"

"Well, I just ran for the truck, jumped in the open door, wrenched the wheel hard over, and it headed for the ornamental lake in front of the government buildings down the street."

"Why?"

"What do you mean, 'why'?"

"You could have run like a chicken too, couldn't you?"

"What, and see my father's beautiful hospital get wrecked? Are you kidding?"

"Then what happened?"

"Well, the truck went over the edge of the lake and plunged in and just about sank. I thought, 'that thing is going to explode,' and I flung myself behind a big ornamental urn thing, and when the truck settled, the hydrogen motor and the storage tank exploded, and all the water went straight up. The blast blew the whole of my uniform jacket apart, and I got showered with fish. I was lying there deaf as a post, and these fish, all these colored fish, were flopping about on the courtyard."

"Made a wonderful holo story, you know that?"

"Well, that was it."

"Well, what was the sequel?"

"They blamed the northern tribes, but it wasn't an assassination attempt at all. They got their hospital. Old Solomon had a team in there the next damn day.

"Turned out the truck blew a tire just before they came past. Driver got the wheel wrenched out of his hand. He bailed out and hoped for the best, and stupid Davvd Ong was given a lovely medal. Mind you, that, if anything, built up the Ong reputation. After that, they used to swear by Ong. 'In Ong's name, I tell you, brother', which was what my father liked."

"You made that sound so easy, Davvd!"

"Well, it was."

"To you, maybe, to you. See, like I said before, you knew what to do, and you just did it. You can't be trained for that, can you?"

"Maybe not, but I think Fleet would like to think it can."

"I'm cold. Has it turned cold or is it just this wetness getting to me?"

"Come here, and I'll give you a hug if you promise not to take advantage of a nice, young, innocent man."

"As if I could!"

"Maybe you just have to try harder."

"Just shut up, Ong, and hug me."

The storm howled around the rock, but the waves subsided a trifle as the tide turned.

Back on E5, Don was looking at his tiny probe's sound and pictures. The gale had roared over the range and brought some rain, but the tribe was snug in the caves, roasting meat over a hot, glowing fire. Annrath had made bowls, which were drying nicely. The little wild pigs played and squealed and grew less wild. Life was good, but they missed the people they had left behind.

Professor Ardan Radnath, Senior Research Fellow for Human Studies on E7, was unhappy. His long-suffering colleague, Dandra Singh, was even more unhappy. They had, using the vernacular, "blown it," in a way that defied their comprehension and their usual slick expertise.

Dandra had a phrase in mind he dare not voice aloud. It was to do with excreta striking the blades of a cooling device, which were revolving at maximum speed while both of them stood very close to it.

"Did you not, Dandra, have that colony very closely monitored?"

"Yes sir, very closely monitored, indeed."

"So, perhaps you could tell me, how does it happen that the colony whom you assured me was immune to influenza, not only was destroyed by it, men, women, and children, Dandra, but that half of that colony disappeared off the face of the planet?"

"Sir, they were monitored, and—"

"And so closely, Dandra, that the bulk of them vanished overnight, taking the virus with them to contaminate everyone they met in the future!"

"Sir, they had been immunized against most strains. Those who vanished were immune from the strain that killed the rest. I would stake my life upon that."

Radnath gave Dr Singh a look that suggested it was only a matter of time before that could be the case.

"Are they loose upon the planet, Dr Singh?"

"No trace has been found of them, sir. They could not have traveled far by foot. All the indications are that they were uplifted by a craft of some kind."

"Dandra, I hope and trust that you too will be uplifted to find these lost souls before you and I find ourselves shackled to a shovel in the dung pits on New Babylon."

Dandra hung his head and cursed ancient gods who he knew had it in for him.

"Sir, how can we be blamed for an act beyond our control? Can we be blamed if a thief comes in the night and steals the chickens or the buffalo?"

Radnath shook his head from side to side, as does an elephant when it is thinking.

"I know that what you say is true, Dandra, I know it, but we have to now inform the Research Federation that somehow we have killed off several human beings and lost the rest somewhere on a planet that was a haven of research, not buffalo rustling!

"Perhaps you would like to write the report. They may accept the analogy of the chickens and the buffalo, but I doubt that it will make them sympathetic. Ten million credits, Dandra, were allocated to this research. A mere drop in the bucket for Wu and Ong Foundation, but even they might suggest that it might have been better spent by those in charge, who have accidentally lost half of the project and killed off the rest!"

"Perhaps, sir, they will understand that a person with your impeccable research record and Galactic reputation would not be held responsible for what was, evidently, beyond your control?"

"Flattery, Dandra, is nice. I may survive the holocaust. How about you?"

"Sir, you and I are both blameless. We followed the protocols, we dotted the I's and dotted the T's--.

"Dandra! You do not *dot* T's! Now listen to me, child of my uncle. When you were caught stealing watermelon, what did you do?"

"I lied, and then I ran. May I ask what you did when *you* were caught, sir?

"I ran and then hid under the house, like a dog that is going to be beaten. Then I waited, because I knew that the person who would want to beat me now, would have forgotten about it later."

"Sir, we cannot hide under a house."

"Listen to me, Dandra. Let us not run away, but let us think of a way, let us say, to allow those Neanderthals to disappear without any blame being attached to us at all."

"We cannot make new ones, sir."

"Dandra, how long has this research project been underway? I have given ten ESYs to it, and it was begun just before I was appointed. Now, I want you to find the figures of births and deaths for the past ten years of this tribe, not just the small colony we knew right here, but the larger ones over the ranges by the great lakes. Find those, and we may have a house to hide under after all. Now, are the dead buried, the caves decontaminated, and every scrap of skin and clothing in those caves burnt?"

"Yes sir."

"Now, Dandra, son of my uncle, you will build a house to hide under, using the deaths from the past two cycles. Those that the virus killed, Dandra, died from natural causes, or a spear wound, or an infection, or an accident. A great deer killed two last year. Do you remember that?"

"Yes sir, theirs is a hard life."

"Dandra, you have seen my wife. She is beautiful and comes

from a very good family. Our son is doing very well at Belvedere. He is studying stardrive engineering, and they speak well of him. Our daughter will soon be a qualified doctor with an honor's degree in robotic medicine programming. I have a house that even the planetary delegate envies. So, build us a house to hide under, Dandra, and make sure that it is one that cannot be pulled down around our ears."

Dandra already had the data coming up on the screen.

Marshall Kurt Schiff, acting commandant of Barracks Ten on Valderia, was awaiting the arrival of one Jackson Wu. Young Wu was there to ask questions, and Commandant Schiff was prepared to give him any answer except the correct one.

Schiff was well trained. The Valderian Military Academy had worked on him ever since he had entered the gates as a raw cadet, and he was now a polished example of what an officer should be, one who could be totally trusted to serve the Valderian ideal. He had seen some hard service, but he was hard, and he had enjoyed it.

He was tall and lean and crisp. His hair was crisply cut; his uniform was crisply tailored and crisply pressed. His boots shone with the kind of glow that could only be achieved by serious hard work on the part of his valet. His high-necked uniform jacket was a blue gray, his buttons gold and crisply polished, and his breeches dark blue. His collar bore the gold badges of rank, and across his left breast there was a small wall of colored silk bricks that were his array of medals.

His office was as austere as he was. It had no holos of cheerful family smiling from the desktop or cheerful bunches of mountain daisies; it was dark wood, severe and angular. The desktop was all polished timber except for the leather pad directly in front of the high-backed hard chair.

Schiff looked around his office and was satisfied. He buttoned a discreet bell, and his assistant, a very young officer, appeared, clicked her heels, and awaited orders.

Jutta Vogel loved the service. She loved her job. She loved the somewhat Spartan life. She loved to hike in the mountains with her jolly fellow officers and sing patriotic songs, and after a long healthy hike, to retire to the mess and drink maybe a couple of patriotic beers.

She was crisp. Her long blonde hair was coiled and plaited into a tight, neat pile around her head. She was fair of skin and blue-eyed, and she always looked, as Marshall Schiff may have observed, "crisp."

She showed in a slightly disheveled young man who was in need of sleep.

Jackson Wu, younger son of the great Solomon Wu, was not in a good humor. He had spent three days and nights on board a Valderian starship, which, if it had been allowed to carry weapons, would have been a cruiser on patrol of Valderian interests across the galaxy. Young Wu was used to luxury. His father was not one to stint on comfort, but the Valderian starship was as starved of luxury as its designers could devise. When it was not shuttling Valderians around that part of the galaxy they liked to think of as theirs, it was a troop carrier.

Young Wu had appealed to his father to let him travel on the private yacht, but his father had been adamant.

"It would be in bad taste to swan around like a lord of creation, when all I want you to do is to ask questions about that fiasco on Beebop. You go on one of their ships; you talk to the man we know was responsible, but who would never admit it; and you ask simple questions. If you want to know if someone is lying, Jackson, you have to look them in the face, boy; you have to talk to them on their turf; and you have to use your nose! Sniff them out, boy, sniff them out, and you might eventually graduate as the diplomat I would love to have in this family!"

The ship had a stateroom that might have been a stable, if the stable had had dull-colored and thin carpets. There were no decorations of any kind whatever. The furniture was dark timber; the bed was hard; the drinks cabinet had contained nothing but three different kinds of Valderian beers, and the food at mealtimes was boring and tasteless. His shipboard companions were mostly Valderian officers going or coming from some military duty, and they tended to avoid him. When he attempted to join in a jolly drinking song with them one night, they had stopped and excused themselves.

He had little sleep.

His bed was hard, and he was constantly awakened by hard boots up and down the corridor and laughter, joint laughter, that suddenly stopped as it passed his door. He was in a bad mood before he reached the office, and now, he was quietly angry. He had enough sense to curb it. As his father had impressed upon him, "Your personal feelings are not the best diplomatic ones."

"Do come in, Jackson; do come in and take a seat."

They exchanged the ritual, perfunctory shaking of fingers, and he sat in the chair offered him. It was plainly uncomfortable, hard and unyielding. He was unshaven. The hot water had run out during his shower on the ship. His suit was rumpled despite the most expensive fabric employed in its construction. His tie wouldn't knot correctly. His breakfast was inedible.

"Jackson, it is an honor to have you here. What can I do for you? Your father has sent you, of course?"

"The family sends me, sir, and I do as I am told. When my father says, "You will do this or that, it is better to say 'yes sir' than to engage in pointless arguments, believe me!"

"He and my commanding officer would get along well, I think."

"Only if your commanding officer did as he was told, sir."

Schiff attempted a smile that came out close to a sneer.

"It would be interesting to get them together, eh, Jackson?"

"May it never happen, sir, for both our sakes!"

"But I am forgetting my manners."

He pressed the bell, and Jutta slid into the office.

"Jutta, some refreshments for Mr. Wu. The flaky pastry ones

and a drink? What would you like to drink, Jackson? Beer? Or maybe fresh coffee?"

The girl disappeared.

"Now, Jackson, what is your mission? I am ready to listen."

"The family Wu, and the family Ong, since we are united in this event, wondered if the slime worms on Beebop arrived there with your knowledge, sir."

"You tread on dangerous ground, Mr. Wu. I will treat your visit here as a diplomatic one, so I will not take offense, but you appreciate that that is the kind of question that is not to be treated lightly. Lighter questions than that one have led to bloodshed."

"Forgive me, sir. I have not had a restful journey, so my temper is not as good as it should be."

"Jackson, I am sorry to hear that. Would you like coffee or something stronger? No, I don't mean beer, but I have some real, Old Earth scotch here, hidden away so my staff is not tempted."

He bent down and opened a door somewhere in the desk and emerged with a bottle.

"I am not a great drinker of these spirits, Jackson, but have been told that a twelve-year ESY single malt is acceptable?"

"Yes sir, but I had better not drink on an empty stomach. I could say things I didn't mean."

"A little later perhaps. Have coffee now and some of the pastries. They will fill the void a little. Now ask me the question again?"

"Slime worms, sir, were found on Beebop and had to be destroyed because they threatened the lives of the beacon staff there—"

"And Fleet did a wonderful job in eliminating them, we see and hear."

"The reason I am here and not Fleet is that we have business interests in the moon. You are well aware we lease it to Fleet as part of its directional beacon network. Fleet would not have responded as it did except that the beacon was damaged and the staff in danger. It would have been an internal matter to be settled by the Ong Wu Foundation, had there not been loss of life."

"And you ask me if the Valderians were responsible, is that it?"

"Valderia produced the slime worm and uses it as a great, living recycler of dangerous waste. You put it on moons or planets that are contaminated, and the worms digest nearly all toxins and expel them as useful faeces, to be dug in or plowed under. The worms on Beebop were not the usual species your government uses elsewhere, with respect, were they?"

Schiff stood, slapped the calf of his polished boot with his riding crop and did a short turn of the office.

"Have you been doing your homework, Jackson, and that is why you lack sleep? I have a confession to make. It is hard for a Valderian to admit mistakes; we don't make many and we tolerate less, but in the case of Beebop, we did make a mistake. Beebop was never meant to host those worms. The sister moon, with which, as you know, we have a lease agreement with your esteemed Foundation, was supposed to be the host, but, how do I explain this? The coordinates fed into the computer on the drone that was used to drop the spawn was that of Beebop and not Beegal. You have to admit that the names are similar. Perhaps the operator was tired, Jackson; perhaps he misread the orders? The spawn went to Beebop. It takes a good half-ESY for them to grow to any kind of maturity and another full ESY for them to mate and expand the population, so you see, we were not fully aware of the critical nature of the situation before Fleet reacted, as it usually does, and went into a red rage about it."

"May I use that as a full record, sir?"

"I did notice the device in your button hole, Jackson, and was aware that you would record this conversation. Of course, you have to be aware that I do not fully represent Valderia. What you have there will be denied at interplanetary level. I have told you to the best of my knowledge what went wrong. Fleet hasn't accused Valderia of anything untoward, remember that, Jackson.

"I have a holo that you can take with you. It explains in great detail the development of the worms and just how useful they are, especially in places that would require hugely expensive resources.

"We like to maintain good relationships with the Ong Wu Foundation at all times, Jackson, and I am pleased you came so I could explain the situation to you. Now, another drink? Another pastry? No? Then you will have to excuse me. I have lots of recalcitrant soldiers to get to work.

"Oh, and by the way, Jutta has been ordered to escort you on a tour of the city and to generally look after you. She is an excellent hostess. You leave in the morning? She will maybe show you some of the nightlife."

He put on the dark blue cap, tapped his boots and left. Jackson stood up. The chair had given him a numb backside.

Jutta came in and smiled. Her smile was as fresh as the mountain air; her cheeks were as pink as a new rose. He smiled back.

"I am sorry, Mr. Wu, that I cannot escort you now because of my duties here, but this evening I would be delighted to show you some of the city. You are staying at . . . ?"

"The Palace."

"A very good hotel. I have never been inside it, but it has an excellent reputation."

"Why not come and have dinner with me? I hate to eat alone, and you can tell me what to order. Some of the food here isn't familiar to me."

She smiled and gave him a neat, crisp, little curtsy.

"Shall I come at mid-six cycle?"

"Yes, do and we can do a short tour before we eat. Will that be time enough?"

"Yes, I think so, Mr. Wu. I shall not be late. Your car is outside; now, if you come with me."

Jackson rode to his hotel, set back from the main square. It was pleasant enough. The city had a faintly regimented air about it with its stiff, uncluttered buildings and organized gardens, but the hotel was at least comfortable. His room overlooked the square, where land cars hissed along. Bright red and black taxis came and went, and he watched the Valderians cross the roads. They never seemed to straggle. They seemed to bunch and march across as lights changed. The local police were static bodies, merely watching, and the street cameras revolved as they did in any city, just watching and waiting. It all reminded him of a barracks.

He showered and changed, found a fresh new suit and bought a bright bunch of flowers in the foyer and had them sent to his room. Then it was to the bar with its disciplined palm trees and uncluttered background, where the bottles of assorted exotic drinks were regimented. He ordered a long gin and tonic, but the barman had poured him beer. When he looked at it with some surprise, the barman apologized.

"I am sorry, sir. I automatically pour beer because that is what we drink here. You surprised me by asking for that drink. It is a long time since I have had to serve it. It is an Old Earth drink, sir?"

"I suppose so. I never thought about it. My parents drink it, so I drink it."

"Add that to your bill, sir? Room number?"

In some ways, the human bar staff, the atmosphere of the place was all rather old fashioned, but he didn't mind that. One became used to a total robotic presence on other worlds where human labor was in very short supply. Here, they had the manpower, and used it. He wondered what the nightlife would be like.

The bell chimed on his inter-room communication device, and a voice announced that a Miss Vogel was at the reception desk. He hurried down and was half expecting her to be still in uniform, but she was wearing a very pretty, very dark, floral-patterned dress that revealed her legs and was low-cut enough for him to be interested in her breasts. She had done something to her very blonde hair, had somehow piled it up, and it had a decoration in it, pinning it together, and her heels were high, making her taller. She looked quite beautiful, and he stood back and smiled in genuine appreciation.

She laughed at him.

"Were you expecting my dress uniform maybe, Mr. Wu?"

"May I say, Miss Vogel, that I think you look very beautiful, and that I am very lucky to have you escort me?"

She laughed a little and gave him another curtsy.

"Please, may I ask for a drink?"

They went to the bar, and the barman made him a long gin and tonic. Jackson laughed.

"Would you like to try one of these, Jutta?"

"I would like to try it. It isn't like beer, is it?"

He shook his head, "No, nothing like beer, and you may not like it, but try it anyway!"

Three gins later, she thought that she quite liked the change from beer.

"Are we ready to go out now, Mr. Wu?"

"Please, call me Jackson. I feel like an old man when people call me Mr. Wu."

"In deference to your family, not every girl gets to be the escort of a young man from your family background."

"Can we forget that, please? I have to put up with that all day from my father and mother. When I think I can just be me, Jackson, student, a young man who just wants to enjoy life, they haul me back in. It's like being a fish on a hook. I can play so far, and then they tighten the line."

They walked a lot. She took him around the music hall district. They watched some obscure street theatre puppet show all about fat soldiers, which didn't impress him but made her laugh. He guessed you had to be part of it to fully appreciate it. His heart quailed a bit when she said "barracks," but she just wanted to show him the horses. Neat and regimented, clipped regimental style. She went to a head hanging over a stable gate, and she beckoned him closer.

"This is mine, Jackson. This is my horse. This is my 'Sergeant.'"

"He looks beautiful, but I know nothing about them."

"He and I ride together on the parades and when we charge the 'enemy.' He will never be really mine, but I love him and think that he isn't just a company horse, but my personal mount. It is strange how a human can love an animal like this, and maybe, he loves me just a little too."

"Maybe he does, Jutta, maybe he does."

He watched her stroke the animal's nose and whisper to it, and he thought she was lovely. He shook his head. "One mustn't get too fond of the enemy, Jackson."

The military museum left him cold. He couldn't appreciate the love of weapons, or the lists of the dead cut into the floors of the Memorial Hall. His feet were tired, and he was getting hungry. He suggested they eat. She took him down a narrow street by a canal with brightly painted barges on it, and suddenly there was a sign. She led him into a warm interior with white tablecloths and red napkins. There were flowers on the tables and much polished wood.

"This is the most expensive restaurant in the whole city, Jackson, and I have never eaten here, so you will have to take the same chances as I do. In the holo mags they rate this as being six stars, and critics go mad about the food. They have a menu that half of the city could never understand, and I need you to translate for me."

"How do you think I will know?"

"Because you are so wealthy that you will think this place is like a taxi driver's café."

Their table was in a quiet corner. The whole restaurant was quiet, even though it had a fairly full clientele. He noted that those in uniform were very top brass indeed. They were bemedaled and heavy jowled and drank a lot of beer.

The menu was partly in French, some in Italian, some in plain Galactic, but the food was very special, and the chef, or chefs, knew what they were doing. Thanks to a very broad and expensive education, Jackson could cope very well. He thought Jutta was impressed.

They ate and drank, and he supplied her with a wine that his family drank, barely noting that the cost was nearly as much as his starship fare and they had a dessert that had Old Earth chocolate and ice cream. The coffee was hot and mellow. He was well satisfied and told her so.

"Ah, Jackson, you have made me very happy, because now I can go back to the mess and boast that I ate here, and that a generous young Mr. Wu paid the bill. They will be green with envy."

He laughed at her.

"Let us do better, Jutta Vogel," and he beckoned to a human waiter.

"What are you doing?"

"Sit and wait just a moment."

A girl with a holo camera appeared, and they sat close and smiled as she captured the moment.

He gave her the credits, and she left with Jutta's address.

"Now you can just show them that as living proof that we were here. No one can accuse you of just big noting yourself without proof, can they?"

She looked at her tiny time band and pushed her chair back.

"I will take you back to the hotel, Jackson, because I have a very early parade in the morning, and the marshall does not tolerate sluggards. We had better take a cab, I think."

At the hotel, he asked her to his room.

"I have a small present for you, Jutta. It isn't a great gift but just a token, because you have been very kind."

"When a young man wants me to see his bedroom, I think maybe he expects me to be the gift?"

"Well, it is a thought, but no, I do have a small gift."

In the suite he gave her the flowers, and she smiled, and then she kicked off her shoes.

"Now, Jackson Wu, can you take orders?"

"I think so."

"Turn your back to me and do not move unless I tell you."

He kicked his shoes off in turn and turned his back to her. She slipped his coat off and threw it onto a chair, then his shirt, and then she loosened his pants and let them drop. She slipped her fingers into the waistband of his underwear and pulled them down, and then ordered him to lift his feet while she took off his socks.

"Now, you must close your eyes tight. Tight, I said."

She took his hand and led him to the bed.

"Now, on your face. Put your face in the pillow. Do not dare look!"

He buried his face in the pillow and felt something warm flow over his shoulders and back.

"That is just a little oil, Jackson. I carry it with me at all times because I am a masseuse. Now keep still and close your eyes."

She kneaded the knots out of him. Her elbows found every muscle and released them into a relaxed and pliant state. She pressed down with her firm hand onto and into his backside, down his legs until he groaned. She flexed his toes until he wept. She rubbed him with a soft towel, and then she said, "Stay very still, Jackson Wu, and I will finish."

He was so relaxed he forgot his naked state and lay there, totally compliant.

"Now, can you hear me? Turn over!"

He slowly rolled over and opened his eyes.

She was beside the bed, totally naked too.

Her nipples were red rosebuds against her cream skin. Her hair was down and long and thrown back. She rubbed her hands.

"Now, I shall finish."

She leant over and worked his chest hard, kneading and bunching. His stomach tightened, and she pushed her fingers into his thigh muscles and into his groin. She gripped his arms and grasped his biceps, then triceps, and he felt the pain of pleasure.

"Now," she said, "it is my turn."

She slipped her hand down his stomach and held his rising organ.

"Now, I am going for a ride, and you are my Sergeant."

She slipped onto him and wriggled herself into a position that impaled her.

"Now, first we walk a little to get us warm. Then we trot a little, like this. We like to trot, don't we Sergeant?"

He was groaning.

"Now we are warmed, we break into a gallop. How far can we gallop, Sergeant, how far can we gallop?"

She rode him hard and fast, and he was helpless. Then she collapsed onto him, kissed him on the mouth and moaned with him.

"Oh, Sergeant, you give me much pleasure. I love to ride, Jackson, and you make a good horse."

He held her close and kissed her neck.

"Please, let us sleep for just an hour or so. I have to parade so early, it is almost criminal."

Light was coming through the window when he woke and felt for her warm body, but it had gone, and her space was cold. He swore, but she was long gone. Nothing was left to take away with him. She had never happened. He swore again when he saw the time. He had a very hurried shower, did not shave, got into his clothes and hurried down to the lobby. He paid his bill and ordered a cab. They rushed his luggage down, what there was of it, and he was at the shuttle launch pad just on time. On the damn Valderian spaceliner, he had the same awful room, and there seemed to be the same awful guests. The food was just as bad, and he was feeling savage after four nights of it. He couldn't wait to get home. What he knew might be vital.

He went to his suit lapel and looked for the recorder. Then he looked on his other suit. The tiny recorder had vanished with Jutta into the night of Valderia. He found the holo cube, slotted it into the machine and learned much about the worms. He also learned that the meat was very high protein and could be made into just about anything. He even recognized the delicate pastries that the marshall had given him to eat. Then he went into the bathroom and was very quietly sick. He was pleased this so-called "diplomatic" venture was nearly over.

His father was amused. It was not what Jackson had expected.

"You did well, my son, you did well. You see, I expected the reception you had, but we really did want to test the water. Sending you was one way of doing it without causing a great deal of offense. You know that Schiff is related to the chancellor? Of course you didn't. If you had you would have been somewhat cowed, I think. No, the news of your little visit will get back to the powers of Valderia, and they will know that we are on watch. We know all about the worms, of course. I didn't want to tell you, but we do have a worm farm or two scattered about the galaxy. They bring in a very good supply of ready cash. When the meat is processed and flavored, it can be made to taste like anything, as you discovered. On some planets it has been the savior of starving masses, and the worms grow fast and need no real artificial feeding if one has the right swamp."

"But you are talking about the normal commercial worms?"

"Yes, of course. The Beebop worms were genetically engineered, Jackson, without approval of the Foundation. That is why we have to watch the Valderian experiment. No, the Beebop worms were put there to deliberately disrupt that beacon. Fleet has guessed that while things were getting very hot and confused, the Valderians sent a large battle cruiser through that quadrant without registering it in that star space. Where and why, only the Valderians know."

"Isn't all that Fleet business? Sorry father, but aren't we getting in a bit deep here? Let Fleet do the dirty work, not us."

"I have to remind you, Jackson, that our huge business interests and Fleet are very closely related. Many of our interests wouldn't have happened if Fleet hadn't hovered about with a cruiser capable of wiping out half a planet."

"I'm not sure I approve of bullyboy tactics. We can get things we want without that, can't we?"

"Nowadays, of course we can, but in the early years when we and Ong were expanding the horizons and pushing hard to get our companies established on lumps of rock that rival forces thought they might take, we needed Fleet, and we paid huge sums to make sure it could afford to be there. But enough of this, how was the nightlife? I am sure your mother would love to know."

He coughed. "Sorry, but I think I caught a cold on that damn Valderian starship. I need to get a drink."

The storm slowly ran down into a large rain depression, which helped to level the waves a little. Maggda had been prowling like a caged leopard, frustrated by the weather and their inability to simply do anything very constructive. She had had Randolph work on her hair, and Davvd had laughed, not at her hairstyle, but the thought that she wasn't going anywhere where it could be seen, and that if she stepped out on the landing pad, it would be blown away in seconds.

"I know all that, Ong! I know all of it, but you have to appreciate that maybe for just a few hours, I can look at my face in a mirror and not feel too devastated. So leave me alone; go and see if we can talk to Fleet, or Joe or Don. Things are quieting down a lot. We may be able to find out when we can get off this rock."

"Yes ma'am!"

He laughed and went to the control panels.

He had suspected that the Wu rental ship that came to E5 was unmanned by humans. It was a totally robotic-controlled ship, but it was larger than, what? Larger than it needed to be for just data collection or an upload of up-to-date core samples. It had come and gone but had stayed a lot longer than most fly-bys usually did. He thought he had found the transport for the "displaced persons" of Maggda's tribe.

He reported to Don, and Don played him the record of the tribal comings and goings. Davvd thought that it was time to try and get back to home base and to somehow see for himself.

Maggda had been looking for her octopus and its shell and was pleased that it had hidden somewhere during the wildest weather but now was back on station. Ong had been right. "Dive deep and cover your butt." She idly speculated about the "clerk" in Fleet who was passing information to Galactic. Obviously not some young low-ranking slave, because he or she didn't need the credits. She got up and went to find the master of the universe.

"What's happening?"

"Don has been monitoring the tribe. They are all healthy and pretty happy, I think. And that ship that was rented out to Valderia, it had to be robot manned. No human listed. It was classified as an "upload data" visit. I think those guys were part of it. They got dropped off here. Now I do know that there is a long, ongoing program with Neanderthals being conducted on E7. They were looking at some genetic enhancement to accelerate intelligence. Had been tried with other primates, but it wasn't a very quick fix, if you know what I mean.

"Take the pill dumbo, and you will be a genius?"

"I don't think it was that simple."

"Damn and I thought I could join the ranks of the smart guys for once."

"Trying to think, Rathbone? No, not Rathbone, it was Radnath. Professor Radnath. He was in charge of the thing, I believe. Now I can get some answers, maybe?"

"Can we reach E7, and what time scale are they on?"

"I want to leave that for a while. I want to get us back to our base. Have to give Foundation a buzz to let them know we are going to be off here and back there. They want to know who is nosing about up here, same as we do."

"I had a thought about the 'clerk' in Fleet Com. Can't we devise some message that would smoke them out? You know, 'Davvd Ong was eaten by a plesiosaur last cycle, so won't be able to pay his mess bill?"

"Non-payment of the mess bill would have them jumping about for sure. The other would leave them cold."

"No good?"

"Not a very good idea, Styxx. What we have to do is to make sure that it gets picked up by our spy. Give it more thought, and we can maybe bait a hook. Oh, and by the way, despite what I said, your hair looks great."

"Thanks, I don't think Fleet would approve of your hair right now. Get your hair cut, trooper!"

"Shut up, Styxx, and come here and kiss me. I need it."

"You must be feeling better. Ask me nicely."

"Maggda, please, pretty please, sidle over here in your slinky way and give me a big, hot, wet kiss?"

"Are you going to kiss me back or is this a one-way street?"

"Get over here and find out."

Don brought the loader over the next morning. The sea had subsided to its normal rush and roar level. They scrambled out of the narrow entrance and climbed onto the loader platform and found a couple of straps. They huddled behind a couple of empty crates; Don revved the rotor, and they headed back to base, clutching bags and Maggda her "dressing gown." At the last minute she found she couldn't give it up. It had a logo on the pocket of Bare Head Island, and she wanted a souvenir. Who knew when she would get back there again?

Going into her bedroom, she felt like she was home. It was strange how secure she felt there and how the presence of Davvd Ong had much to do with that. She greeted the robots like old friends. Their expressionless faces could easily have held smiles of welcome.

Marshall Schiff was humming a jolly little marching song and keeping time with his whip against his boots. From behind his desk in his hard upright chair, he watched as Jutta brought in coffee and a few cream-filled pastries on a regimental plate. She set the tray down on the table and clicked her heels. He smiled. She was looking, what word could he use? Well, "crisp" was reasonably suitable.

"Good morning, Jutta! You look pretty and wide-awake as usual. Did you have problems with your escort last night?"

"No sir, he was the perfect gentleman." She felt in her skirt pocket and dropped the tiny recording device into the ashtray.

"Did he entertain you well?"

"We ate at the Blue Boar. It was wonderful!"

"Well, he didn't stint there, did he? That place has the finest cuisine in the city or even the planet, they tell me. I seldom eat there. There are usually very high-ranking officers pigging it, and drinking too much beer, and then they want to ask me too many questions and are trying to curry favor. I think I prefer the mess."

"Yes sir."

"At least he got you back in time for parade this morning, eh? I did wonder if you would be missing, but then I thought, 'That young woman knows where her place is!'"

"Yes sir."

"There's a thought, Jutta. Imagine it. You and young Wu together. What a coup that would be! Just think, if you joined his family and brought the Wu's into a union with the best families of Valderia, what an alliance that would make!"

"Are you matchmaking, sir?"

"Well, Jutta. He has so much worldly wealth that you could buy the Blue Boar and its entire staff and eat like a queen every night of the week. However, since you betrayed his trust and stole that little device, I think he might not see you as bride material, eh?"

"No sir, I think not."

"It is a pity. He is such a pleasant, sharp, and personable young man too. I suspect you will never hear from him again, Jutta, so just remember you did your duty. Now forget him and get on with your career."

"Yes sir."

"That will be all. I shall ring when I want this table cleared."

"Yes sir."

That night she thought that maybe, however silly it seemed,

she could quite well enjoy life with young Jackson Wu. Now that he hated her and all she stood for, she knew her dream would remain just that. She looked at the flowers, and wiped a tear away. How silly could she be? She had only known him one night.

Although she was already very mature in ESYs, Jackson Wu's mother was beautiful. The family wealth and access to any kind of rejuvenation that she desired or her husband insisted upon had made her a woman who had kept her figure and looked much younger. She was blessed with a good bone structure, was active and fit and wore good clothes. She loved her sons, Horatio and Jackson, and if they used enough wiles, they could get just about anything they wanted from her. She, however, was ruled by Solomon, who knew exactly when to curb any excesses.

They lived in opulence, but the boys were brought up to understand that one just couldn't pick credits off trees. Horatio had climbed the ladder to achieve his modest rank in Fleet, and Jackson would finish his studies at Belvedere and be channeled into a political life. Solomon felt no qualms about arranged marriage or directing his offspring to where he wanted them to go. His plans for the family fortunes and his growing empire left little room for individual sympathies. The master plan encompassed his offspring and enveloped them, rather than the reverse. He saw Jackson in his diplomatic suit as a young planetary delegate sitting in the Galactic Parliament, making sure that Wu Foundation didn't get less than it deserved.

Jackson was studying political sciences at Belvedere, but it wasn't Jackson Wu who attended classes but Jason West. Subterfuge had to be employed where anyone who knew the Wu family could whisk him away and demand an enormous ransom, and he did have a panic button he could press if that kind of thing came up. He wasn't a showy young man, kept his place, didn't follow the family rule of "nothing succeeds like excess," and he played his Jason West role well.

His professors knew who he was and over-compensated,

making his workload a tough one. He was happy at Belvedere. His change of identity meant he could go drinking with his classmates when he had time. He could date the girls and get laid every now and then, but generally, he worked hard, studied hard and felt that Jason West was a pretty straight kind of guy.

His mother was tending to orchids in the vast conservatory. In fact, the android she called "Crystal" was doing the tending, but mother was hovering, making sure that the "girl" was getting it right. The android was one of the very latest from Wu Robotics and Artificial Intelligence Labs. It was uncannily human. Even its "skin" was warm. Its smile was warm, and the eyes were bright and varied the focus all the time. It had distinct facial expressions. His mother had dressed it in a becoming blue housedress and neat shoes. It had a strange female aura about it. He had a brief thought that it might be good in bed too but quickly put that aside.

"Now, Jackson, tell me what you achieved on Valderia. Your father says you did well, but he won't elaborate, of course. What happened?"

"I was treated well. The marshall was polite, lied a lot, fed me slime worm meat without my knowledge, and I had a terrible journey there and back. I ate at the best restaurant—"

"Ah, so you ate at the Blue Boar! I have fond memories of the restaurant, Jackson. Your father took me there once when we were a lot younger, and he was doing some complicated business deal with the Valderians. If I remember rightly, he even bought me flowers, which was so surprising I think I cried with pleasure!"

"It sounds very romantic, mother."

"Well, he wasn't always so tied up with Galactic company business that he ignored me or the family. Did you dine alone?"

"No, the marshall gave me a young officer to show me around, and we walked a lot and talked a lot, and I went to bed early because of the very early parade the next morning."

"Well, that was kind of the marshall."

Well, yes it was, but that same young officer stole my data

record pin, so I have no real record of the interview, which makes me look pretty stupid."

She raised her eyebrows.

"Shall I continue with the next section, madam?"

Mother and son both started. The voice was so plainly human, without a trace of any mechanical or electrical impulse, that they both laughed.

"Thank you, Crystal, please continue."

His mother led him away to the central stacks of shelves and whispered, "That girl, android, robot, or whatever she is, is so human, Jackson, that she frightens me a little. The other thing is, she or it brings out the mother in me. We were walking in the garden yesterday, and without thinking, I put my arm round her waist like I used to do with Su Lin, and she felt warm, and I had to stop and sit down and just cry."

He reached out and hugged his mother. She sobbed a little before she pulled away.

"I had such hopes for Su Lin and Davvd, you know that? I could see my grandchildren playing here and laughing, and it was all destroyed in one instant. Gone, forever."

She wiped her eyes, and sniffed.

"You see this flower, Jackson? It comes from a jungle that was created on Mars. It is a wonderful example of how beautiful things can grow where there was nothing but dust, and now there is luxuriant life."

"It is a wonderful flower."

She held his hand and pressed it.

"When you are ready, I would love nothing more for you than to give me a wonderful daughter to take the place of Su Lin, and a couple of grandchildren. Sorry, my son, but mothers think like that. Horatio will never do that for me, you know that? I just feel that in my bones. He isn't made of the right stuff; he is just a hard-nosed 'officer.' Do you know what I mean? You are a much more sensitive boy. When you meet the right girl, Jackson, you will know. It doesn't matter where she comes from, she will be like this orchid, and you will be hard pressed to resist her. There, that is enough mother talk, I am getting maudlin. I think it is time for coffee. Crystal? Would you make us some real coffee? We need it."

Jackson spent his small amount of free time before he shuttled off to Belvedere in the study of the mansion. He lay back in one of the great leather chairs and thought about Jutta.

"Damn Jutta!"

He couldn't understand why she had got under his skin so quickly. His mother was just mourning for Su Lin, and Jutta was hardly another Su Lin, but the image of her with that horse and how she had whispered to it suddenly translated itself into a mother and a child, and he knew that he was being a bit of a sentimental young fool.

She had been sent to steal any evidence he may have gathered, was "on duty" even when she made love to him. How could she do that? Was she just carrying out her orders, or was she being a dutiful whore because the marshall had told her to be one?

He tried but couldn't see her as a whore. Did she make love to him because she wanted to, because she wanted to please him as he had tried to please her and to hell with orders? It preyed on his mind so much that eventually he swallowed his pride and went into the vast communications dome atop the building and sent her a message via her barracks.

"Jutta, I can forgive but never forget. May those flowers stay fresh forever. You are in my heart, always. Jackson."

He felt that he was overdoing the sentiment, but when he thought of her and her pink-cheeked freshness, her rosebud nipples, and her tender mouth, he was helpless. What was it that he had tried to do? "Don't get too friendly with the enemy, Jackson."

He made a resolution *not* to tell his family, whatever happened.

Jutta was about to leave her room for her morning duties when her Tri D comm screen lit up, and chimes of martial music told her she had a message. She was going to ignore it because she was late for her lecture to new female recruits on the dangers of unsafe sex, when she saw that it was an interplanetary coded one.

She swore. There was a lot of traffic across the galaxy, usually selling stuff she didn't want and couldn't afford. She wished she could afford a whole set of Second Skin, but her salary wouldn't allow that. Maybe it was Horst, her brother, on some Valderian tin can the other side of nowhere, who had suddenly remembered her birthday.

She entered her code and Jackson's message came up, complete with a little cartoon of a pony with flowers in its mouth.

"Are you coming down, Jutta?" Her friend, Maria, was at the door.

"What?"

"What's the matter? You've gone very pink."

"Coming, I"m coming. Right now."

Her lecture to the new recruits was memorable for its almost incoherent commentary and long silences while she looked out of the window.

What the heck was she going to do about Jackson Wu? She made up her mind that whatever happened, if anything did happen, she would keep it from her family and definitely from Marshall Schiff. Definitely from him, at all costs.

Maggda felt at home. The weather had changed to a cool breeze, and she noticed that leaves were turning gold and red. From the rear cavern entrance, she could see across the plains to the wooded slopes of the range where color was rioting. She had organized her beach across the stream and had Joe make her a table and a comfortable chair from raw timber. Davvd watched the building of these constructions and had shaken his head. The building done, she dug up by the roots some flowers that had big bell-shaped blooms and what looked like bulbs or tubers and put them in a small bucket, which she spray painted dark blue and brought them in under the lights. She went through drawers and sorted cutlery into sets. She found yards of white canvas in the stores and had Joe make a couple of tablecloths and napkins. She wished she could carpet some of the cold floor but decided she had better stop before Davvd went mad with her.

He was coming and going and sometimes swearing, so she assumed his tussle with E7 wasn't going too well.

"Tell me your troubles, Master of the Universe."

"I will very shortly, but I want you to do me a message we can leak to our little clerk in Command. It has to be something that is an attention grabber but not hysterical. I will get Don to send it fully coded to the admiral so whoever gets it will have to decode it to make sense of it. I can put in my code so the admiral will know it is really from me, but we can hide source if we want to. So think about it, Styxx. Go sit on the beach and think.

"How are you going with, what's his name? Radnath?"

"Something smells there, something very fishy, but the figures are all there. I daren't accuse such a big name scientist of lying, but he is lying about something, and I can't pin it down. If we could talk to the Neanderthals or whatever they are, we might find out, but I am sure these boys and girls came from E7. That is the only place this side of the galaxy that fits. Radnath is doing a long term 'accelerated intelligence' program. It started with genetic DNA mutations, then they introduced a drug program, and that's about all he will tell me. I haven't told him we have some of his gang here, and I am sure they are some of his, until we are absolutely clear about it. He says they have no missing persons. They have all been accounted for, and he sent me the data, but . . . why don't I believe him, Maggda?"

"Because you are a natural skeptic, right?"

"I am going to have a drink and talk to Don about getting close to the tribe without stampeding them, if I can. Go work on your message, and then we can see if we have got it right. Maybe 'missing in action' might be a good start?"

"Who were you in action against?"

"Think of something, not someone. Vague but believable, right?"

She sat out on her beach and wrestled with it. It had to be something that would cause Don to transmit it to the admiral, and that would be because he, Don, couldn't get in touch with Captain Ong, right? Ong had to go, but where? No, wait. Ong had gone *somewhere*, where he *couldn't* send any messages.

A large green and blue fly settled on her pad.

"Unable to contact Captain Ong. Missing while visiting Bald Head Island prior to Force Ten storm in that area. Wreckage of low level recon vehicle recorded on beach behind Bald Head Island after storm abated. No messages received from Captain Ong after that date."

She looked at it carefully. Wreckage could be identified if they screwed down the satellite images. Now, he wasn't "dead" as such, but "missing" and had sent no messages since that date. Vague enough but serious enough to make one wonder. Gales and storms would have been recorded by the satellites, so could be verified.

She could hear Simon somewhere, saying, "It's not just what you say that sells a story, Maggda, it's what you don't say that is just as important."

She found Davvd working out on a piece of equipment in the bare-assed gym.

"I need to get out of here and stretch the legs and lungs, Maggda. Tomorrow we can go for a walk. I have a plan."

"Take a look at this and make changes where you think fit."

He looked at it for a while.

"What do you think? See, I figure that we have to say things that they will check on. They can get all this from satellite records, right, but the real information is that you are on E5 and missing. Two very juicy pieces of news. Now when the admiral gets this and sees your code identification in it, he'll know you were behind it, but the spy won't, will he? If I wanted something to stir up Galactic, then this would do it."

"You do good work, Styxx, remind me to reward you."

"Ha ha, Ong. You're a bit stingy, so I won't be surprised if it works out at nothing much."

"Want a real close eyeball view of your tribe tomorrow?"

"How close?"

"Close enough to smell them."

"And how do you propose to do that? We dress in skins and roll in the dirt, and we walk into the cave and say, "Hi guys, just passing by and thought we would drop in?"

Your trouble is, Styxx, you have too much imagination to be a really good reporter."

"Say that again, and I'll hit you with that weight."

"Make sure you can lift it first."

"How, Ong, how? How do we get in there without freaking them out?"

"I suspect the same way they got in there. Tomorrow, Ace Reporter of the Lacy Undies, all will be revealed. Trust me."

"Go and get showered. You smell like a Neanderthal."

"Yeah, good, isn't it? Want to give me a kiss and smell the pheromones?"

"Can I do that in the shower?"

"What, so I get all hot and sweaty again? Go away and tempt me not. Ask Joe what he has on the menu for tonight. I can't wait to spill it on your lovely white cloth."

She hit him with a sweaty towel and went off to the kitchens.

At the end of tiring, boring day watching new recruits attempt to assemble field weapons that were never going to be fired in anger, if indeed they would ever fire again, then watching as they were chased over a steeplechase course that Jutta was pleased she only rode on a horse, she went off to the mess to eat. Her mind had run on about Jackson Wu all day and for why? Well, for one thing he wasn't a Valderian. He was Old Earth. The fact that he belonged to one of the richest families this side of anywhere had nothing to do with it. She had felt strange about Jackson Wu from the moment they met. He had shaken her hand briefly, and it felt like an electric shock had gone up her arm. Nonsense, of course, but she had felt something, static off the damn carpets probably, but it had unsettled her a little.

She went to the bar; the barman poured her a beer, and she shook her head. He was an old corporal and had been on the bar for the past ten cycles so he knew what she drank and what everyone who came past twice drank.

"Can you make me a long gin and tonic, Schnell?"

He looked at her quizzically.

"It is an Old Earth drink. I have discovered that I like it."

He went down below the bar and down the steps, leaving his off-sider to serve. When he came back, he held some bottles in his hand and was smiling.

"Here is the magic 'Gin'; here is the magic 'Tonic.' Now all we need is ice and a lemon, cut and squeezed a little, and--

"Top the glass right up, please, Schnell."

This is on your mess bill, ma'am?"

"Yes, of course, why?"

He put in the details on the touch pad.

"One of these costs as much as four beers, ma'am."

She gave him a strange smile. "I don't really care."

She sat with Maria during the meal, and Maria could see that whatever it was that had come over the Tri D Com screen had affected her.

"Why don't you tell me?"

"Tell you what?"

"What was it that came over the Tri D this morning? You were blushing like a virgin."

"I can't tell you."

"If I buy you another couple of those things, will you tell me then?"

"You can't afford it."

"How do you know?"

"Because I was drinking those when I was escorting Mr. Jackson Wu the other night. He paid, of course."

"Schiff ordered you to do it, right?"

"It was an order."

She knew that Maria was going to get it all out of her sooner or later.

"You know what we did as little girls at that horrible school when we wanted someone to keep a secret?"

Maria took a lapel pin off her tunic.

"Give me your hand. Now I prick both our fingers, and we mix our blood."

"Not here, you dumb--everyone will think we are mad!"

"Your room then."

Maria looked at the flowers.

"Wu bought you these?"

"And we went to the Blue Boar."

Maria put her hand to her mouth.

"You went there? What is it like inside?"

"Very special, and he could read all the languages on the menu!"

"You have to be kidding. Who knows those Old World languages now?"

"He does. He impressed the waiter no end."

"Can I just ask what he was doing here with Schiff? What would a young guy like him come out here to talk to him for?"

"It was something very secret because Wu recorded the conversation on his lapel recorder, and I had to steal it for Schiff."

"And how did you do that?"

"Well, we went up to his room in the Palace, one of the executive suites, and it was lovely, and I stole the lapel recorder."

"The Palace! You have lived the high life, Jutta, first the Blue Boar and then the Palace. Then you just thought you might go to bed with him."

"Well, he bought me those flowers, and was nice, so . . ."

"You went to bed with him."

"Well, yes, I had had quite a bit to drink, and when he was asleep I took it and got dressed and came back here, ready for parade."

"Was he, well, good, you know? Did he make it last?"

Jutta blushed, and Maria seldom saw her blush.

"Well, I think he was as good as Sergeant over the jumps."

"You lucky bitch."

"But I thought he was gone. I thought he would hate me for what I did to him, and then he sends me this."

She turned on the machine and showed Maria the message.

"Seeing that, Jutta Vogel, I don't have to ask you what you did in bed, do I?"

"I think it was the wine and the gin and tonics. I just didn't care that much."

"And what now, you little randy vixen?"

"If you tell anyone, Maria, I swear by the Sacred Blade of Valderia, I shall kill you!"

"You mean that, don't you?"

"I really mean it. Now let us be serious children and swear it the way we used to swear it."

"Give me the pin."

Captain Horatio Wu was about to go off shift and hand over to his colleague, Captain Thrift, when the console detected a routed message to the admiral's desk in his personal code.

"Are you going now, Horatio? Give me the pad and I'll sign in."

"Ah, just a minute, Colin. I may have to fix this last entry up before I go, but you can take over."

They exchanged signatures and recorded the change of shift. Horatio went to his office and brought up the message. It was in the admiral's personal code rather than Fleet, but Horatio had no feelings regarding privacy. He wanted to know who was sending coded messages from E5, a research moon worth damn all in his opinion, and how would they know how to set it anyway. As far as he knew, the whole place was pretty well robotic controlled with only an occasional human dropping in there for research data off the recorders.

He saw the source, and it was from a damn robot. He read it with increasing interest. Ong had been on the moon! Ong had gone missing and was probably dead. If he had been less inhibited he might have screamed with joy.

He copied it into Galactic and then sent the original on to the admiral at Fleet.

He also sent the message to a satellite above Alpha Six, and it automatically routed it to the desk of Simon Brent on Mars.

"Cover the tracks. Horatio." Then he sent a simple mail to Brent. It was a demand for credits at his usual central European bank on Old Earth. He had to add that touch even if he had never cashed the credits. It might throw any sniffer dogs off the scent. He went out whistling and had an expensive meal, then called a girl who was always ready to give service for credits. It was going to be a good night.

The admiral had Sonna clearing out files from the long past. Many were still bound in paper and plastic covers. They had graduated to the lowest cabinets, which gave the admiral a wonderful view of his young captain's rear end as she bent over and hauled out totally useless material that he ordered to be shredded.

She sniffed, pushed back her hair, stood up and saw the lights on the pad indicating a personal coded message.

"Are you going to put this through the decoder, sir, or shall I?"

"What is its source?"

"Looks like something from E5."

"E5. Are you sure? Ong has been down there for days, and we've had nothing. He should have been finished there and on leave last week."

The decoder hummed its little tune, buzzed and spat the plain Galactic information out.

The admiral looked at it and then looked again.

"What is he playing at?"

"Sir?"

"What do you make of this?"

She read it twice and checked the coded numbers.

"I would say that he had this sent. He isn't missing because he worded this, and he got the robot to send it as a distress signal, maybe."

"What does he want us to think?"

"Well, knowing how smart he is, sir, I would suggest that we just sit on it and wait to see what happens. Maybe we should just send a confirmation to the base on E5, which he will get anyway if he is alive and well. It's obvious that he doesn't want anything personal to go to him right now. It's the kind of thing one does if you suspect your codes have been broken, don't you think, sir?"

"Just come here a minute, Sonna; you are covered in dust."

She allowed him the pleasure of dusting off her uniform so he could feel her breasts.

"I think you're right. Who the hell could break that code? There is only one place it goes through, and that is the com satellite station. Who, or what it is, has to be close to this office."

"Could be a totally electronic device, something planted?"

"Maybe you could crawl about on your hands and knees again, Captain?"

She gave him a wry look and picked up the Com Pad. "Security can come and sniff around. I am not going to ruin my stockings or my dignity, if you don't mind!"

Davvd Ong looked at the confirmation that Don had handed over and smiled.

"Maggda, we may have our fish. All he has to do is take the bait. Don, monitor newscasts out of Galactic Media. Just set that up on automatic so we can run it at our leisure. Now, where is Joe? I need him to help me set up our 'gods from the stars' charade."

Maggda looked at him. "Are you well, Ong?"

"I am feeling very well, thank you."

He grinned at her then went off into the recreation area and sat on the battered leather lounge. She joined him and sat close, and he put his arm around her.

"What are we going to do, Lord of the Universe?"

"Think about it for a minute or two. If you had to abduct a dozen or more Neanderthals off their home turf, how would you do it?"

"Hit each of them on the head with a club and then, well, tie them up, and—"

"Those boys are hunters and tough cookies. Walk in there with a club, and you'd get squidged. No, what happened was that they stood and let it happen. My guess is that a robot of some kind, make, or brand knocked them out with some sonic pulse, stunned them all, then loaded them onto that research ship and brought them here. Gave them all lovely sharp weapons; didn't actually harm any of them. They think this very generous man from the stars, or gods, or whatever they believe in, brought them here for some reason, and they might believe it was a gift from heaven. Who knows? All one has to do is set the cannon to stun, not kill, and you have immediate crowd control. They all fall down, can't move, and then they are put into the ship, and zoom, here they are."

"How long does the stun last?"

"Not too long, why?"

"Well, how far is E7 by star drive, days or weeks? If you think they were uplifted off E7, then they would have to be fed and watered like cattle, wouldn't they?"

"Two ESDs, max."

"And that is why they are here, not somewhere the other side of nowhere."

"You get better looking by the minute, Styxx. How smart and beautiful can you get? You've been on the smart pills, right?"

"Don't be silly, wonder boy. You have to feed and water them. Now if it was going to take weeks, you would need a whole damn supply chain to do it, or a starliner, or whatever. You suspect it was a survey vessel big enough to fit the tribe in, and they wouldn't suffer much in a couple of days, would they?"

"These are people who are used to a fair bit of hardship, right? Two days with some basic food and they wouldn't notice it."

She stroked his face. "That scar has gone. You're as lovely as ever. Now, boy genius, how are we going to get a close-up of our tribe?"

"Well, the plan is pretty simple. We wait until it is nearly dark, and they have gone into the cavern, cave, shelter, or whatever. Then you and I and Don and Joe take the loader, and we flit over there with all the lights on, and we come down out of the night—"

"And scare the whole lot of them totally witless, and they run screaming off into the night. Damn good plan, Ong."

"Wait until I have finished! We don't get that close, Maggda; we come down in the meadow, a longish walk away. Don and Joe are lit up, and they have the stun guns; they walk across the meadow up to the caves. Now think about it. These boys and girls have seen that loader buzzing about with Don at the controls or Joe, but they haven't seen any humans, have they? So it isn't that strange, and if we land it far enough away, they won't feel immediately threatened."

"So far, so plausible, now what do we mere humans do?"

"We are going to get dressed up in those lovely, silver decontamination suits hanging in the lab lockers. We land, and then we wait until Joe and Don have a short head start, and we follow. In the dusk we'll look just like Joe or Don, right?"

"Then what?"

"Joe and Don get close, and then they zap them. They all fall down. We go and get a close look and get them all recorded as individuals, which is what real scientists would do. That is really important, that we make a record of them all,"

"Sniff the dung?"

"You betcha, babe."

"It all sounds too damn easy, Ong. It has to go wrong

somewhere. Who was it said, 'The best laid plans of mice and men . . . go down the tubes'?"

"I have no idea. Go find a couple of suits that will fit us."

"I think it's a case of one size fits all.

"Well, you know what that means, nothing fits anything or anyone. We might have to get Joe to tailor something."

She went out and heard the ding-dong tones from the console. The admiral had sent a reply.

Simon Brent, high in his plas-steel tower on red earth Mars was wondering what the heck to do. There was a message that gave away Captain Ong's location, if that could be believed, and although he might well be there, he might well be dead. Simon knew this wasn't a case where one could check the facts or the sources, and that scared him. He was itching to go ahead and blow this information across the galaxy. They had unlimited footage of E5 and storm activity picked off the satellite, and he could do a kind of historical docco of the moon and Ong and make it into a biggish story. He had experts on his staff who would think all that was easy, but he wasn't prepared to blow it and end up a damn fool sued by Ong Foundation. It was the kind of information that, if it were true, was dynamite. If it was just a vague damn rumor, he was going to regret ever touching it. He wished he could dial up Maggda and ask her what she thought about it. She might have some really good ideas. The trouble was that he had no idea if she was alive or dead either. It looked like both Maggda and Davvd Ong were gone forever, and he had never told her that he loved her, if what he really felt was love. He didn't think he had ever really experienced it, but he thought she might have stirred it in him. He went out of his office and had a coffee and looked out over the landscape. It sometimes helped.

Jutta and Maria were hunched over the small writing desk in Jutta's room.

"Are you really sure you want to send Mr. Wu an answer?"

"I don't know."

"Jutta Vogel! You are an officer in the Valderian army. You are supposed to be able to make decisions. Do you or don't you?"

"Yes, yes, but what do I say? One night, that's all we had together. One night of, well, passion, and I betrayed him."

"And you can't just write him off, can you? Keep feeling his hands on your—"

"Shut up, Maria!"

"You write, and I will write, and we will compare them. All right?"

They sat and scribbled. Maria had the giggles. "I remember writing 'I love you' notes to half the boys in high school, and they ended up fighting."

"And you got suspended for three whole weeks, do you remember that?"

"Yes, but it was worth it."

"Your parents were so angry, I thought they would kill you."

"And then Rolf, you remember lovely, big, blond Rolf? We made love in his father's barn, up in the hay."

"You did what?"

"It was my first time. I don't think I enjoyed it that much. I was covered in scratches from the hay stalks and itched for days."

"Serves you right."

"Sometimes, Jutta, you can be very pious. Now, listen to this. I have tried to tell him you are interested, and that you would love to see him again, but it isn't too strong."

"Jackson, your heart is bigger than all Valderia. How can I make things up to you? I don't deserve your affection. Jutta."

"That makes me weepy. Put in after the last line, 'After I betrayed your trust.'"

"Right, so we have."

"Jackson, your heart is bigger than all Valderia. How can I make things up to you? I don't deserve your affection after I betrayed your trust. Jutta."

Jutta wiped her nose.

"Can't I put in, 'I want you so badly, my nipples are burning'! Something that will make him jump a starship and come knocking on my door first thing in the morning?"

"And you criticize me for having big Rolf?"

"Sorry, I was just trying to make you react."

"You know, Jutta, that this isn't a game. I mean, don't play with the affections of a guy like Jackson Wu unless you mean it. The Ongs and the Wu's are the most powerful families on this side of the galaxy. Young Wu could get very angry with you, and you could just, well, disappear one dark night."

Jutta laughed and then became very quiet.

"You make him sound like some gangster."

"Not him so much as his family. If they find out he has fallen for a Valderian tart, and they object to the slur on the Wu family name, they could get really heavy, Jutta."

"I am not a tart, Maria! I don't go sleeping around, and you know that. What about *my* family name?"

"I know that, you know that, but he is a well-known, highly influential young man. I love you, my dear friend, but when the media says he was shacked up with some girl called Jutta Vogel, everyone will say, 'Who?' and assume you were there for hire. Schiff ordered you do it, didn't he?"

"He didn't order me to make love to him, just to get the little device. Now I don't know what to-do. I just wanted to tell him I was sorry and, well, hope he likes me. I am so confused. You make me frightened, Maria."

"Oh come on! So far no harm done. He obviously thinks you are pretty special. Send the damn message and sit back and see what happens. I mean, you are just being polite and friendly, you haven't got as far as, 'burning nipples,' have you?"

They both laughed, and Jutta sent the message. She was nervous about it, but in the back of her mind, she thought he might respond as she hoped he would.

Ardan Radnath was counting the hours.

"In two days and four cycles, Dandra, we can leave here for some well-earned rest. I will be pleased to not have to duck questions from E5 about our project. Someone there wants to know too much about starship movements, well, research vessels, and I feel it is because something has alerted them to some discrepancy. I hope and trust, Dandra that the house is strong enough for us to hide under?"

"Oh, yes sir. It would take a genius to find out where the dead and the missing overlap. It is quite wonderful what can be done with statistics! Read the data, and everything is as smooth as a baby's fundament, sir."

"If you say so, Dandra, if you say so."

"There is one small, a very small, pimple on the smoothness, and that is when the Valderians come to count their subjects."

"What do you mean, Dandra?"

"Sir, statistics are one thing, but a physical count is another."

"Ah yes, Dandra, but they won't be doing anything like that. They will check the figures, find them accountable, and go away. They have never questioned those in the past."

"Ah, well sir. I suggest that this time they will want to see a really live humanoid, since they did administer, or rather, we did administer those drugs to the group, and they have since vanished."

"They died from natural causes, didn't they, Dandra? The statistics show that. You said so yourself."

"I think that although it is statistically true, when a whole experiment dies from 'natural causes,' it may be considered a step beyond simple carelessness."

"Dandra, go and pack your bags and contact the shuttle that is coming down to do pollen counts tomorrow. With luck we can squeeze on it and catch the freighter to New Babylon and then home. With luck, we may be listed as vanished by natural causes also. Hurry, man, hurry. I think our house is about to collapse on our heads."

They boarded the freighter after some fuss about accommodations. They were bunked in with the captain and first officer and shared their table.

"May I ask, sir, what made you travel with us rather than the regular starship?"

"Of course," said Radnath. A sudden death in the family, my cousin on New Babylon."

"Going back for the funeral?" asked the first.

"Yes," said Dandra.

"Sudden death, was it?" asked the captain.

"Very," said Radnath.

"Struck by lightning," offered Dandra.

"Lightning?" said the first.

"Yes," said Radnath.

"Unusual way to go, that," said the captain.

"Milking his cow under a peepul tree in a storm," said Dandra.

"Killed them both," said Radnath.

"Probably curdled the milk as well," reflected the captain.

Jackson was feeling a bit light-headed. The message from Jutta had been a real surprise, but one that had made him euphoric. The trouble was he had no idea what to do next. He erased the message from his mother's pad, packed his bags and caught the shuttle to the ship for Alpha Six and Belvedere.

His tutor met him with a smile.

"The end of session assignments have been put up. I hear you had a couple of days in Valderia recently."

"Who told you that?"

"I think you told one of your friends."

"Nothing is secret, is it?"

He sat through the tutorial with interest. He had had a very good grounding in the family politics and their interests, but Valderia was somewhere else, a bit of a mystery in many ways. He had been given the task of an essay on the "Rise of Valderia, Post Star Drive Expansion."

"When the star drive was perfected, thanks to Ong and Wu, about four centuries ago (ESY's), Valderia and its associated 'empire' were discovered. The inhabitants of the planet were humans. How they had evolved there, arrived there or just been created there was still the subject of great debate. Their DNA, their totally humanoid characteristics suggested that a race unknown had seeded Valderia with humans centuries ago. The Gods from the Stars was a legend but not a religion, so whatever it was that had transported the human seed had long vanished. The Valderian psyche leant towards a love of the military, great self-discipline, pride in the race, and a desire to spread and conquer. With the sharing of the star drive, the Valderians had colonized seven planets or moons and had become a colonial power, subjecting the more primitive humanoid races that lived there in a state of slow development to Valderian rule. The Valderians exploited the resources of their colonies and did little to develop the infrastructure of their subject planets or moons other than establish bases that were devoted to the military.

Scientific research was carried out and was directed to both biological researches, generally with military uses in mind, and by participating as partners in other planets' research projects where there might be useful advantage, especially for the military.

Ong and Wu Foundation funding had set up research projects on four planets controlled by Valderia. Valderia had a research project involving 'accelerated intelligence' based on E7. That was very hard to define. The record was obscure even though Wu/Ong research had put up ten million for a long-term study. Where was that leading?

The government of Valderia was a military-based structure with a chancellor as head of planet; twenty-four high-ranking officers formed the Council of the High Command; twenty-four business and civilian delegates made up the numbers to forty-eight representatives. Local government was made up of area councils with their numbers dependent upon population figures, usually with a military governor or chair. They had taxing rights.

Public citizens could vote for changes in laws or government decrees via their local members. There was no set time for authority to change hands. The economy was stable. The Valderian credit was on par with the rest of the galaxy and traded throughout as a strong currency. The rule for the most part was one of a stern but basically benign authority. Its education system favored a military ethos, but the basics were soundly taught. Graduates from its universities were fed into industrial development, star drive engineering, scientific-based agriculture on the subject planets, or into the military academies. Academic pursuits led to research posts. Trades were considered a lower tier of educational endeavor. There was a class system based on the military model. Valderia was respected, criticized in whispers and suspected of many violations of human rights but was never brought into a galactic court."

Jason West sighed, dragged as many authorities as he could find to back his research and thought of a rose red-nippled Jutta. What was he going to do?

He came to the conclusion to do what he knew Davvd Ong and his sister, Su Lin, had done. Carry out your affair but keep the families guessing, if you could.

Jason looked at the "first families" of Valderia. No wonder his father had sent him to Schiff! Schiff was the nephew of the damn chancellor! He would be a prime candidate to put his hand up when the old man died. He carried a lot of weight on Valderia, and there he was doing duty as a mere barrack commander? Did that make sense? But then again, hadn't Davvd Ong played the recluse in his role as a mere captain in Fleet?

He wrapped up his essay, knowing it wasn't going to get him an "A" but a "Pass" would be good enough. He wanted that out of the way. He wondered how he could get to Valderia again to see Jutta.

Davvd was having mild hysterics as Maggda got into the decontamination suit. It was his turn next, but her swearing and groaning had made him laugh. It made her look like some grotesque, living refrigerator.

"Laugh away, Ong. Wait until you get suited up, buddy boy!"

He struggled into his suit and was aware that his contortions were equal to hers, so it was her turn to laugh.

"The one good thing, Lady of the Lumps and Bumps, is we don't have to cart the damn decontamination pack on our backs."

"What are you going to put in there then, a papoose?"

"I would have thought that was your role, Miss Styxx."

"No, I have no desire to drag a helpless child about with me, thank you, Ong. What is the status? Is good ol' Don up and at them?"

"The boys should be ready. Let's stumble outside and see."

"Have you thought, Master of the Universe, that if it is this clunky walking on polished rock, what it's going to be like out there in that long meadow grass?"

"You always wanted to live dangerously, so you're about to find out."

"No, Davvd, seriously. I wouldn't be much of a star god falling on my face, would I?"

"I think if we stick right behind Joe and Don, the grass will be trampled enough for us mere mortals. Come on. It's getting dusk. His little bat in the cave will let us know when they are all inside, and we can make our move."

"Davvd, I am not at all sure about this. I feel very nervous."

"If it's any consolation, so do I."

"Are you just saying that to make me feel good?"

"Probably."

"There are times, Ong, when I hate you."

"I feel like that about me too, some of the time."

"I hate you!"

"Come here, and if I can find out what part of you is front and back, I'll give you a big hug."

Don entered. "The vehicle is ready, sir."

"Stun guns?"

"Sir."

"Set on just stun?"

"Yes sir."

"Let's give this gig a whirl."

Outside it was getting quite dark. They clambered ungracefully onto the deck, hung onto the straps, while Joe and Don sat up front behind the crude windscreen.

"Fire her up, Joe."

The rotors turned, and the noisy motor caught, and they clattered into the dark night air. It took no time to arrive over the meadow. They could see the glow of the cooking fires spilling out into the night. Don switched on the landing lights and the working lights, and they descended into the grasses, swathed in bright blue light.

Suddenly, the entrance to the cave was filled with human forms, blinking in the glare of the lights.

Don and Joe climbed off the loader and walked towards the group, their stun guns by their sides, and Maggda and Davvd tried to stay in their heavy footprints. It seemed to take forever, but they were suddenly there in range, and the males began to move slowly toward them. Davvd said "now," and there was a blue glow and the hunters and the women and children fell like ten pins.

They moved into the entrance of the cave. Maggda, trying to hurry, fell flat on her face, and he hauled her up.

"No hurry now. Just be quick and efficient."

He had no idea of what she said. Her ugly mask was twisted about her head.

They lay as if asleep. The children twitched a little; the men still held the long spears, and suddenly, three little pigs scampered out of the dark and came to nuzzle the children, making them start.

"Don, record all this please. Get close-ups of all the tools and equipment."

The knives were in sheaths, leather and wood, and hung on

the belts. The skins were tanned, and the smell was no worse than a clean stable. The women and children were clean as if they had bathed that day. Maggda said, "Look at these."

Close to the fire were three large and one smaller red clay bowls. They were dry and hard but still "green."

"I wasn't aware these guys were into a clay culture, were you?"

"Record all this, please, Joe, Don, don't miss anything."

They examined the beds and the coverings, the wattle and daub walls, the rock base, and the handprints on the bare rear wall. White ochre, stencils, the hands of the warriors, hunters, and their family.

"Joe, go and bring the gift I made up, will you?"

"What gift? I didn't know we came bearing gifts."

"I had Don make them up."

"What are you giving them, Ong?"

"Something you would appreciate if you were living in a cave and had no makeup except ochre."

Joe came into the cave with a handful of what appeared to be bones.

"What is it, Ong?"

"Bone combs. Now if you want to do the honors, put one in each of the women's hair. The rest put on the stone, just there."

Don, Joe take blood samples and identify what came from whom. Record all this, boys, and then we can scuttle off before they wake up."

A child moaned, and a man groaned.

"I think we have done enough for one visit. Now beat a stylish retreat, get onto our star car and get the heck out of here."

They rose up into the darkness, lights blazing, did a slow U-turn and headed back to base. Joe doused the lights, and they clattered through the dark. Maggda looked back. The tribe were getting to their feet and looking toward the skies. They didn't seem to be in much of a panic.

Last night, after we had eaten, the star people came. They were bright as the stars, and their eyes lit up the meadow and they walked towards us as they had done before we left our old home, and we felt a sharp pain, and we slept and could not move. When we awoke, the fire had burnt down, and it was getting cold, so we closed our cave to the winds and made a larger fire to last all night. The star people had left other gifts. The women laughed when they found that with these gifts, their hair could be untangled. The children didn't like them much, but the women thought their gifts were special. My hair was untangled by Annrath with her toothed bone, and she laughed at my face. She is a special woman, and I care for her.

I feel that the winter is not too far off. We see the color of the forest and the small animals collecting nuts and hiding them for when the snows come, so we know it will not be long. We wonder why the star people have come back with more gifts, but they did not hurt us. It was just like the first time they came. We have carried more rocks up from the lakeside to build a bank so the wooden walls we have made will not move in the winds or the snow drive into the cave. We have made those stronger.

Annrath has made a circle of stones and has put her clay bowls inside it, turned over so they will not fill with ashes, and she and the boys have piled the wood all round them and up very tall. She has made us bring back branches every time we go into the woods. We have slung the deer we have killed on the branches, and we carry them back that way, on our shoulders. The geese flew away, and the great owls fly low at night now. We must kill more meat and dry it and catch more fish before the white snow falls, and the game disappears. At the end of the winter, I shall be a father, Annrath tells me. That will be strange. I must keep Annrath warm while the snow falls so our child does not suffer. I care for Annrath. She is a special woman.

Davvd Ong, Maggda, and Don were in the laboratory.

"These guys were vaccinated with an anti-flu virus and something else before we found them. All their blood samples show traces of what I think, and Don seems to trace, is something that is doing things to their DNA, but I haven't the brains to know what it is. I think these guys have come from E7. Radnath was very tight-lipped about it all, but he and the Valderians were doing research into accelerated intelligence, so maybe . . ."

"How do we find out? Why not get a link to E7 and get onto Radnath and put it to him. Tell him we have a small tribe here, and has he lost any lately?"

"I think that if we had a safe com link I would tell the admiral, but if some slinky bastard is decoding our stuff, then we have to sit and wait a bit. Let your bait get taken, Goddess of the Lost Tribe of E5, and we shall see."

"And I thought we would be off here in a couple of days, now that we have these 'Neanderthals' tied down."

"You have had enough of me, is that it?"

She went over to his chair and kissed him on the mouth.

"You know what I mean. Let's get off this damn moon and go live it up at your uncle's ritzy place and go fishing and sleep between silk sheets, and I can have real makeup and slinky underwear and drink real drinks, not Uncle Joe's home brew."

"You want a hug?"

"Ahh, you just say things like that when you know I'm feeling suicidal."

"Does it help?"

She hugged him, and he held her so close it hurt.

"Maggda, when this is sorted, and they let me go home, I am going to come calling, babe, and I am going to come to your apartment in the early morning when you are in the shower; you are going to come to the door in your Bare Head Island dressing gown, and I am going to pick you up and carry you into your bedroom, and I am going to put you on the bed, and I am going to lean right over you and . . ."

"Why have you stopped, for Aton's sake, I'm dying waiting here. Are you going to take me like some raging bull or not?"

"And I am going to say, "Can you do breakfast. I'm starving!"

She wrestled to get out of his arms, but he held her tighter.

"And when we have had breakfast, Maggda Styxx, I am going to have you!"

She went limp, and he held her up and kissed her.

"Is that a promise, Ong?"

"It is a firm promise, Ms. Styxx. Don here can be my witness."

"We could get some practice in now."

"Wait. I have to wait, you have to wait, and all good things come to—"

"Those who think there is some virtue in damn waiting . . ."

"Nothing would give me greater pleasure than what we both want, but just go with me. I have to see this thing through first."

"Are you under damn orders?"

"Will let you know when I walk in your apartment."

Marshall Kurt Schiff, Defender of the Blade, First Class, etc., etc. had been announced and was sitting in his uncle's office in the Chancellery.

His uncle, Field Marshall Heinrich Nobel, sat behind the huge desk in a green leather chair that was more throne than mere furniture. His desk was bare except for two com pads, a stylus holder set, and a gold plated clock, a gift from the battalion that he had once commanded. He was an austere man but not unkind in his Valderian way. He loved children, dogs, and horses, and occasionally his wife. He tried to keep his finger on the pulse of things, but outside of the armed forces, his interest waned. He had experts to do that side of the thinking. He was suspicious of "advisers," but the complexity of the modern day to day had forced him to accept their role. Schiff was counted as one of the few he trusted to tell him the truth. Schiff, for his part, would only tell the chancellor what he thought he might like to hear. Schiff, however, was always aware that the old man always checked. He knew that a direct lie, that could be challenged, would be. If one had to lie then make sure it was beyond the old man's expertise and a long way off.

"Sir, I have come to ask for advice," began Schiff. He knew that this kind of crawling paid off if handled the right way.

"When you open a conversation with that, Kurt, I know you want to screw something out of me, or maybe you have made a dreadful administrative mistake, or there has been a debacle that needs covering up somewhere."

"Because you are the one man I can come to without causing a ripple through the cosmos, sir. I need direction."

"Well, explain, don't just sit there waving your crop about."

"Valderia has, as you know, a research project being carried out on E7, the research facility leased to scientific ventures by the Ong Wu Foundation. The Foundation, ten ESYs ago, gave Valderia ten million credits to carry out a long-term study there."

"It was some nonsense to do with taking those backward tribesmen from where was it? And turning them into intelligent beings by 'accelerated development'. Wasn't that part of it?"

"Well, sir, as usual you have grasped the essentials of it. The specimens, humanoids, were at an early stage of development, mainly verging on Stone Age hunter/gatherers. We had to employ outside research personnel because the Foundation wouldn't allow us to do this without having external checks and balances. And because we needed the finance."

"Well, what are you here for? Aren't you behind that project?"

"Yes sir, I am, but I keep a very low profile because the military is not normally involved with these purely scientific ventures, and as far as the Foundation is aware, our civilian, totally objective observers conduct the research for us."

"Well, what do you want from me?"

"Advice, sir, as I said in the beginning."

"Our project ran into problems a short while ago when our research team on E7 discovered that our sample experimental group had contracted the Old Earth influenza. This decimated the group, even though they had been vaccinated against just about anything. The survivors were moved to protect them and us from any adverse Foundation criticism and funding withdrawal, but we had a simple logistics problem."

"So tell me!"

"They were moved to E5, a research moon, again leased from the Foundation."

"What was wrong with that?"

"E5 is strictly a 'flora and fauna' station usually manned by robotic staff. No humans are allowed there off base because of the danger of contamination. We believe that the presence on E5 has been recorded by the robotic staff, and Fleet has been alerted."

"Didn't cover your tracks, did you, Kurt?"

"Advice, sir?"

"You are in charge of this mess, aren't you? You got yourself into it, now get yourself out of it. But if you give us a bad name, Kurt, there is an advance garrison commander's job going on the ice moon, Calypso. They need a man like you out there. Two of the last garrison commanders have committed suicide, and we can't think why. Do I make myself clear?"

"Perfectly, Uncle. Do I have complete authority to sort this mess out?"

"It sounds as though you are going to need it. See my ADC on the way out, and he will get that signed up. I am not going to say 'best of luck.' You may need more than that, boy."

Schiff saluted, left and smiled. With complete authority, he could do more than sort that little mess out on E5. First, he had to get Fleet off the scent before they sent a damned human observer down there to foul things up. With luck, he could uplift the whole damn sample that was left and cart them off to the back blocks of one of the colony planets. Keep Fleet out of this, Schiff, and you will be fine.

Back at his office he was a bit put out because the lovely little Jutta was chasing up other duties, and he would have to find another assistant. He decided to leave it until the morning, when she would be back on duty. He was fond of that girl.

On E7 the automatic response unit accepted a message from Valderia and equally automatically sent a reply confirming that there were no human authorities on the planet at this time. This information reached Schiff almost at once, and he was perplexed.

He brought up his files on E7 and saw that Professor Radnath and his assistant, Dr. Singh, were not on leave until another four cycles. So where, ask Aton, were they?

He ordered communications to try the university at New Babylon, but they cheerfully assured him that the persons he sought were working on E7. Two brains lost in space. He was not happy at all. He would have to divert either a military starship to drop off someone to look for them, which was added expense, or wait until the idiots spoke to him. What had seemed like a simple question and answer session had begun to look like a conspiracy of silence.

He asked for and received satellite close-ups of the caves where his "tribe" had been, and the space was as virginal as a hole and pile of rocks could be. Well, at least there were no bodies lying around anywhere. He idly checked the numbers of the surviving tribe that his robotic crew had moved to E5 and found that they too had disappeared, listed as "death by natural causes." Some were skewered on the horns of big deer! He had personally seen the drop-off on holos. They had all been alive and well then. His instructions to give them better tools had been carried out to the letter. What had happened to them? Were they still on E5 or not?

He had a sudden and chilling vision of the ice moon Calypso, frozen fingers falling off inside the pressure suit, and strong men just walking off into the white hell of frozen gases . . . he shuddered and tried to pull himself together. Who could he send to find out what the love of Aton was happening? He put aside the armed platoon at once. Go down there with an armed cruiser and violate the sanctity of a Foundation moon reserved for birds and beasts, and he would end up on Calypso for sure, despite his family ties. Then the remark his father made in a fit of temper one day crossed his mind.

"If you want something done right, do it yourself!"

Well, he discounted that for a start. Stay calm, Schiff, stay calm. No humans down there, just a few robots at each station around the moon. When humans did get down there, their presence was closely monitored. They had limited range, they didn't go crashing about, but robots could and did range freely. It had to be a robot, same as those who transported the tribe. Get in there, find the lost tribe, get out, and report to Schiff. No food to supply, no shelter to provide, not even a portable toilet.

He whistled his little marching song and spoke to his transport officer at the shuttle base. That done, he ordered a very expensive robot from Stores. His authority from the chancellor overrode the duty officer's reluctance. It was a brand new model, not a scratch on it, and it had cost a fortune. Just a matter of time now. Get his tin man onto E5 in one piece, and he was halfway home. His euphoria was such that he rang the florist in the city and ordered a bunch of flowers to be delivered in the morning. That would make young Jutta's face light up!

Jutta was pink-faced and happy. Maria even heard her sing in the shower. Jackson was sending her happy, fun things, which hinted of feelings that indicated his heart and his brain needed fine-tuning. She was sending him hints that, given the time and place, they could do things together that would make him blush.

At Belvedere, Jason West slogged through his work, ignored his friends, brushed off very obvious attempts by pretty, young women who thought that if they were wanton enough, he would notice them, but he kept dreaming of cream breasts and rosebud nipples. He wasn't sleeping well. When he spoke to his mother on the Interlink and she saw his face, she told him to get more sleep. He very nearly told her that he thought he was in love, but common sense prevailed. In love he might be, but he had to make sure before he committed himself, and to a Valderian, no less.

Schiff was at work early next morning. His flowers were arranged in a tall vase he had appropriated from the mess; he awaited the click of heels as Jutta came down the corridor. She entered the office, clicked her heels and smiled. She took in the flowers and frowned a little.

"Please, Lieutenant, I have flowers here for you."

Her face broke into a smile that spoke of extreme pleasure. She took the card and read it. She looked at him, broke into tears and made a noise that could only be described as a dying wail. She fled the office, tears streaming down her face, making enough noise to bring every serviceman to office windows, and he was down the corridor after her.

"Jutta, what have I done?" I just wanted to give you pleasure!"

It was a fatal thing to say or shout after her. He suddenly became aware that everything was going to be misinterpreted. He spun on his heel and banged the door behind him. He sat at his desk and shuddered at the thought of the court martial, where the commanding officer had attempted to violate a young female officer and had bought her gifts to sweeten her up. Visions of ice and snow flashed before his eyes. He picked the flowers up and threw them into the waste bin and roared like a lion in anger and frustration. No one came near him for four whole cycles.

Jutta fled and found Maria, and they went quickly to her room.

"What has happened? What has he done to you? For Aton's sake, tell me! Did he put his hand up your skirt or grab your breasts or what? I have to know!"

Jutta sobbed a little, wiped her nose, and sat on the bed and composed herself.

"Well, what happened?"

"He gave me flowers."

Maria looked at her. "He gave you flowers. Is that all? He gave you flowers!"

She nodded.

"Didn't touch you up; didn't suggest that you could make him a happy man if you did as he asked you to?"

Jutta began to cry.

"I thought they were from Jackson. I thought they were from Jackson, and I was just so disappointed when I saw they were from Schiff! Oh, Maria, what am I going to do? He will kill me! I have made him look such a fool, made myself look like a fool, and half the barracks think Schiff assaulted me. I am in terrible trouble. I want to crawl away and die."

"Go and wash your face, make sure you are neat and tidy like a good officer should be, and when you are 'parade respectable,' we will march down there and apologize, and you will tell him."

"I can't."

"You can, because if you don't, I will. Keep acting like a dummy, Jutta, and you and he will be ruined. He isn't a bad man, and he doesn't demand much, and I know he likes you. He was just trying to be kind. Now get yourself respectable, and we will go down there. Now, hurry up!"

It was the worst moment in her life. Schiff was angry and bemused, but he listened. She told him she thought the flowers were from her "young man," and although they were lovely, she was disappointed that they were not, because she was expecting him to send her flowers.

Maria hovered.

"You see, sir, Jutta and her young man are apart, and they don't meet very often, so they send each other messages all the time, and she was expecting a small gift. And you were trying to be kind, sir, and she was very emotional, and you didn't know, and it was all a big mistake, sir."

Schiff sniffed and stood up. He came round the desk and stood in front of Jutta.

"Lieutenant, would you accept my apology. I was just trying to . . . make you smile. I was thinking that maybe I should be kinder to you because sometimes I am a bit harsh, and you never complain, and your smile, well, it makes me smile too. I am so sorry I offended you."

Jutta burst into tears. If he had been a tyrant she would have stood firm and defied him, but to have this hard man saying it was really his fault, was too much.

"Sir, I am so sorry. I feel such a fool, and how can I undo what has happened. I have made you look bad, I know that, and I wish I hadn't."

"Would you retrieve those from the bin, please, Jutta. Take them to your room. Take seven days leave. I do know what it is like to be disappointed when you have your plans go astray, and emotional ties are even harder. Take her away, Maria. I think we both know that next time we will be a little more open. Now get her out of here before she lets down the whole army and starts crying again."

In her room, Jutta flashed off a message to Jason West at Belvedere.

"I have seven whole days free of the barracks. What do you want me to do?" His reply was swift.

"If I put you on a starship, you would be three days coming and three days to get you back, and that would only leave one day, but if I can come, then we can have four days together. I shall be at the Palace and will contact you then. My heart is beating faster. Jason."

She showed Maria.

"Are you going to go and bed down with him at the Palace?"

"Why did you think that, Maria! If you must know, I am going to take him home to my family!"

Maria spluttered into her coffee.

"Dear Aton and by the Holy Blade of Valderia, I think you are either mad or just so besotted that your brain is addled! What will your parents think? I can just hear them now, 'And where did you two meet, Mr. West?' 'Well, we got to know each other when we were both stark naked, and she rode me to death like her cavalry mount on the bed in my suite at the Palace!' 'Oh, that's nice. It's so good when young people know how to enjoy each other's company.'"

"Sometimes, Maria, you offend me."

"Are you sure you want him to meet them?"

"No, but I just have the feeling that he will want to. He is that kind of man. I will tell them the truth that we met when I had to escort him after he came to see Schiff. You know them, they won't bother about what he was doing there. They will just assume it was army business and leave it at that."

"He may find it a bit of a comedown on the farm after the luxury he has been used to."

"I am not ashamed of my family or my home, thank you! I think he will just accept it for what it is, and if he doesn't, then I will know I have made a mistake."

"Has it got that far? Are you really serious about Jackson Wu?"

"I don't know. I just feel very close to him. He sends me messages, and they are like love letters, and all he says is that he misses me, and I do the same. I know it's crazy. I went to bed with him for one night, and it seemed like we had been making love forever. How do you explain that?"

"I don't have to; you do. You know that when he gets here, he will expect you to make love to him again, don't you?"

"I don't care. I told you, he makes my nipples tingle!"

"You, Jutta Vogel, are a lost cause. I've never met anyone who does that to me, not even blond Rolf!"

They went down to the mess. Jutta drank a couple of gin and tonics. They made her feel better.

Marshall Schiff inspected his robot. The Stores supply officer hovered about in a kind of panic.

"This is one of the latest from Wu industries, sir. It is equipped with a human response circuit and a full 'experience' learning module. It learns as it goes, and it responds as well as we do to most situations. It is self-charging, but it still needs a bit of sunlight to keep it alert. Artificial light is fine though. It has just about everything built in. Can record and make tri-dee stuff. Can store and project holos, is very strong and very stable, and what I like about it is that it, well, looks almost human, don't you think?"

"That, Bruno, could be a distinct disadvantage. I know I asked for this 'superman,' but have you something a bit, well, shop-soiled and about three models back? For what I need, I want a rugged, all-terrain, heavy-duty, go anywhere model that won't suddenly go all girlie on me."

"Are you sure, sir? I have a couple of Mk Fours, and we haven't taken them out for a while, but I am sure they perform really well. One of them is multilingual; the other one is just Galactic. Well, all the Old Earth stuff is getting a bit, well, obsolete unless you run a fancy restaurant, sir."

"Scrub up that multilingual one, see it is charged up, and when it is, buzz through its code so I can program it. Now how much space will there be on the vessel it will be piloting?"

"Do you want that in an accurate measurement or a sort of 'about so big,' sir."

"Will the space be enough for about, say fifteen humans to lay down in?"

He ruminated a bit. "Yes, but they won't be running about much."

"Food and water for say five ESDs."

"Just field rations, sir, and no fancy cooking. Plenty of water."

"Right, that should be fine; let me know when you are ready to shape up and ship out."

"I need the authority, sir."

Schiff handed him the plastisheet document signed by the chancellor. "Will that do?"

It did well enough.

The basic model Mk Four was as rugged as Don, without the sensitivity. It was made to serve the demands of the military, not make philosophical decisions. It did as it was told, learnt as it went and was very reliable. Schiff was satisfied. He was pretty sure it would be able to root out the lost tribe and get them to a suitable site where Fleet and the Foundation wouldn't be looking over his shoulder all day. He went to his quarters and awoke in the early hours as the shuttle took off to take his "tin man" on its journey to E5. He had tried to program it for all contingencies. He wished it bon voyage. Way above the planet, the shuttle docked with a dented military vessel of indeterminate age and providence. It powered up, set coordinates and vanished into hyperspace towards E5.

Davvd Ong was checking the media for reports of his demise. None had come through. He sat up as Maggda came in with another potted plant.

"Are you going into a full-on gardening mode, Ms. Styxx, or is it a temporary aberration?"

"It is a pretty little thing, and it makes my bedroom seem less angular. What are you doing?"

"Well, no fish, no hook; whoever it is hasn't taken the bait as yet."

"You know why. No verification, no means of checking it out. Simon used to stress that you check your sources all the time. I'm prepared to bet he has turned this over in his mind since he got it, *if* he got it, and has decided it is too dangerous."

"Right, you are the expert. Tell me what you would do to make Simon shout this all over the galaxy media?"

"Tough call, Ong. Let's think. He needs some kind of verification. If he had someone from Galactic on the spot . . ."

"I get it. How are we going to let him know that the great Maggda Styxx is right here on E5 without everything going pear-shaped?"

"Let me think. Can we send a simple holo, say of me telling him to get that story out, straight to Simon at Galactic? That would bypass Fleet, and our spy wouldn't know, and he is expecting that news to break any day, or isn't he?"

"Well, the admiral knows I am here and safe, that's one up on our slimy bastard, so we could do a simple holo, squirt that off to Mars, and Simon would be a lot wiser, right? He might be mourning you, you never know. Just wondering if *all* traffic from here goes through Fleet or remains commercial. I have to ask Don; he knows more about that than I do."

Don confirmed that he could send a holo straight to Galactic. Staff sent family messages, but they usually self-censored; anything that wasn't got edited by the machine anyway. It was just to protect research data.

"Okay. Let me get a script together, and I will be ready in about five."

"No histrionics, just a simple confirmation, right?"

"Don't tell the expert her job, Ong."

"Sorry."

"Simon, I am on E5, came down with Davvd Ong. There was a huge storm. Davvd hasn't come back. I am looked after by the robot staff. This is all top secret stuff, but if you got a leak from Fleet source, then it must match this information. Davvd is gone, and it is lonely here. This is strictly legitimate. I miss you."

"Don, play that back, please?

It came out a bit out of focus, but a genuine plea. Davvd was pleased.

"I'd buy that. He'll have that and the E5 logo on that console behind you so he does know where you are, and on top of that, he'll have the E5 code front and back. Send that off, please, Don, and we'll all hold our breaths."

"I want a bonus, Ong."

"What now?"

"If I sidle up to you and push my body against yours in a very suggestive way, will you give me a tongue-in-cheek, big wet kiss?"

"Maybe. How suggestive are you going to be?"

"Very."

"Don, can you make a holo of this please? I'm going to collect 'moments of sheer suggestiveness' . . . from now on."

"Get ready, Ong; I majored in it at Second Skin, remember?"

"How can I forget? So be gentle with me."

They were laughing too much for real passion, but it helped to make life a bit more bearable.

Joe was announcing their meal was ready.

They ate. It was meat cooked under pressure, very tender

130

with vegetables she didn't recognize, and a dessert that tasted of an exotic fruit. Ong behaved himself and didn't mess her tablecloth.

They retired to the battered lounge for coffee. Don was at the console when bells chimed.

"There has been a media release, sir. It says you are dead. Do I need to arrange your funeral, sir?"

"No, but thank you, Don. Keep monitoring that channel; there might be a lot more."

There was more later. Simon had done as he had wanted to do. Made a docco of the moon and the storm, and he had incorporated Don's message. It was very moving. Lots of footage of the hero Ong in various battle zones, the worm episode on Beebop, and finally a reference to the death of his wife and parents. Maggda sat with tears rolling down her face.

"Just imagine what it will be like when you finally do go, Ong! I hope I won't be there to see it."

"Well, Lady of the Lace Knickers, we do know that the spy we want is someone up there in Fleet Com HQ. Now we have to pin him or her down."

"Can't you get onto Fleet and get a rundown of likely personnel? Oh, sorry, that stuff would be classified, right? But there must be someone watching the place who would know. How are we going to tip off the boss?"

"We have done our best from this end. Now they have to do their bit, set their own traps, do their own checks. I am not Fleet's Sherlock Holmes, Maggda. I just want to sort this little mystery out right here and take some leave."

"Okay, but may I ask who the heck is 'Shylock who'?"

"Ask Don, I want to rest. Call me early, Joe."

"Yes sir.

"Same for me, Joe."

"Yes, miss."

She went to her room and paused by his door. He was showering, but on his bedside table was a tri-dee of Su Lin. She went quietly on her way. It had reminded her that he was still very much in mourning in his own quiet way.

It grew cold around the cavern, but the fire warmed them, the skins covered them, and the hay that they slept on was deep and warm. The little pigs snoozed next to the children, and there was peace in the world. That was set to change.

Maggda sat watching the tri-dee screen as the cameras outside the base slowly scanned and swept the landscape. As she watched, it began to rain, a gentle shower that spread across the valley and the meadows, and the afternoon sun created a wonderful rainbow. She felt that things could be much worse. This moon was beautiful. The wild life couldn't have been more natural, even though most of it was imported from other planets across the galaxy. She wondered what winter was going to be like or if there was going to be a winter; whether she and Davvd would be back home before too long. He had been very quiet since the news of his disappearance and probable death had been released. She went to the kitchen and found him cutting bread that Joe had baked that morning.

"Get some while it's fresh," he said, offering a slice of buttered bread thick with honey.

"You're dripping it all over the floor, Ong!"

He found a wet cloth and cleaned up.

"Davvd, a couple of questions. First, do we get a winter here? Second, what happens to the Ong dynasty now you're dead?"

"What do you want answered first?"

"Either one."

"First one is easier. We get a winter. It snows. It gets very cold. We all stay inside and keep warm. It lasts for about the same time as an Old Earth winter, and that is why this moon was chosen to be a habitat for quite a few Old Earth species. If you ask Don or Joe they will give you precise details of temperatures, snowfalls, wind velocity, and when the first birds come back from the south."

"Ong dynasty?"

"Have you got a week or so to listen? It depends a lot on the admiral getting a coded message to my family, relatives, etc., and to Solomon Wu. I am hoping and hoping and hoping that he has enough sense to let them know I am alive and well, but because I am on duty down here, everything stays tighter than a duck's backside.

If that doesn't happen, then my Uncle Max gets power of attorney, and he gets to be nominal head of Ong business interests. Now Uncle Max will hate that because he has just made his fishing lodge so beautiful that he just wants to stay there and retire from any kind of business cut and thrust. Solomon will be either very happy or very angry, depending on the combined business ventures that eventually need my signature seal. His wife will cry a lot. She is a lovely, soft woman. His son, Horatio . . . his son . . ."

"What? What is the matter? You've gone white."

"His son, Horatio, his son, Captain Horatio Winston Wu, is a Fleet captain like me!"

"So what's that to do with the price of eggs?"

"He is an officer who works at the com station above Alpha Six. He decodes, he transcribes, and he encrypts, and he has access to just about every damn signal that comes or goes anywhere. He is a brilliant, natural decoder. He speaks all the Old Earth languages, and he is security cleared to level six!"

"Oh, Davvd, are you saying one of your own family is selling Fleet out? That can't be right. He couldn't, could he? And why, for the sake of Aton's breath, would he? He doesn't need the money, he is so damn rich—"

"You said it, babe. He doesn't need the money. Our spy doesn't take his credits, does he? You know why? Because what he would get from Galactic would be peanuts! He just ignores them, but he has to go through the ritual of asking for the credits. I am prepared to bet that Simon has had a demand for credits and that he paid up."

"Whoa here, sidelocks! You can't just pin a spy deal on your brother-in-law just because he works for Fleet up at com station, can you? What is his motive? He doesn't take the credits, so money is out of the question. So what does he want?"

"Sherlock."

"What? Is that a motive or a security code?"

"Never mind, Maggda. It just seems very circumstantial that Horatio is in a position to just pluck what he wants out of the message bank and use it. He has the means; he has the expertise; he has all the power of a vast com satellite at his beck and call; and he has high security clearance. No one would question him."

"Motive? What about the motive? You keep ducking the motive!"

"You tell me."

"How come you have never mentioned this brother-in-law before?"

"I honestly forgot him."

"How?"

"He and I are Fleet. He started, oh, about a semester behind me in the academy, could be a bit more. We were never close. He had his crowd, I had mine, and we would meet at parties or stuff like that, but we never really were socially side by side."

"So?"

"So nothing. He went into Signal Command; I went into Deep Space Command. I did neat stuff like how to blow up a planet or two, how to pilot a battle cruiser, and how to quell a rebellion on a strange planet with nothing more than twenty troopers and a couple of tins of soup."

"Don't give me that bull, Davvd. I know how much you have done, remember? What is this crap about two tins of soup?"

"Don't you dare laugh. We were sent to Vitari Five. There was a tribal revolt against the governor. The planetary delegate was kidnapped and was being held in the hills, not just for ransom but to change some laws because they were screaming that their leader had been discriminated against by the government."

"Get to the damned soup, Ong!"

"Okay, my commander was a veteran. He had lived out there. Anyway, we got ambushed, and they were going to hold us too. Then old man Dixxon, he spoke to them in their own dialect, and he told them that we had come in there to destroy all of them, raze the place to the ground, and that we would all sacrifice ourselves if they didn't release the delegate and resume talks."

"So? Was that true?"

"And they all wet themselves laughing. We were all wetting ourselves for other reasons, and they fired off rifles into the air, then Old Dixxon took off his back pack and pulled out two large tins of soup, which was part of the ration pack. No labels, just shiny tins, and he said, 'Now you know what this is, don't you? This is the two-part pack of a fusion bomb.'

"So he puts one tin down on the ground next to the other one, and he pulled his communication ear shell out of his tunic pocket. He sticks one end to one tin and the other end to the other tin, then he stands up and pulls his little com radio out of his tunic top pocket and taps a code into it. It played a little song, then it said, 'Local time is' whatever it was, and he puts the com radio on top of the first can and put the plug from the ear shell into it.

"Then he gets a stick off the ground, sticks it into the dust and scratches a mark at the end of the shadow. Now, all those big, hairy guys were watching this. They didn't look too different from our Neanderthals out there, to tell the truth. Then he did a very smart regimental turn and said, 'Line out from me.' So we lined out. Then he said, 'Kneel down and take your helmets off, and if anyone questions me, I will personally shoot them.'

"So we knelt down, and we were facing the sun. Then he kneels down too, next to the tins, and says, 'Sergeant Boyce, I want you to lead this holy choir in the regimental anthem, and you mules had better follow him so close there won't be a quaver between you. Now put your hands together, close your eyes and tilt your heads back, Now, Boyce, one, two, three, lead off.'

"So, Maggda, we sang the anthem, and Boyce had a wonderful baritone voice, and when we finished, Dixxon held out his hands to the sun and screamed, 'We come to you, Aton, we come to you!'

"None of us dare move, and the damn sun was hot, and we heard a heck of a lot of noise and shouting and land cars roaring about, and then their chief must have appeared. Dixxon stood up, and he pointed to the mark in the dust, and the hairy bastard shouted something, and they brought the planetary delegate over. So Dixxon ordered us up, we got our helmets on, and then Dixxon and the hairy bastard embraced and kissed each other, twice on each cheek. Then we formed up, Dixxon carefully picked up the soup tins and put them in his pack, and we got the hell out of there. And when we were on the ship going home, the planetary delegate says to Dixxon, 'I think you could teach me a lot about diplomacy.'

"Dixxon said, 'Yes sir, diplomacy first, fear later. Works all the time.'

"I never see a big tin of soup without thinking about that."

"Davvd Ong, do you expect me to believe that?"

"Maggda Styxx, look up the Fleet records. It's all in there."

The nights get cooler. We do not know this place, but we think the winter is coming. The leaves turn, and last morning there was frost on the grass.

Annrath made me light her great fire, and it roared all day. She and the women fed it all the branches until all of them were eaten by the fire. It was so hot the women brought meat to roast beside it. It burned all day, and when it became low, Annrath told me to let no one touch it or to come near it. She was very fierce. I know Annrath is a special woman. She thinks differently than the others, and they follow her lead. I am proud that she wants to be my woman.

Don recorded the fire, but it was just a small blaze and didn't spread, and Davvd accepted it as something the tribe was doing and ignored it.

Maggda went down the gully with Joe and collected plant roots that he could cook, and she brought back colored leaves on thin branches to make a table center dressing.

Davvd smiled. She was strangely at home in this underground den of scientific endeavors. Joe had cut his hair back to Fleet standard, and she had had hers styled from a picture in a magazine found in a drawer that must have been many ESYs old. It suited her. She was searching for dress designs. He thought that she would have an uphill job with nothing but service denims as a base, but she was determined. He suddenly realized that he was getting used to her being there all the time. Every now and then he would just hold her and kiss her and then let her go. It was all he dared do to show his increasing affection for her. They joked a lot, but she had made no more overt suggestions that they have sex. He kept stumbling over memories of Su Lin and her sensuousness, and he was in no real emotional state to forget one for the other.

She may have read his mind and his mood, because she kept a little aloof. She would reach out and hold his hand every now and then. Or give him a brief and gentle hug or sit with her arm over his shoulder as they sat on the old lounge. He felt like an old married man, comfortable and secure, and if he could get rid of the need to take her to bed, he would have felt complete.

At the Wu household, there was consternation. Solomon was angry and very irritable and was doing his best to alienate everyone and everything around him. His wife, gentle Sylvia, was distraught. Now she had lost the last link to Su Lin.

Davvd had gone, and she turned to her android as a human friend. She had already had its hair style changed to that of Su Lin, had had dresses made from material that Su Lin had chosen, had had shoes fitted that Su Lin had worn and liked and had created a daughter so completely in her mind that Solomon feared for her sanity.

Jackson was irritable too. Having planned to get away to see Jutta on Valderia, he was torn between his mother's needs and his own.

He went to his mother's suite and was momentarily startled at the appearance of Crystal. It was like confronting his resurrected sister. His mother was sitting with her arm around the "girl," who was nestled close and doing some complex needlework, exactly as Su Lin did when she had spare time.

"Don't say anything, Jackson. Your father thinks I am mad, I think I am mad, but I have to have some emotional comfort, and Crystal helps to do that. I can talk to her, Jackson, about things your father would become angry to hear. I can have her warmth beside me day and night. When I wake in the night, she reaches out and holds my hand, and I need that."

"Can I give you a hug, mother? I love you, so you can do what you want to do as far as I am concerned. If this 'girl' makes you happy and feel better, then I think she must be good for you."

He was a little unsettled by the smile that Crystal gave him. She was so real that he knew why his mother was captivated by 'her.'

"Crystal, please make us some coffee. I must talk to Jackson."

"Jackson, did you come here to comfort me?"

"Yes and no, mother. End of semester, finished the exams, and I am on holiday for a few weeks."

"Then you can stay and keep me company."

"Well, first I have to go back to Valderia. The officer who stole my recording device wants to make amends. Acting on orders, it seems, so says an apology is due. I mean, I can't nicely refuse, can I? I do have other things to sort out too. Business things."

She looked at him with wet eyes.

He felt he was betraying her.

"Mother, listen to me. Davvd isn't dead as far as anyone is concerned, just missing. The other thing is, what was he doing on

E5? I am prepared to bet that Fleet put him there on some secret mission. What we don't know was if he was really alone down there, do we? There could be a platoon of Fleet commandos looking for him right now. I don't think we should write off Davvd Ong just like that; do you?"

"Horatio says he is dead and gone, and he should know. He's also in Fleet."

"That doesn't mean much, mother. Different branch, different circumstance, and Davvd was undercover a lot. Only a few top brass knew where he was most of the time. No, I think whatever they tell you, you shouldn't give up hope. He could have faked his own death for some security reasons. Who knows?"

Crystal came in with a tray.

"Have some coffee with us, and then I suppose you are off to Valderia. Does your father know about this?"

"May I ask you not to tell him? I just want to do what I have to do and do that very quietly. If he finds out he will want me to get involved in something to do with his business, and I just want a few days away from that, from college, and from bad news."

"I promise not to. There is a lot I don't tell your father either, would you believe?"

They laughed, and Crystal joined in, then she handed his mother the little plate of sweetmeats.

"Can I tempt you, Sylvia?"

His mother said, "They look very tempting, don't they? Thank you, Crystal."

He kissed his mother goodbye and very nearly pecked the cheek of the android.

He knew why she was so taken with it. It could have been his sister.

He packed a small bag but put in a business suit at the last minute. He didn't really know what he was letting himself in for. The robotic butler booked his stateroom on the next Wu starship through to Valderia, and he went and sent Jutta another short message.

"I am coming. My heart flies ahead of me. Jackson."

Jutta sang. She contacted her mother on the farm.

"If I ask nicely, may I bring a young man home to meet you both? I don't know if he will come with me, but if he does, will you mind?"

"Well, Jutta Vogel, this is a big surprise. So where did you meet this young man? On the parade ground?"

"If he does come, mother, I will tell you then. I love you all."

Her mother smiled. "She has some young man now, Gerhardt. I wonder what he will be like. Knowing her he will be like the other boyfriends she has had, simple and penniless."

He laughed. "Well, Rachel, wasn't I just like that when you took me home?"

She threw the wet dishcloth at him, and they both laughed.

There was an alarm chiming from the console. Davvd Ong heard it, but Don was already taking care of it.

"What do we have, Don?"

"There is a vessel in orbit. It is not registered as a Foundation vessel or a Fleet ship. It doesn't have approval as far as our records are concerned."

"How big?"

"A small supply vessel or an equally small gun ship. Or a scientific delivery and pickup one."

"Can we see this thing, please, Don?"

"Only a radar probe image. The high cloud blurs everything."

"Show me anyway. Well, I can't see much either. Get me a recognition chart. It may be on one of those."

A set of charts came onto the screen.

"Discount those bigger vessels, Don. Just show me the tonnage of that thing if you can, and we can take it from there. Does it respond to an identification challenge or not?"

"Robot controlled, no human aboard. It has sensors working."

"Oh, Aton's breath, you know what this thing is, don't you? It is the same damn ship that brought our tribe here! Now it wants to take them back! Watch it like a hawk, Don; if it moves a damn centimeter, scream!"

"What's the excitement about, boys?"

"We have big trouble. Up there is a vessel that I believe has come here to scoop our little tribe up and take them either back to E7 or somewhere else!"

"Who, what? How do you know?"

"Because it just fits, that's all. The tribe wasn't spooked by us because they had experienced robots before. This thing brought them here. Whoever is behind this is doing all this illegally. They think there is no human here. There wouldn't normally be any right now. All the staff would be back home writing up papers and sorting records, so this damn thing can come here and snatch what it likes, when it likes!"

"Davvd, are you losing your mind? You were sent here to find out what was killing animals, right? You, Don, and I found out who and what it was. You kept saying these are illegals. This ship is going to take them back, which is what should happen, and now you are getting, well, emotional, aren't you?"

"I am angry that who or what is behind this is doing it without going through channels, or in other words, without doing the right thing. Someone stuffed up; someone tried to cover their tracks. They might have got away with it except Don picked it up, and you and I confirmed it. The other thing is, I am torn between getting our tribe back to their real home and their real safety."

"There is a pregnant woman there, you know."

"I know. So how do you feel?"

"You really want to know? Shitty."

"See? You feel the way I do right now. They are people just like us. They are a living, human experiment, which I find a bit hard to take, even if Foundation approved the concept a long time ago."

"Doesn't make it right, does it?"

"I guess it would be if these poor souls hadn't been screwed about. They would have lived out their lives on E7 and been none the wiser."

"Sorry, but if the experiment had worked, they would have been, wouldn't they?"

She saw the look on his face.

"Sorry."

"Has that thing moved, Don?"

"No sir."

She had a small flower in her fingers. It was closed tight. "You know what this is? I've looked it up. It is a night-flowering moon daisy."

"I know what you are going to say. That ship isn't going to move until it gets dark, same as we did. Would bet my pension on it."

"What is more to the point, my softhearted hero, is what are we going to do about it? Whatever it is, it had better be good. How can you stop a mass transportation? There is just me and you and these two. You can't knock out a robot with a stun gun, or can you?"

"Logistics. Consider the logistics. The robot lands the craft, same as we did, in the meadow. The tribe comes down to 'greet' the man from the stars, as they were about to do when we zapped them. They fall down. Now how many bots are there on that ship? Do you know, Don?"

"There is one giving off a signal. If there are others, they are switched off."

"Let's say just one then. Now, it has to get the bodies out of the cave entrance or off the meadow and into the hold of that ship. My bet is that it would use a loading cart. It could put three or four onto the cart and just go up the ramp and dump them off. Three or four trips, maximum."

"So what do we do?"

"I don't honestly know."

She gave a little wail and banged the desktop. "How do we stop something like Don, for example, doing what it is ordered to do?"

"Ask Don."

"Don, can you tell me? If you were that robot that was programmed to take the tribe back, what would stop you without causing total destruction?"

"I am not aware of its design or origins, Miss Maggda, but if it is a Wu Industries model, then its plasi-positronic brain is close to mine and Joe's. There is a basic core that is expanded or modified according to what it would be specified to do."

"So?"

"Both Joe and I are sensitive to power surges. We are not capable of withstanding violent electrical shocks. In cases like that, both Joe and I would protect our circuitry by switching off immediately. We would, effectively, close down for a while until we could detect that the threat had passed or been eliminated. Our brains would not be damaged, but our mobility circuits would be switched off."

Davvd sat up.

"So you would react just like a human hit by a stun gun pulse might? Fall down and not be able to move?"

"Yes sir, but we are immune to stun guns."

"Wait a minute, Lord of the Universe. When I tried to follow you in here when we first arrived, I came into the rear entrance, I got zapped, and it stopped me dead in my tracks. What was that?"

"A simple force field, a few sensors, and when your body passed between them, you completed the circuit, and the current flowed and zap!"

"It hurt."

"It doesn't carry much power. It is the sudden zap that makes you back off."

"Could we stop our friend up there with something like that?"

"I think we would need a lot more zap to do it. Don, do we have a small, powerful generator in stores?"

"There are two mobile and one stationary for emergency power. We have used them very little, but they are ready to be used."

"What are you thinking, Davvd?"

"Say we set up a power source on the loader, and we have a net like a big loading net, and we bare-wire that so we can maybe throw that over our friend when he emerges from the ship. We get the net over him and throw the switch, and he gets zapped. Doesn't get damaged, just immobilized. We immobilize him, and we, well, after that I am open to suggestions. Would that work, Don?"

"It sounds a very feasible plan, sir. May I ask how you get him into the net?"

Maggda laughed. "Good thinking, Don. All right, tell him, Davvd."

"He will attempt to do his kidnapping after dark. He will bring that ship down in the meadow, and the tribe will come out to greet him. We, with our trap set up on the loader, are hiding in the rear of the meadow in the dark. He comes down all lit up, and the glare will actually hide us. Now, we take off as he lands, and we hover above his ship. Hopefully he won't be looking up, and the noise of the loader will, hopefully, merge with his ship. Now, he is programmed to do his job, and that will be a number one priority. We should be able to sling that net over him and power it up. He falls down, and we have him."

"Hopefully."

"Don't be negative, Maggda; I can't think of anything else. I did think we might be able to put that net down in the grass so he steps onto it, and we send the power through it via a long cable, but, of course, we don't have an exact landing spot, do we?"

"Just a thought. That loading net is heavy, heavy, heavy! I couldn't lift it, let alone throw it, could you?"

"No, but Joe or Don could tip that off the loader, and the weight of it would probably put him off balance before we even throw the switch. We have the element of surprise, don't forget."

"Would you be surprised, Don?"

"Surprise is a human reaction, and if I were truly human, I would be. My reaction would depend upon sensing a threat that

I could eliminate. In those circumstances, I think I would be unable to identify the threat quickly enough to avoid the net falling on me, and rendering me immobile."

"So you think that it would work?"

"It would appear to be the only logical method we have so far devised, miss."

"So, it's all we have. Don, Joe, get that net wired up, get enough cable to allow us to drop it off the loader to the ground. Make sure those wiring joints are not going to break as we drop it. Get it onto the edge of the loader, say the right-hand edge, and Joe, what power will we need?"

"The smaller generator will be sufficient, and it will be less difficult to wire up, sir."

"And it will give us more room on the deck too. Make sure it starts and stops as it should. So we had better get started; it will be dark sooner than we think, and our boy will be here before we are ready for him."

Annrath has been to look at her fire. It has burnt for two whole days, and the ashes are still glowing, and she can see her bowls glowing within them. One has broken, but the other three are whole. She keeps laughing and talking to the other women. She has told me that soon we can make more things that will be of use to us now that she has learnt how to make the clay into stone. She says we can make perfect spear points from the clay and turn them into stone, and they would be sharp, but they would break if they were dropped, so I think that would be a useless thing to do.

With our sharp knives we have cut grasses, and the women have ground the seeds into a paste as we did at our last home, and they bake them on flat stones in the hot coals. We have filled the cave with hay to keep us warm during the winter. We have made a great pile of wood close by to burn. We have smoked a lot of fish and dried a supply of meat, enough to feed us if the snow stops us hunting. There is nothing else we can do. We await the first snow.

The dark descended. Davvd and Maggda turned off all the

lights in the complex and went out to the loader. Joe and Don had pulled the net into a neat, folded form on the edge of the loader. Wires snaked back to the generator. Davvd hit the starter and it purred into life. He switched it off quickly.

"Ropes, do we have ropes to tie our friend down once we stop him?"

"Yes sir, all coiled here, sir."

"What would I do without you two?"

"Be three parts helpless, Davvd?"

"Not in front of the boys, Maggda, they think that I am pretty useless anyway!"

Above, in the void, power surged, and the ugly ship applied retro-power to its drive and began the plunge to the surface of the moon. With no human feelings to consider, its entry was brutal, but the pilot was unmoved, merely registering G forces but not affected by them. The coordinates were already set, and the ship changed direction, making corrections until it hung five hundred meters above the meadow. Then it switched on a full array of landing and identification lights, docking beams, and spotlights until it became a source of blue white power, then it dropped, located the position in the meadow and settled in the deep grass.

The lights penetrated the cavern, and they stood to see the star men. They pushed open the "door" and filed out as the star men appeared, then there was another noise. Against the glare they were blind, but something else was there somewhere in the gloom. There were blue sparks, and the star man fell out of sight into the meadow grass. Two more star men appeared, then suddenly all three were lifted up into the darkness. The noise went away over the trees, and there in the meadow was the shape of something they thought they recognized.

"It is what brought us here," screamed Annrath, "and it has come to take us away from here."

"We will not go," growled Manta.

146

"We will not go," said Olan. "We will kill the star man."

Suddenly, all the lights went out, and what remained was a blacker shape against the overall blackness. They went back to their cave, closed the door and were ready to fight, if that was needed.

"By Aton's breath, Maggda, that was easier than I thought it would be."

"You mean you didn't think it would work?"

"Kept thinking of Dixxon with his soup tins and wished he were here to come up with something better, to tell the truth."

"Better take a look and see what we have, Davvd. Are the boys securing our pirate?"

"Let's take a look."

In the loader hanger, Don and Joe had pretty well put everything back. Joe was lifting the generator back into its hidey-hole, and Don was coiling ropes. It was a big robot, taller than Don, with a blued steel appearance. It stood exactly as the boys had left it after raising it off the deck.

"Any identification, Don?"

"It is a military robot, sir. It is an army issue for the Valderian army and has been used by them as a pilot and for heavy-duty traffic work. Very rugged and pretty well indestructible in normal circumstances."

"A bit like you guys,"

"Yes miss, but we think faster."

"Have I told you lately that I love you, Don?"

"No, miss."

"She does, Don, she does. She might be going to kidnap you to serve her when we get away from here, so watch your back!"

"Yes sir."

"Now what, Lord of the Planets. Do we just stand him in a corner as a conversation piece, or what?"

"Approximately how long will he be comatose?"

"In Old Earth time, sir, about half an hour."

"Good, let's get ourselves a drink. I can use one. What brew do you have Joe?"

"I have a mead made with honey and herbs that is mature. It is sweet but dangerous to human health, so please don't drive after drinking, sir."

"Have you noticed that Joe is getting funnier by the minute, Ong?"

"Well, what do you expect after you see the people he hangs around with? Let's have that drink, Joe. Might give us some ideas."

They sipped their drink and looked at the military machine. The only indication it was "alive" was the small blue LED in the center of its "forehead."

"You know, this is a pretty elaborate piece of equipment. I would suspect that there aren't too many on active service right now. They cost a lot of credits, and they only get put into the field when there is a full-scale panic on."

"I think it is going into recovery mode, Davvd. Are we safe?"

"Humans are always safe with robots, you know that. Just stay calm and think of it as another Don."

The eyes began to glow, and there was a faintly audible hum as it routed power. It moved slightly and turned its head. It recorded the scene and the humans in front of it.

"Do you have a name?" asked Davvd.

"I am Serial 447, sir, of the Valderian Army Corps."

"Where are you located, 447?"

"Army Barracks Ten, sir."

"Are you on active duty all the time, 447?"

"No sir, I was assigned to Marshall Schiff for special duties, sir."

"Are you allowed to tell us what those duties were, 447?"

"To locate certain humanoids on this moon and transport them back to E7 to their rightful place of residence, sir."

"Do you know how those humanoids came to be here, 447?"

"No sir, that information has been listed as 'classified,' sir. I was given my orders. I was not given any background information, sir."

"Probably wasn't seen as relevant anyway, Davvd. This guy is just a shuttle pilot trying to do his job; he knew just enough to do the job, and that was it."

"Yes ma'am."

"What are we going to do with you, 447?"

Jackson willed the starship to Valderia, and it flew there exactly as it should, on time to a millisecond. The shuttle deposited him at the landing dock; he took a taxi to the Palace and asked for the room he had on his last visit, and it was his. He bought a large bunch of flowers whose name he didn't know from the florist in the foyer and had a large bottle of gin and some tonic sent up to his room .Then he had a thought and asked the receptionist if she knew where he could buy his "wife" Second Skin underwear.

She smiled. "Why here, sir. Just down this corridor is the boutique. They have them there." He almost trotted down and into the shop. The lady who served him smiled when he said that it was for his wife, but she made up two sets in the size he thought would fit Jutta.

"But sir can exchange them if they are not quite right, you know that." He hoped he wouldn't have to do that. "Are you sure about the color, sir? Ivory is always welcome, and the midnight blue is very alluring."

He asked for them to be sent to his room and fled after paying. He knew now why women desired them so much. He went back to the foyer.

He had told her exactly when he would be arriving, so he knew that she knew. His time band told him that even if she walked in right now, he should have time for a drink.

The barman smiled.

"I know sir, one long gin and tonic with ice and a lemon slice."

"I wish my memory was as good as yours!"

"Thank you, sir, but in this job it comes with the territory. I like to think I get it right most times. Are you alone, sir?"

"Hoping not to be."

"Yes, now I do remember. You were with a young lieutenant in the army. She drank gin and tonics too. Went quite pink, a very pretty girl, very pretty, and if I'm not mistaken, she has just walked in."

"Make me another one of those, please, for old times' sake."

She was wearing a very pretty, very floral dress with a low neckline that had a wide lace collar around it. The skirt was full, and he thought she probably had full petticoats beneath it because it stood out from her legs. Her hair was braided up, but she had inserted a tiara of small wildflowers that were like a halo on it. Her stockings were white and were woven with a pattern of small roses. Her high-heeled boots were of shiny red leather, and she blushed a bright pink smile at him.

"Oh, Jutta, you look wonderful." He held out his hands, and she grasped his. "I want to kiss you."

"Please, Jackson, can we wait just a few moments. I want to have a gin and tonic with you again."

The barman smiled and passed over the glass, and she thanked him.

"Do you know that this dress is a traditional dress, and it is worn by brides on their wedding day?"

"Are we getting married?"

"Not today but I love this dress, and I just had to show you."

"You make it look very ordinary, because you are so beautiful."

She held his hand tightly.

"I have been wanting to see you again so much. How can you want to see me after what I did to you?"

"It wasn't you, was it? Schiff made you do it. I couldn't get you out of my mind. My studies have suffered; I sleep badly. All I can do is think about you. My mother thinks I have been ill. Now finish your drink. I have a present for you."

150

She began to giggle. "No, Jackson, not again!"

"No, different, I promise you."

Out of the elevator, she looked at him. "Same suite?"

"Same suite." He palmed the door lock and let them in, and she saw the flowers in the great silver vase.

She put her arms around his neck, and he kissed her long and hard, and she shuddered a little.

"What did I do, what did I do?"

"When you kiss me like that, well, my nipples tingle!"

They laughed.

"Now, Lieutenant Vogel, can you take orders?"

"Yes sir."

"Turn your back to me, Lieutenant, and close your eyes. Don't you dare look."

"No sir."

"Now, take your clothes off and put them on the floor, all of them."

She slipped out of the dress and the heavy petticoats and was left with her stockings and her boots.

"All of them."

She wore old-fashioned garters, and she pulled them down and rolled down her stockings, and she was stuck at her boots.

"Sit on the bed, Vogel."

"Yes sir."

"Now give me your boots."

He pulled her boots off, and she was pink and cream, and her nipples were jutting like rosebuds. He leant over and kissed each one in turn.

"Now, I have a present for you. It requires a whip and for you to turn over so your lovely pink bottom is revealed in all its glory."

She scrambled off the bed and hid behind it, one arm hiding her breasts, and the other cupped between her legs.

"You dare to touch me, Jackson, and I will scream so loud the windows will break!"

"Oh. Jutta, my little sweetheart, look in that drawer beside the bed, and you will see your present."

She kept her eyes on him and opened the drawer and took out the box, gold and black with gold ribbon, and she squealed.

"Second Skin! You bought me Second Skin! Oh, Jackson, do what you want with me. For Second Skin I would even put up with the whip."

"Come over here." Now take out the light colored set and put them on. I didn't know what your size was, so I guessed."

"How did you guess these?" She cupped her breasts.

"Well the lady brought in a bowl of oranges, and I picked the one I thought—"

"Liar!"

She slid into the underwear and paraded. Her pink nipples showed through the synthetic spider silk, and she glowed.

"When that model, Maggda Styxx, was wearing this underwear all over the channels, I never thought I would ever get to wear it too. When my friend Maria sees me in these she will kill me from sheer jealousy."

"Do you want to go out to dinner tonight?"

"Can we go to the Blue Boar again?"

"We can go wherever you want to go. It's too early to go out now. What do you want to do?"

"I want you to have me anyway you want."

She stripped off the underwear; he threw his clothes off onto the floor; and they clambered into bed. For a short while they clung to each other's warmth, and then he made love to her in a gentle, loving way until she moaned in his arms.

As they lay together Jackson sighs, "Can this go on forever?"

"I don't know. I feel very happy right now."

"I feel very happy."

"Will you marry me, Jackson?"

"Let me kiss your nipples again, and I'll tell you later."

It was dusk before they emerged, but the shops were still open, and it suddenly occurred to him that she was wearing an old style wedding dress, and he was suited up in a quite formal suit.

They took a red and black taxi into the city center, and he watched for dress shops. He stopped the cab at the door of a very stylish looking establishment with a name he thought he remembered. He thought his mother had clothes with this label.

"Can I buy you a dress?" I don't want the waiter to think we just got married."

"You want to buy me a dress from here? This is Maxxi's."

"The clothes look like they would suit you."

"Jackson, this is Maxxi's!"

"Sorry, I thought they looked all right. If they are rubbish, let's look somewhere else."

She grabbed his arm and whispered in his ear.

"In the same way that I could never afford, Second Skin, I could never afford anything from here."

"Perfect choice then. Let's go in."

"Are you really sure?"

"Do you want a dress or not?"

They went inside. The assistant was tall with a severe bobbed hairstyle and a tailored suit that clung to her very slim body. She looked down from her high-heeled elevation through black-rimmed glasses that made her look as if she was examining a specimen in a laboratory. Her smile was bleak.

"Do I offer my congratulations on your wedding, ma'am?"

Jutta frowned. "A friend's wedding. We all wore traditional dress. It was lovely, wasn't it, Jackson?"

"Quite beautiful. I love those old traditions, don't you?"

"May I help you, madam?"

Jackson waved his hand about the store.

"Madam would like two dresses that will suit her complexion and her choice, of course. One is to be for daywear and the other for evening when we dine at the Chancellery. Can you find something that suits?"

The assistant blinked. "If you are dining at the Chancellery, I can show you some very suitable clothes. Come this way please, madam."

They were at the Blue Boar, and she was drinking her first gin and tonic when she laughed at him.

"Did you see her face when you told her we were dining at the chancellery? It was wicked of you to do that. I never thought you had that sense of humor, but now I know. Those dresses and the underwear, do you know that my whole salary for a whole year wouldn't buy those?"

"I didn't think about it."

"Jackson, I have to go back to the officers quarters tonight because my leave really doesn't start until tomorrow, then I am really free. We can go back to your room now if you like, and we can . . ."

"Get some sleep tonight, and we can play tomorrow."

"I want to take you to my home. I want you to meet my parents."

"Oh, Jutta Vogel, you scheming vixen. Does this mean we are engaged?"

"Will you come out and meet them? We can go up the mountain and see the lakes, and . . . they will want to meet you, I know they will."

He took her to the barracks, and the taxi took him to the Palace. He crawled into the rumpled bed where her perfume rose off the sheets, and he felt tired but happy. She was very desirable and he felt great warmth for her. He wondered what his mother might make of her.

The next morning Jutta was about early, packing her bag and thinking of what she and Jackson would do. Maria came by and came in.

"I heard you banging about. I thought you were on leave."

"Starts this morning."

"So did you meet him last night?"

"Let me show you something. Close your eyes for moment."

She pulled the Second Skin box from her bag and hid it behind her.

"Guess what Jackson gave me last night."

"Are you being vulgar?"

"Don't be smart, just guess!"

"Flowers?"

"How about these!"

She gave Maria the box.

"In Aton's holy name, what did you have to do to get these?"

"Oh, he beat my bare bottom with a whip, but it was worth it."

"Tell him he can beat my bare bottom too if he buys me these!

"And, Maria Schmitt, these!"

She took the dresses from her wardrobe and held them out.

Maria took the day dress and held it with reverence. It was cream and draped like a static waterfall.

"Oh, Jutta, this is so beautiful."

"It is real silk from little worms, and those pearls all over the bodice are real, freshwater pearls, sewn on by hand. The buttons, Maria, are really gold. Now the next dress —"

"He bought you *two* dresses from Maxxi's? He must be insane or so much in love with you he is losing his mind and his credit balance at the same time!"

She held the blue evening dress against her and turned around. It had gold threads running through the silk and black embroideries at the neck and all around the sweeping hem.

"You know what this dress is for, Maria? It is for when we dine at the chancellery. He told me so,"

"Liar!"

"I can almost believe him. That is what he told the lady at Maxxi's."

"So what are you going to do with him?"

"I don't know. I told my mother I might bring him home to show him off."

"And what then? Is he going to sleep with you at your home? Your mother will have an attack."

"Well, Horst is away, and his room is free, and there is the small room above the stables . . ."

"This boy of yours, Jutta, is probably heir to millions of credits, and you want to put him above the stables like a stable hand?"

"What else can I do?"

"He is free, you are on leave. Go away with him and do a nice little tour of the mountains together. He gets separate rooms, but you both sleep in one, and you show your mother that he has his room and you have your room and that you are as virginal as the fresh winter snow."

"If she believes that, she is simpleminded, Maria."

"Never, but she is a mother, and she trusts her daughter to be discreet. That is the difference."

"And my father?"

"He will ask if the boy has lots of money, and you can tell him he has enough to buy a small planet or two and not ask for change. Then he will clap him on the back and shake his hand, and then he will send you on your way and wish you joy!"

"Somehow I think you are right!"

Marshall Schiff was impatient but controlled. He had duties at the barracks, but as soon as he could, he had set a series of tasks for Maria to carry out and went to communications. She was replacing Jutta on the roster, and although she wasn't as decorative as his pink and glowing lieutenant, she was an excellent second best. Schiff was not a predator, but he liked the girls who shared his office and duties to be sharp and pretty. It made a good impression on higher-ranking officers and distracted them so he could be on top of the situation. He was waiting for a signal from his robotic probe to E5.

"News from 447?"

"None, sir. The ship orbited E5 then went off the screens. It does that when it enters the atmosphere, sir. We assume it landed, but it hasn't resumed orbit or left the moon, so it must be on the ground somewhere."

"What, by Aton's name, is it doing down there?"

"Well, sir, it could be a malfunction of some kind. That 447 is capable of diagnosis, but if it required some spares that it didn't carry . . ."

"What about weather?"

"It could be waiting for a break in a storm, or maybe there is an electrical disturbance in the upper atmosphere that would keep him grounded. We should have had a routine signal telling us that the situation is normal, but we have had nothing."

Schiff slapped his boot savagely with his riding crop.

"Keep me informed. I want to know immediately if there is any contact with that damn ship."

"Yes sir!"

Schiff went back to his office, asked Maria to make him coffee, and he sat and tried to make sense of it. What the heck had gone wrong? He felt that something had, and it didn't smell good. If it had crashed, there would be a signal. If it had malfunctioned, then 447 would have sent a coded signal. He forced himself to wait. Think of something else.

"Maria, your friend Jutta Vogel. Is she seeing her young man?"

"I think so, sir. She told me she was going to take him to meet her parents."

His eyebrows rose.

"Is she engaged, Maria? If she is, that happened in hurry! Who is this Don Juan who can sweep the pretty Jutta off her feet, do you know?"

"She just tells me that his name is Jason, sir. I think he comes from Old Earth and has some business here that he is taking care of for his father."

"For a moment, Maria, I thought you were going to say Jackson. She met young Wu when he was here on . . . business, let us say, when he came to see me. Now that would be a union!"

"I am sure she said his name was Jason, sir."

"I think I made a comment that she should snare young Wu! He and she would make a pretty good match, and that is aside from his money."

"I wouldn't know sir. Do you want me to take the tray away, sir?"

"Yes, thank you, Maria,"

He smiled to himself. Jason and Jackson were pretty close. Jutta was such a pretty girl and really quite smart, but when it came to subterfuge, he didn't think she would or could conjure up a trail of deception of any real depth.

He made a small bet with himself that Jackson Wu was getting the pleasures of his young lieutenant's flesh and feeling very pleased with himself.

The desk com chimed, and he saw it was from com.

"Sir, the ship has gone into orbit, and it has signaled that it will be leaving there in seconds."

"Is that all?"

"Automatic signal, sir, to notify the beacons before it makes the jump. Nothing else."

"Thank you, Captain."

Now all he had to do was wait.

Davvd and Maggda were sweating. Don had gone out to the ship to set the control, and it had arrived in orbit shortly after.

"Thank you, Don."

"Sir? I simply set the drive to take it home. 'Return to base,' so it may be a deviation of its original orders."

"What else could we do? We can't have that sitting about down here like a garden ornament. The satellites will have registered it anyway, but now that it has gone, maybe we won't get any 'please explain' calls."

Maggda came in with a mug of coffee and put it on the desk.

"Right then, Master of the Universe, what are we going to do with 447?"

"Do you have any ideas, Don?"

"Technically, sir, we have stolen a very valuable robot property of the Valderian armed forces. It carries a penalty of twenty electrolashes and hard labor for a very long time in the mines of New Babylon."

"Oops!"

"Maggda, what do you think, apart from 'oops'?"

"Who knows he is here? Apart from Schiff, who knows? Is Schiff going to issue a warrant to get him back or what? Schiff sends an illegal ship here, right, so he isn't likely to make a lot of noise, is he?"

"Schiff isn't a pussy, Maggda. Did you know he is related to the chancellor of Valderia?"

"Oops!"

"I can think of a worse expression. He pulls a lot of weight. Fleet watches him like a hawk. He keeps a low profile as marshall of number ten barracks, but . . ."

"In reality, he does Davvd Ong impressions?"

"What?"

"Well, like you. He seems to be able to go where his chancellor puts him and plays down his importance."

"I think you overrate my importance. I am just a damn sniffer dog most of the time. Smell something bad and bark, that's me."

"All right, I believe you. Now what do we do with 447?"

"Any robotic suggestion, Don?"

"Joe has him servicing the loader. He is programmed to carry out all kinds of repairs. He can service anything if you show him the manual, and he has all the Valderian ones in his memory.

"Does he cook?"

"Be serious, Styxx."

"Can we give him a name? I can't go around calling it or him 447 all the time."

"You think of one, and Don will tell him, and he'll answer to it, right, Don?"

"Yes sir."

"How about Randolph?"

"I thought you hated that name."

"Well, it grew on me. How about Rex? Short and sweet and masculine.

"Suits me. What do you think, Don?"

"Very masculine, sir, and it suits his character."

"Did you hear that, Davvd? Don is into character assessments."

"You have hidden depths, Don."

"Thank you, sir."

Maggda laughed, picked up the mug and went into the kitchen. She wondered what twenty electrolashes would do to her skin and winced.

Maggda was flicking through the information sheets on robots Don and Joe that she had found in a dusty file. What struck her was that both Don and Joe were really quite old, and obviously, newer models would have more efficient systems, but she really doubted that. Close your eyes, and Joe or Don were as human as one could wish them to be or, she reasoned, had wanted them to be thirty-odd ESYs ago. She smiled at the archaic style of the information sheet.

"ROBOTIC INTELLIGENCE"

"Robotic intelligence, thanks to extensive research by Wu and Ong Foundations, has increased since the first fully operational robots came onto the market.

"The robotic brain is not based wholly on the human model but has been structured to take the best of both electronic and human traits. The human brain uses minute electronic impulses to function, and the robotic brain, built into a matrix of a gel-like fluid, is served by electronic impulses that can generate new circuits, as their programming desires. To make this more flexible, an artificial hippocampus was created by Young and Bartlett (see footnotes) to allow acquisition of increased learning and memory. This was produced by the ability of the gel matrix to assimilate proteins and chemicals within the hippocampus. This led to the creation of artificial synapses that fed on proteins already present in the matrix.

"Ong and Wu laboratories (see footnotes) also discovered that animal brain tissue in the form of selected T cells could be implanted into the sterile matrix, and grown alongside the synthetic one and with the introduction of proteins, could affect the growth patterns in the synthetic organs to give increased memory and 'creative responses.'

"Research using human brain tissues and experiments on human subjects was banned in C3498 (Old Earth Cycle) by the Galactic Court. It was found that in some cases researchers had used non-volunteer subjects and against Convention Article 47 (see footnotes), had removed organs and live brain tissue.

"Limited research using human specimens who volunteer for 'Accelerated Development' is permitted under the Act in limited numbers and under strict controls approved by the Galactic Court and the Wu Foundation.

"Wu Laboratories stepped up research into a full artificial brain and this led to fully self-operating machines. The D series and the J series were created as full general-purpose robots in C3552. Because of the expense in producing these models, a limited number were made. These were seen as ongoing research models and used by research laboratories and specialized business companies. They have been used as advance exploration members in many roles.

"Further research continues, and the development of a highly advanced android has been put into place. It is projected that models of the android series 'Crystal' will be available within five ESYs. It will have many very human characteristics and be virtually unrecognizable as a machine. To comply with artificial intelligence Standard #2329 A.I., these models will have to bear the manufacturer's mark on the soles of their feet or behind the artificial earlobe.

"For further information, go to Inter.gal ARTI.@Ongwu."

She resisted the prompt. It explained a lot about Don and Joe. She went to find Davvd. He was talking to Rex.

"This boy has seen lot of action, Maggda! He has been in more combat zones than I have."

"Aren't they supposed to be noncombatants?"

"Oh yes, but as a mechanic and as an ambulance driver, Field Aid pilot, and a 'pick up that bomb and eat it guy,' he has seen it all."

"How come he is off duty and reporting to Schiff?"

"Came in for service, and the war he was in stopped, so he was put in store. Schiff signed him out."

"How are you feeling, Rex?"

"I'm pleased to serve you ma'am."

"Would you like to get back to barracks, Rex?"

"I have no emotional links with my last location, ma'am."

"That's good because you may have to stay here a little while until we decide your future."

"Thank you Ma'am."

"Davvd, Light in My Darkness, what are we going to do now?"

"Tomorrow morning, Wick in my Candle, we are going to see our tribe, and we are going to let them see we are just like them."

"I had a horrible feeling this was going to happen. How good are you at dodging spears and the odd rock being bounced off your skull?"

"But you don't know, do you? We go prepared!"

"Yeah, we do what those old knights of old did, we wear armor?"

"Better than that, beautiful Miss Styxx!"

"We take stun guns. Now you are talking, Captain Ong!"

"No, we go armed with language!"

"Language?"

"Well, enough to say hello and 'I want to speak to Olann and Ogarth and maybe Annrath."

"Where did you get all this stuff, Ong?"

"What do you think Don has been doing all this time? His little bat up in the cave has been listening to the tribe. It has been analyzing the language, and it isn't too complex. He has been downloading it into the translator. We get plugged into that, and we go and we say, 'Top of the morning, boys and girls,' the translator puts it out in 'caveman,' we bring gifts, and we get to be buddies."

"When was the last time you used one of those things? Ask where the toilet is, and you get sent to an undertaker!"

"C'mon, Maggda, have faith. These things are highly refined research tools, kid. Are you with me or not?"

"Just hold my hand and tell me when to run, okay?"

"I need you there because you are a woman, and they respect their women.

Rex is going to be sitting at the controls of the loader. At the first sign of trouble, he picks us up. We walk across the meadow and up to the caves, and we wave. They will see us coming for a long way. They will see we are not carrying spears or knives or anything they can't handle. How does that sound?"

"Why do I have such faith in you, Ong? You keep doing this stuff, and I believe you, why?"

"Well, there isn't much choice, I guess. Sorry, but let's face it, isn't this more exciting than walking about nearly nude selling undies?"

"Oh shut up, Davvd, and let's get some language under our belts. How do you ask for a stiff scotch and dry?"

The translator wasn't nearly as bad as she had thought. They played games, going back and forth from Old Earth to Galactic to instant Caveman, and it worked quite well until she asked where the toilet was.

"I think it said, 'Out the back behind the big rock,' right?"

He laughed, "Just don't ask too difficult questions. Don has worked hard on this stuff, you know that."

"Thank you, Don. I am not very grateful, am I?"

"I like to please you, Miss Styxx."

"The feeling is mutual, Don."

"Now what are we eating tonight, Joe?"

"I have no idea, miss. I asked Rex to do it."

They both groaned and went looking for a stiff drink.

Jackson had given some thought to his appearance. He wore a decent jacket and a burnt orange waistcoat, and a check shirt with a green cravat. His pants were fawn cord, and his boots were brown and highly polished. He was attempting to become, in appearance anyway, a young Valderian officer, off duty but still bearing the almost military stamp.

He wandered down the mall under the hotel and found a "Gentleman's Tailor."

"Yes sir, and what can I do for the lieutenant this morning?"

"Will I need a hat? I am going up to the mountains for a few days, and I don't know what to expect as far as the weather goes."

The elderly salesman was obviously pleased to offer advice.

"Sir, I can sell you a wonderful hat that will serve you well whatever the weather. Most of the younger officers wear them off parade. A wonderful hat, sir, and it will never wear out."

He produced a brushed, green felt hat with a narrow brim, a dark green band, and a patterned feather as an accent.

"Now try this one, sir, and it will complete your outfit."

Jackson tried it on, and it fitted well.

"No sir, never tip it back. Just pull the brim down a trifle, and it will feel better and look better, and you know why? When the brim comes down a little, one has to look up, and it makes one stand erect, as a young officer should, sir. Head up and eyes front."

"You know your business. Thank you for telling me, I think that is excellent advice."

"No sir. Thank you for coming to me in the first place. Now, will you need a coat?"

Jutta beheld him in the foyer with wide eyes.

"Jackson, is that you? You've joined the army!"

"I've been buying clothes. I have no idea what you've told your parents, but if they thought I was, well, 'army,' they might like me better."

"Are you nervous?"

"I don't know what you've said about me, do I?"

"Well, Mr. Jason West, you will just have to come with me and find out."

"Don't make slips, Jutta, I am Jason from now on. I don't want anyone to know I'm wandering about Valderia as Jackson Wu, please."

"Don't be so nervous! Lieutenant Vogel will take good care of you!"

She took his hand and walked him out to the land car. He threw his bag in the back, and they climbed in. She programmed the drive controls, and the car slid away from the curb and out into the traffic flow.

"Now it knows the way home, we can talk. My mother is expecting a young gentleman, and you certainly fit the part! I hardly recognized you with all these Valderian clothes. You look just like one of my male colleagues from the barracks in his civilian outfit."

"Have I gone too far?"

"You look just perfect. Kiss me and I will feel better, then I will contact my parents to let them know we are on our way."

"Jutta, we have to stop somewhere. I have to buy them a little present of some kind, don't I?"

"See, I told them you were a gentleman. In the next little town before we get onto the highway proper, we can find something."

The car hissed along, and at the next small town, Jutta stopped it, and they walked past the shops.

"Flowers for your mother?"

"Not very original."

"What then?"

"There in the window, there!"

It was a cooking apron, with a large striped cat on the pocket with a mouse in its mouth and a smile on its face.

"Are you sure?"

"My mother just loves to cook, and she always needs aprons. When she puts that on she will think of you, believe me."

"And your father?"

"Ah, that is much easier. Come down here to the knife shop, and I will show you just what he needs. A few days ago he broke a favorite knife that had belonged to his father, and now he is like a man without a right arm. Buy him a new one, and he will think you have been sent from Aton."

They bought and settled back into the car. It left the town and joined the highway where it picked up speed, with the automatic controls keeping them safe from other vehicles and on course. The countryside lost its urban sprawl and became wooded, with mountains as a backdrop. They left the expressway and climbed a pass over the ridge and down onto a flatter plain overlooking the villages in the valley. The car turned down a rougher narrow road and pulled up at the front of a large, whitewashed, black-beamed, and slate-roofed farmhouse. Outbuildings stretched away behind and to the side, and a rough-coated dog emerged, wagging its tail.

She gave him a quick kiss, "My home, Jason, my home. I hope you love it as much as I do."

They stood in the wide doorway. He could see where Jutta had inherited her looks. Her mother was a pretty, plump-faced woman with a smile so much like Jutta's that he immediately thought of what his father had once said. "If you want to know what a woman will look like in twenty-five years, look at her mother." She radiated the same kind of unaffected, open-faced warmth without favor that Jutta did.

Her father was going grey, had a weathered face, and a body tending to thicken. He wore old cord trousers, battered boots, and an ancient leather apron that he was trying to take off, but the knot had beaten him, so it stayed.

They climbed out of the car. The dog came over and stood up against Jutta's skirt, and the father growled at it. It sniffed his legs and wagged its tail and went back beside the master. Then Jutta was being hugged and kissed, and he stood there feeling a bit lost, then her father held out a hand that was hard and gnarled but warm, and he put an arm about his shoulder and said, "Come in, come in. We are pleased to see you safe."

Then her mother took his hand, kissed him on the cheek and said, "Come in, come in." They muddled themselves into the kitchen where there were chairs beside a long table with a white cloth and a small vase of flowers in the middle, cutlery that had bone handles and looked like museum pieces, cream and blue side plates, and a black cruet set that looked like little cats.

Her mother whisked away his coat and hat and Jutta took them out somewhere, and he was alone; they were looking at him, and he felt very shy. He sat and didn't know what to say. He had felt more at ease with damn Schiff.

"I brought you a gift, Mrs. Vogel, and you, sir, and I am not sure if they are suitable or if I did the wrong thing, but Jutta has them and . . ."

She came in with the packages, sat beside him and handed them to her mother and father, then she reached for his hand, and he felt better. She was as soft as a sponge cake and stronger than plas-steel, and he clung to her hand like a drowning man.

Her mother undid the brown paper, found the apron and laughed.

"Did Jutta tell you that I needed another one? She did, didn't she?"

Now, Gerhardt, what did you get?"

"Jutta Vogel, how did he know I was lost without my knife? You told him, didn't you?"

And she said, "Yes Papa, yes Mama, but I knew you would be

pleased. Jason has been worried about meeting you. I think I made him afraid you might bite him."

Then she kissed him on the cheek and squeezed his hand as tight as she could, and they laughed a little.

"Well, boy, we thank you for the kindness. Now have a drink with us and tell us about yourself."

It was the moment he had been dreading.

"Come where we can sit in comfort, come into the parlor."

The room was old-fashioned, the furniture was old fashioned, the décor was old fashioned, but the chair was deep and comfortable, and they sat. Jutta and her mother left and brought drinks on a big wooden tray. Her father said, "Will you take beer with me?"

And he didn't know how to refuse.

"I am at the university at Belvedere, and I have two more years to go, then my father wants me to go and do post-graduate work in the Diplomatic Institute, so I have my future planned for me."

"And what work would you do after that, Jason? It seems like a long time to study, and I don't understand it, so what work will you do, and will it pay well?"

"Papa! It isn't fair to ask him that!"

"Well, I didn't mean to offend, but his father must have some money somewhere to keep the boy all those years. What does your father do, Jason?"

"Papa!"

"Well, my father is a businessman, and he has many interests all over the place, all over the galaxy, I think. He can afford to send me to the best schools and to the Diplomatic Institute because he wants me to be a diplomat and a planetary delegate. That is what he wants me to be."

There was a long silence.

"Jutta, did you know this?"

"Yes, Mama."

"And I thought you were bringing home a simpleton, like your father!"

168

They laughed, drank their beer, and her father clapped Jackson on the back and said, "I don't really know what it all means, young Jason, but I think you may have a better future than any of us, eh, Mother?"

Her mother laughed and gave her daughter a warm kiss. She kissed Jackson on the cheek and said, "May Aton guide you, both."

Jutta grabbed his hand and pulled him out of the room.

"I want to show you the farm before it gets dark as well as your room at the 'Jutta Palace Hotel.' It is a little smaller, Mr. Wu, but the horses underneath do warm it; we have changed the sheets, and it doesn't leak. We think you will be very comfortable there, but there will be no spanking of bare bottoms. Is that understood?"

"Yes, Lieutenant Vogel."

She laughed, and they did the tour. And when he and she climbed the tight wooden stairs to his room, he pushed her onto the bed and held her tight and kissed her for a long time, until her mother came into the yard and shouted for them to come down to dinner.

Maggda was prepared for her tribal visitation. She had dressed in her "Joe the Tailor's" outfit, put on some clean boots and a bush hat decorated with cutout flowers made from the fluorescent flags hung around the loader to warn of blades and surge. She had sewn them on while waiting for Davvd to finish his usual check of the scanners, the satellites, and the signals. She was nervous.

He wandered into the rec room and looked at her.

"Did you put those flowers on that, or did Joe?

"I did, with my own little, needle-pricked fingers, Ong. Now go on, tell me not to wear it, and you can go play meet the cavemen by yourself."

"Hey, whoa, are we a bit defensive this morning or what? If you had waited for me to take a breath, I was going to tell you that it looks very cute."

"Cute?"

"No, exquisite, and better than Maxxi could have dreamed up. How about that?"

"Give me a big wet kiss, Ong, and I'll believe anything. I hope this little excursion works out all right, for all our sakes."

"Trust me."

"I hate that expression, Davvd. Last time I heard that I had some guy trying to get into my pants."

"I never said that."

"With you it might be different. Are we ready?"

"In about five. Rex has the loader out; Don is monitoring; Joe is giving us a final download onto the translators."

"The gifts?"

"Ah well, yes, the point is I can't decide. I can go for mirrors for the women, but the guys . . ."

"What did you have for the guys?"

"Bows and arrows."

"Bows and arrows?"

"It is the next stage of development, Maggda. The bow was a weapon used for centuries for hunting and warfare. The thing about the bow is that it can kill game from a long distance, it is quiet, and it needs no shot or powder or any kind of electronics. It can be made by anyone with pretty limited skills, and it will still work. Kids make them when they play, right?"

"Joe made some up, right?"

"Right, quite sophisticated ones, with arrows. He got the specifications from his files. He demonstrated one for me. I'll show you."

He fetched a sturdy plank. It had an arrow in it that had pierced the timber.

"I tried it, and it takes a fair bit of strength, but Joe thinks any of those guys could use one in no time. Winter is coming, and they will need help to stay on top of it. I mean, some clown gave them knives they can never replicate, but a bow and arrow they can. It needs a lot of real skill to get to be an ace with it, but so does anything."

"And Captain Ong is going to demonstrate this new weapon of mass destruction, right?"

"Sort of."

"How many?"

"Times or bows?"

"Both."

"If we do it right--

"No, if *you* do it right!"

"It will be enough for about three arrows. Then one or more of them will want to try it, and all we have to do is make sure the arrow isn't pointed at us. Joe made up enough bows for all the men."

"I feel bad already."

They had the bows bundled but not strung; the arrows were carried in a hard tube. They went out to the loader, and Rex ran up the motors. They lifted off and over the ridge and the woods and put down on the edge of the meadow, where the caves were in full view. They could see men on the ledge outside the cavern, armed and alert.

"You carry the mirrors, I will cart the bows, and we just walk slowly towards them. Smile, and keep smiling; it is a universal sign of good faith and greeting . . ."

The grass smelled sweet, and there was the scent of autumn in the air. Wood smoke was climbing up from a fire down beside the lake. A couple of birds flew low overhead and screeched, and she jumped.

"Hold my hand, Ong, hold my hand!"

"Can't Maggda. Have my arms full, and these bows are awkward to carry."

"Oh damn!"

"Not far, trust me."

She gave a low wail, and then they were just a few meters from three, large, hairy, and skin-covered hunters.

Ong put down the bundle and held out his hands. The hunters hadn't moved. Davvd switched on the translator and spoke very clearly.

"We bring you gifts. We bring you gifts to help you take more game. My woman brings you gifts for your women."

There was a movement when they heard their own tongues. Joe had actually recorded their dialectal nuances, so it came as a surprise to hear Manta's voice coming from these strangers.

"What tribe are you from?"

"Where do you live? Why do you come on the star man's bird? What do you want with us? We will not go back. We will kill you first."

Maggda was shaking, but she smiled so hard her cheeks ached.

"Our tribe is called Ong. We live beyond the forest, and we saw you come here. We would share with you. Winter is coming, and the cold will be here, and we want you to live. The star men brought us here too, but we are close to them, and we share with them."

Davvd sat down in the grass, crossed his legs and took out the bows. Then he took the cylinder of arrows and shook a couple out. Maggda sat beside him and became aware that the grass was wet and so was her backside.

He handed the arrows to the hunters. They sniffed and felt the sharp points and inspected the bird feather fletching. They shrugged and looked at him. He took the plank of wood with the arrow through it and handed them that. They examined that with greater interest.

"Now, Miss Styxx, may Aton help us."

He stood and bent the bow, bracing it against his foot, and hooked the string onto the notch. Then he took an arrow from the pile and slipped it onto the string. He grunted as he bent the bow and pulled the arrow's feathered end back to his lips, and then released it. He aimed towards the lake, and the arrow hissed away into the air and was almost lost to sight before it fell.

There was an audible intake of breath. He put the bow down and showed them the plank again; then he picked up the bow, slotted another shaft onto the string and this time aimed toward the rock face. Out on the flat ledge was a large skin drying on a frame, and he elevated the point and released it. The arrow hissed away, and it struck the stretched skin low down and penetrated it. This time there was a gasp, and hands were held out. He gave them the bows, and they shouted, and the rest of the tribe came out of the cavern. Maggda gave the women the mirrors and asked for Annrath. She considered this the moment of truth.

The woman was fresh-faced, strong, and pregnant, but she showed very little fear.

"What does the sky woman want with Annrath?"

"I come to see you are well and that the baby grows strong, like your man. I come as a friend, as any woman might when her friend carries a child."

There was silence, and Maggda thought, *I knew I would blow this, I just knew it!*

Then Annrath came and took her arm and dragged her into the cavern.

Davvd was showing the men how to string the bows, and how to hold the arrow and pull the string with two fingers. It took very little to explain that this was a very powerful tool, and they were soon firing arrows across the meadow. He took the plank with the arrow in it and set it up a good bow shot away in the meadow. Before many minutes had passed, they were having target practice. Because they were strong, the bows were like toys, but the speed of the arrow impressed them, and they observed the flight with a hunter's eye. He suddenly thought that he had a lot of explaining to do to when the questions were asked.

They were pleased. They stamped their feet with pleasure and struck his back with an open hand, which he guessed was a sign of friendship even though it threatened to collapse a lung. They examined his clothes and his boots and kept saying *"the star men,"* and they pointed to the loader on the edge of the woods.

"We are like you, and we come from the stars, but the star men follow us and are part of our tribe."

He didn't think that was really convincing, but they just grunted and examined the way in which the bows and the arrows were made, and he knew that they would soon be making their own versions. He looked for Maggda, but she was gone, and he realized she would be with the women.

The woman, Annrath, took her into the cave and led her to what was obviously her space against the wall, not far from the fire. She shooed the little pigs away, and she took Maggda's wonderful hat off her head and placed it on her own, then laughed at her image in the mirror. The other women and children joined in, playing with their mirrors and chattering away. Then Annrath pulled away a skin and showed Maggda a set of three bowls. They were red clay and had been fired to a hard ceramic state. Maggda picked one up. It was heavy, but it was a wonderful cooking pot. It had no glaze, but it was impressive. Maggda pointed to Annrath and the bowl, and she smiled. Annrath went through the pantomime of how she made it, and Maggda laughed and nodded. Then Davvd's voice came from the translator.

"Are you alive and well, Miss Styxx?"

"Yes, Davvd, and I need to talk to you."

"Then say your farewells, kid, before you end up staying the night and eating raw deer meat. Too long and we could lose our novelty value."

"My man calls me, Annrath."

"Then you must go. What are you called, star woman?"

"Maggda."

Annrath repeated it.

"I will welcome you again, Maggda."

She handed Maggda her hat, but Maggda gave it back to her and put it back on her head.

"My gift to my friend, Annrath."

They walked to the entrance and down to the meadow. The men were standing with the bows raised above their heads in a sign of farewell.

Maggda took Annrath's hand and squeezed it, then she clasped Davvd's hand and walked with him to the loader.

She let out a great sigh as they climbed aboard.

"See, Styxx, no spears in the chest and no rocks off the head. Now do you trust me?"

He put his arm around her, and she pressed closer to him.

"Why do I trust you so much, Ong, even if you are such a smart-ass?"

"I couldn't have done it without you. You were wonderful. Welcome to tribe Ong."

She kissed him, and he held her tight. Maybe this was more exciting than parading about half-nude in see-through underwear. She thought that she could be having worse experiences, and then she laughed. Poor Simon. She was living the story of a lifetime, and he would never get to publish it. She went and showered then found Joe and made sure that Rex wasn't to cook again. It was a culinary experience that she wouldn't have wished on a caveman.

Jackson went to sleep with the sound of the horses down below in the long stables, the occasional snort, and the stamp of a hoof. He snuggled down into the bed, which was no worse than any he had to sleep in at college.

Jutta had seen him to the stable door and had kissed him goodnight, but refused to go any further.

"Tomorrow, we will go walking, so get a lot of sleep, Jason West. You will need your energy!"

He fell asleep quickly, which surprised him, but then drinking strong beer with her father may have had something to do with it.

Next morning, the sound of buckets and boots woke him early. Someone was whistling and clanking about, and he guessed it was either her father or a farmhand going about his duties. He looked about and found that what looked like a part of the wooden wall was actually a door to a neat paneled bathroom with a big brass showerhead and taps and a polished steel mirror.

The water was hot, and he shaved and dressed and was pulling on his boots when he heard Jutta calling from the yard.

"Breakfast now, get out of bed!"

He went down the stairs and nodded to a red-faced, sturdy looking lad with a bucket of oats. The boy grinned at him and raised his cap.

The dog came over and asked to be petted. Jutta was waiting at the kitchen door, and he looked at her.

She looked back at him.

"Oh, the boots will do well, but you need a good sweater. We walk today!"

She was wearing a pair of delightful short leather shorts with flowers painted on the pockets, hiking boots and socks, and a sweater that showed her figure.

"You look like you mean it, Vogel!"

"Breakfast. What do you want to eat?"

"Whatever you eat, please. When I am at college I usually oversleep and miss it and have to rush to classes."

"My mother will make you eat. She will try to feed you up."

They went into the kitchen and sat at the long table. There was just the two of them.

"Gerhardt starts early, and his horses need attention, so he eats before the sun gets up, and I eat with him. Now what are you going to eat? You will need something if you are walking to Grunvald and back."

Jutta ate some cereal that looked as if it had been swept off the granary floor, eggs with some thin-sliced ham, toast, and a cup of coffee with fresh cream in it, and he had the same. He felt as if he was bursting, but she laughed at him.

"Today, Jason, we walk, and as Mama knows, it won't take long to walk all that off, will it, Mama?"

She went out and came back with a small pack on her back, another one for him, and a long staff for each of them. She kissed her mother, and they walked down the rough track a little way and found a narrow path that speared off across the meadow.

Down below the town was a collection of toy houses with a blue river winding through and some blue smoke coming from a few chimneys. It didn't look that far, so he was confident. She set a good pace. The track went down, came to the edge of the meadow and went up and over the ridge.

"First we have to go up because there is a gorge, so we go up and then across, and then we zigzag down. It isn't that far."

He was wondering if his breath would hold out. She stopped and clung to his arm and kissed him.

"On the way back, Jackson, there is a barn with hay in it; we will need a rest, and we can make love and no one will know. So keep walking."

It cheered him to think of her naked in his arms; he watched her pert backside in the leather shorts, and it gave him his second breath.

It was a very long way, he realized that now, and when they stopped to take a drink from the bottles in their packs, he asked her how often she had done this walk.

"Horst and I used to walk down to Grunvald twice a week to pick up letters; then of course, we bought the electronic mail machines, and we had no need. I walk, or march, a great deal in the army, you must know that, so my legs are good, and," she laughed, "it keeps my bottom tight!"

"Now, we go on, slowcoach. Left, right, Jackson."

It was not unpleasant. He fell in with her pace and had longer legs; it was sloping gently downhill, and they covered the kilometers in good time. They emerged in the main street of the town from a narrow tunnel of overhanging trees and went into the square.

It was a pretty town and very old. The shops were hardly modern, but he liked that. She told him to sit on a bench by a fountain in the square, and she went off, to return with two small tubs of ice cream with strawberries on top. She sat beside him and they spooned up the cream.

"Horst and I did this after we walked here. Sometimes, if it was very cold, we would have coffee, but it was usually ice cream."

"Where is your brother now?"

"On some cruiser out in the back of nowhere. He is on active service. There is a war of some kind on the outer planets, or planet? Valentine? Or some name like that. I just hope I don't get sent out to fight out there."

"You? Surely not."

"I am on the list, Jackson. I have yet to serve off planet, so I could get called at any time, and I would have to go, you know that."

"What made you join the army?"

"Well, Horst did, and I love horses, so I joined and I am with horses, just like here."

"Aren't your father's horses enough?"

"You haven't seen them, have you?"

"Of course I have, I nearly slept with them last night, didn't I?"

She laughed and gave him a strawberry flavored kiss.

"Papa will show you his horses tomorrow, Jason; now come on, it is a long way back."

The trail was uphill; he looked up at it, and it appeared to go straight up to the mountaintop. She set a good steady pace, and he walked behind, using her as a pacemaker. She had lovely legs, and he knew she was fitter than he was, and he wondered if they would have the strength to make love or even get back to the farm. The wind grew cooler, and he was glad of the sweater. He thought his legs would fall off and his back break, when she said, "Look, there is our barn."

They had changed tracks along the way, but he had been concentrating on putting one leg in front of the other and hadn't noticed.

"Come," she said, "we can rest a little, but we mustn't be too long because I think it may rain."

The barn was a windbreak half-filled with fresh hay off the adjacent meadow. He flung himself down, and she lay beside him.

"I am sorry," he said, "but I am too tired to make love to you now."

"I knew you would be, but kiss me, Jackson, and make my nipples tingle."

They lay locked in each other's arms, and he kissed her and felt her shudder a little. She pulled up her sweater and gave him her breasts, and he kissed her rosebuds, then she said, "No more, or I will just want to have you, and we must get back. Come on and let's march, Private Wu!"

The track wasn't too overpowering after that, and eventually it joined another that led to the back field of the farm, and they were home. The dog barked, they greeted it, and it went into the kitchen to tell her mother.

"He always tells me, don't you, Wulf?" So, how was your walk, Jason?"

"She is stronger than I am, Mrs. Vogel, much stronger. I am not that unfit, but she is a superwoman."

"No, Jason, she was just born here, and walking was what we all had to do. Walk or die, that was all there was to it. Now go and get changed into something comfortable, and I will make you some fresh coffee, and I have baked a few little pastries that will tempt you."

She flapped her new apron at them.

"You see, this has inspired me. See how this cat smiles?"

He went up to his room. His bed had been made, and he felt guilty that he hadn't done so himself, but he had been called away. At his college he had to because his father had insisted that he didn't hire servants; his mother had approved, and he felt it wasn't much of a chore anyway.

He used the bathroom, and it was sparkling. He wondered if the Vogels had a girl to do the cleaning. He thought he might ask Jutta. He would have to be discreet about it because it may cause offense.

They dallied the rest of the day. After the evening meal, which was wonderful with venison and pasties, fresh vegetables, coffee, and a wonderful dessert whose ingredients he couldn't't guess, they moved to the parlor. Jutta and her mother cleared away the debris, and her father offered him beer, but he was so bloated that he refused, politely.

"Of course, I should have offered you wine! We have a cellar full. My father kept a good cellar, but he was an exception. We drink beer because the Valderian is a beer drinker, and I think the government encourages it. It is supposed to be patriotic to drink beer all the time!"

Jason laughed. He was getting to like her father.

"May I ask you about your horses, sir?"

"Tomorrow, Jason, I will show you my horses."

"They are not the ones in the stables under my bed?"

"Oh no. I have my special breeding horses. I will show you in the morning. Jutta hasn't mentioned them, I hope, because she would have spoilt it for you."

"No sir, she just said that you would show me."

"In the morning, I will show you. Do you ride, Jason?"

He suddenly had a vision of Jutta naked, riding him like a cavalry mount, and he shook his head.

"We do have horses on the estate; they are for guests who my father knows would like to ride, but I am not a horseman. As children, we never had the time to really get to like animals much. I and my brother were sent to private schools; we came home on holidays and had--he was about to say 'robotic staff' but checked in time--servants to care for us. I think my mother had a dog once, but we never had real pets."

"What a terrible life you have had, Jason!

Jutta appeared with a tray.

"Jason has had a terrible life, Papa?"

"Terrible! I don't know how he has survived this far, Jutta. He has suffered so much that I fear for his sanity. He needs someone, and I can't think who, to take care of him and to be kind to him and take him for walks. Do you know of anyone?"

"Maybe. But that someone would have to be strict with him, don't you think, Papa?"

"Oh yes, very strict."

Her mother came in wiping her hands on her new apron.

"Someone with an army background I would think, Gerhardt?"

"Now that sounds a perfect solution."

Jutta came over and kissed his cheek, and they all laughed. His family had never been like this one.

Marshall Schiff heard the cruiser come down and slapped on his cap and hurried out to the landing field. The ground crews were crowding about, the fuel trucks were holding back, and it was busy. He went into the Control Office and lounged against the wall. The duty officer saluted but was busy with stuff on screens and ignored him.

"When can I board the ship, Captain?"

"Well, when it gets a bit cooler. It virtually dropped out of the sky. The pilot could be drunk or plain stupid. Can I call you, sir? Sorry to be a bit distant, but I have a shuttle coming in with wounded on board, and I have to get them into Med Care very quickly."

Schiff turned away. Nothing he could do except go back to his office and wait. It hadn't been a good day. He found a bottle of Old Earth scotch and poured himself a large slug. Maria was tidying the desk and putting reports onto the computer/recorders. He moved out of her way and went to the hard chair.

"What news of Jutta, if any?"

"Oh, she has taken Jason out to meet her parents, you know, sir, at Grunvald. They have a farm there. Her father has horses, and as you know, she loves those."

"Not just horses, if I am right?"

"Big horses, sir." They have been genetically improved, I think the expression is."

"What do they do with them?"

"Well, they can do the work of large machines, and they can go over terrain that machines find nearly impossible. Can't tip a horse over as easily as you can a tractor on those slopes, and I think their farm is just about all up hill and down dale. He sells them, of course. I think we have some working for us, doing heavy work. One horse can do the work of several men out in the field. We take them out to the backward planets. Don't require fuel or roads, sir."

"Has she said anything more about her man?"

"He bought her some special underwear!"

"A sign, Maria, of a bit more than mere friendship, wouldn't you think?"

"I really don't like to ask, sir."

"And neither should I. I can tell by that look, Maria that I have been imprudent, and I apologize."

"I am sure she wouldn't mind. She showed me, and I was green with envy!"

The comm pad chimed, and he glanced at it and went out to the field.

The duty officer met him before he ventured onto the pad.

"May I ask, sir, where the ship went?"

"Why, that has to be classified."

"Empty, sir, no pilot, no freight, no nothing." He looked at his pod. "What happened to that 447 we signed out to you, sir? Wasn't that piloting this heap of scrap when it left here?"

Schiff slapped his boot with such force it hurt his leg.

"No robot?"

"No sir. The hold is as clean as the hold on this kind of crate is likely to be."

"How did the thing get back here?"

"We've run the recorders. It went to E5, we think, but there has been an erasure, so we don't know if it actually touched down there or just orbited. Then it was re-programmed, and it did a simple return to base maneuver. Did you send it to E5, sir?"

"Like I just told you, Captain that is classified."

"Right, sir, I never heard you mention E5, but there is one small problem outstanding, and that is the 447 one. What do I tell the Stores commander when he asks for it back?"

"You say I can't remember ever seeing a 447 go out of here."

"Well, I can say that, sir, but I may have to mention that your signature is on record as having received one 447, which brings the ball back into your court, if you don't mind my saying so, sir. The thing is there will be a lot of questions being asked very soon, and I want to know where we stand with this."

"I will personally deal with this matter. I will personally talk to the Stores commander about it. Does that satisfy you, Captain?"

"Of course, sir. I think he is on his way here now. Isn't that his ground car?"

Schiff was quietly fuming, very aware that the duty officer was just waiting to see the great Marshall Schiff go head to head with the Marshall Commander of Stores.

He stood stiffly as the Stores commander left his car and came over. Marshall Ghent was a big man, gray haired if his shaven head could be described as hair, built like a bull and of the old school of the military. He was taller than Schiff and quietly contemptuous of the exalted relationship that Schiff enjoyed with his uncle. He considered that Schiff was just there to tell tales to the chancellor and to push his friends, rather than fulfill any real military duties. He and Schiff were socially apart, never made contact in the senior officer's mess and avoided each other as much as possible. Ghent had come up the hard way, from junior officer to a field commander, and was now semi-retired, as Stores commander. Each considered the other's position faintly inconsequential. Their mutual contempt was well known.

"So, Schiff, what kind of balls-up is this?"

"Don't talk to me that way, Ghent. Remember where we are and who you are addressing."

"I know who you are, but what I don't know is where you've put a 447 robot that you signed out and sent off into the damn wide blue yonder. What authority did you have to play games like that, for Aton's sake?

"The highest one, Ghent. The highest one."

He took the Chancellors plastisheet authority out of his tunic pocket and waved it under Ghent's nose.

"So this gives you authority to steal a 447, does it, Schiff? What you take you bring back, not leave around somewhere out in the damn back blocks of the galaxy. So where did you lose it, eh?"

Schiff was red faced.

"Its location is classified, Ghent, classified! Do you understand that? A bit out of your league, but I think you know what that means."

"I think, Schiff, that you have lost the damn thing or damn well sold it! There was nothing on that original requisition to indicate it was going to be used in a classified operation, or that it was expendable, was there?"

He held out his hand, and the duty officer handed him a flimsy. Ghent glanced at it and handed it back.

"Now listen to me, Schiff. Pin your ears back and listen. I want that 447 back here by the end of the week, and I don't give a damn how classified it is. Get that thing back here, or I will personally roast your chestnuts!"

"Don't threaten me, Ghent."

"Going to run to Uncle, are we, Schiff? Think he will be impressed when you tell him you owe the army seventy thousand credits for losing a 447? End of the week, Schiff, or I light the grill."

Schiff turned on his heel and with his back to Ghent, quick stepped off the pad. He thought he could hear laughter, and his ears reddened.

His ear com rang its little chime, and he stopped.

"Yes Maria," he barked, and immediately regretted his bad temper.

"Sir, I have a message in 'clear' from the chancellor that says, 'Talk to me as soon as possible,' and another from Wu Foundation, which I decoded because it was marked urgent.

"Read it please, Maria."

"'Please explain irregularity with Accelerated Human Intelligence on E7.' Coded from the director."

He was silent for a moment.

"I am on my way back to the office, Maria, thank you."

She took the bottle of scotch, polished it and a glass and stood them on his desk. Then she slipped out to the outer office and hid behind her screens. She didn't want to be the target for any flack that might come her way.

He came in and saw the bottle and the glass, and despite himself, smiled. He poured himself a stiff belt, sat down in his straight-backed chair and rang for her.

She was a little hesitant, but he smiled.

"You look after me very well, Maria."

"I try to please, sir."

"You know, Maria, you and Jutta Vogel make life worthwhile for me, here in this Aton-deserted hole. You know that I have no wife, don't you?"

"Ah, yes sir."

She wondered where this was leading.

"I have very few people I can trust or talk to, and you know why?"

"No sir."

"Because my uncle is the chancellor."

He knocked back a half glass of the single malt and stood and looked out of the window across the bare and dusty parade ground and the ugly barracks.

"Don't be offended, Maria, but you and Jutta give me a little piece of fresh beauty every day. You are young and pretty and fresh, and you cheer me along, and it makes this place a little sweeter. Now I am sorry. I shouldn't burden you like that. Forgive me, I forget myself."

She stood with her hands clasped in front of her and said.

"You can talk to me, sir, if you think I am worth it."

"You don't know how I envy you, Maria. You leave here at the end of the day, and you are free. You can go out and see a lover or have fun in town, and no one will say that you have let down your family. My family is like a sack of bricks on my back. The chancellor haunts me. I see his frown all the time, answer to him all the time. You may think that being related to the head of planet is a noble and honorable thing. Well, it is a very mixed blessing, Maria, a very mixed blessing."

"Can I do anything, sir?"

"Join me at my table in the mess tonight for dinner."

"Sir?"

"Just join me, look pretty and laugh at my jokes. I have a score to settle with that bastard Ghent!"

She wondered what it was going to be like. She had the thought, "Just watch your back, Maria, and smile a lot."

"Thank you, sir. I shall be honored."

"No, Maria, you will honor me. I shall expect you."

"Half cycle six, sir?"

Jutta was shouting down in the yard.

"Get out of bed, you lazy boy, your breakfast is ready!"

Jackson was up and showered and dressed, and his legs felt as though he had walked up the side of a mountain. They ached, but he had made his bed and tidied his room and hung up his towels, and he thought that would show that he wasn't just a rich kid with poor domestic skills.

He went into the welcoming kitchen, and Jutta was already eating her horse feed cereal.

"How do you eat that stuff?" he asked.

She looked up from the bowl with some surprise.

"This is what you should eat at breakfast. It exercises the bowels, Jason."

Her mother laughed. "Do you want to hear that kind of talk at breakfast? That is what the army has done to her, taken away her manners."

"Mama!"

He dared to give her a chaste kiss on her cheek, and her mother smiled.

"Eat your breakfast, and Gerhardt will show you the horses. Now, one egg or two?"

They finished, and Jutta helped her mother clear the table.

Her father clumped in, in his working boots and leather apron.

"Oh, good. You are ready to see my horses, Jason?"

"Yes sir."

The big shaggy dog walked with them down past the barn, and back behind that, was the real stables, as Gerhardt called them. It was a large building with tall double doors. Gerhardt pushed one open and beckoned Jackson inside. There was light from a few small skylights, but it wasn't bright, and suddenly, Jackson was confronted by horses in their stalls, looking at them as they approached down the central aisle.

They were so enormous that he felt cowed. These were animals that rivaled the size of the Old Earth elephants he had seen on holos. Their heads were huge, their nostrils like caverns, and their eyes made him feel nervous. He followed Gerhardt very quietly, a little way behind him. Their hoofs were the size of buckets, and when they stamped and snorted, the floor shuddered. Gerhardt stopped in front of a monstrous dapple gray, fished in his pocket and held out an apple. The great head came down, and the tongue picked the apple from his hand, showing the great yellow teeth.

They went down and out of the back door, and they sat on a bench in the sun. The boy who had greeted Jackson the morning before came whistling by with a large shovel and a broom and smiled.

"Good boy, Johann, keep them clean!"

"Now," said Gerhardt, "ask me the questions."

"Only two," said Jackson. "How and why?"

"These are the genetic remains of the great horses that were used centuries ago to carry fighting men into battle on Old Earth. Huge beasts, capable of carrying a man dressed in great sheets of metal to protect themselves from one another. Of course, never as large as these! Now for the why.

"I bought a big horse, a mare in foal, to work with me on the farm. Some of the fields are steep, the machines were dangerous to use, but a horse, you see, Jackson, can pull a plow nearly as well as a machine, and it costs about the same in feed as a tractor.

So I brought the mare home, and she was cheap, and I wondered why.

"Well, when she foaled, the birth was hard, and the foal was very large. The horse doctor took a blood sample, and he called me and said, 'Your mare is quite normal, but the foal was treated in the uterus. It has had its genes modified, and its offspring will probably inherit the trait. The mare you bought was from the agriculture research farm at Vinnsbruck. They were playing games there, Gerhardt, right up to the last week when it closed down, and they sold the stock.'

"So, Jason, I had this stallion, and when it bred with my normal mares, their foals were all large, and boy, with each generation they got larger still, until these, these are the final part of the breeding program. Someone played games with the genes of these animals, and here they are, bred for size and strength, and they need a special role."

"But what do you intend to do with them?"

"The big grey plow, we had to have a special harness and a plow made for it to pull, and it can tow a loaded wagon up the side of the mountain without any help. It can work in any weather, and he never seems to tire. I love that horse. The others, we work them, and we hire them, and despite their size, Jason, they are wonderfully docile, and they never seem to fret. Jutta told you that we sold a few to the army?"

"No sir."

"These big horses, they can do the work that Old World elephants did in the forests, you know? The army uses them as ambulances out in the field. They put a kind of frame over them to carry four stretchers and a medic. It looks a bit strange, but if you want something to pick up wounded where a truck won't go and where a loader can get shot down, the horses win. I am fond of them, Jason, because they are really, well, lost on their own. Nowadays everyone uses machines or robots, but I am just a lover of living things, and I would hate to see these animals abused or shot because they are too strange to live."

The dog came and put his nose into Gerhard's hand, and he scratched behind its ears.

"What do you say, young Jason?"

"They overwhelm me, sir. They are so huge that I can't think of them as just horses."

"That is the trouble. People hate things to be different. They want something they can feel safe with, something, well, familiar. These wonderful animals terrify them."

"If one stood on your foot, sir?

"Well, you would have to use two wooden planks for a shoe, I think!"

He laughed and stood up, and they wandered back to the house.

"The interesting thing is, Jason, although I wear these steel boots when I go near them, they have never trodden on me. They know their size and strength."

"I wonder why someone would want to create something like them?"

"That, boy, is nothing! Horst tells us that on some planets where the army is 'putting down' rebellions or some such government nonsense, he has seen troops who are like damn robots! They have had something done to their brains, the poor bastards! A lot of them are, well, sort of backwoods tribesmen, and they seemed to Horst to be acting as if they were on strings. He hated it. Someone is out there, boy, creating monsters to kill, not like my horses, to help us all to live."

They came to the door, and Jutta came out and kissed him on the cheek.

"So, what do you think of my father's little pets?"

"Overwhelming"

"But he loves them, don't you, Papa?"

"Have you made the coffee? If not go and get us some. Jason needs it after his little tour, don't you, boy?"

"Yes sir!"

They went inside, and she squeezed his arm and whispered,

"I honestly think he likes you, 'boy'!"

"Don't tell him, but I think I like him too!"

It was something he really felt was right. He wondered what his father was doing.

Marshall Schiff was an unhappy man. He felt as he had once when as a child, he was accused of breaking a window in the school, when it was his enemy, Mark Blumb, who had thrown the rock.

The chancellor was in an irritable mood and obviously suffering from either bad digestion or just his usual constipation. He was short and not very sweet.

"What are you doing down there, for Aton's sake, Kurt? I hear rumors that you sexually assaulted one of your office staff? I trust that is a lie?"

"Sir, I never--"

"Now, I have an official complaint from the damn Wu Foundation. You still haven't sorted out that problem on E7, have you? And now it may have spread to E5? The damn foundation is talking about cutting off research funding. That will please your two tame researchers on E7, won't it? Apart from setting back a ten-year program to zero.

"Next thing, Kurt, they tell me that you have lost an army robot, a 447 model worth 70,000 credits. How in Aton's holy name can you lose a bloody robot! Did you just put it down somewhere, and it wandered off?"

"Sir, I didn't—"

"Now listen to me, boy, I am giving you seven days to sort this whole crap mess out, or you go back on active service."

"Uncle, not the ice moon, spare me Calypso."

"Who said anything about a damn ice moon? I said, active service, guns and bombs, and people killing each other for the glory of Valderia, Kurt, or have you forgotten? That's what you got all those medals for, remember? You may not care that much, but we have a full-scale rebellion going on, on Valentine."

"Valentine?"

"Pay attention. Valentine, a lovely little planet in a solar system the other side of nowhere, next to nothing else, and the reason we are there, just to keep you up to date, Kurt, is because it is strategically vital to us in that part of the system."

"Well, yes sir, of course I have heard about it."

"Think about it long and hard, Kurt, long and hard. The staff tells me they need to replace a few senior officers out there. They keep getting killed off. Now do you think you can let me have some good news for a change? Seven days, or you can pack your bags!"

Wu Foundation was slightly less threatening. It requested an overdue report from Professor Radnath, and it pointed out that there was some discrepancy in the data it had received. It asked for confirmation or otherwise as to whether there were any humanoid experiments being carried out on E5. Satellite surveillance had suggested that there were unauthorized humans there, not registered as credited researchers. Was this true? Please confirm or deny.

How the heck was he to know?

He drank from his scotch supply and whiled the day away. He changed into his dress uniform and bought a small corsage and waited at the mess entrance for Maria. She appeared in a dark blue dress that showed off her white breasts, and he clicked his heels and gave her the flowers, then pinned them to her bodice. Out of uniform, she seemed a different person, almost a stranger. Her perfume hung about her like a cloud. He offered his arm, and they went to dinner. The reaction was more than he had hoped for.

It was the condemned man telling them all to go and get screwed, and he loved it. The gossip was coming and going, and if Maria frowned a bit, he cared less.

"Is that the girl that he put his hand up her skirt?" asked Ghent.

"No, that one was the blonde. Don't know about this one."

"Pretty. He may be a bit offside, but he knows how to pick a pretty woman."

"Is she one of ours?"

"Junior officer," offered someone from Admin.

"Been keeping her undercover?"

"Or under the covers, eh? Haw, haw, haw!"

"Lucky beggar. For a while there I thought he might be a bit of a pussy, if you know what I mean."

"Well, why don't you ask him? I fancy seeing you with a cavalry sword through your ribs."

"Ah, let's leave it, should we? I think the port is coming."

Schiff was a good dancer. They danced to all the old favorites from the Valderian brass band past, and despite her misgivings, she began to enjoy herself out on the dance floor. Good wine and a pleasant meal helped, and Kurt Schiff was genial to the point of warmth. She had never seen him like this and wondered why he wasn't married or had a lover somewhere. He was a good-looking man, very 'army,' but she had met worse.

He escorted her back to their seats and gave her a little bow.

"Maria, thank you."

"Sir?"

"For just being you. Can you see their damn faces? Schiff with a pretty woman and enjoying himself as though he hadn't a care in the world."

"Sir, I don't understand."

"A rock through a schoolroom window, Maria. Don't ask me to explain. In seven day's time, you will probably have a new commanding officer for the barracks. My beloved uncle, the chancellor, thinks I should do more for my country. You have heard of Valentine?"

"Yes sir, sort of, it is, well, isn't there a rebellion against the Valderian occupation, or something, going on there?"

"Sort of, yes. The army is getting the worst of it right now. We only had a token force there anyway, and we totally misjudged the feeling of resentment that our removal of their provincial government caused. So we are going to put in a few thousand more troops, and we are going to crush the rebellion, and Valderia will fly its flag on an ugly rock out in the middle of nowhere, to prove that we are the power that will not be cowed by a rabble!"

"What will happen to me, sir?"

"Nothing, Maria, nothing, if I can help it. You will just have to do your best for the next body to take my chair."

"But, sir, are you sure you are being posted out there?"

"Unless Aton gives me a miracle, probably yes."

"But when did this happen? Why didn't I know about it?"

"I am just one of many, Maria. I heard that eight hundred will be shipped out of here by the end of the week. Several general duty officers and three robot medics. They have all received their orders; mine is just a matter of time. I have had the movement order posted, and the selection has been made for the other ranks, but I am still waiting for the blow to fall."

"I am sorry, sir."

"This is a hell of a place, Maria. Dust, dirt, and a lot of personal backstabbing, but it is heaven to what we are going to find on Valentine. I have seen the holos, and they are not the most exciting of locations, believe me. Apart from which there is a hard winter there now and frozen battlefields. I hate the cold, Maria. I once nearly froze to death on a ball of ice when our shuttle had to ditch on it. I shudder when someone says they love the snow!"

"Sir, I think I had better go to my quarters, if you don't mind?"

"Oh yes! Sorry. I thank you for your company. You made me very happy just by being there, you know that?"

"Thank you, sir."

"Right, go and get some sleep. I still have reports to send out, and I think I may have some scotch left."

She didn't know why, but after a moment's hesitation, she kissed him on the cheek and fled.

They had finished dinner. Jutta had helped clear away, and

they had moved to the parlor. Jackson was drinking a very fine red wine that Gerhardt had brought up earlier and decanted.

"So, are you a connoisseur?"

"No sir, but this is excellent. We do have wine at home, and although I drink very little of it, I do recognize a good vintage when I taste one."

"This is one of the old man's better choices. It comes from across the valley from a little village called Uphaaven. They had good vineyards there, but that was so many years ago most people have forgotten. The old man bought the entire vintage. It was a favor really. I think his friend was in debt, so he bought it all, rather than make him lose face by giving him the credits."

Mrs. Vogel appeared and sat down with Jutta beside her and the dog at her knee.

"I want a word with you, Mr. West!"

"What has he done, Mama?"

"I went to make his bed and to change his towels, but a fairy had come in the night and did it for me!"

Jackson was a bit red-faced.

"Please, Mrs. Vogel, I didn't know *you* had made it before. I have to do that at college, so I just thought . . ."

"Jutta, we have here a civilized young man. He is not only polite, but he thinks of others. You can bring him home here anytime you want."

"Thank you, Mrs. Vogel."

"He isn't a bad sort of boy, is he, Mother?"

"No, Gerhardt, I can think of worse."

Jutta's com pod chimed, and she went out into the kitchen to answer it.

There was a muffled scream and then silence. They heard the connection broken off, and she came into the room, white-faced.

"I have to take Jason back to his hotel. I have orders to be back at barracks by 0800 in the morning. They are shipping out lots of troops to, my guess, Valentine, but it is classified. I am on the list of general duty personnel who have to be ready to move. It seems that High Command has drafted over two thousand of our troops already. I have to get back now, or I will never have time to do everything."

She flew into her mother's arms and sobbed and then, tear-faced, kissed her father.

She went to Jackson, and he held her tight.

"Is there nothing you can do, Jutta? Can't you just talk to Schiff?"

"That was Maria, not personnel. She says that he is on the list too! We will be on the same transport out of here!"

It was a dismal farewell. He kissed her mother and shook her father's hand, and he wished him well.

They slung the bags into the ground car, and she programmed it to make its way back to the hotel. On the way they held each other tight, he kissed her, and she cursed the army.

"You see, Jackson, I talked it up. I never thought I would have to go. There must be big trouble out there, big trouble, to cause this kind of commotion right through the army."

They went to bed subdued and made love. She sobbed a little, asked him to kiss her nipples, then got dressed and told him to stay there. She went out and got back into the car, punched in the destination and went back to the barracks. On the way it rained. It seemed appropriate.

There was heavy rain overnight, and the stream behind the cavern came up and rushed down the gorge. Maggda went to see if her bridge had been washed away, but it was still just above the water level. With the weather turning cooler each day, her little sunbathing excursions to her "beach" had been curtailed.

She was at a loose end. She had amused herself by teaching Rex to cook or rather, had allowed him to scan all the research complex's cookbooks, which simply went into his memory. She was going to spring an exotic meal on Davvd, with Rex as chef, and see the result. She had also been coaching him how to answer when questioned as to where he had been. It was just a matter of time before Davvd sent him back, so she was giving Rex some answers. They were hardly those of a military 447, but it amused her.

Davvd was too busy preparing reports for Wu Foundation and Fleet and being a god-like figure for the tribe to have much time to talk. It came as surprise when he found her in the rec room coaching Rex.

"What news, Master of the Universe?"

"Two things, Lady of the Long Legs."

"Talk to me. I haven't had a word out of you for two days."

"Been very busy, busy, busy. The thing is, I am sending you back to civilization, and . . ."

"What did I do to deserve that, Davvd?"

"Let me finish. I am sending you on a mission, Styxx. I have a heap of stuff that the admiral needs to get, and we can't send it because the code is broken, you know that. Now, we don't know if our thief is behind bars or still on the loose, so you will have to go back and explain the situation here, mouth to ear, otherwise it could go astray."

"And what are you going to do here on your own?"

He laughed.

"I have more to do than I ever realized! Don't forget, I was supposed to be here, alone and incognito."

"That was before things got complicated. You could have cut and run back with the evidence and passed that on to some tame 'expert,' couldn't you?"

"There are things going on here that I still don't understand. You came to me and told me about Annrath's pottery. Now that is a big breakthrough. Clay culture is a pretty big leap forward for these guys. What is even more impressive is that she grasped the concepts so quickly. Won't be long before she sees the need for a closed kiln and mass production."

"She is a very smart lady."

"They are not your 'normal' Neanderthals. I don't like to talk about them like that, but they are, according to Don's research, straight off Harvallo."

"What and where?"

"It is a planet owned by Valderia, or 'administered' might be a better word. Seventh quadrant, out the back end of Regis galaxy. I wouldn't have known, but Don dug deep. He did a DNA comparison check on the blood samples. They were brought, as far as I can guess, to E7 as part of a nebulous long-term experiment in 'accelerated intelligence.' Wu Foundation put up a lot of credits to get it running. They had two salaried staff on E7 to supervise it, Radnath and Singh. They would know more than anyone else what was going on, but they are no longer on the planet. Another damn mystery."

"What next?"

"I shall miss you."

"Wait a minute! What devious scheme have you hatched now, buddy boy? Haven't said I was a willing volunteer, have I?"

He came over and gave her a hug.

"I suppose you think that if you hug and kiss me, Ong, I am going to go along with this forced eviction, right?"

"When I explain it, you might. You leave here. Send you up in the pod that we came down in, still in orbit ready for occasions just like this one. You and Rex board the *Double Happiness* as if you never left it. Probably get your luggage back if they haven't offloaded it."

"So Rex rides with me, to where?"

"You both go to Alpha Six. You get to talk to the admiral at the HQ there and have a neat little holiday. Rex gets sent back to Valderia, Barracks 10, on the next Valderian liner or troop carrier that comes through. After you download all the stuff to the admiral, you can go to Mars and talk to Simon. Of course, Miss Styxx, you will be bound by the Fleet Secrets Act, so be very careful what you tell him, or you could end up . . ."

"New Babylon in the dung pits?"

"Something like that."

She walked about the rec room table and frowned.

"When?"

"Tomorrow morning, our time."

"Tomorrow morning!"

"Reason is the *Double Happiness* comes through and can do a diversion stop then. They pick you and Rex up, and the pod sits in orbit in case I need it. You swan off in the luxury suite, eat in first class, go home to Mars, check the potted plants in your apartment, talk to Simon and get your hair done by someone who gets paid to do that stuff. So what do you say?"

"You promised me you would chase me round the bed when I got home."

"Give me a kiss, Miss Styxx, and I promise that when we get this over and done with here, I shall be there."

"I have to go in the morning?"

"Sorry".

"If that is the case, then we are going to have a good day of it. I want to go and talk to Annrath, and then I have a surprise for you tonight."

"You still have to go in the morning!"

She had Joe make a really special table centerpiece of yellow and red leaves that glowed against the freshly laundered, white canvas cloth. She polished up the old cutlery and tasted a few of Joe's home brew specials before she settled on one. Wine glasses were the usual specimen jars, but she found two quite small ones and polished them up. She went to the kitchen and checked before calling Davvd in from the console.

"This looks very civilized, Styxx. What's on the menu?"

"Ah, you had better ask the chef."

"Joe?"

"Well, no, Rex is on duty tonight!"

"Rex? Are you mad, Styxx? Last time he cooked he used sump oil to fry the meat!"

"Rex, can you come in here please? Master Davvd wants to know what you have cooked."

"Miss Styxx brought home a haunch of venison, sir, from the tribe. I have marinated it for two hours in the stock that Joe supplied me. It has been baked in a slow oven with wild radish roots and fresh herbs. The artichokes are those that Joe grew here. The other vegetables are native. There is a side salad of the kind that Miss Styxx says you are fond of, and I have made a pudding with a lemon sauce that is, according to the recipe, 'piquant and not too sweet.' I have prepared coffee. I have found some dark chocolate squares to go with that, sir, or if you prefer—"

"What have you done, Styxx? When he gets back they'll put him on kitchen duties instead of stacking bombs!"

"I just thought he deserved better. Can you serve that now please, Rex, and if you could carve, that would be wonderful."

The meal was superb. The meat tender and not dry; the vegetables retained their freshness; and the lemon pudding was of the kind that mothers make.

They drank their coffee and sat on the battered lounge, and he put his arm round her.

"I shall miss you, Maggda."

"With luck, Ong, we'll be seeing each other quicker than we think. Get this mess sorted out here and come to Mars and surprise me. I promise to wear nothing but my 'dressing gown.'"

"Hopefully you're right. Now what else have you got to surprise me with?"

"Oh, I almost forgot! Rex, come in here please. I need you."

The robot came in and stood in front of the lounge.

"Yes, miss."

"Now, 447, where have you been?"

"I have been on holiday, sir,"

"Where did you go on holiday, 447?"

"My holiday destination is classified, sir."

"You dumb, stupid, chunk of metal, answer me!"

"Verbal abuse is the resort of a person with a poor intellect, sir."

"I'll have you melted down, you insolent rust bucket."

"Yes sir, but you would have to write off 70,000 credits, sir."

"You have gone too far, Maggda, but wouldn't you love to see the face of the poor officer who tries to get any sense out of him now!"

"I'm leaving in the morning, Ong. Hug me and kiss me and touch me in places my mother said not to let a man touch unless he showed me the engagement ring."

"I shall miss you, you vixen."

"Shut up and kiss me . . . no, not there, but here."

"Vixen."

He kissed her and then pushed her gently, but reluctantly, away.

"You had better get to bed, Maggda. Starships don't wait for late passengers."

"Spoil sport," but she went to her room and packed a bag and crawled into bed. She was excited by the prospect of going home, even though she knew she would worry about 'her tribe' and Davvd and the 'boys'. In a strange way, she was looking forward to seeing Simon and the office again, as well as the red soil of her native land and her parents. She slept, dreaming of holding Joe's hand in a red dust storm. Outside, it rained harder.

In the damp meadow stood the bright yellow pod with the ramp down. Rex was already aboard.

"Did you have to put that yellow ribbon round his neck with the thank you card?"

"Couldn't resist it. Are you going to kiss me goodbye or not?"

He held her tight and kissed her like he meant it.

"Take care, Styxx,"

"Take care, Ong."

The ramp slid closed, and after a few seconds the pod fell slowly upwards, accelerating as it went, out and up into the deep blue of the sky of E5. He turned away, and on the edge of the meadow, some of 'his tribe' was waving. He waved back and then went back to the cavern, and he swore. He felt suddenly very lonely.

The rain came down again. The stream rose, and water flowed over Maggda's bridge, loosening the rocks. It turned with the current and was swept downstream and out of sight.

The pad outside the barracks was a seething mass of men and ground cars, loaders and piles of stores and baggage, stun canon, laser long-range guns, and noise. The duty officer had five Admin robots hovering, monitoring and acting as air traffic controllers. A troop transport took off. Dust blew everywhere, and Major Schiff screwed his eyes up. Demotion was automatic once he left the base. It helped to hide his relationship with the chancellor, but he was sore that that bastard Ghent was relishing his discomfort.

A battered scout ship came down close by. The duty officer checked his ID pod and shouted to a ground staff sergeant. There was head shaking and arm waving.

Schiff had his small pack on his back and was in line with the other officers. He turned and saw Jutta at the end of the line. They moved forward as another transport readied for takeoff. He turned again and saw, to his horror, that the battered scout had unloaded a robot, a damn 447 robot, with a bright yellow ribbon around its neck, and what looked like a card fluttering on a string.

He nearly broke line, but the transport opened its ugly door, and they began to file into the dark interior. To their right, four hundred men with heavy packs were going into the carrier section four at a time. He glanced back. The robot was being escorted off the pad by a junior officer.

It was, he was sure, the missing 447, come home a day late to save his hide.

He and his fellow officers went forward to the enclosed section of the carrier. There were seats for them, albeit cramped, but the other ranks were herded like cattle into just enough space to sit on the floor.

Jutta had a seat across from him, but he nudged the male lieutenant next to him and made him swap his seat for hers. She gave him a wan smile.

"Jutta, we share the same fate, it seems."

"Yes sir."

"Cold comfort for both of us, I think."

"Yes sir."

"How are your family taking this?"

"Not very well. You know that my brother is on a cruiser off Valentine."

"I knew that he was with the army but had no idea he was close to Valentine."

"That is where we are going, isn't it?"

"High Command keeps that under wraps until we leave the planet. They will tell us once we are on our way."

"Do you have your command yet, sir? I thought we might be together again."

"I am like a leaf in the stream, Jutta. I think we will get briefed once we get on the surface of Valentine. I gather the situation there is very fluid. No one knows until we get there."

The red lights came up; they felt the craft fight gravity and rise, gathering speed into the morning skies, up into space where the huge Valderian liner sucked them aboard. They were given simple boarding cards, showing a place to sleep and a place to eat. It was Spartan but cleaner than the carrier. She found her way to the junior officer's quarters, where she met her cabin mate, a pleasant girl with a very tanned face and a red nose.

They shook hands, exchanged names, and Jutta asked Kristen where she had come from.

"Look at me, Jutta! Off the farm! I was seconded to the army farms out at Veerladen. They send the defaulters out there to work, so I spent a lot of time amongst the cabbages, and that wasn't just the ones with roots! But you know, I loved the open air, and of course, the boys who were sent there were hardly criminals, just a few who had stayed behind with a girl, or who had had enough of being pushed around. I just supervised. We had some big sergeants and corporals as guards, who drank a lot of beer and played cards with the so-called prisoners. It was a very healthy kind of life. I spent most of my time on a tractor; that's why I have a shiny nose! Now, how about you?"

They exchanged stories and packed their gear away as best they could, then the bell rang for lunch and they joined the crush, found their table and hoped that the food was edible.

447 was escorted off the pad and told to report to Stores. He was met by a sergeant who laughed at the ribbon and the thank you card.

"So, 447, where have you been?"

It was impossible to find out, so they found him a space and signed him back onto the books.

Marshall Ghent was not amused by the ribbon or the card scrawled in a girlish hand. He wished he had Schiff here to see 447 to add to his discomfort. Maybe Valentine would get rid of the pussy for good.

The shuttle dropped the senior officers off first. The landing area was snow blown, windswept, and freezing. The two of them scrambled onto a land truck, and it churned off through the mud and slush down a rutted road to the base. They passed a few vehicles blown apart and wrecked by the side of the road, and Jutta thought she heard thunder. The driver laughed, "Wish it was, ma'am; guns, big guns, over that ridge."

The truck slid to a stop outside an entrance to what looked like a mine tunneled into the hillside. Great trees had been split and used to shore up the short tunnel into the interior. Inside there was light, and it was marginally warmer than outside in that fierce wind. The duty officer was a hard-faced female major, who handed out the paper work and told both Jutta and Kristen to go behind the desk down the tunnel to stores to get their winter gear. They both emerged wearing great hooded and padded coats, thick gloves, knee-length, fur-lined boots, and they carried a bag of heavy underwear.

"Now, my children, get along the track. There is a field medical station there, and with luck, there will still be a hut standing for you to bunk in. You two have been assigned to Field Med Three.

There is a major there to tell you what duties you will have to carry out. If you don't know much about putting on bandages or sewing up cuts and wounds, then you will have to learn quickly!"

"Are there no trained med staff, ma'am?" asked Kristen.

"Yesterday, my chicken, there were three. This morning two were killed, and the third taken off planet to specialist care in the hospital orbiting up there." She shook her head and looked up.

"So duck a lot and wear your helmets and your field armor. Welcome to Valentine. I know you will get to love it, if you live long enough!"

"Who is there now, ma'am?"

"There are two robots, a major in charge of surgery, four walking wounded who are helping out, and an ambulance called 'Jane.'"

They headed off into the wind.

Kristen said. "I think she has gone a bit gaga. When they call an ambulance Jane, you know they are, well, a bit shell-shocked."

They staggered down the lane with their heavy bags, slipping through the slush, and there was another hole cut into the hillside. Beside that there was a hut, walled all round with sand bags and rocks, and behind that a track led down under a solid roof just above ground. The snow was falling fast, and they could barely find their way into the Med Center. It had heavy doors and no glass.

The major was wearing a white coat that was covered in blood. He took it off and threw it into a bin.

"Good to see you, girls. Major Heinemann, or Max if you like. Jutta and Kristen? Lovely names. What can you do? We've lost all our trained staff. Dead or so badly injured, that poor Bette had to go aloft. Are you med trained? Well, that makes it a bit hard, but the robots can train you. Don't mean to be rude, but you can watch them sew a wound, splint a leg, and stuff like that. They are good, and you'll learn quickly. Start in the morning. First light or when we ring you. Go find your hut and make yourself comfortable. I think they've changed the bedding."

The hut was bleak. It had four bunks and lamps beside the

beds. In a corner were two bags with tags on them and black stamps. They didn't have to read what it said. They knew it said "Deceased." There was a black iron stove but no wood, and Jutta knew they would freeze if they didn't warm the place up.

"Come on. Let's find something to burn, or we'll die in the night."

They hugged their padded coats close to them and went out into the snow and round the back of the hut. There were a few small branches, and they collected those.

"We need something solid, Kristen. Something that will burn for a long time."

They trekked round the back of the Med Center.

"Crates and pallets, look!"

"How are we going to break them up?"

"Get a couple back first. There must be something in the hut. Come on before we freeze!"

They dragged a pallet each back to the hut and struggled to get them through the door. Once inside, they hunted for an ax or a tool of some kind.

"Poker! You stand on it, and I'll lever the planks off."

It took some working out, but they ended up with some planks and some hard bars. They were too long to go in the stove. Frustrated, they sat on the beds, and then there was bang on the door. The major came in with a saw and an ax.

"Sorry, we take these out of here when the place is empty. The poor beggars up in the line will steal anything that will cut a hole or chop ice. Let me help you. There is wood, but we store that too. Come on, and I will give you a barrow load."

They soon had the fire roaring, and the hut warmed up quickly.

"It's a good thing this place is so small," said Kristen, "or we would need wood all night."

"I just want to get some sleep. I have to sleep."

Jutta took off her heavy clothes and put on long-legged

underwear and a thick woolen, long-sleeved shirt and crawled into the nearest bunk, pulling the thick covers over her. She fell asleep. There was thunder, but it died away as the darkness fell. She dreamed of her mother and cried in her sleep. Kristen dreamed of cabbages.

Jutta and Kristen used the bathroom at the rear of the hut. It was bare and cold, but the water grew hot enough after a minute for them to get warm in the communal two to a stall shower. They ended up scrubbing each other's backs, and then they hurriedly dried and got dressed. The snow had piled up during the night, and they began to trudge through it to the mess hut, when Jutta heard a noise, and stopped.

Kristen was impatient.

"Come on, Jutta, or all the food will be cold, the coffee all gone, and we will end with nothing."

"You go on. I thought I heard . . ."

"I can't wait for you. My feet are freezing," as she scuttled up the path.

Jutta heard it again and laughed. It was a horse snorting, and it came from the big shed.

She crunched her way to the big doors, and they were locked. She went through the deepening snow down the side, and there was a green painted door. She turned the handle and went into the gloom.

In a large stall was a giant red horse. Above and to the left of the stall was a platform full of hay bales. She heard a cough, and she shouted, "Is anyone there?"

A head appeared over the edge of the bales, and then another, covered in straw.

"What are you doing there?"

"Corporal Heinz."

"And Private Webber, ma'am."

"What are you doing there, Heinz?"

There was a muffled cough.

"Ma'am, we are her handlers."

"Ambulance orderlies, ma'am."

"Get down here so I can talk to you both."

"Yes ma'am."

They came down a rustic ladder fastened to the wall, both in their straw-covered heavy underwear.

"You are what?"

"Orderlies, ma'am," said Heinz. "We look after Jane. We have our billet up there because we need to be near her, and she likes to have someone close.

We go out with her to pick up the wounded, keep the harness and the stretcher frames right. She, well ma'am, she can't be left alone. She has to have company."

Jutta had wet eyes.

"When I was a little girl this horse was in my father's stables. Red Jane was her name. My father used to pick me up so she would take an apple out my hands. And I would stroke her big nose. My father bred this horse, and I never thought I would ever see her again."

"Gerhardt Vogel. Your father is Gerhardt Vogel, ma'am?"

"Why yes? How did you know?"

"Well, I come from Grunvald, ma'am!"

"Oh, what a story! I have to tell him when I get home. May I touch her?"

She went to the stall, and the huge red mare lowered its great head. She held her hands to its nostrils, and it put its ears forward, and she rubbed its cheeks.

"Do you remember me, Red Jane? You are wonderful."

Then she suddenly felt hungry. "I must eat, boys, but I will be back." She fled up to the mess hut. The coffee was stale and cold, the eggs like rocks, and there were no fresh rolls, but she felt much better for some reason. Home had come to Valentine. Kristen wasn't that impressed, but she didn't care.

Schiff was bundled up in his heavy coat with a fur-lined hood over his battle helmet, heavy gloves, and night glasses so he could detect where the men were in the growing darkness. It was snowing, and he swore, cursed his uncle and Ghent, the army, and his own stupidity. How could he have grown so complacent and so sure of himself that he couldn't see the fall coming? He had been living in a fool's paradise, throwing his weight about and acting like an arrogant junior officer instead of a mature and cautious senior member of the officer corps. He hated his uncle for being the chancellor. If his uncle had been a farmer growing crops on the sunny side of the Vinterland valley, none of this would have happened.

He was moving up the line, through the dugouts, when there was a great roar of sound, and he was blown off his feet and into the snow. The sonic blast missed him by centimeters. He was lucky to have just received the fallout. A muffled and helmeted soldier pulled him down into the cover of a mound of mud and asked him if he was all right.

"Sonic cannon, sir. One of ours that they took when they overran us last month."

He staggered to his feet, his head ringing, and kept low until he found the dugout where a group of officers were looking at screens, poring over maps, clicking data up on pods and mumbling amongst themselves.

There was a general there who reminded Schiff of Ghent. He was from the same mold, pure army, without any vestige of humor.

"Schiff, isn't it? Been waiting for you. Now listen, Major, I have given you one hundred and fifty men. Coming up to the front now and they'll be digging in along here."

He pointed to the map and the screen, and then set up a tri-dee of the terrain.

"The Valentines re-took that ridge yesterday, and we have to get it back because, as you can see, the only all-weather road cuts through there, and we need to move supplies, and they can blast anything that moves along there. You will get them cleared out of there tomorrow morning at first light so we can re-fortify that ridge. Any questions?"

"Cannon, heavy lasers, what do we have?"

"What you can find, Schiff. Your boys have their usual laser rifles, some sonic launchers, and if they can get it up there through the mud, a fast-firing launcher."

"Tanks, do we have any?"

There was muffled laughter.

"Schiff, we had a supply of ten tanks when we came here to put down this little rebellion. Five were destroyed on the first day because they ran into a trap that strips the tracks off. Five backed out and got destroyed by 'tribesmen' firing a kind of small, explosive, heat-seeking shell right down the gun barrels. When those hit the shells in the breech, the turrets blew off."

"What you are telling me, sir, is that we fix bayonets, charge up the hill and wipe them out in hand to hand, like the good old days?

"You get the picture, but before you wet yourself, we will be sending in a huge barrage before you attack. Won't just be you. Farther down the line we have two more groups going in with you. Red on your right, Green on your left, and you are White. Get up there and tell your juniors what's happening and hope your NCOs are up to it too . . . Here, take your orders and these maps and get it sorted. Try not to get killed. We are running out of body bags."

Schiff went to the dugout and briefed his officers and saw a straggling group of weary soldiers coming up the track. There were a few sonic blasts, but they kept low and once in place, began to dig in. He saw a field kitchen being set up, and realized he was hungry, cold, and wet. He set his juniors the task of scavenging for weapons behind the lines. The thought of sharp plas-steel cutting into his guts made him feel faint. He crawled into his dugout and onto his bunk. An orderly pulled back the canvas and offered him a muddy cup of coffee and a coarse bread roll with sliced sausage. He was past caring if it was dog, cat, or horse. He wondered if he would survive the morrow.

The Fleet starship, battle destroyer *Golden Sunrise*, located the planet of Valentine and slipped behind the sun. A Valderian cruiser in orbit about the planet had been firing missiles down to the surface in contravention of the Galactic Code of Conduct. It was accepted that a rebellion, if it was a "rebellion," against the government set up by the administrative power, namely Valderia, could be put down but only by surface action, not by an off-planet source.

Golden Sunrise was put on alert and sent to observe.

She moved into a tighter orbit and was immediately picked up by the screens on the cruiser. She moved closer and was now plainly visible, eyeball to eyeball, by both crews. The commander of the Fleet destroyer was amiable.

Captains of starships formed a unique club. It was as it had once been, when great sailing ships met on a vast ocean, and their skippers hailed one another as friends without ever having met, but these two had been on interstellar courses together.

"Konrad, are you still commanding that old tub?"

"Peter? Is that you, you old bastard?"

"Konrad, what are you doing out here? You used to do business on the seventh quadrant, so what brings you here?"

"The usual, Peter. When the High Command says I have to piss in rainbow colors, then I try my best. What brings you here? Is this Fleet showing muscle, or what?"

"Galactic Federation, Konrad. We are following up a complaint. Gone to the top levels now. Valderia hasn't been a good boy."

"Not my plate of eggs, Peter. I just do as I am told. The politicians screw things up all the time, not us."

"True, Konrad, true, but I have to advise you that if you fire off one more missile onto that Aton-forsaken rock down there, I shall have to destroy you. I am pretty sure you get the picture. I am acting under orders too, old friend, and there is nothing personal, you understand?"

"Do I have options?"

"Only two. One, release another missile, and you and your crew become star dust. Option two, you tell your High Command that in order to save your ship and crew you have had to leave the vicinity of Valentine."

"How long do I have?"

"Would you like to come over for lunch?"

"Sounds pretty civilized."

"Good. Come over and you can tell me about your boy. Is he doing well at university?"

The general swore.

The Valderian cruiser broke orbit, powered up and went back to Valderia. It had problems with the star drive and dare not risk the vessel any further.

Konrad thought that the swordfish fillet may have been grilled a tiny bit more, but that the wine, as usual, couldn't be faulted.

He wished he had more potential enemies like Peter.

Major Schiff went with his troops into the snow-covered battleground that the barrage had pounded and found very little opposition. There were dead soldiers, some covered with mud, but they looked hardly fresh. Schiff saw no corpses that could be classed as today's body count. There were occasional bursts of laser cannon fire from dug-in positions, and he lost a few, but he became aware that there should have been a hail of fire, a withering storm cutting down his tired men, but there was nothing. It was then that he realized, with a sickening, gut-churning consciousness that they were all going into a huge and terrible ambush.

He screamed into his com pod. "Halt the advance! Take cover, dig in now! For Aton's sake, dig in, you bastards, dig in!"

He flung himself down and saw his band do the same. To the right and left across the wasted landscape, Red and Green persisted with the advance, and then the whole world turned upside down. Red and Green were simply blown away and bodies were flung like straws across the hill.

A huge force picked him up off the ground and threw him back like a rag doll. He felt the force pass him and the debris and dust, rocks and corpses crashed about him. Four huge sonic mines had exploded in unison. The blast was devastating.

He thumbed his com pod, and to his intense relief, he could hear most of his officers responding. They had gone to ground just in time. He staggered upright and called them on. Something struck him on his left side, and his armor didn't help. He was totally unconscious when he hit the ground. His face was turned to the bleak sky, and large snowflakes fell and melted slowly on his cooling face.

Red Jane went off on her mission. There were others doing the same.

The general was white-faced and almost incoherent. He had sent his troops into an ambush that even a junior officer would have seen coming, but he had ignored it. He now had no support from space; he had lost that too. His cruiser had slipped away with some bullshit about "star drive malfunction." He was dealt a further blow when an encrypted message arrived. It was from High Command. The Galactic Federation was sending observers to Valentine. He was ordered to hold his position, not advance, and to "sweep up the mess." By Aton's breath, what was going to go wrong next?

The dead and the dying were scattered like leaves across the battlefield. Schiff was just one of many. Some frozen to death; some bleeding to death; some buried in the mud. Field stations took them in, patched them as best they could and sent them on to the base hospital or to the shuttle that took the worst cases up to the fully operational hospital in orbit.

Jutta learnt to do things she had never been trained to do. The robots had their work cut out, but unlike Jutta and Kristen, they had no need to eat, drink or sleep. They cut and stitched and scanned and sealed and repaired. The major was like a cheerful machine. He encouraged the girls, and he managed to inspire them with some creative surgery that the robots were not programmed to do when a soldier came in who was in such a terrible state that death seemed the only option. The deaths increased, and they passed them on, in the body bags, back down the line. They thought of the families, and Jutta thought of hers, and of Jackson. She wondered if he was aching for her as she was for him.

Then suddenly, Major Schiff arrived. They had found him alive because the wound had stopped bleeding in the frozen air.

Red Jane was plugging her way through the mud and the wasteland. They had one stretcher to fill, and they nearly passed the corpse, covered in mud and snow, when Jane snickered her little warbling song. Webber swung down.

"Are you sure about this one, Jane?"

"Brush the snow off its face, Webber; take a reading. She isn't wrong too many times."

Webber scanned the body, and with the snow off the face, he suddenly saw an eyelid flicker, and the scanner recorded a very faint pulse.

"We got a live one, Heinz."

"Right, let's get him up here, and we can get back. Full load, time to go."

They loaded him on to the stretcher frame and plodded back, the rhythm of the great hooves rolling the bodies gently back and forth; pain came and went, and Schiff went back to blackness.

They cut his clothes off him, warmed him with a thermo blanket and assessed the wound through his body. The laser rifle had cut a neat fused hole through him, piercing liver and lung and a rib. They patched and sewed and spliced. They re-grew organs and stopped further damage, but he was destined to go aloft.

Jutta found him in the transit ward behind the med center and held his hand and kissed his cheek and cried a little. "Sir, it's terrible to find you like this! I didn't know you had come here until now."

He could hardly speak. Seeing her made him feel totally weak and helpless but full of hope.

"Jutta, you beautiful and wonderful girl. I didn't know you were a nurse?"

She squeezed his hand.

"Here, Major, I am nurse, surgeon, cutter of firewood, mother, sister, and I hold the hand of the dying, and become all of those."

"What has happened to us, Jutta, and what of young Jackson Wu?"

"I miss him very badly, sir."

"So it was Jackson Wu, wasn't it?"

"We had to call him Jason, sir. My parents think his name is Jason West. I daren't tell them that he is the son of Solomon Wu."

"Probably a wise decision. How did your parents take him?"

She laughed.

"My father calls him 'boy,' and my mother thinks he is charming and a fine young gentleman."

"Which he is, Jutta, which he is. Do you think you will meet his parents soon?"

"I think I will be terrified when I do. This war or whatever it is we are fighting for, Aton knows what, might last forever."

"It is a bad war, Jutta, a very bad little war. I can see that it won't be long before the Galactic Federation gets involved, and we will be getting our backsides kicked out of here."

"I just wish it comes soon, sir."

"So do I, Jutta, so do I."

They moved him out that afternoon, and he underwent surgery on the massive hospital ship that circled above their heads. The prognosis was good. He would be back on Valderia sooner than he thought.

He didn't know, but they had recommended that he get a bar to his Blade of Honor medal for saving his troops from an ambush that had wiped out just about everyone else.

Ghent heard, was incensed but was forced to admit that hated though he was, Schiff may have some worthwhile qualities after all.

Maria felt relieved that he was alive. In her books her new boss wasn't worth anything compared to Marshall Schiff. Maria received a coded message from Valentine. It was sent to her, not her C.O., so she brought it up on her screen and read.

"Schiff was hurt, and we treated him. He is on his way back to you. I am working in a field dressing station with lots of blood and guts. I miss you, but I miss J.W. more. Send him a message to say I am alive, and I miss him. Love, J."

Maria was feeling better. Her new boss shared nothing, so she wasn't going to share much with him, but it wouldn't hurt to tell him that Schiff was coming back. The news left him cold. "I suppose they'll find a hole for him to crawl into," was all he had to offer.

Maria called Jutta's family, knowing that they would be kept in the dark anyway, and told her mother the news. Maria could hear her calling her husband and telling him that Jutta was all right.

Then she sent a message to Jackson and hoped that he would be reassured. She was pleased she wasn't in love and apart from her lover. She thought about Schiff. She wanted to help him somehow. That was strange.

Jackson was at home when the message came from Maria. He had passed sleepless nights and was due back at college soon, and he felt lost. It was all right when he could just reach out an electronic arm and touch her, even though she was space time away, but being cut off from her completely had made him feel empty.

He went to find his mother. She was watching Crystal sew. It was an elaborate embroidery of three flowers intertwined on green silk. Crystal never had to pick up a stitch or correct tension. His mother was fascinated by the process.

"I love this girl, Jackson. She is so clever. When she does anything, it turns out right, every time."

"Because she isn't really human, mother. Humans make

mistakes. Its part of what makes us what we are. Our mistakes and failures are us."

"Did you come in here to give me a lecture?"

"No. Can I talk to you without Crystal listening? She records everything we say and do, you know that."

"I don't believe that, but if you want her to go . . . Crystal, would you go into the other room, please? I have to talk to Jackson."

"Yes, Sylvia." The android smiled a perfect smile and rose like a real young woman from her chair, carefully put down her needlework and left silently.

"Can I tell you something, mother?"

"Are you in trouble, Jackson?"

"No, Mother, I have to tell you something. I don't want father to know, so please don't tell him. I didn't want to speak in front of Crystal because she does record all we say and do. It isn't that she spies on us; it is just the way she is made. She is made, Mother; try to remember that."

"You did come here to give me a lecture. I won't give her up, Jackson!"

He smiled. "You know that you said to me that if I found the right girl, I would know, and that I should hold onto her. Do you remember saying that?"

"Yes, I do. So who is this wonder woman?"

"Do you remember, I told you that a young officer had stolen my recorder? Do you remember I was going to Valderia for an apology?"

"Yes, I remember that, and you came back in a hurry."

"Well, I think that I have fallen in love with this young officer, and--

"By Aton's breath, Jackson, are you trying to tell me that you love another man? Please don't say that. I want grandchildren!"

"No, Mother, the young female officer is a lieutenant in the Valderian army; her name is Jutta, and she is quite beautiful. I have met her family. I think they like me. I think her father likes me, and I like them so much, and they made me feel so much at home that I didn't want to leave, but she has been posted off planet to a war zone . . ."

"Do they know who you are?"

"No, Mother, they think my name is Jason West, like my college name. Jutta knows who I am because she was the one who escorted me when I went to see her commanding officer. That's when we met."

"Don't tell your father just yet. Do you really love this girl? You have to know for sure, Jackson. Are you sure you have had long enough to know?"

"I think about her all the time. I just want to reach out and hold her hand. I love the way she does her stupid hair. I love the way she walks. I love the smell of her, even after we walked up a damn mountainside. I just love to see her just doing ordinary things. She goes right through me, Mother. I want to bring her here to show you, to meet you and Father. I want her, very badly. I don't know if that is love, but it makes me feel terrible when I can't see her or talk to her or feel her beside me. Is that love? I don't really know, but it hurts like hell."

"When you tell me it hurts, then I know that there is something more there than you just having sex with her. Oh, don't look so shocked, I know more than you realize! I was young too, you know. Now, have you told her you love her?"

"No, and she hasn't told me she loves me. It's just that we, well, 'know.' Am I making sense?"

"Where did you say she was?"

"The Valderian army is fighting some battle on a planet called Valentine, and she was posted there. Her friend Maria sent me a message saying she was all right and missing me. I can't do much except hope that anything I send to her, Maria can pass on. The army won't allow personal contacts because of security. Valentine is such a long way away that there is very little contact with anyone or anything out there right now."

"Now listen to me, Jackson. You have your education to finish, and when you have done that and found a position somewhere that your father approves of and have some future, then if you still feel the same way, then marry her. I wouldn't stand in your way, you know that. Just don't tell him yet. If she can wait for you and you can wait for her, then it will last. I am dying to meet her. Show me a tri-dee of her."

Crystal came back and picked up her sewing, and the stitches came together with a precision that was so correct that the piece lost its personality and became just another beautiful piece of machinery, just like its maker.

They told Schiff that he would be leaving them soon.

"Send you home, Major, and you can rest up with your family, eh?"

"Thank you, Major."

"I expect they will be pleased to see you. If you hadn't been found when they did, you would have been another statistic."

"I suppose so. Just the luck of the game. Aton smiled on me."

"Well, take care of yourself. When you do get home, take it easy for a while, and good luck!"

Home. Where was that, Schiff wondered? Was it the rather bleak quarters on Barracks Ten, maybe, or the apartment that he rented downtown, with a twice a week housekeeper who cleaned and collected surface mail for him but barely spoke to him.

He had never had a home like Jutta or Maria. He knew that they had parents who loved them, wanted to protect them, were concerned about their lives and their welfare, their diets, and their clothes. Their families spread love and warmth like blankets.

He thought about his mother, his lovely, talented mother, and his distant father, the doctor. He had a dim recollection of his mother kissing him and giving him a toy, a kind of dog with floppy ears. He couldn't have been very old. His lovely mother and distant father.

His mother was a musician. A brilliant cello player courted by

218

orchestras worldwide, even interplanetary wide. She played at the great concert halls, opera houses and salons, and at the invitations of the super wealthy. She was a soloist they made holos of, a musician who stood out anywhere. She was famous. He remembered her as dark and slim and beautifully dressed, and that was about all.

His father was an army psychiatrist. Very quiet, very good-looking, and unassuming. He worked with the depressed and the traumatized from the battlefields, and he had published papers that were of scientific merit and well received by his peers. He had been seconded to the army psychiatric division and given a salary that was the envy of the university men who could never hope to match it. The reason came later.

His mother was a party animal. She loved to drink and flirt and grew depressed when her current lover left, and she would drink until another came along, but it never seemed to affect her platform poise or her incredible skills. She had met his father after a great party where there were army men and women who had idolized her, flattered her, and then she had gone to bed with someone who left in the early hours, and she couldn't even remember his name.

She was so depressed she rang the only person she could remember from the night before with any clarity, and the psychiatrist talked to her and bought her lunch, and she went to his office and seduced him.

It was a strange affair and talked about, and he and she forgot that one could still make children by healthy sexual intercourse, and Kurt Schiff had come along.

Neither of them wanted a child. She wouldn't have an abortion; she had some strange conviction that this was part of Aton's will; and she carried him through the pregnancy and even used her condition to gain adulation on tour.

When Kurt was barely away from the breast, which was that of a young woman who had been hired to do that for his mother, he was put into a daily crèche at the hospital and looked after by a series of "mothers." His father would come in and pick him up and then hand him back. He was bright, and he learnt quickly. He almost forgot his real mother. His father hired a lady to look after him, a foster mother who was plump and warm and seemed to smell of apples all the time. He attended the local school, and he became aware that there were things that one could do and those that one couldn't. When his enemy at school threw the rock through the window and ran to the teacher and blamed him, he learnt that there were those one could trust and those one should never trust.

His mother went to Old Earth on a concert tour of some kind and never came back. His father didn't seem to notice since she was seldom there anyway. He graduated to the only place his father could think of—Cadet Training School.

He was a bright cadet. The rules were simple and easy to follow. He was academically quite gifted, so that put him into the officer class, and he rose to graduate as a young lieutenant with "promise." His father came to the graduation parade, and that was the last that he saw of him. He went to New Babylon and was murdered by a patient in the psychiatric hospital for mentally ill combatants.

Schiff was a very good strategic planner, and his grasp of what to put where and how made him a very high scorer in battlefield games in the training center. When he was posted to an actual combat zone on the dust and sand and red rock landscape where Valderian oil interests were threatened by a native population with the temerity to consider the oil fields theirs, then his skills came to the fore. He never felt that he was actually killing real people because the screens were so much like the game that he couldn't make the transition from those to reality. When he was driven through the carnage, he felt sick. He had thrown the rock that had broken the window, and there was no one to blame.

He served on an ice planet. He felt terrified the whole time he had to go out and direct fire; he felt that he would die in the ice and be lost and mummified like an ancient animal that the soldiers had dug out of the ice.

When he received medals, he was embarrassed. He was presented to the chancellor, and it was then that he was told that this head of planet was his uncle.

His father had enjoyed "royal" patronage. He felt in some way betrayed.

He was posted to a planet where the army was setting up a headquarters division, and he was part of the planning team. He shared a room with another young officer in the raw, temporary complex, and when that fresh-faced and lean young man had undressed and pulled back the sheets on his bed and had asked him if he wanted to share with him, he discovered that there was more than one kind of love.

He had refused; his companion had not been offended and had turned over and slept. Schiff found another billet and felt more comfortable .He went to his offices and there was an older woman major in charge. She was slim, hard, and good-looking. She bullied him, but he learned a lot. He learnt more when she invited him to her quarters for a drink before dinner. When she opened the door, she was wearing a very short and thin "undressing gown." She had bullied him and taught him how to please her. He was a tame performing animal, and she showed him how to do things that he would never forget. They never had a "love" affair. It was a meeting of two sexually deprived people seeking gratification, and it could never last. She moved on, he finished his work, and forgot her.

He went to Alpha Six and joined an office where the army had set up a secret listening station to monitor coded messages to Fleet. What he discovered much later was that Fleet knew more about his work than he did. When he received a message wishing him "happy birthday" from Fleet, he knew he was in the wrong league.

He came back to Valderia, took up a position as a major in the officer training section of Barracks Ten. His uncle contacted him, and he found himself in charge of the barracks with the rank of marshall. The other officers saw that as sucking up to his uncle, but he wanted to forget his relationship, and he tried hard. It hadn't worked too well. He didn't want the job, but he couldn't refuse.

He rented an apartment in the nicer part of town, hired a housekeeper, and had the occasional liaison with young women who were like him, a bit lost and hoping for affection in any form. He felt lonely a lot of the time.

His uncle had called him in and told him that he was needed to supervise an off-planet project connected to "Accelerated Intelligence." It was a long-term project and just required supervision. He would have two researchers doing the work; all he had to do was check results and see if they had made progress. He had a virtual blank check, which made him wary, but it sounded like a break from the routine stuff that he had to deal with every day, and he accepted it. He did read a background study paper that made him even more wary. It considered implanting electrodes into the brain so that the subject could be controlled like a robotic drone, but it wasn't conclusive, and he put it aside. Wu Foundation had funded the original scheme and was still handing out cash, but they were asking for more and more ongoing information when he was called off to Valentine. Now he was going back, and it didn't make him the happiest of men. To make things worse, Jutta Vogel was going to be absent from his office space, if he had an office space to go back to! He slept as the starship went into drive and fled Valentine for Valderia.

On the battlefield, snow and the rain had turned the hillsides and gullies into a morass. Some sniping took place, but the heavy sonic attack cannons were silent. The rebels had dug in and were consolidating their positions. It was a war being fought in an ancient style, with foot soldiers slogging through mud with equally primitive weapons, confronting one another in close quarters combat. Vehicles bogged down, and the spy drones were shot down with ancient, smooth-bore guns that blew the sophisticated airborne craft apart with a hail of shot, stones, and jagged metal. Men came into med stations shot with crossbow bolts, which were just as effective as laser rifles. The general was fuming, but he held back from bringing up mass launchers, which would have torn apart the enemy positions, simply because he had no idea where the rebels had gone. His satellite showed nothing but mud. Its heat seeking sensors revealed blurs that were possible troop concentrations, but were meaningless. Snow obscured the landscape as the wind picked up, and drifts of white covered the carnage with a virginal blanket. The fighting shifted from his sector to farther afield, and he tried to make sense of the reports, and then it swung back again. He was awaiting reinforcements to replace the men who had been killed in the ambush. They were all late. High Command was holding its breath.

Schiff had saved most of his small force and then had been shot out of action himself. All he needed was some damn "observers" from Galactic Federation to complete his misery.

There was a break from the casualties, and Jutta and Kristen could spend time with Red Jane and her boys, as Kristen called them. Heinz was a cheerful boy, and he acted as a foil for Webber, who was a bit dour. They did nothing but deal with death and destruction as their duty demanded, but they could sideline that when they were off duty. Their billet was up the ladder and under the roof of the great horse's stall. They had a simple bedroom and behind that, another room with a wash basin and steel tub and an iron stove set on bricks. They were worried to death that it might burn the whole place down around their ears, so they only lit it at night.

"Who is in charge of this setup?" asked Kristen.

"The major down at the admin office, but she leaves us to do what we have to do, ma'am. We just get down there to get supplies and what we need for Jane, and she leaves us alone."

"I suppose she thinks you do a good job, or she would be kicking your backsides," said Kristen.

"The thing is, ma'am," said Webber, "getting anyone to do our job isn't that easy. See, Heinz here, he knows about big horses, and I grew up on a farm, so I am used to animals. Red Jane trusts us, and if these big horses don't trust you, you won't do anything with them. They could trample a tank to death if they got it into their heads, couldn't they, ma'am?"

"I think you could be right, Webber," said Jutta. My father loves them. They are his pets, really. He will be so proud that one of his 'girls' is out here doing a wonderful job, and of you too, for looking after her so well."

The snow provided a blanket for the rebels to come very close to the defenses. Dressed in white with soft felt boots and carrying the explosives on their backs under the white sheets, they penetrated the outer perimeter. The sentries registered something on the heat seeking screens, but the images were blurred by snow and ice, and the sentries were cold and reluctant to get out into the blizzard to check. Six of the rebels penetrated the perimeter and planted sonic mines under the snow. Any disturbance was covered quickly by the cold, white blanket. The rebels crept back to their deep dugouts, drank their harsh spirits and waited.

Field Station Three was sending the last of their critically injured up to the hospital. There were a few casualties coming in, but there was a period of being able to cope. Jutta had been given instructions by the robotic surgeons and knew how to do things she never thought possible. She was considering that maybe a career in the medical corps might be a future option, but she wondered if she could stand the blood and pain for any length of time. Kristen just wanted to get back to her cabbages and her minor criminals. The robots never felt sympathy, but they knew how to restore the life pulse, even though it was in a purely mechanical way.

The general pulled back the cold and the weary and replaced them with fresh troops off the transports. They took no new positions, just held the line, and the army filtered back to their billets, and snow continued to fall. As they fell back, the laser cannons cut some down; laser rifles picked off the unwary; and Jutta, Kristen, and the med team were again occupied.

Heinz and Webber went out across the plain and avoided the trails where snipers lay in wait. They crossed the muddy ground and picked up casualties and brought them back. Then Webber was shot through the thigh, and Heinz brought him back. Webber swore, and they patched him up and told him he would probably be able to run a marathon again. He told them it would be his first if he did.

Jutta went to the stiff major and asked if she could replace Webber until a replacement could be found. The major looked at her as if she were mentally ill and asked her if she was.

"I grew up with those horses, ma'am. My father bred them and still does. I grew up with Red Jane, and she knows me."

"Vogel, Gerhardt Vogel? Jutta Vogel, now let me tell you something. People get killed very quickly out there as you well know. I know you aren't a trained medic; neither is the Kristen girl, but you do a good job; your major tells me so. Why should I give you permission to go out there and get killed when we will have a replacement in a day or so?"

"It is freezing weather, and the wounded will die of frostbite and just from the cold. A day lying out there will increase the casualty rate by over fifty percent. Heinz and I could save four or five every trip. I am used to the animals and don't need training, and Red Jane trusts me, ma'am."

"You are a pain, Vogel. One trip and that is it. One trip so you can experience what it is like to wet yourself when the shooting starts. One trip and no more, is that clear? Don't put that horse or yourself or that brave bastard Heinz in trouble, or I will certainly see you court-martialed."

"Thank you, ma'am."

"Get out of here, Vogel, before I change my mind."

Heinz looked at her with some surprise.

"Are you sure you want to do this, ma'am?"

"Do you think I can do it, Corporal?"

"Well, ma'am, you know Red Jane, and you are pretty fit, and you don't, forgive me for saying so, seem like someone who would want to run when the shooting starts."

"Is that a compliment, Heinz?"

"Sorry, ma'am."

"You know what the major thinks of you, Heinz?"

"No ma'am."

"She thinks you are a brave bastard, and if I cause you trouble, then she will court-martial me!"

"Well, ma'am, I have been called a bastard before now, but brave is pretty good coming from her!"

They laughed together, the com chimed, and they went out into the snow. Jutta stepped up into the foot strap, and the great horse went up a steep hillock and then another and plowed on until they reached the killing fields.

Every now and then a shot would pass close by. A hiss in the air, an explosion, dirt thrown up and over them. Red Jane with her acoustic helmet took it all in stride. Jutta kept wanting to duck from something she couldn't see, and they picked up four wounded in varying states of injury, and they started back. She felt a blow on her armor that numbed her leg but wasn't injured. Then they came over the hill and down the side and crossed the track, taking a direct line to the med. center. Willing hands unloaded, and they turned back and made another trip. Jutta hoped the major wasn't looking. Another four came down from the battlefield. The rebels were not directing a great deal of fire in their sector, and they came home unscathed.

Heinz slid off Jane's back and helped her down.

"Are you all right, ma'am?"

"Got hit by something and my leg is numb, but I am fine, thank you, Heinz."

"May I say something, ma'am?"

"Anything you like, Heinz."

"You may not be as quick as Webber, ma'am, but you are

better looking, and I think you did a great job. I don't care what she says up there, but I would go out there with you anytime."

"That is a compliment coming from you, you brave bastard!"

They laughed together, saw to the great horse's needs and went to see Webber. He was pleased to see them. They didn't tell him she had taken his job.

Jutta received a cryptic message from Maria.

"J.W. asks Aton to look after you. He misses you terribly, and he has told his mother."

Jutta wondered how that was going to be received.

Schiff went to his quarters in the barracks and tried to think of it as home. It was stark, and his loneliness increased by the minute. Two junior officers came to see him, but it was from courtesy rather than kindness, and his orderly was given a briefing as to how to care for him. He was weak as a kitten, and moved with care. He had been ordered not to drink anything alcoholic and knew that his doctors were right, but he craved a shot of the single malt as a sailor craves sex after a long voyage.

He pressed the com button and called Maria. She had some trouble finding an excuse to leave the office but came over to see him and was shocked to see him so pale and weak. Just the sight of her made him feel better. He was on the ugly lounge, wrapped in a rug, and she held his hand for a moment.

"Tell me about it, sir. I want to know."

So he told her, and it helped more than she realized.

Heinz and Jutta were finished for the day. They had helped seven wounded off the field, and it was then that Heinz noticed that Red Jane had a loose shoe. They had taken off her stretcher harness and were walking her up to the Heavy-Duty Vehicle Pool to get the robot to fix it. They had shoes and a working forge there, so it was just a ramble across country with Jutta sitting behind Heinz. They talked about this stupid war and when it might end, what they both would do when they got back home.

Sergeant Schroeder, or B.M., as the men called him, was happy. Supply had just delivered him a brand new, huge earthmover painted a mixture of gray and vomit green, and he was going to do what his gang had tried to do a week ago, and that was to clear a small landslide that had blocked what was euphemistically described as a "highway" to the main base. They had checked out a vehicle to do it last week, but it had run into a hidden track skinner under the dirt, then a sonic mine flipped it off the road and into the drainage ditch. The driver, encased in the vehicle's armor plating and his body armor, had been deafened, bruised and disorientated but lived. The vehicle had been declared a write-off.

Schroeder loved the big mechanical machines. Brought up on Valderia in a trucking company business, he was at home with anything that weighed as much as a small suspension bridge and had an engine to match. His new machine was a delight. It had a hydrogen powered, twenty-cylinder engine, and was turbocharged for those difficult jobs where one needed to shove a house out of the way. "Big Mouth" Schroeder was on his way to fix last week's setback. He had two boys riding with him whom he had nicknamed, "Mop" and "Bucket." They were from the islands in the Sea of Valderia, and they spoke a different language, were block like, heavily tattooed in the strangest places and were assigned to his workforce this week because they had objected to the security force telling them to stop throwing beer bottles at noncommissioned officers and urinating in the flowerbeds. They had weeks to serve their sentences, which was a kind of poetic one since they had been given the latrine cleaning and digging jobs. Schroeder couldn't pronounce their names, so Mop and Bucket sufficed. They were a cheerful broad-grinned pair, incredibly strong, with a girlish sense of humor. Sober, they were great marksmen, and he had watched them with a laser rifle picking the pips out of cards at fifty paces. They rode behind the armored cab with rifles at the ready as the dozer rumbled down the track towards the first disaster area.

Heinz and Jutta watched the huge machine go by, and then he walked Jane to the side of the road opposite the entry to the machine shop. Jutta's leg was giving her intense pain, so she sat up on the horse while Heinz went in to pick up the shoe. The horse was at peace; she was grazing on a patch of grass that had come through the disturbed snow and was docile and at ease.

When Schroeder ran the blade of the dozer over the sonic mine hidden under the snow and mud, Mop and Bucket had dropped off a short way back, as his thumb had indicated, and escaped the first force. The heavy machine was stood on end. Schroeder was thrust up and then sideways; his blast helmet was squashed down onto his head. The dozer, still under power but with only one track, screwed sideways off the road and fell on the other wreck. Schroeder was deaf, shaken, and had no idea who he was or where he was. Mop and Bucket were thrown a few yards along the road and rolled into the snow banks. Schroeder fell out of the cab, twisted his ankle in the wreckage and crawled away, and as he did so, flames flickered from the engine. He hobbled away and threw himself into the deeper snow as the flames roared skywards. There was a dull thud as the hydrogen went up. Bucket was trying to stand and fell over his rifle, which discharged and drilled a neat molten hole in the generator of the large wind-driven turbine at the rear of the workshop. That caught on fire and then exploded.

Heinz was deaf, shaken, and confused, and Jutta and the horse had gone he knew not where. He slumped back onto a large tire and openly wept. Mop and Bucket were openly laughing.

Red Jane exploded into violent action as the sonic blast swept over her and leaped fifteen meters up and over the bank, with Jutta hanging onto the strap around the great body of the animal. The horse was in panic. Its ears assaulted by a noise that was driving it mad, it could do no more than run to escape it, and it ran, with

Jutta trying to stop it, but Jane could neither hear nor feel. She leapt through a small wood, crashing through the trees like a bowling ball through the pins in a bowling alley. Across a great wide meadow with wrecked artillery and smashed bunkers, then through a small lake where waterfowl attempted to fly, but many were caught on the surface and crushed. Over a wall of rough stone in a single stride, through a shed that shattered into splintered planks, and across a road in front of a slow-moving truck that veered off into the ditch. Jutta hung on. She had ridden her father's horses, so she knew the gait, but this was horrendous. Over a plain covered with rocks that somehow she avoided, over another wall, and then suddenly, there were a hundred or so animals attempting to flee and milling all round her great hooves. She was covered in foam, her head was singing, but she was run out and exhausted. She stood still, trembling all over, and hung her huge head. Then Jutta, her face covered in blood from a nose that had connected with Red Jane's neck and also trembling with exhaustion, became aware that there were people around her, people in white robes and hoods, and they were all carrying guns. She could sit no longer and slid off the horse, and, landing on her injured leg, fell awkwardly into the dung and remembered no more.

Maggda luxuriated in the huge bed in her suite on the *Double Happiness*. She ate the best, and while he was still there in her room, talked to Rex. Then he was dropped off with her on Alpha Six and sent on. She would have loved to see what happened when he arrived on Valderia.

She located her luggage, still secure, and went to the most expensive hotel she could locate in the capital and having found a suite to her liking, went to a hairdresser and a manicurist, had an allover wax job, bought the most expensive make up she could find and sent the bills to Simon. She settled into her room and contacted him on Mars and told him when she finished her business here, she would be home. She gave no further explanation, and hoped he would be excited to see her.

230

"Some hopes!"

The admiral was looking at the latest inquiry report from Security's probe into the leaking of information from Signals, orbiting above him. It wasn't that the spy leaked what could be considered top secret but that there was a leak there at all, and it all led to Captain Horatio Wu. Galactic Media was the end of the line. There seemed to be a pattern to the leaks because anything that referenced Captain Davvd Ong was sent out to that office. The motive was obscure, but the fact that Wu and Ong were related hinted at a rivalry that needed to be squashed. He thought that a change of scenery would give Captain Wu a warning without any adverse publicity, and he looked for a suitable situation that would cut him off from any further temptation. To do that would require not just his decision. It would merit a full meeting of his security staff. He had a long discussion with Simon Brent at Galactic and sent a couple of heavies to see him who flashed their IDs so quickly that he never could remember their names. They only had to be seen in his office to cause so much speculation, which he ducked a lot and answered no questions. His staff was divided as to the Fleet Security call. Some hoped he would be disappeared, and others hoped he wouldn't because they had credits to collect. Simon thought of Maggda and knew she was somewhere out there winding handles. Get her back here, and she might tell him the truth.

Maggda took her holo cubes and all the coded stuff that Davvd had prepared and made an appointment to see the admiral. It took time. Although her face and her bottom were common currency across the holo channels, she still had to go through the scans and iris checks and the background information that Security knew anyway but would subject her to again. Everything Security loved to load onto any unsuspecting visitor. Finally, she was admitted to the annex. After the annex, she was shown into an elevator, and from there she was ushered into an outer office that was totally devoid of human life. A large robot registered her presence by a flickering LED, then the inner doors opened, and as she passed through those, she was scanned again, until finally, she was in the "old man's" inner sanctum. A very pretty female officer there welcomed her, and then she met the man. Admiral Upshott was tall, immaculate in his Fleet uniform, and pleasant faced, graying at the temples, with the light tan that was very fashionable right then. He could well have done holo commercials as a lawyer or a doctor on a soap. His was the kind of face that starships used to attract passengers on "fly with me" posters or recruit young bodies to Fleet service.

The pretty young captain was a little in awe. Maddga Styxx, *the* Maggda Styxx was here in person and looking better than she did on Tri Dee screens. Her clothes, if she knew anything about anything, had come from Maxxi's most expensive, and Ms. Styxx wore them as if they were overalls, with a careless offhandedness that suggested they were merely "clothes." She half expected her to disclaim, "What, these old things?"

Admiral Upshott looked her over and saw her under lights, with just a wisp of spider silk between her and total nakedness, and sighed.

Maggda had seen that look before and smiled. She could pretty well do as she liked with this man from now on. That boosted her confidence.

"Now, Ms. Styxx, tell me the story. Captain Sonna will get us a drink.

So Maggda told him, and she gave the cubes to Sonna and asked what Davvd had to do now to get back home.

It became clear that Ms. Styxx was not just breasts and a bottom with a body that sold underwear. Ms. Styxx was shrewd, asked questions and actually wanted answers. The admiral became wary. This woman worked for Galactic and was good at her job, and she would want more than a two-cent press release to hold her off.

"Of course, Maggda. Do you mind if I call you that? I can't go on being formal with someone I seem to know quite well after all those commercials you appeared in. Do you mind?"

"No, I don't mind."

"What I can tell you, and you can tell no one else, is that Galactic Federation has taken an interest in what is happening on E5 and E7 and will probably be getting even nosier if they find that what Captain Ong is playing with now turns out to be bigger than just 'experiments.' They don't tell us much more than that, but we have been monitoring not just the so-called 'experimental data,' but what appears to be happening on Valentine, for the Feds."

"I don't want to see the 'Ong tribe' destroyed by bureaucratic bungling.

"The Ong tribe?"

"Well, that's what Davvd and I call them. We wanted to have them listed as 'Displaced Persons,' which would automatically give them some rights outside of the experimental framework. Federation has to protect the weak from the bullies, or doesn't it?"

"They seem to have won you over anyway!"

"Well, it isn't quite like that. Those people were ripped out of their home environment, and something set up, we think, on E7. Then something went very wrong, and we mean very wrong. They told us about a sickness that came and killed a lot of them, and then the 'Star People' came, and brought the healthy ones off to E5."

"How much real contact have you had with these people?"

"Too short and too long. Look at the records that Davvd has made, and the holos, and see for yourself. They aren't just a backward tribe of so called 'Neanderthals'; these are real living human beings that someone has been tampering with, and we think, for all the wrong reasons."

He looked a bit grim.

"The research project was an accredited program. It went through the scrutiny processes. They approved the research team. They suggested Singh and Radnath, who had had a lot of experience with animals and apes, and the retarded."

"With the objective of screwing up their brains?"

"If you read the objectives laid out in the original research submission, no."

"You know what Davvd and I think? We think that this original submission was a ploy to raise millions of credits for what would be real and beneficial research, but that someone or some organization hijacked it. Once they had the loot, they changed things to suit themselves."

"You don't sound like someone who walked the catwalk, Maggda, more like a staffer on a crusade."

"Yes, well, Davvd Ong does that to people. Hang around with him long enough and you get virtuous. Problem is we interfered a bit with these people too. On E5 it is winter, and we had to give them an edge to survive, but don't take my word, look at records and judge from those.

"Did you know that Radnath and Singh have disappeared off E7?"

"Sorry, Admiral, but you will have to read the reports. Talk to Davvd, he has his finger on the pulse down there, if there is one."

"What were conditions like there?"

"Idyllic in one way and rough in another. I really loved the sheer natural beauty of it. The center has everything, and the two old robots that originally were part of Davvd's family, well, were like 'family.' It got to the stage where I thought they were. Then, of course, we had some excitement when we got attacked by a plesiosaur going to Bare Head Island Research and nearly got eaten, and Davvd saved my life. We got stuck on a rock in a huge storm with not even what we stood up in and had to find old stuff in the lockers, and the best thing I could find was an old lab coat for a dressing gown until our bags washed up, and we could more or less get dressed again . . . so, all in all, it was pretty routine, really. You will just have to look at the stuff that Davvd gave me to bring here. I can't be as precise as you would want, I know that. Sorry."

He laughed. "Sonna will look after you for a minute or two. I have to go and chase up a few things. Have another drink, make yourself at home, and I'll be back."

Sonna looked at her and smiled. "I'm just wondering how many women would find themselves naked with Davvd Ong and not get carried away."

"Well, Captain, it wasn't quite like that, even though I may have made light of it. He was cut all over his body from the seashells on the rocks and dripping blood everywhere. All I was wearing when it happened was my underwear, don't you dare ask why, and I got hacked about pretty good too. The robotic team out there on the Bare Head Island Research base patched us up, and I can tell you, if you want a really exciting new experience, get dragged through an oyster bed and find yourself lying naked on a slab while a tin man called Randolph works you over."

"Sorry, Maggda, I really didn't mean it like that."

"How were you to know? Next question is did we or didn't we, right?"

"The thought did occur to me."

"I can tell you, first up, that Davvd Ong is still mourning his wife. He won't admit it, but he is. I saw holos of her, and she was so beautiful that I winced. He is a very loving man, Captain, and if you must know, we hugged a lot and kissed a lot and laughed a lot, and he gave me the key to my bedroom and let me sleep.

"Now, something else I have to tell you, I tried hard to seduce him, I really did, and I know he wanted me, but he is just too strong. I think he invented 'virtue,' but we made a promise. When all this crap is over and out of the way, he is going to call on me, and I promised that all I would be wearing was that grubby old lab coat, and he was going to make me very happy. He promised me. So, Captain, he had better keep his word!"

And they laughed.

"I learnt a lot from Davvd Ong. He is utterly reliable and strong, and he hates injustice. If you want to get marooned on a place the other side of nowhere, and you need someone just to be there for you, pick Davvd Ong."

"Shall I add you to his fan club?"

"List me as number one. He gets a bit reckless at times, but he has it all worked out, and it works. His tribe took to him like he was a blood brother. Those guys are suspicious and wouldn't think twice about putting a spear through you if they thought you had pulled some double deal on them, but they trust him and, hopefully, me. There is a pregnant woman there I worry about, and winter is going to come any day, and she is smart! Boy is she smart. I need to know if she is all right. I feel like a den mother. Spend some time back in the Stone Age, and I get all maternal!"

Sonna laughed. "I envy you, you know that?"

"Well, don't. I really sold myself to Second Skin for more credits than I ever had in my life and wonder now if it was worth it. It isn't easy seeing your butt and your breasts in tri-dee on the screens, believe me. Now I work for Galactic; I have some kind of purpose. The media can be a real help just by telling the truth, or it can screw things up by lies. I made a promise to myself to just be straight all the time, and I think my boss understands that. So far he hasn't fired me!"

The admiral came back in.

"All the records and data that Davvd Ong gave you are being assessed, and my team is pretty sharp, so we will know a lot more than we did."

"Can I get a message out to Davvd?"

"Sonna will handle that for you. Now I have to get back. Thanks for everything you have done. Just remember that if you speak out of turn . . ."

"Ten years in the dung pits on New Babylon, Admiral?"

"I think we understand each other, Maggda."

"To Don, E5. Contact confirmed this end and 447 sent home. Heart condition needs your professional help via physical contact. Emotionally stretched. M."

It went across the starways, and Davvd smiled and then

thought of her physical presence and how much he missed her being there. They would just have to wait.

Kurt Schiff was depressed and lonely. He had been given a better reception at the mess than he normally received. The wounded warrior with a bar to his medal helped in a society that respected that, but it wasn't warmth, and he needed that. His orderly was an older soldier and had been selected to "keep an eye" on him. He would report to the major at the med center if Schiff did silly things like get drunk and ruin his recovery. Sometimes being related to the chancellor had benefits. Schiff walked. He did the two circuits of the parade ground every day, as directed by his doctor, and ate sparingly. He tried to watch holos and couldn't. He tried to get to see Maria, just because she was a little warmth and a mine of gossip, but her new C.O. kept her away from him. He knew no one he could confide in or even cry on, and he felt more like doing that now than he had as a child. He busied himself with his task of the research project that had fallen apart on E7 and now on E5, and the more he looked at what Singh and Radnath had been heading towards, it simply didn't make sense. Radnath had a brilliant record. He had "brought to life" the most severely retarded patients by directing nano-robotic probes into the brains of those whose synapses were like a traffic accident on a busy interchange and by drugs and cell manipulation had cleared them.

Schiff was no scientist. He was a man who could take a puzzle and locate the component parts, and he knew where credits could be spent wisely or thrown away, and he found the records had parts missing.

High Command had had a finger in the pie because Radnath had coded that into a few reports. They had sent him some "volunteers," whom Radnath had been grateful for on record but had held private doubts about. After checking DNA, Singh had made notes about the "origins" of these volunteers and expressed doubts. Radnath had sent a query to High Command about a "change in the direction" of the original research brief they had "requested,", but there was no record of what that meant or a reply. Schiff became more and more frustrated. He was stuck on the bare barracks and not able to confront the two people who might throw some light on what had happened, or what was expected to happen. He went to his weekly consultation with his doctor at the medical center feeling irritable. His orderly marked the bottle of scotch with an invisible line that could be checked by ultraviolet, just to make sure the major didn't weaken.

At the med center, they ran the scans over him and checked his wound, and the major smiled at him and told him to get dressed. She asked him how he felt, so he told her. He had to talk to someone. She listened, and behind his everyday list of frustrations, she was thinking of his dossier. What she really wanted to do was to give him a deep psyche probe and get to the bottom of his miseries and iron those out, but she knew that he would refuse, get angry, and that would reverse anything she could recommend. She came back to earth when he asked when he could travel.

"Well, Major, that depends on where and when."

"I have to go to a research planet to do some catch-up work for my uncle."

"Some sort of hush-hush work, I take it?"

"That kind of thing, yes."

"Out of the question for another month. I want that liver of yours to get right. Doesn't matter about the rib, that will heal itself anyway, and the lung is going nicely. Are you walking? Good, but getting off planet wouldn't be advisable now. Too much in transit stress. Just keep walking, get some fresh air, eat simple meals and don't, whatever you do, Kurt, think about the Scotch!"

He swore. She hesitated.

"May I suggest a change of pace? This isn't something I normally put on the therapeutic list, but it might work for you. Shift your gears a bit. Now, take this card, and if you think you can, make a call and make an appointment. No obligation, I can assure you." She handed him a buff card, and he read it.

"COMPASSION AND COMFORT"

"Stress therapy consultants."

"BY APPOINTMENT ONLY"

The number was on the reverse.

He looked at the major, with some degree of anger and surprise.

"You think I need this, do you?"

She smiled at him. "When you respond like that, Kurt, ask yourself, not me. Now, you don't have to do anything. Keep that card and when you get so hemmed in, make an appointment. I worry that you are getting to feel like a trapped animal. Can't do what you want to do. Have to carry out orders that physically you can't carry out, haven't got a shoulder to cry on, can't have a soothing drink. I would feel the need to go and break something, and when you do, make a call before you do."

"What kind of organization is this?"

"Private and expensive, and they know what they are doing."

"Can't you tell me anymore?"

"There is a number you can ring, isn't there? Get it straight from them."

He walked back to his quarters and then did another two circuits of the parade ground. Maria saw him through the window and felt like shouting to him to come in and talk to her, but she had so much work to do that was out of the question, and her new boss wasn't a man one could talk to.

Schiff waited two days and then contacted "Compassion and Comfort."

A polite and cultured voice took his name and asked him who had referred him, and he was given an address. The office was in the expensive end of the city and was light and airy with flowers on the desk and a pleasant landscape tri-dee on the wall. He sat, and the receptionist whose name badge said "Trudi" consulted her screen and said:

"I think you might like to see Suzanne. She can see you at the end of the week, before midday. Would that be all right? Do you have a private address in town? That makes things easier. She will contact you about details. Now, we do have to have payment before any consultation; did the major explain that? No? Well, I am sure she did mention fees. That will be six hundred credits . . . do you have your cube? Thank you. You can claim part of this fee, you understand."

"Is there anything I should know before this consultation?"

"No, Major, I am not the consultant. Suzanne will explain everything you need to know. Thank you for using our services."

He left, and she sent the scan of his personality probe and his tri-dee image to Suzanne. She privately thought that Suzanne was an excellent choice.

He met her under the clock in the little square off the gallery district. It was pleasant with lots of baskets of flowers hanging from shop fronts and a delightful and ancient little fountain in the center. He wore his red flower in his buttonhole as requested, and she had hers. It was like playing spies, and he felt slightly silly. She was about his age and very trim. She wore a very businesslike, expensive black suit with a red blouse and black stockings and higher-heeled, sensible shoes. Her hair was beautifully cut and styled, and she was pretty in a mature way. He liked the look of her immediately. She wasn't some silly young girl with a new psyche degree, which he assumed she had. She smiled and held out her gloved hand and looked at him at arm's length.

"Kurt. Come and have coffee. If I don't get my fix before lunch I fade away. Come down here."

She led him down an alley to a shop that was old, with lots of varnished wood, and took him to a table by the window. A waitress appeared, a human one, with a little white cap on her blonde head, and smiled.

"Gretchen, would you bring us my usual coffee and another for my friend, Kurt, and some of those little pastries, you know what I have. Thank you, Gretchen."

He looked at her, and she observed him, and they drank their coffee.

She said, "I feel a bit awed. Here I am having coffee with a man who has just been awarded a bar to his last bravery medal."

He shook his head. "Do you mind if I ask you something? Do you know my doctor?"

"Your major? Yes, I know her. She and I were students together."

"You did medicine together?"

"She went on to surgery and joined a team of volunteer surgeons and then joined the army. My career diverged."

"You went into psychology?"

"There are two kinds of hurt. One is when, like you, you get shot and physically injured, which is bad enough, but the other one is when the world seems to be out to get you. No amount of surgery is going to help that."

He sat and said nothing, just looked at her calm and pretty face. She pushed her chair back.

"Now, you and I are going shopping. My mother's birthday is tomorrow, and I want you to help me choose."

She took his hand and drew him out of the shop and into the alley.

"My mother has a painting by an artist called Gunter Sachs. She loves it, and I know that he has a small exhibition at the gallery down here. So you and I, Kurt, are going to choose a painting together."

"I am not the greatest authority on art, Suzanne."

"Neither is my mother, Kurt, but we should be able to find one she likes. There is one criterion, and that is it mustn't be too big!"

Her hand was warm, and her grip was firm, and he was led like a child and never even noticed it.

Sachs was a traditionalist. Suzanne looked at them all and then whispered to him, "This one?" It was a lovely little work of a bridge, with children playing in a square behind it and in the far distance, some white-capped peaks. She squeezed his arm.

"She will love it. She has one of what could well be a view of the other end of that street. Do you like it?"

"Yes, I do."

"Good, now I will pay for it, and we will attempt to get a table at the Blue Boar."

He laughed a little, and she raised her eyebrows. "How did I know you would want to have lunch there?"

"Because you recognize that both you and I have impeccable taste!"

She held his hand, and they secured a table at the Blue Boar and ate. He, very sparingly and with regard to his wounds, and she with appetite. They lingered, and finally she said, "Where is your apartment. I want to freshen up."

They took a red and black ground car, and he hoped his cleaning lady had done her job. Once there, she looked over his bachelor apartment and smiled.

"Bathroom?"

He showed her the way and then sat in the big leather chair that was his one real comfort.

She emerged, looking fresh.

"Bedroom?"

"Through there."

"Come with me." She stood by the bed and removed her clothes. She hung them neatly over the end of the bed. Her underwear was expensive and plain but pretty. Her breasts were full, and he looked at her, just exploring her with his eyes, and she said.

"Get your clothes off, Kurt, and get into bed with me, or we will get cold." He did as he was told.

She rolled over onto her stomach and said, "My back, just rub my back gently for me. I have an old injury that needs a light massage, and you can do that for me, can't you?" Her flesh was warm and firm and he gently massaged her.

"Up a bit, just a bit more, oh, that is wonderful. You have a light touch, Kurt, thank you."

She rolled over, and they pulled the covers over themselves. She was warm, and he could feel her generous breasts against his chest.

"Rub my back".

He rubbed her back and her neat backside, and she bit his ear very gently.

"Just hold me for a little while. Can you do that?"

It was pleasant just to have her warm body next to his, to feel her hand on his back, to smell her hair and to suddenly feel relaxed. It had been a long time since he had experienced it.

"You need some warmth and affection, Kurt. Your hurts are hard to heal when they are in the head. This scar down here, that is nothing. Why don't you talk to me? I know who your uncle is. That is a big load to carry. Talk to me and rub my back a little."

He held her and talked to her and told her how frustrated he was. She listened and prompted and recorded it all on the tiny instrument in the gold pendant around her neck. She turned over and asked him to hold her breasts. He had his face in her hair and his hands on her firm and generous breasts, and he said, "Why do I trust you so much? I have known you for half a day, and you can drain me dry. I never tell anyone how I feel."

"Because you feel threatened. You can talk to me because I am neutral. I am not part of your army rules and standing orders, and I will always listen to you." He laughed a little and kissed her neck.

"Are you my afternoon wife, Suzanne?"

"Yes, Kurt, I am your afternoon wife. Talk to me."

"Give me advice."

"You need a woman, Kurt. Not some reckless bitch who is a neurotic with the idea that sex is all there is to life. You need someone to give you support. You need a woman to tell you that although things are looking tough, she will be there to reach out to you, and be a little mother to you sometimes. Kiss you and keep you warm and encourage you when you feel defeated, and romance you when you both need it. That's all the advice I have right now. Now, put your hand down . . ." They made love slowly and with regard to his physical hurts. It wasn't that screaming passion that he had felt at times with others, but this was warmth and gentleness, and she and he found pleasure in the slow sensuousness of it. They lay side by side, and he rubbed her back without being asked. It seemed the natural thing to do. Then she kissed him quickly on the mouth and went into the bathroom. When she emerged she had made up her face and fixed her hair.

He watched her dress. Even the neat and methodical way she put on her clothes and finally her shoes gave him pleasure. She then came over to the bed and reached for his hand.

"I have to visit my mother, and I have to go. Be kind to yourself, Kurt."

She went out, and he heard her heels on the marble and the door close, and she was gone. He couldn't lie there without her. He showered and dressed and went back to the barracks and his quarters and almost reached for the scotch bottle but drank water instead. He felt very relaxed. Nothing seemed to be big enough to worry about. His cleaning lady came and saw the soiled bed and grimaced. She changed the sheets and sniffed Suzanne's perfume and shook her head. At least this one must be well off. That perfume wasn't sold to the poor and needy.

There was pain. It was dark, and there were arms about her and a naked body close to her, and she thought it was Jackson; she reached for him and became aware that there were young breasts against hers; she stiffened, and a voice said in Galactic, "You will not be harmed. I am here to hold you and keep you warm and to care for you. You fell from the animal, and your leg is injured, and your clothes were covered in dung. We washed you and have tended to your wound; we have put you in a warm bed; and I am told to hold you. You will not be harmed."

Jutta stiffened her lip and tried hard not to weep. "Where am I?"

"We call this place Yellow Ford. This is where the river is shallow enough to take our animals across to the pastures. We have not been able to do that for a few days because your army has been bombarding us."

"Please, don't blame me for the army."

"We don't blame you or the animal or your servants. We know that you go out to save lives, not kill people. You have saved the lives of our men too. Why should we hurt you?"

Then Jutta cried.

Her naked companion held her close. "The pain is bad, we know that, but to lose your friends is worse."

"The horse, the big animal, what happened to her?"

"She is safe. We took her across the river. She has even had her shoe repaired! She will miss you?"

"I shall miss her more."

"The men tell me that the fighting is going to stop. Your soldiers are not advancing; they have stopped. They say that there will be a real end to the firing. They say that the Galactic Federation is sending delegates. We have heard that on the newscasts."

"How long will that be, I wonder."

The girl slipped out of the bed and lit a small lamp that threw a yellow light around the room. She was naked, slim, and young with small pointed breasts and short hair. She found a sloppy robe and threw it on and hugged herself. "It is cold down here. We are underground. Everything is covered with snow. We cannot light a fire here because your army can see the heat, and then it bombs us, but I will find you a robe and skin to cover you."

She went into the darkness and Jutta turned her injury to the light and moaned. Her thigh was yellow and blue-black and swollen. It was so painful she could barely touch it. She did not dare to stand on it, but she had to. Where was the toilet? The girl came back with a robe and soft sheepskin and led her hobbling to what served as a bathroom. Then she returned to the bed and tried to get warm, and eventually, she slept. She had no idea if it was night or day.

When the message came through, Maria was white-faced but stayed calm. She wanted to scream in grief, frustration, and anger but held her emotions in check. Jutta had been listed as "missing in action, believed killed."

She knew that the Vogels would get that too, and she wondered if the parents would stay sane. She rang Schiff's quarters and told him. He was very quiet.

"Thank you, Maria. She was very brave, you know that?"

"Yes sir."

"It is a hellhole out there. It is cold, Maria, so cold that it is like death itself. I believe that Aton has forsaken the place."

"Just as long as he hasn't forsaken our Jutta, sir."

She switched off the com and went to the bathroom and wept a little.

When Jackson saw the message, he went cold. A chill went up his spine, and he shuddered. He knew it wasn't true. How could she be gone? Then he knew just how Davvd Ong must have felt when he lost Su Lin, and he went to his mother and told her. She hugged and kissed him, and he openly wept.

"What can I do, mother? What can I do?"

"You will do what I and Davvd Ong did when we lost Su Lin. You will grieve, and you will be empty, and you will mourn, and then you will learn to grieve inside, and you will go on living. Your Jutta will still be with you, deep inside. Your Jutta may be alive somewhere.

"Missing" means missing, not found dead. So just ask Aton to smile on her, wherever she is, and wait. That is all you can do."

He sent a message to Maria. "Tell Jutta's parents that all our hearts are broken and sign it Jason."

What else could he do?

Schiff roused himself and using his influence to the full, asked to know what had happened to Lieutenant Vogel. How had she been killed and/or missing? Where and when? When they told him, he understood and felt a little better. The great horse had bolted; she was riding it and had not been seen since. He told Maria, and she told the Vogels and then Jackson. Had Aton smiled on her after all?

Schiff went to the med center and saw his major. She smiled at him. She had already had a report from Suzanne.

"Did you know Suzanne when you were in med school?"

"Did she tell you that, Kurt?"

"Why didn't she go on and finish her degree?"

"Well, perhaps she did, Kurt, but she didn't tell you that, did she? What is more important is that she was good for you?"

"Too good. I can't stop thinking about her."

"Was she good for you?"

"Putty in her hands, Major. I talked to her, and she listened, and I was a child at a mother's knee. She could tell me anything, and I would believe her. Was she trained to do that, or is that just being Suzanne?"

"Why don't you ask her?"

"I am afraid to."

"What are you afraid of?"

"I spent one day with her. One day. It was as if Aton had made that day for me. If I try to repeat that, will it turn out to be better? I doubt it. She gave me a wonderful day, and I don't want to spoil that".

"Are you going to tell her that, Kurt?"

"I don't think she and I will ever meet like that again, so probably not. I just have to thank you for letting me have that one day with her."

"All part of the service, Kurt, and you know that I didn't send her to you, don't you? She chose to do that, not me."

"I won't forget your kindness, you know that."

"How's the wound? Too much exercise can be as damaging as none, you know that."

He managed to smile and went back to his dull quarters.

Horatio Wu received a summons to meet with the admiral. He immediately thought of what he might have not done to cover his tracks, but the admiral was all smiles.

"Sit down, Horatio, please sit down. I have wanted to speak to you about the family. Are they all well?"

"Yes sir. I think everything is fine. My mother mourns for my sister still, but mothers do that. Jackson is doing well at Belvedere, I think. He hasn't talked to me lately but we are a long way apart." He wondered what this was leading to.

"How would you feel, Horatio, to be offered another job?"

"Another job, sir?"

"I have a tricky decision to make. I have been approached by the Galactic Federation to nominate a delegate to help oversee the cease-fire between the Valentinians and the Valderians on Valentine. We had a short list, and you were on it. I did say that your position here is a vital one, but there was talk that, without putting too fine a point on it, your family connections would be a powerful influence on the discussions. I think the family name might bring home to both parties that the federation means business. We can't have these wars going on all over the galaxy because someone wants to throw their weight about and flout the conventions. Do you see what I mean? The other thing is that you would serve two purposes. You are Fleet, which gives us both a Fleet representative as well as being identified with Wu Foundation. A kind of double-edged sword."

"Well, sir, are you sure I am suitable? It would mean a big upheaval, and . . ."

"Yes, it would. You aren't married, are you? The other thing is you speak the language, so won't need a silly box around your neck at the talks. Always an advantage, that."

"When do I have to make a decision, sir?"

"In about thirty seconds. I have to get this off any minute. They have to draw up lists, fix the protocols, divert starships. Yes or no?"

"Well, yes sir. Thank you, sir!"

"Always looks good on the record, Horatio. Not everyone in the service gets a chance this big so early in their career. I know your father will be pleased. Give him my regards, will you? Get off and pack your bags. Probably tomorrow afternoon? The shuttle will pick you up, and you will go on the . . . ?"

Red Crane, sir. An Ong starship," said Sonna.

"I have to thank you, Horatio, for doing this for us at such short notice, but I am sure you will serve us well. Sonna will see you out. Good luck and goodbye, Captain."

Horatio Wu knew that he had been hustled, but what can one do if the guy who has you by the seat of your pants and your collar has just heaved you down a flight of stairs and is the one who pays your wages? He left, signed off and made his way to his quarters. His bag was easy to pack. All he ever wore were his uniforms. He looked up Valentine and discovered that where he was going was under snow. He didn't think he would be building on his tan out there. Horatio looked at his Pod and tried to digest the briefing notes. It was too complicated for him to grasp at once, and he was too ruffled by his sudden departure on the Ong liner, *Red Crane*, to get settled. He knew that if he blew this assignment his father would personally send very big men in dark suits to educate him, and he didn't dare that. He was aware that his meddling with the admiral's coded messages had got him thrown out of his job, and he was thankful to have "Wu" tacked onto his name. That saved him from a spell in the dung pits and total disgrace, at least. He went back to his notes and sighed.

"Valderia assumed control over Valentine with the death of the Valentine Planetary Delegate and the political turmoils associated with his replacement. The Valentinians failed to elect a representative within the allotted time scale, and Valderia was given the authority to restore political stability. The Galactic Federation set guidelines that allowed for free elections to be held once the situation became calm. The population of the planet, which is basically tribal herders and farmers with some organized agriculture, is spread thinly, and there are few modern industries. Mining takes place in the mountains. Much of the industrial base is owned by outside interests and pays royalties to the Valentinian authorities, both at a planetary and local level. There has been resentment against the off-planet ownership of the mining industry and the export of wealth. Valentine is classified as a grade C planet, with aid coming from Wu and Ong Foundations to improve educational and medical facilities. The University of Valentine is totally funded by Wu and Ong foundations. The Valentinian military is made up of tribal groups under a supreme commander from the largest tribe. This in itself has caused some tension. Open elections for this position failed to elect a leader whom all the tribes could trust. There is a military training college, but this is not large and is devoted to tactical training and not raising an elite officer class. Service in the armed forces is made up entirely of volunteers. Before the Galactic Federation brought Valentine under its wing and set up planetary delegate status, intertribal warfare was common. Further notes, lists of leading figures in all aspects of government, military, and industry, are contained in Appendix A . . ."

He ordered a stiff drink and sat in the most comfortable chair he could find in the lounge and watched the women go by. To hell with Valentine!

Jutta was in pain but sleepy. She didn't dare ask about her leg. Her doctors had left her to tend to other wounded and dying, and she had Romana to look after her and to talk to her. Romana washed her face and sponged her body, combed her hair and then brought a mirror. Jutta almost screamed when she saw her face. Her nose was swollen. Her eyes were blackened. Her jaw was bruised, and she had a cut upper lip. She looked like a prizefighter who had lost his bout.

"It will all heal, Jutta. It will all heal!"

Jutta tried a smile.

"What do I look like? If my mother saw me like this she would weep."

"And your lover, what would he say?"

"He would . . . Did I say I had a lover? Did I tell you when I was doped up and out of my head?"

"I thought that someone as pretty as you would have a man somewhere. I am sorry if I upset you."

"No, Romana. I have a wonderful lover, but I wonder if we will ever be together again."

"Of course you will! When this is healed up and you are well, you can go back to him."

"Maybe, Romana, maybe." She wondered what Jackson was doing right now.

Jutta awoke and was hungry. There was warmth in the dugout or cave or whatever it was that was underground. She could smell wood smoke and food cooking, and she wanted to get to the bathroom. Her leg was too painful to bear weight, and she called out for help. The girl from the night before came in and helped her, but when she saw Jutta's leg, she helped her back into bed and told her not to move. She was hungry and shouted again, and another older woman came and brought her a bowl of boiled grains and goat milk. She would have eaten grass, but she was grateful. Then the girl came back with two men who stood by her bed and ordered the girl to pull back the covers. The younger of the two pulled up her robe and told her not to be silly. "I am not here to harm you, girl, but to help you." he said in Galactic. He felt along her swollen leg, and she cried out when he squeezed it a little. Then the older, bearded man with gray hair did the same, and they went to the side of the room and whispered together. The girl knelt by the bed and whispered to Jutta.

"The young one is Jonas. The old one is Ibrahim, my father.

Jonas wants to cut your leg off, but Ibrahim is telling him to let him save it. Both are doctors, Jutta."

Jutta began to sob. She was aware that her wound was not healing, but she didn't think it could be this bad.

Ibrahim came to the bedside and felt her hot and swollen limb again, and then he said in Galactic, "There is a lot of infection. The bruising would normally have gone down by now, but there is damage to the blood vessels that will lead to gangrene. Here we have nothing to treat that except herbs. Our major hospital was destroyed by your bombs and sonic cannon. We have very few supplies here. Now we have to resort to old remedies, ancient ones. Old, but sometimes good, sometimes bad. It is all we can do, trust to Aton and hope. Jonas says that if we leave the leg, it will become so infected that it will not be possible to amputate it, because the infection will spread to the lymph glands, and you will die anyway. You are strong and healthy, and that is good. Will you trust me to treat you? I will give you a strong sedative so you will sleep and feel little pain; I will let loose the little beasts on your leg, and they will hopefully cure it. The little beasts are not pleasant, but they have been used here for centuries and maybe will save you. I trust Aton to guide me. Will you let me try? Or lose your leg now?"

She was feeling so ill that she just nodded. She was exhausted and cold and had given up any hope. "The beasts," she muttered, "give me the beasts." Jonas gave her an injection, and she slipped away into darkness.

"First, Jonas, we use the little beasts, and when they have done their work, we pack ice all round the leg. Then we see if the work needs doing again and then ice again. It would be better if we could get her to her own doctors, but . . .

"The snow is so deep it will swallow you. She just has to stay here. I will fetch the beasts."

The little beasts, the size of a tropical cockroach, were kept in a cage with a fine mesh. Ibrahim picked them out, one by one, and placed them on Jutta's thigh after making tiny pinpricks to draw a little blood. The little beasts crawled to the blood spots, extended a proboscis and began to extract the dead cells, the blood, and the poison. Strong men had fainted at the sight of them doing their vampire-like work, and the needle-like pain was intense if one was conscious. The two doctors sat and waited as the little beasts became full, and then they picked them off and put them into a jar. Ibrahim went to fetch more.

"Do we have enough?"

"It is enough. After they work, we use the ice, and I have one ampule of antibiotics. I have been saving it."

"She is the enemy."

"She is like my daughter. How can you hate her when she worked to save lives?"

"There, that beast is full. Take it off and put another on."

"They like their work, Jonas."

"Then they get thrown to the chickens, Ibrahim. It is a sacrifice few of us would make!"

Jutta stirred, and the men watched her closely. Her leg was changing color. The little beasts' extended guts filled with bad blood, and Jonas removed each one and placed another in its place.

"That is the last of them, my uncle."

"When she is ready, we will use the ice. Get Romana to fill a bag. We will see how well that does."

Jutta came back to the world after flying with the great cranes of the marshlands of Valderia. She could see her parents' farm down below, and they waved to her and called out, "Come home now, Jutta, come home. Don't fly away from us now!" She wanted to swoop down and hug and kiss them, but try as she may, they became smaller, and she grew lighter. Slowly the sky slipped away, and she could see the yellow light of the lamps. She had no idea where she was. She looked at the two bearded men with startled eyes and would have moved, but they held her and calmed her. The pain in her leg was intense, and she moaned.

"The pain is from the little beasts, my daughter. They have done most of the work, we think, but they are savage. Now we are going to pack your thigh with ice, and it will hurt also, but you are strong. We shall feed you, and you will feel better. Jonas will give you a sedative after that, and you will sleep again."

He held an instrument to her ear. "You are a little feverish, but if we can drop this infection, that will pass soon."

Romana, the slim girl, came and held a bowl of something hot and savory for her to eat and spooned it into her mouth as one does with a child. Then she gave her goat's milk to drink, and Jutta asked to be helped to the bathroom. She went back to bed exhausted. They put the ice pack on her leg; she winced from the cold, but her leg quickly became numb, and it felt better. Jonas felt her forehead.

"I will give you something to make you sleep again. We want you to rest while, hopefully, the leg begins to heal. When you wake you should feel less pain." He gave her an injection, then took the ampule from Ibrahim and injected that also.

"I think we should try to tell her army that we have her, Jonas."

"If she lives, my uncle, if she lives. She has to fight for herself now, and it is not over yet. If you tell them she is alive and well, and then we tell them she has died, who will they blame? Wait and let Aton decide." He jerked his head back. "I trust no one these days, especially those out there trying to kill us all."

Romana was watching Jutta sleeping. She tried to imagine what she looked like without the great bruises around her eyes and the strapped-up nose that Red Jane had inadvertently broken. She wondered about her family. Did they think she was dead? She thought that Jutta would look beautiful if she recovered. She had held her naked body in her arms and wondered if she had a lover to hold her as she had done. She felt a kinship with this sad enemy soldier and knew she shouldn't, especially if Jonas were to find that out. He would have let her die, covered in filth and blood. It was Ibrahim who had rescued her, her compassionate father whom she loved. Jutta stirred briefly and then went back to her heavy breathing. Romana left her and went to help her mother in the kitchens. Outside, the snow had stopped. The weak sun lit the great drifts that covered those still left dead on the battlefield and created a world of beauty out of the carnage. Aton smiled.

The major at the med center was reviewing Schiff's dossier. Suzanne was right about him. He was a lonely, somewhat lost soul despite his family background and perhaps, because of it. He needed warmth, but where would he find it? His parents had given him nothing much to build on. His brief relationship with Suzanne had made him aware of his needs rather than his frustrations, which would be a step towards his normalcy. It was a pity that Suzanne couldn't give more of her time. The major punched in her number and saw the smiling face.

"How did you get along with our melancholy major?"

"Basically, I mothered him a bit. He is a really pleasant man, you know, once you get past his army hang-ups."

"Anything dangerous?"

"I didn't detect anything. He is still a bit fragile after he got shot up, but I don't think he will go into a deep, death-dive depression. He seems to be pretty normal as far as physical, sexual contact goes. He was kind and gentle and listened, and he was able to talk to me."

"A lot of that is due to you, you know that? He really respected you and what you did for him. He is afraid to see you again because he had such a wonderful time with you that he thinks to try and repeat it may be a mistake."

"Oh dear! Maybe it was a bit of overkill."

"Would you see him again for another consultation? I am serious. Would that be a bad move?"

"Hmm, have to think about that. Do you think he needs me again?"

"You are the expert."

"Look, I will listen to his recording again and get back to you. You know that Compassion and Comfort is very strict about too much real bonding."

"You will let me know? Could you face another session with the boy hero?"

"No problems there. I have had much worse experiences. In some ways he reminded me of my late husband."

"Let me know."

"Take care"

"Bye."

Schiff was working hard to locate Radnath and Singh. They had to be somewhere, and he thought that they may have been like naughty children who run home when trouble gets too much for them. Radnath lived in style, so he started with him.

New Ganges on Alpha Six was the home of researchers, university dons, authors, teachers, and philosophers of the mystical kind. It was on the river. Large houses of the more opulent type sprouted like sacred lotus along the banks. The agent working for Schiff soon found and sniffed his man out. He didn't seem too surprised to see him. When Radnath was given a first-class ticket to Valderia and a room in the Palace, he found himself unable to refuse. That with a gentle warning that breaking his contract could spur a legal battle that could leave him bankrupt, made him very helpful. Radnath was suddenly calm. He had known all along that they would track him down, and he hadn't even bothered to hide his address. It would be better to just get the whole thing over and done with. What struck him as strange was that Schiff seemed to be as much in the dark as he was about much of the direction of the project. He contacted Singh and told him the house was falling in on them, and there was no place to hide.

Outside the research cavern on E5, the snow was falling. Light and non-lasting, it blew across the meadows and fell like icing on the branches of the near-bare trees. Deer took shelter in the pine woods away from the biting wind. The water birds had headed south as the moon spun away from the sun and dodged the gas giant that had spawned it. Up on the great northern plains, the woolly mammoths dug the grass out from the snow and began their southerly journey down towards the warmer climes. Great herds of deer traversed the edge of the mountain range and fed amongst the heather on the high slopes or on what leaves remained. Wild boar rooted for the fruit of the oak and beech trees. Fruit fell off the wild apples, and the Ong tribe collected those in woven baskets.

Davvd caught a ride on Joe's loader to see his friends and crunched his way across the snowfield to the big cave. Snowshoes would be his next project, he thought. The men had mastered the bows, had made stronger ones and could bring down an animal with ease. They had reinforced their entrance wall; it was tight and moss-packed: and very little wind blew into the warmer interior.

Annrath had been firing bowls and platters and her "fireplace" was her sacred site. Her bowls cooked meat and herbs and vegetables. Joe showed them what was edible and what was not and made a store of things they could plant in the spring. They had reluctantly accepted Joe as part of Davvd's tribe, but because he couldn't be hurt and always brought food or things they could use, he was now welcomed. The younger children spoke to him as a friend, and he spoke back to them. Learning the language for Joe was child's play. Davvd took a little longer but had studied and studied and had finally discarded the translator. The women asked about his woman, and he told them she had gone away to the stars again. Annrath grew large and asked when Maggda would be back. She wanted her to be near when the child was born, and all Davvd could say was that he hoped she might be back too. They allowed him to hunt with them, and he was quick but hadn't had those skills born in him as they had. When he brought down his first deer, they clapped him on the back and roared. He wanted to be sure they would not be too disadvantaged by the winter, but they assured him that they were not going to be. They were snug, had great fur coats, thick boots, and great caps, and they laughed off his concerns. He was sure they knew better than he did, and he wished he had the lady of the lace knickers to share all this with. He sent a long coded message to the admiral and asked for the authority to get Maggda back and to make holos so they could be sent to the media to reveal what had taken place here. He felt that if he publicized the illegal import of the tribe, it may flush out more information. He went and had a drink of one of Joe's special brews and sent a message to Galactic. Had Maggda forgotten him?

Maggda with a mission arrived back at Galactic and kissed Simon, demanded a drink and flaunted her beautiful Maxxi clothes. He looked at her and thought he had never seen her looking so well and sharp and told her so.

"Simon, you know that your leak in Fleet has been sent to New Babylon and is doing ten years hard labor on a tread mill?"

"I had Fleet heavies here. They just said that it might be good for my health to not use anything else that came my way about your Davvd Ong. I thought that it might be wise to forget him for a while."

"Simon, that is wrong thinking, babe. I have been pestering the admiral to get permission for us to make some really serious docco's down there and to use those to tell the story. Davvd needs the publicity now to shake the birds out of the brush, and if you knew how badly I want to get back there, you would give me the big Okay."

"You know I can't do anything until Fleet gives me the go-ahead. By Aton's breath, Maggda, don't stuff around with those boys. You play it very straight. What gets me is that you got away with stowing away, living with Ong, and they just told you not to be a naughty girl."

"Yes, Simon, but you don't have my legs. Apart from that, the admiral likes me. I am working on the plan that Davvd thought up. He gets the man to come round on the publicity angle, and Fleet gets the limelight; Davvd Ong stars again; and we, Simon, good ol' Galactic, get the scoop of scoops. I have been there; it is totally photogenic. It reeks of holo sensation and tri-dee magic, and wait till you meet the 'Ong Tribe.' They are a natural set of stars. I got to know one woman there, and she is wonderful, and Simon, she is getting close to producing her first born. Can you see that on the screens across the galaxy?"

"No, Maggda, no, I draw the line at close ups of childbirth!"

"No, Simon, I didn't mean it quite like that; for Aton's sake, do you think I would do that? No, Simon, but think what a real human interest plug that would make. If that isn't a winner, I don't know what is. The whole moon is a nature docco, Simon. I have been there, Simon, I have been there!"

"Get the admiral's go-ahead, and I will give you the money and the gear, and you can go back to 'Wonderland.' By the way, you blew the original story, so you owe me twenty-two thousand credits for all that Maxxi gear and running up bills that will send us broke. Do you still want to go?"

She went over to him and ran her hands down the front of his pants.

"See, Brent, I knew you still cared for me!"

"When that clearance comes through, Styxx, then I want you out of here. Just looking at you costs me credits."

She swung around and gave him a parting kiss. "Yeah, but who else is as good, Simon, who else!"

He reluctantly had to admit that she was right.

Schiff asked Radnath to eat with him in the mess. Radnath couldn't refuse, and they had a pleasant meal. Radnath refused wine but drank juice. Schiff led him to the lounge, put him into a large leather chair and sat opposite him. "May I ask, Professor, how we got into this mess?"

"It has become a mess, sir, because of those who know little, assume they know much and have used our research for their own ends."

"Professor, are you trying to tell me that you think the

Valderian High Command is using your research without your knowledge? Is that it?"

"I am in no position to accuse anyone, sir. What I do know is that early research, which we abandoned as unethical if applied, is being used elsewhere. You have to understand, sir, that we do not live and work in isolation. I have many friends who share the kind of research that Singh and I are carrying out, and we share papers and results. We knew that data processing between the neurons carried the key to the direction that we were moving towards--"

"Sorry to interrupt you, but I am not a scientist. I was given the job of an overseer, administrator, and accountant, if you must know the truth. I am as much the meat in the sandwich as you are. I have people who add up numbers and pay bills, but I do not control High Command."

"But you have very high connections, Major, do you not?"

"Did you choose your uncle, Professor?"

There was silence.

"Now let us get down to hard facts. You had a number of your so-called Neanderthals on E7. Legitimate bodies, all being treated in some way."

"We had moved to nano robotics. We had developed a method of transferring essential proteins—"

"Stick to the hard facts, please. You had several of your subjects die from an old, almost obsolete and prehistoric influenza virus. I know this, and you know this, but where did this virus originate. Do you know?"

"We have regular supplies delivered to the station. Some is food, of course. Much is chemical and biological. We are funded as you well know, Major, by Ong Wu Foundation, and you pay our bills. Now Ong Wu uses the Valderian commercial freight carriers to do that."

Schiff said nothing, but he nodded. His thought was that the commercial arm of the service was really just another part of the Valderian armed services, and that High command held the purse strings anyway.

260

"Where do you suspect that this virus came from?"

"It could only have been introduced in the supplies. It was a strain which we had not vaccinated against. How could we? It was listed as a 'dead' strain, an eliminated strain."

"Next question. Who would want your subjects to be killed off?"

"If I said your High Command, you would then ask 'why?' Am I right?"

"So?"

"Singh and I had reached a plateau. We were waiting for our subjects to show changes, but this wasn't something overnight. We knew that what we had started was something the subject brains would develop as a maturing process. As old cells passed away, the new programmed cells would emerge, and the neurons would both increase their internal activity and—"

"Stop! What motive?"

"High command had its experimental work finished. It didn't need this leg of the research. If it could eliminate our 'specimens' and discredit us, they would simply advise Wu and Ong that we had completed our research and that it had been, literally, a dead end."

"Explain what you mean by High Command having its experimental work finished."

"We had shown that as with brain disease and very retarded subjects too, that it was possible to insert electrodes into certain parts of the brain by nano surgery, as indicated by scans, and leave them there. They could be operated by remote signals, for example, instead of drugs to counter epileptic fits. We could switch off certain areas and actually control an individual's movements and the will to respond to fear, for example."

"What does that mean?"

"Imagine a regiment of soldiers who can be told what to do via transmitter. Imagine a troop of soldiers told to take an enemy position against bad odds but showed or felt no fear at all. You

261

would have an army that would be formidable. A commander could control them from his desktop. It doesn't stop there. If you could cut out, say pain, for short periods, you could get these soldiers to fight on regardless."

"Do you know this as a fact or is this just hypothesis?"

"Sir, I have no holos of this taking place, but in the more remote parts of the galaxy, I know your armies have troops like none other before them. People talk, especially when men get killed, and the surgeon's scan of their bodies reveals unusual changes to the brain. If I were there, I would draw my own conclusions. What you would have would be 'human robots,' without the problems associated with robots in an active role, killing people. The Galactic Federation's Conventions are very strict about that, as you know. No robot can be used to harm a human. That is a basic rule, and anyone who flouts that will be, well, very sorry."

"Do you know where your lost tribe is now, Radnath?"

"I suspect that they were moved to the nearest habitable research planet, or moon. It would have to be uninhabited, or they would cause problems. I think you or your High Command took them off to E5!"

"I was responsible, but I was like a puppet on a string. I tried to get them back, Radnath, but someone got to them first. I was made to look like a fool and ended up getting shot on Valentine. I suspect that Fleet knows more about you and me and High Command than we can guess. Someone did a very good job, Professor, and that's why I am a major again, and you are, seemingly, redundant!"

"I still have a contract, Major, and so does Singh. We didn't leave our positions; they left us, in a manner of speaking."

Schiff smiled. "Your salary will go on being paid into your accounts, so don't worry. You and I have a job to do now, do you know that? We will have to find out what or who has taken over your role. I expect to run into Fleet, don't you?"

"You would know more about those political intrigues than I would, sir."

"Could you travel?"

"In what connection?"

"If I asked you to come with me to E5, would you be able to?"

"That is an uninhabited research center, isn't it, just robots with a base that records and stores data? But there is accommodation there? It can accommodate seven personnel when they are all in residence. It hasn't been used much because most of the monitoring is done either by robotic staff, the new satellites, or on-ground sensors. I asked about it. Met with a strange response from Ong Wu, but the general feeling is that it is going to be taken off the restricted list. I think Ong Wu will allow limited ecotourism soon. I kept getting told that decisions are 'pending.'"

"Will it be safe?"

"Don't expect a woolly mammoth will come and trample us, do you?"

"Respect the intellect of the elephant and fear his power, sir."

"I will remember that. Now I have to take you back. I have a meeting to attend. Thank you for coming to see me. I am sure that we can sort this mess out soon."

He saw the man out and had a drink and thought about what in the name of Aton he was going to do next.

Ramona had helped Jutta out of bed and taken her to the bathroom. There was a large tub filled with hot water, and she helped Jutta into it and then sponged her all over with a soap that did smell. It reeked of the liniment that Jutta's father had made for his horses, so Jutta laughed. It was the smell of the stables and made her wonder when she would see them again. Ramona toweled her dry and helped her into the shapeless robe that covered her and kept her warm. "Back to bed and rest." she said.

"I am hungry."

"You will have to wait. My father says that appetite is the first sign of recovery."

"How is my leg?"

"The color has nearly all gone, but there is a little infection where the beasts did their work, but the soap will kill that. Can you walk?"

Jutta sat on the edge of the bed and stood up slowly. Her leg ached, but the pain was bearable. She took a couple of steps, then two more.

"Good, my father and Jonas want you to be able to walk. So, you will have to walk every day. You only have four days before we have to say goodbye to you."

"What does that mean, Ramona?"

"They are going to take you away from us. The army will come and put you on a transport with the others and take you to Pushtak."

"Pushtak, what is Pushtak?"

"It is a camp for prisoners of war. Much as I would like you to stay and talk to me and keep me company, we cannot keep you fed. My father has told them you are still weak, but the snow has stopped, and the roads have been pretty well cleared, so they have a tracked vehicle that tows a large trailer, and you ride in that, to Pushtak."

"How far is Pushtak?"

"About two or three days away, but that depends on the roads and the cease-fire."

"Will we be fed? And how will we keep warm?"

"You will have to ask Jonas, I think."

Jonas smiled. "We think you have had enough of being treated like a princess, fed like a baby and living in the lap of luxury. Pushtak will be home for a while, I suspect, until they get round to exchanging prisoners, and that depends on this Galactic Federation doing its work. You know what they can be like, arguing over a dot or a crossed T for weeks."

"My big red horse, what will happen to her?"

"I think she has already been classified as 'spoils of war.'"

"What will happen to her?"

"An awful lot of meat on that animal; she could feed us all for a month!"

Jutta was red-faced and speechless.

"Jonas is saying that to upset you," said Ramona. "She is too valuable to eat right now, but if things get tougher, then we may have to."

"But she is trained to bring wounded off the battlefield. She can tell when a man is alive or dead. How can you just dismiss her?"

Ramona reached for her hand.

"He is just being cruel. I know that they are already making a harness for her, and she can plow some of the fields that our tractors can't. She will be well cared for, Jutta, don't worry."

Jonas nodded. "Get her up and walking Ramona, so her legs get strong. It is a long hard way to Pushtak."

So Jutta walked. She had good legs, and the exercise helped to pump blood through her injured thigh. They gave her back her clothes and she dressed. Ramona took her out of the deep bunker into the fading snow. It was bitterly cold, but her Army issue clothing was strong and windproof. She trudged the snowy lane, back and forth, and asked to see Red Jane, but she was too far away to walk there. She saw others doing the same, some women but mostly soldiers with limps or still bandaged arms, hands, and heads. The sun came out on the second day, and she turned her face to Aton. Then it was the night before, and she was given a good meal and warm goat's milk. Ramona gave her a homemade bag of sheepskin with a change of underwear, a pair of hand-knitted stockings and a little bar of the liniment soap. They laughed over it.

"What could I give you, my friend and enemy, other than this? When you smell it you will think of us here, and remember us."

"I know that you sacrificed a lot just for me. I am the enemy, and yet, you protected me and cured me and slept with me, and I won't ever forget you."

"They will come early, Jutta, so have your clothes ready and take this bread, and I will leave you some milk. It will be freezing cold and rough, but you will have company at least."

They hugged each other, and Ramona left wet-eyed, and Jutta crawled into the rough bed, wrapped herself up and tried to sleep. The morning came too soon. There was the rough clatter of the engine and loud voices and doors banging, and a soldier came in and called her out, "Come, come, we have a long haul and a lot more to get on board."

Outside was a strange vehicle that resembled a long, converted farm cart. It was dirty, covered in a canvas roof, with a ramp at the back. Already there were people clambering into the trailer, and ahead, a large farm-tracked vehicle growled and thudded. She joined the others inside, and they forced her forward. There were rough benches filling fast, and she was squashed up into a corner. More came; there were more shouts; suddenly the whole contraption lurched and was on its way. It was full. Some were already on the floor. It was impossible to stand. The tractor rumbled out of the "village" and was on the road. If it hadn't been for the canvas roof to keep the wind and the rain off, they would have frozen. Being squeezed together helped to keep them warm. She was jammed between a large sergeant with a deep scar across his face and a young female corporal who seemed afraid to get too close to the officer. Jutta said, "Come close, and we can keep each other warm," and the girl smiled. They rumbled for three hours, and then they stopped. More shouting from outside, then the order to get out and line up. The same scramble out as in, the same chaos of lining up. It had begun to rain. Then they were ordered to file past a mobile canteen. A plastic cup of soup and a slice of bread were dished out, then another line and a cup of water. A woman sergeant was handing out the water, and Jutta asked for a toilet. The woman pointed to a low wall behind her. She went back, and there were three other women there. Then they were all loaded on again. Such is the nature of the human being to establish its territorial space that she found herself back in her corner with the corporal. Her leg was giving her pain. She was cold, but there was no respite. Another three hours and they were all exhausted. There was a shuddering halt, and they climbed stiffly off the trailer and lined up. It was nearly dark. In the lights of the tractor was a large barn, and they were herded inside. Some of the men were detached to bring in more straw and spread a deep covering. Jutta and her companion went to the rear wall, away from the draught from the doors, and sat with their backs to the wall. It was very cold. A guard appeared with a lantern and held it high.

"This is it for tonight. No food until morning. We haven't any, so we share the pain. Two water buckets up here and a ladle. Get down into the straw. It is going to snow again." Jutta lay down, made a pillow of her bag and covered herself with straw as deep as she could, and her companion did the same. It was too cold to sleep. Jutta asked her companion how she became a prisoner.

"I was with the mobile kitchen, and we were going to feed the boys up at the front, so we hauled it up there. There was a counterattack, and all our boys retreated. We were left there, and these rebels in white sheets suddenly appeared and got our sergeant and the cook with a stun pistol. They fell down in the snow, and I was left standing there, with a soup ladle in my hand. Then these four rebel soldiers came over and held up their mess tins. I gave them hot soup, and when they had that, they packed the trailer up and took it and me with them!"

Jutta had to smile.

"What about you, ma'am?"

"I was with a field ambulance called Red Jane, and--

"The big red horse?"

"Yes. We were getting her shoed when a mine blew up. I was sitting on her back, and she bolted and took me to the enemy lines. I had been hit by something. The armor saved me, but my leg was in a bad state. They healed it up for me, and here I am."

"And the lovely black eyes and the nose?"

"Blame the horse. Hit my face against her neck when she took off across country."

They huddled together, got back to back and pulled the straw over them as much as they could. It was a very cold night.

Corporal Stumm brought Jutta some water in her plastic cup that she had kept from the day before. "I don't think we will eat for a while. If the guards have nothing, then I wouldn't expect us to get much, would you?"

The doors banged open; they staggered out, and found a wall and joined other women. Then it was back to their transport. They occupied their corner again. The big sergeant had found it easier to lie on the floor. They rattled and groaned on. Snow fell, and then was replaced by heavy rain that drummed on the canvas. Four hours went by. They were tired, had sore backs and backsides and when they stopped, were too tired to move. "Out if you want to eat!"

They were outside a farm. Under a lean-to shed, there were tables with soup cans steaming and bread and mugs. Behind the makeshift kitchen was a dry floor, and they took their soup and sat down in the dust. The rain poured down and spouted off the ancient tiles. Jutta and Mary Stumm sat together and made the most of their slim meal.

"If I can steal a mug, that would help. We need a water container or a food bowl, and that would serve for both."

"Will they count," asked Jutta?"

"Wait and see."

As they filed out, a sergeant was collecting mugs, and Mary managed to drop her mug on the floor instead of the large bowl. He cursed and put the bowl down to pick it up. Jutta slipped her mug under her coat. The crush behind her pushed forward, and they made their way to the trailer.

"Thief!" said Mary.

"Whose idea was it, Stumm?"

"This is good. Now we have two containers. When things get

tough, it is the little things that can make a difference."

"I think I will stick with you, Stumm; you have a natural talent for survival."

"Thank you, ma'am."

The rain eased. They made a stop to refuel the tractor, but they had to stay on board. Then they stopped again for a toilet break. They were allocated a space behind a tall hedge. They climbed back on board again. They rumbled on. By mid-afternoon the rain had started again, mixed with sleet. When they did grind to a halt, they were put into another barn. It was another night in the hay, but at least it was shelter, and they slept. Fatigue had won. It was a cold morning, but outside there was a line of prisoners getting a hot drink of some herbal tea and a slice of bread from a mobile kitchen that was set up under canvas. The rain had stopped, but it was bitterly cold. They were hustled along and back into the trailer. Before they boarded, Mary pointed ahead; there were more trailers like theirs. There were a lot of souls on their way to Pushtak. The camp at Pushtak was an old army camp, hastily brought back to life to house prisoners of war. The patched roofs and a few boarded windows suggested essential repairs had been carried out. Jutta and Mary looked around and smiled.

"You know something, Mary Stumm, this is just like the dump that I left behind."

"You must have been in Barrack Five, Jutta."

"No, Barracks Ten."

"Are they any different?"

"Wait and see."

They were being processed, and Mary went off into the "other ranks" section beyond a high wire fence. Jutta joined the ranks of officers queued up, waiting to be listed. When her turn came she was scanned and iris identified, much to the amusement of the young rebel sergeant who was taken by her black eyes and strapped nose. Then it was a pinprick to draw blood for DNA; then it was a tri-dee image and a number tag. Eventually, she filed out past a table where she was given a pillow and two thin blankets and a card with a number. It was going to be home for the time being. She found her hut and went inside to find ten female officers already making themselves at home. She avoided the bunks by the windows, knowing that the cold would strike through those, and found one in a corner. Along the end wall were lockers, and the women had begun to each claim one. Jutta chose one; she had nothing much to put in it but her sheepskin bag, but it cleared the space. She was expecting more to come and fill the bunks, but they were the sum total for her billet. She made her bed on the straw mattress and sat. They all did the same and exchanged stories. Hers was the most amusing, and they laughed when she told them how she had been taken. When she thought about it, it did seem faintly ludicrous. In the back of the billet was a washroom with two showers and two toilets, no mirrors and no toilet paper, and the water was cold. In the center of the billet was a large iron stove but no fuel in the buckets, and they wondered if they would get some heat.

A large woman sergeant in a badly fitting uniform came into the billet an hour later and ordered them to sit. She had a list of names, and they answered in turn. "Now", she said, "you will not change bunks. We have you recorded as being where you are. Every morning, two of you will go and fill the fuel buckets. Every morning, one of you will replace the toilet roll and burn the waste. All fuel is costly, so don't waste it. Every morning, you will be called to parade for roll call, and then you eat. If you miss roll call, you do not eat. If you are sick, then you will not leave roll call but stand until someone takes you to the medics. You will be required to do at least one hour of exercise each morning and one in the afternoon. If you fail to do that, you will be given extra exercise under strict supervision. I have to tell you that it involves a heavy wooden tread mill. Escaping. We would welcome your escape since it would free us from having to feed you, and since there is nowhere to escape to, your life expectancy outside Pushtak has been estimated at three days. The cold or the bears would kill you. Food is limited, thanks to the Valderian army making war on us. Whatever you are given to eat is what we are forced to eat. We share the pain. Who is the senior officer?"

A gaunt, short-haired major put up her hand.

"You are now in charge of this billet. If the rules get broken, then you will be punished as the responsible officer. That will involve the tread mill. You will see that the billet is swept and kept clean and that the fire is kept clean and has enough fuel. The billet will be inspected once every week on a random daily basis. The beds must be made up, and clothes put into lockers. Now, any questions?"

The major said, "We need a table and some chairs, and a mirror. We have not been issued with towels."

The sergeant made notes.

"You two, come with me. Now get your fuel in and get the fire lit. It heats the showers. Welcome to Pushtak, girls!"

Jutta and her neighbor in the next bunk found companionship. A week passed quickly. The food was never going to be on the menu of the Blue Boar, but it kept them alive. Jutta wondered if her parents or Jackson knew where she was.

The Valderian media covered the cease-fire with a slanted propaganda angle, but then it released a list of prisoners of war. The Valentine branch of the "Flag of Compassion" published names and tri-dees of its prisoners; Maria saw Jutta and gasped. Had she been beaten up? She had two black eyes and her nose, her pretty nose, looked awful. She was still alive and although not exactly well, still had a sparkle. Maria sent a call to Schiff, and he saw her for himself.

"Well, he said, she may look a bit the worse for wear, but I think she is still our same old Jutta. Have you told her parents?"

"I sent them the tri-dee. At least they know where she is. I think that with some luck, they will do an exchange. It just depends on the Galactic Federation observers doing their job. Am I right, sir?"

"And if our High Command doesn't get even more stupid than they are now!"

"Sir?"

"Forget I said that, Maria. I never said it."

"No sir."

"Maria, will you have dinner with me tonight?"

"Sir?"

"No, not at the mess. May I take you to the Blue Boar? I really would like to do that. I need company, and right now, I can't think of anyone as well suited as you, and we both need a break. Can you come?"

"Well, yes sir, I think so. Sir".

"No uniform, and that's an order. Wear that blue dress you wore to the mess. I will wear a suit that has been tempting the moths, but I think is still smart enough not to shame you."

"Half cycle six, sir?"

"Half cycle six."

"Thank you, sir"

"No, Maria, you deserve the thanks, not me."

Maria shook her head. He had even remembered her dress. What was happening to Kurt Schiff?

Radnath had sought out Singh.

"Listen, son of my uncle, I am going to find our lost souls on E5. As you well know, it is a place where much has been done in natural experiment. It is a place where outcomes are only scientific after the event and not before. Put the wheels in motion and then watch."

"Feed the monkey the magic weed and watch how well he dances?"

"In a manner of speaking, oh yes indeed, Dandra. I have spoken to Schiff. He is as much worried as we were. Now we must find the lost souls and return them to E7."

"But they are now, what we might assume, undertaking an unmonitored and natural experiment, are they not, sir?"

"Mistakes made cannot be undone now. What we have to do is to cover our heads against the rain, Dandra, son of my uncle."

"We may need a large hat, sir."

"Oh yes indeed, Dandra, a very copious hat, but we are getting used to weathering storms, as is Major Schiff, I think."

"May Aton smile upon us, sir."

"May Aton smile upon us, Dandra."

Davvd Ong was feeling a little better. He had been looking at all the latest information that Joe and Don had compiled about E5. E5 had been given a limited time span for the breeding programs and had almost arrived at its potential. Animals that were now in large numbers could be taken and were being taken back to the natural habitats, where the genetic diversity within their numbers ensured that they would be free of in-breeding problems. The list went on. What was encouraging was that a meeting of the Foundation and the scientific community was due, and Davvd could present them with the reality of his tribe. He was hoping that they would be allowed to stay, and maybe more would be allowed to come and live there. He hoped Maggda was doing her work with the admiral. A lot depended upon her.

So Maggda had worn short skirts and low-cut blouses and cajoled him; he had asked for more information from Galactic, and Simon put a team together in a hurry, and the information, spin, persuasion, went back and forth. Finally, the man had been to his peers and higher life forms, and Galactic had permission from both Ong Wu and Fleet to publicize the plight of the tribe that had appeared on E5 literally overnight, but censorship still lurked in the background.

"There are possible links with Valderia here. We won't tread on anyone's toes just yet, and they won't ruffle our feathers. That may be the most mixed metaphor you'll hear for a long while, but I think you get my drift, Maggda. We don't want an intergalactic incident to come out of this. Is that clear? Now I have a list of equipment that Ong wants. He wants to replace a 'dragon fly observation vehicle' that he says was written off. Do you know what that was about?"

"I think it might be better if you just accept the fact, sir, and give him what he wants," said Sonna, and she winked at Maggda.

"Don't forget, sir that he has to do the job, has done more than his brief asked and is down there facing it all alone."

"And you have to be there to direct the publicity angle, right, Ms. Styxx?"

"Yes sir. I know what has gone on, he knows what is going on, and an outsider now is going to have to start from scratch. The way I see it, publicity that Galactic can generate will bring the scum to the surface, if there is any. What Davvd wants more than anything is to find out if there were dangerous and obscene experiments made not just on the Ong tribe, but on many more like them. If he wants that, then Ong Wu Foundation would want that too, wouldn't they?"

"Let us do things one at a time, Maggda. You take care of the media angle and let us liaise with Ong Wu. Now, I am sending a large pile of supplies on a Fleet ship to E5 in the next day or so. Get your gear packed and ready to ship out with it. You can go with it. It won't be *Double Happiness* but adequate for the short time you will be aboard. Now, is there anything else?"

"Tailored uniform denims for me, three sets; heavy winter gear, thermals, and all-weather gear for a delicate young lady like me."

"Sonna will handle all that, won't you, Captain?"

"My pleasure, sir. Now, tell me the sizes, and we can get that done by this afternoon."

The Fleet freighter *Morning Glory* left for E5 the next afternoon. Maggda had a small, pleasant cabin, and the officer who normally called it his own, was bunked up with two others. The ship was using the best Ong Wu power drive so far developed, and it scorched its way to E5 in 2.35 Old Earth days. It delivered its load and Maggda onto the snow of the meadow, then Joe and Don came out and brought her and it to the cavern. The tribe watched

274

progress and speculated that the star woman had returned. They wondered what gifts she had for them.

Jutta had done her morning's exercise with her friends and went back to the billet. The Untidy sergeant appeared, pointed to her and said, "Out."

Jutta wondered if she had transgressed but marched with her companion to the administration offices, a rough-looking shed tacked onto a long hut at the camp entrance.

"Mail for you. Lieutenant Vogel. Sign here. It has been opened by security, of course. Still, it may cheer you up, eh?" She had a square package and two letters. One from Jackson sent via 'space delivery' and the other from her parents, forwarded via the Military Postal Service. She felt a little emotional. The square package was a tri-dee of Red Jane and Ramona, and the letter from Jackson was short but sweet and promised hope in other ways. She discovered that his brother, Horatio, was on the Feds' committee and on the planet. She had very little hope of meeting him, but it gave her some hope. Her parents expressed the usual parental love and told her to be strong. Now that she was alive and well, they said, "Stick it out and you will soon be back with us!" She felt lighter and sang and found some fresh flowers. Jackson wanted her, her horse was loved, and her parents loved her. Aton was smiling.

Major Angela Hoffmann had a visit from Major Schiff.

"When can I go off planet, Major? Things are getting to the stage where I may have to take the risk, and soon."

"Get up here, and let's have a look at you." She ran the scan over him and felt the wound and looked at the function of lung and liver on the screens and told him to sit up. "How far and how long, and will you have someone or thing to monitor you?"

"To E5, but don't know how long or if there is a medical unit still functioning there. It is an expedition to find facts and open-ended."

"What do you want to find on E5, Major? It's a robotic-monitored research moon, isn't it? Lots of birds and beasts and nature in the raw. Hardly your scene, I would think."

"Major, if I could duck it, I would. I no more want to go there than I wanted to go to Valentine. I have this bad gut feeling that when I get there a woolly mammoth or something with horns will tread on me or gore me to death. Apart from which, it is going into a hard winter right where I want to be, and I hate the cold."

"Duty?"

"I am not supposed to talk to anyone about this, but I can trust you. If you must know, not strictly. I made a mess of a little job my uncle dropped on me and have to sort it out, sweep up the mess and tell him that Valderia is safe again. It is one of those lovely little interplanetary screw-ups that I was caught up in, and my uncle being my uncle, blames me for it."

"And you have to go to E5 to fix it?"

"No other way. So when can I travel?"

"Four days. Make your plans, but the liver is a bit weak still. Four days and you can fly away. Are you still feeling stressed? You seem to be tense. I thought you were on the mend after seeing Suzanne."

"If I could take her with me, I wouldn't be."

"Could you risk seeing her again?"

"What's the risk, Major? She is like a masseur I used to go to, except that she manages to fix me mentally and physically at the same time."

She raised her eyebrows.

"I know that she is a very highly trained psychotherapist, and that you think I need some tender loving care. My father was a psychiatrist, and I am not stupid."

"Kurt, you would get angry if I suggested you have a deep psyche probe, wouldn't you?"

"Do I need it?"

"Do you miss your mother?"

"I never knew her. Is this what you think is biting me, deep down?"

"The scans they did when you were being fixed up off Valentine show an anxiety level that shouldn't be there. They did a scan; it showed you might need help. That came to me, and I asked Suzanne. She confirmed that you had a minor problem."

"A minor problem?"

"A minor problem."

"And what do you think I can do?"

"Do you want to see Suzanne again? It won't be easy because of the regulations that Compassion and Comfort has in place."

"When? It would have to be before I ship out."

"Want to leave it with me? I can contact you anytime during the day, can't I?"

"A minor problem."

"A minor problem, Kurt. Leave it with me."

He left and wondered what his minor problem might be. He didn't love his uncle, and his mother was never there, but he thought he functioned pretty well. He went and sent Maria a small bunch of flowers. It made him feel better.

"Suzanne? Can you see him just once more?"

"I know; I got all that data you sent me about his mother. You know that she lives not far from my mother. She knows her."

"How is he going to react when he finds out she is still alive and living just across the square from you in Valhalla?"

"Probably hate her guts. Want to risk a confrontation?"

"Well, his mother knows all about him. She is terrified that he will hate her if she just turns up. I think you are right about filling in the gaps, because he has never been whole, has he? A kind of orphan emotionally. He is a sensitive soul, and he needs a stable relationship. Then he will be a pretty good officer and a very good member of the aristocracy. Might just accept that he could do good things if he got into a position where his rank pulled weight, you know what I mean?"

"You know that we wouldn't be doing all this for some ordinary soul, don't you?"

"I like to think we would but maybe a bit lower key."

"Day after tomorrow, same time, same place. Yellow daisy."

"I will tell him."

He went to the Compassion and Comfort offices, and Trudi was a little short. "We are a little concerned about the visit, Major. We don't encourage consultations too close together." He paid his six hundred credits, and she confirmed that Suzanne would see him and sniffed.

He was in the square a little early, and he hid behind a pillar. He turned his back to the sunlight and looked at her reflection in a shop window. He wore his best suit, forsaking the uniform that had become a burden to him. She was wearing a sky blue suit with a deep pleat in the front of the skirt and so beautifully tailored that it fitted without a wrinkle. The jacket fastened at the front with a short gold chain to two gold buttons, and she wore a white lacy blouse and stockings, with blue shoes and a small bag to match. She had a wide-brimmed lace hat that let the sun make freckle light patterns across her cheeks. She was beautiful. She had a long-stemmed yellow daisy in her gloved hand and twirled it in a lazy way. She was at ease. A well dressed man stopped and spoke to her, and she laughed and pointed to her time band. He bowed and left, and a minute later, another, older man spoke to her. She waved down the street, and he bowed and walked on. Schiff had the thought that she was a lighthouse for lost ships.

She held out her hand. He looked at her, and she smiled, then broke the head off the daisy and set it afloat in the fountain. "Are you going to risk seeing me again, Kurt?"

"When I am with you, I don't feel any risks. The world could fall down and I wouldn't care."

She laughed and made a little curtsy. "Can we go to coffee now? I have a different place called Bruno's. They have a different blend there." She led him away and across the street and finally to Bruno's. It was atmospheric with a small dance floor and a stage at the back, and they sat and watched the world go by. She was watching him closely, and when a young woman came onto the stage with a cello, she appeared to look the other way. He listened and watched. He had stiffened when the music began, and he reached for her hand.

"My mother used to play that. I could hear her playing but very rarely watched her. She liked to be alone, and I was very young."

"Brahms, she is playing a little piece by Brahms."

"My mother was very famous, did you know that? She could command a huge price for her performances. My father, did you know, was the chancellor's brother?"

"I didn't know that."

"It wasn't well known. My father never mentioned it. We never went to the Chancellery except on 'business'. My mother was really a 'countess', I suppose."

"Tell me about her."

"I really didn't know her, Suzanne. The strange thing is that when I hear the cello, I have a little pain inside me. I never play her record discs, and I have them all that I inherited when my father died. I sometimes wonder what happened to her. She went 'missing' on Old Earth. My foster mother used to tell me that she would come back one day, but she never did. Now, I can see her as a bit of a wild woman, and I suppose she was. I suppose I will never know what happened to her, and I am afraid to find out."

"Lunch! Where do you want to go?"

"I want to go somewhere you would like, but not the Blue Boar!"

"You eat there too often?"

He laughed, "No, but I would like a change. Take me to somewhere simple." They ate spaghetti at a wine bar with an accordionist who pestered them at their table until Schiff gave him twenty credits, and then they took a robocab to his apartment. He had bought a great cut glass bowl and filled it with flowers and had asked his housekeeper to put floral linen on the bed. She had given him a look that suggested he was a little mad but had complied. The apartment smelled of freshness for a change.

She stood and looked at the flowers and smiled. "Did you think I needed those?"

"I just wanted to please you."

"You are a kind man, do you know that?"

"With you, maybe. I have been called a lot worse by junior staff."

"Never!" she laughed.

He watched her undress. It gave him enormous pleasure just to watch her take her clothes off and put them methodically away, hang up the jacket and skirt and her blouse, and then she was standing in just her stockings. She had two old-fashioned, wide, lacy garters, and each had a silk yellow daisy, and he smiled. "I love those."

"Then I shall keep them on. Get undressed and get into bed with me." She laughed when she saw the sheets. "Do you think we needed cheering up, Kurt? I love them; now come in here and rub my back."

He rubbed her back and kissed her a lot, and she turned over and asked him to hold her breasts. He could smell her hair, and he didn't care if they made love or not.

"Tell me about your mother."

He didn't know what to say. His mother had been a distant, beautiful, and often angry soul who came and went. She had spats with his father, who was never one to fight, so she won all the arguments that he could remember. It seemed to be a long time ago. They made love quietly apart from their mutual deep breaths. She clung to him after and told him not to move. "Just hold me tight."

He knew that she must give herself to other men, but he didn't like to think about it. He held her and thought that no one would appreciate her as much as he could. He alone, he thought, could appreciate her and her elegant sophistication. She urged him to get dressed, and he followed her through the bathroom. She dressed with her usual care and refused to give him one of her garters. "I don't give souvenirs, Kurt. Now, are you dressed?"

"What are you doing?"

"I am taking you to meet my mother. Don't look at me like that. I am not going to marry you, but I have to see her, and it won't hurt for you to come with me. Behave yourself, don't tell her we have just climbed out of bed, will you? Act like Kurt Schiff, next in line to the seat of Valderia, and smile a lot. Can you do that?"

"Yes ma'am."

"Now come here and kiss me before I put on my lip color."

"Yes ma'am."

They took a robocab to the best part of the city, and he looked at the charm of the place with its very fashionable older style apartments, the brush hedges, and the iron rails. She palmed the door lock, and they went into a gray marble hall and then climbed stairs to the first floor. She knocked, and her mother came to the door. Her mother was a slightly faded beauty, and he could see Suzanne in her, but she was younger than he thought she might be. She was very elegantly dressed, bright eyed, and beautifully groomed. The apartment was furnished with very elegant furniture and on the wall of this anteroom, two small paintings. He smiled when he recognized the one he and Suzanne had chosen.

"Mother, this is Kurt, and he helped me choose your painting. He is a major in the army and is a gentleman sometimes, and he has promised to be on his best behavior for you."

"Has she been bullying you, Kurt? She bullies everyone, but sometimes you don't even notice it. Now come in and sit down. Can I get you something . . . No? My daughter is inclined to push people about, have you noticed that?"

"Yes, but when she does it, I think it might be good for me. She has a way of taking control that is hard to fight."

"Suzanne, he obviously doesn't know you that well, does he? He likes you, that is obvious. Now you are related to the chancellor, aren't you, or shouldn't I mention that? The way she is looking at me the answer is 'no.'"

"I have had to live with it all my life. One can't choose one's relatives, and I didn't choose my uncle, but he is the supreme commander, so I have no choice but to do as I am told."

"You were wounded on Valentine? I think Suzanne told me. Have your wounds healed? You got a medal . . .

"Just a bar to an earlier one. I didn't do anything terribly worthwhile except to tell my troops to duck."

"He is a modest man, mother."

"I can see that. Now, I want you to meet a friend of mine. Come with me, Kurt. I will introduce you." She took his hand and led him into the next room. It was larger and had dark green leather seats and an elegant polished wood coffee table and standing in front of the fireplace was a woman whose face he had seen as a younger version on a hundred or so music discs. "Hello, Kurt, my son."

He stood, transfixed.

"Mother?"

"This isn't fair to you, is it? I treated you so badly as a child and then left you, and all I could think about then was myself."

"You really are my mother?"

"I really am your mother."

"I thought that you were dead. Years ago, I thought that you were dead."

"Shall we sit down? I know Suzanne's mother, Rose, from when we were students together. I have followed your career, my son, all the way, but I was terrified that you would just want to kill me if we met. I have been living here ever since my second husband died on Old Earth. Your father left me very well off, did you know that? And I had my own wealth, of course, and you have a large sum to come to you when you marry. It was his will."

"Just tell me why didn't you come back? I don't care about the credits!"

So she told him.

He left with Suzanne. She looked at him critically.

"Are you all in one piece, Kurt?"

"You set me up, didn't you?"

"You will have to forgive me, but neither I nor Major Hoffmann knew your mother was alive and well and living back here on Valderia until the other day. I didn't connect the Freya Schiff my mother knew with you at all. Then when I talked to your major, she mentioned that you never had a mother's influence, so she looked and traced her to here and my mother. It was a pure coincidence.

"You wouldn't lie to me about that, would you?"

"Don't you trust me anymore?"

"Come back to my apartment with me. I need to hold you, and I want you to give me some 'compassion and comfort.' Then I might tell you I trust you again."

"Will you rub my back and kiss my breasts?"

"You are a hard woman to please, you know that?"

"I have to be home by seven cycle. My mother is taking me out to dinner."

"I shall just have to make the most of our time, won't I?"

She called for a robocab, and they went to the soiled bed and the smell of flowers, and he told her what his mother had told him, and he felt better.

Your father was a wonderful man. He understood me. I was young and wild and famous, and everyone in the business flattered me. I performed at places most musicians could only dream about. Then you came along, and I was torn between what I should do, and what I could do. I should have given you lots of love and been there for you, but my career was so exciting that I couldn't stay at home. So I left you to be cared for. Your father did his best, but he couldn't have you in his arms all day. He tried hard, I know that, but his duties made it impossible. I went to Old Earth, and it was the most exciting time of my life. I liked to party, and I flirted, and I slept with men who flattered me, and became rather dissolute. I suppose I was carried away with being famous. I loved the attention, and although I wanted to know how you were, you were so far away that it became impossible.

Then your father was murdered. It was a terrible blow. I loved him despite of all we had been through. I had a long concert tour coming up, and I was under a heavy legal commitment and couldn't break it. So I went on tour, and I met a pianist who played with me, and we merged. He was getting over a bad marriage, and I was lonely, so we merged, and that is the only word I can use. We just got together, and he understood what I was going through, and I understood what he was going through. He wanted to stay in Rome, on Old Earth, and I couldn't leave him, and we married, and he wanted children and I didn't. Eventually, he took a mistress who gave him three bouncing bambinos, and we parted. I came back to Valderia. I had been writing all those years to Rose, my old friend, and she found an apartment near hers, and I have lived here ever since. What could I do for you? You were an army man, an officer who had family 'protection,' so what could I offer you? I watched your career and your triumphs and felt proud but couldn't do anything. Now I am older, and you are a mature man, and you have no wife, no children. Is there no one?

And he could give her no answer. He just felt that maybe she deserved to be given another chance, another means of making her feel better and somehow make amends, and he could only do that by forgiveness.

Maggda was working. This required her to script an introductory newscast for E5, include all the location shots and have Joe set up camera drones to fly over the whole area. It was taking time. Davvd went to see his tribe to explain what the activity was all about. He told them that the star people who had removed them from their old home had saved them but were forced to bring them here, and that they may have to go back.

This caused problems, but he said that he wanted them to stay. He seriously didn't know what would happen if there was that kind of conflict. Maggda made her first pilot run and anchored it, and they sat and watched it.

"You, Lord of the Universe, come a bit later. I want to show where we are, who the tribe are, location, and then we can explore the rights and wrongs. Look at that snow and those hills!"

"Can we run those from here?"

"No. First it has to go through Galactic, then Simon will get them to add background information, 'fill ins,' and then he will push it out. Maybe in a few days? So we keep adding on here. We interview Davvd Ong."

"No interviews with Davvd Ong."

"So how am I supposed to make this creditable?"

"I interview Maggda Styxx. For example, 'This is Maggda Styxx on the Research Moon E5. Tell us what happened, Maggda, and how you come to be here with Davvd Ong. Was it an accident, or did Fleet give permission?'"

"Fleet gave me permission to publicize this event, because it was Davvd Ong and the robotic staff here who discovered there were humanoids here that shouldn't be here. Fleet sent Captain Ong to investigate, and I followed. See Ong, not a single lie."

"Slippery Styxx, very slippery, but you ducked that well. You know I can only be quoted or seen in a shot somewhere, but I never speak to the media, you know that. This way, you become a star, and I just add backup. What's wrong with that?"

"About twenty thousand credits if I don't get you to do an interview. I owe Galactic more than that."

"Just voice over your footage, how's that?"

"I'll ask my boss."

"Hey, don't look so grim. I have to follow my orders, and much as I would love to do what you want me to do, I have to stay low and not stir up the dust. Okay?"

"Are you going to give me a hug and kiss me or not?"

"You poor little thing. Come to Daddy." There was a chime, and Don entered the rec room.

"Sir, we have a visitor. A Valderian military vessel is asking permission to land two humans for research purposes, on the normal channel."

"Life becomes more exciting by the minute, Don. Permission granted, and ask them to identify themselves for the records."

"Yes sir."

"Radnath and a Major Schiff, sir."

"Maggda, see what the cat has brought in! We get two birds with one stone, and we haven't even sent a single broadcast out yet!"

"This, Ong, I have to record for posterity, but please don't tell them, will you?"

"You think they won't be aware of what you are up to?"

"We shall just have to try, Davvd, just have to try.

Schiff and Radnath had had an instructive voyage. They had talked and had grown to respect each other in a way neither thought possible. It had gone from a suspicious blame game to a mutual realization that both of them may well have been used as scapegoats. Schiff was anxious to find out what the "lost tribe" had been expected to achieve in terms of their development under the Radnath and Singh regime. Radnath ducked the specifics but spoke about "environmental influences" in terms of pushing the subjects to learn faster.

"Let us say, that we have a group that were given the kind of cerebral 'opportunity' that would enhance brain function. The work we did with rats and some primates showed clearly that if we pushed the subjects into a more, for example, 'threatening' environment, we could measure the activity and see that the best of them overcame fear and employed strategies to minimize the dangers. The apes began to increase the use of weapons. They made weapons from branches that were heavy and often spiked to chase away a robotic leopard which was stalking them. They employed strategies to actually ambush this threat. They used skills which developed from the enlarged neuron interchange to become creative. The rats, when threatened by a robotic snake, pushed bedding into the narrowest portion of their habitat and urinated on the head of the snake as it came towards them. We saw examples of rats decoying the snake and offering one up as a target, and then other rats attacking the tail of the snake, very viciously. These behaviors are indications that the brains were functioning above the mere instinctive and conditioned levels. A conscious, and group, decision was arrived at, as the best way to defeat the threat."

"What about these so-called 'Neanderthals'?"

"We had an environment which mirrored the one they had come from, and they were already a cooperative socialized group. They hunted together, shared food and protected their females from abuse. They didn't have the same kind of social mores that we have. They did share women, and the 'alpha male,' if I can use that archaic term, was able to have sexual union with several females. The women often refused these advances but accepted the status as a normal one. Our research group was given nanosurgery implantation to improve the interchange of neuron activity, which spikes when a new task is required. The neurons are miniature computers in their own right, not just exchange mechanisms, we all know that. We just enhanced the means for them to function better. When we 'lost' our tribe to influenza, we were at the stage of enlarging the environmental challenges. We were going to put them under a food stress situation where game would be scarce and their shelters inadequate. We would see when and how they adapted, for example, to the making of traps to hold and secure animals rather than running then down and having to kill them. We could scan brain activity so we could adopt measurements to show what, when, and where increased activity was taking place. Increase in the ability to plan and build more efficient shelter was measurable. We saw that the shelter would be one that could be transported, so as to give a mobile base for women, children, and hunters, so as to follow game more readily. We saw that as an essential need, as you and I know. Shelter, food, warmth, and Comfort."

They would land in the morning. Schiff was not looking forward to the cold. Radnath was hoping to have a warm bed and decent food, but he had small hopes. He had lived under these conditions before and knew what to expect. They dropped down into the meadow and were witnessed by Ong's tribe, who waved bows and spears. The ramp fell open, and they emerged to be met by Davvd Ong, Maggda, and Joe. Schiff overcame his immediate surprise and regained his composure when Davvd extended a hand and introduced himself, Maggda, and Joe, and then they loaded the baggage, and Joe transported them to the complex. It was an emotional experience for them all.

Maggda played hostess.

She showed them to their rooms and turned up the heat. Joe had made sure nothing was astray. She offered them some of Joe's Special Brew. Schiff accepted just one. Radnath had a fruit drink that Joe had sealed six summers ago. She drew them into the rec room with all its battered charms and the artificial flowers that Joe had made and placed in her vase. It cheered the place up. Schiff relaxed noticeably after his brew.

Maggda sat closer to Schiff and asked him what it was like on Valentine. He stiffened a bit, then smiled.

"I think I was lucky, really. I was shot out of there, so was shipped out and back to Valderia. I have to take things easy for a while, that's all. It is a hellhole. I wish I could say, 'My country, my planet, my Chancellor, right or wrong,' but it hurts a bit. The thing was, we thought the enemy were dumb bastards . . . forgive the expression, but that is what we were told, and they may have lacked sophistication, but 'dumb' never came into it. We landed a small force there, and they had the numbers and the techniques to destroy all of us. Now don't quote me, and I know you have every damn recording device doing that, but I trust you to be discreet. Our troops didn't believe in it, and I didn't believe in it. It should have been handled by the Galactic Federation outside of Valderia's interests."

"Which are, of course, all that mineral wealth."

"Of course, there are vast oil fields in the interior, and who can survive without that even today? Gold, uranium and iron ore, tin and lead and bauxite . . . it's all there. We set up companies to mine it; the Valentines were getting royalties, but, again, they wanted to take over the whole operation. The excuse about the planetary delegate and the tribal conflict was just to give us a means of gaining total control. You have to appreciate that Valentine doesn't have a huge industrial base. Just about everything goes off planet. They were jerked into the 'modern' mainstream when it was discovered they had all the wealth just lying there. Indium, ruthenium, tellurium, selenium, gallium, and neodymium. A gold mine of rare minerals. Who could resist that? Now, what about you?"

"You must know more about me than I do about you. Major."

"I have seen more of you than most women I have ever known, 'Miss Second Skin,' but that doesn't explain anything. I find you here with Captain Ong, and that tells me more than a holo of you selling underwear!"

So she told him, and he laughed. She was warming to him.

"May I ask about your uncle?"

"I'd rather you didn't. You see, Captain Ong and I are a lot alike. He comes from a family that has vast wealth and power, but he has to duck and weave like me. The only real difference is that my uncle is my commander in chief, and I have to follow orders. Davvd Ong takes orders from his superiors, who owe his family a lot, so he gets cushioned. May I have one of those fruit cocktails that Radnath seemed to like?"

Professor Radnath went through much of what Joe could tell him. Davvd sat and listened, and Radnath soaked it all up. "Of course, what has happened here has turned my and Singh's game upside down in many ways. I believe that the major gave the tribe the knives to give them a head start, which it did, and you have pushed them along too, but from what I see here, they didn't need much pushing. When I meet them, then I can assess them for myself. It was tragedy, you know. Singh and I believed we had made a kind of breakthrough."

"What about the earlier disasters?"

"Disasters? There was a line of inquiry which we terminated. It was used with great effectiveness against disease and brain damage, but we recommended it only be used in controlled, clinical conditions. The Valderian High Command took the results off planet, I believe. Major Schiff wouldn't have been informed about that. It was all on a 'need to know' basis. He was the paymaster, you understand, and liaison with Wu Ong Foundation. We went into panic mode when half of our subjects were killed off by the virus. 'When the buffalo tramples your garden, climb the highest tree.' We thought that we might be next, you understand. That virus had to come from somewhere, and the only real contact we had was with supply ships from Valderia."

Maggda was making noises about food, and Radnath was amused by Joe.

"So this is your chef?"

"He is a brilliant chef, aren't you, Joe?"

"I have been told I am, Miss Maggda."

"Joe has made a vegetable curry for you, professor, and for the rest of us, we have to make do with fish. It was caught yesterday in the lake. He does wonderful things with fresh fish. We have wine, which I brought in with me, but Ong here prefers Joe's Home Brew, which is a savage concoction of herbs, fruits, and spices straight out of the forest. He thinks that he is being a traitor if he doesn't enjoy what Joe makes for him."

So they ate lunch and watched the outside scanners do a tour of the immediate surrounds. It helped Schiff and Radnath become acquainted with the location. Across the snow, the hunters went out towards the thicker forest, armed with bows, and Radnath looked at Davvd.

"I know, I know, but they are out there with mouths to feed, and we are in here enjoying the comforts of high tech civilization. I had to do it."

"So maybe you can forgive me the knives, Captain?"

"I think I can drink to that, Major."

The day closed quickly and darkness fell, and they retired to the basic comforts of the rec room lounges and drank coffee and fruit juice.

In the morning, thought Davvd, we shall see what the tribe makes of these two.

Horatio Wu was discovering that he was not a born "committee" man. Now he was faced with the onerous task of being a diplomat, a chairperson, a calmer of tempers, and also supposed to be alert and functioning as a Fleet representative, albeit as a secondary role to that of the Federation. They moved in groups of twelve about the planet battle zones, inspected the carnage, filled the robotic scribes full of data, and when free, drank a lot and moaned to each other. Horatio learnt the basic rule of how not to sink into a morass of trivia and red tape, and he delegated a junior official to do much of the legwork for him. His delegate was a lover of the non-important fact and spent much of his time collecting facts that Horatio was sure would impress the Federation with his thoroughness in accumulating so much data, but it was of little here and now use. He received a short comm from his younger brother, which said, "Find Jutta Vogel on Valentine at Pushtak Prisoner of War Camp." There was no further information. Personal communications were limited. His eager beaver told him that he was going to visit Pushtak for an inspection. It was because they were anxious to exchange prisoners, and that was becoming a priority. His committee was examining the treatment of prisoners from both sides, and if Pushtak came up, he may as well find out what had prompted Jackson to contact him. The place was currently a quagmire of slush, mud, and sludge, and they couldn't get a local vehicle in there. The shuttle landing pad and airfield had flooded, and everything stopped. Horatio was not upset. The delegates were housed in the best hotels and ate well. The rest of the population were on the verge of starvation, but he didn't care that much. He ordered another drink and hoped the rain wouldn't stop.

Schiff and Radnath were having breakfast when Davvd appeared and sat with them. They expressed satisfaction. Joe had looked after them well. Davvd couldn't help but ask about Beebop. "I saw your adventure," said Schiff. "I felt sick when that worm got you and your sergeant, but have to admit that when you got yourselves out of there, I was relieved. Of course, you are going to blame Valderia for that, and I admit that it looks that way. Can I tell you in strictest confidence what happened? Professor Radnath comes into this, but he doesn't know how, so I will tell him. The beacon site was seeded with spawn twelve months earlier by a remote that wouldn't have been noticed anyway. It dropped the spawn close to the beacon, and then it was just a matter of waiting for the worms to mature. It takes about twelve months or so, old EST. When they began to disrupt the work of the beacon, then Valderian space forces slipped a freighter through loaded with Radnath's 'Neanderthals' from Harvallo. It would be illegal to ship those from Harvallo to E7 without formal clearance, but the High Command had taken most of Radnath's earlier 'subjects' off there for work off the planet."

Radnath was shocked.

"Where did they get taken? I understood they were to go back to Harvallo. We had told High Command that they were to be returned!"

"The army had use for them."

Radnath was silent.

Maggda said. "You know that we kept 447 here, don't you?"

"Oh yes. Thanks to you delaying his return, Miss Styxx, I was demoted and sent on active duty to Valentine, was shot through the body, liver, lung, and a rib. I have just been declared 'fit for duty' again. I was accused of losing that damned robot. My old enemy, Marshall Ghent, took great pleasure in rubbing that into me."

"Kurt, I think we both know that being a combatant isn't easy. You got yours, and I got mine, but I got away with it; you got shot up." said Ong.

"I envy you your freedoms, Captain. You at least can do your work for Fleet without getting criticized from the top all the time. I have to be aware that if I make big mistakes, then that will be seen as a reflection on the chancellor, and on Valderia. You don't seem to have those restraints."

"I have others. The Ong dynasty is like your chancellor or High Command. It doesn't like mistakes either. Since my mother and father and my wife died, I am like another Kurt Schiff, and it isn't easy."

Maggda coughed, and they looked up. "We had better get our winter gear on. I think Joe wants to get the trip started. How about it Professor?"

They got into their cold weather outfits, clambered on to the open loader, and Joe ferried them to the tribe's cave complex. The tribe had gathered and were waving bows and spears above their heads in greeting. Maggda waded through the snow to the cave's flat rock shelf entrance and embraced Annrath, who was bigger than before. "Oh, Annrath, my friend, how wonderful you look!"

"Tell me it is going to be a girl, so that he can blame me for not giving him a son to become a hunter, like him."

Davvd stood and told the tribe that he had friends who had come from the stars to see them, and then Radnath pushed back his hood. There was a growl from the tribe and the brandishing of knives and spears.

"They think you are the one who killed off the others back on E7, Professor. Just stand back and show them your hands are empty, and I will try to explain."

It wasn't easy. Davvd had to call on Joe for help a couple of times. Then Schiff asked Davvd to tell them that he was the one who had brought them here to save them from the sickness, and Radnath was not responsible. It was a moment that Maggda didn't want to happen, but it had. She suddenly grabbed Annrath's hand and turned to the hostile groups. "Please, Annrath wants to offer you food and shelter. Come inside in the warmth. She and her child are getting cold. Come in, come in!"

And it was over. They all went into the cave, and then Radnath wanted to know all about her bowls and the fires, the bows and the hunting, how they felt, and was anyone ill. They ate dried meat and tried to look as if it was the best that Blue Boar could serve up, and Radnath felt better. He took his personal scanner from his pocket and ran it over Annrath and asked Maggda if she wanted to know if it was a boy or girl that she carried. Maggda held Annrath's hand and asked her.

"Annrath, my friend, do you want to know if your child is a boy or a girl?"

"Can the man from the old world tell?"

"Yes, he can."

"Then I will wait. I don't want to know. Having a child is something that has to be left to the mother. I will see when the child leaves my body and suckles my breast. That is the time to know."

"I agree," said Maggda. "That is the time." Now, Annrath, my friend, I have something for you." She felt in her coat pocket and pulled out a simple, crocheted, baby's hat. "This is for your baby's head to keep it warm after it is born. You must keep it clean and dry. Your baby will love it."

Then Annrath hugged her and made Maggda wet-eyed, and they went out with Schiff and Radnath to watch the hunters use the bows and to try themselves, which filled them with a better understanding of the skills and strengths involved. It began to snow, and they said their goodbyes, and Joe ferried them back to the comfort of the base. Joe made hot drinks from something he declared was wine, which tasted of honey and herbs and made them feel very warm. Radnath made copious notes on his pod; Schiff looked at Maggda with different eyes.

"You know, Davvd Ong, that this woman is more than just a beautiful body that can sell underwear, don't you?"

"Oh yes, Kurt, I know. She has been a great help to me, and we have shared a lot."

Schiff looked at Maggda.

"Does he share your bed, Maggda?" She shook her head.

"No Kurt, he doesn't. No one shares that right now. I have my door locked, and he has his, and that is what we both want. But when we get this mess here stabilized, shall I say, then I shall give him the key."

Schiff laughed. She fixed him in her gaze.

"And you, Major, do you have someone to share your bed back home?"

He seemed a little surprised at the question. "No, Maggda, I don't. I have someone to share things with who has shared my bed, but she will never be mine, unfortunately."

"We are both lost souls then. May I give you a kiss to try and make up for subjecting you to all that humiliation after losing 447?"

"I would welcome it."

He thought that being kissed by Maggda Styxx was nearly worth Ghent's sarcasm. They talked into the night. Schiff became more human in their eyes and Ong and Maggda in his. It was a form of bonding that helped them all. Radnath held fears for the subjects that the army had spirited away, not to their home planet but to Aton knew where.

Maggda wrote her script for the documentary. She included Radnath and Schiff and hoped they would play ball. If she got this right, she was hoping Simon would write off her debt to Galactic. Don compiled data that gave her facts and figures on animal populations and the science of E5, so she had some hard facts to back up her story. With luck, things might work out right. Aton could well smile upon them all.

When the star people came again, they gave us weapons called 'bows,' and we can now kill game without the long spears. We have short spears to put into the bows that can be made to fly a long way. My woman, Annrath, has made friends with the star woman called Maggda, who brings her gifts and is waiting for the child, as we all are. Annrath has made bowls, which we can cook food in, and small ones to eat from. She is a special woman. She says she knows what to do. It is in her head. Winter is upon us, and the snow gets deeper. We have seen beasts in the far hills that have long noses and red hair and long teeth, and they would feed us all if we could kill one, but they are so large that we are afraid to shoot our bows at them. The deer are easier to kill. The great bears have gone into the caves up on the mountain slope and under rock. They sleep when the snow comes, Olann says. We have a warm home now. We have made the walls so thick with moss and rushes that no wind or snow can enter. The silver star man with no face who is called Joe made us two travois with the wood like two flat stems, and there is a frame. He calls them, 'sleds.' They slide across the snow and can carry our meat when we come back from hunting. He showed us how to make them. We can make our own now. The star man called Davvd showed us how to walk across the snow with special frames on his feet. He left them with us, so we can make our own. They teach us good ways. Then Davvd and Maggda brought the star man Radnath and another star man called Major, and they came to talk to us. We didn't trust Radnath, but Davvd told us he was going to help us and that he was pleased with Annrath. He told her he could tell her if the child would be a boy or a girl, but she told him she didn't want to know. She told him that it was not for him to know. It was women's business, and they went away, but Davvd says that they can be trusted. We trust Davvd and Maggda but no one else. Davvd says many more star people might come and not to be frightened or to try to kill them, because they are coming to help all of us. Annrath is wearing her special hat that Maggda gave her, and she says that when she wears it, Maggda can see into her head. She is mad, but I care for her. We want the child to be strong. There is not long to wait.

Jutta walked and sang. She sang some of the songs that she

had sung in the mess after special dinners and marching songs, and it helped them to walk. She was slimmer and strong, and even though the food was basic, it was a comfort to know that her guards were all eating the same food. They had suffered much. She had more letters from Jackson and begged message sheets from the sergeant, who laughed and squeezed her arm.

"He is special then, Lieutenant Vogel? I remember being young and in love too. May Aton get you back together soon."

Jutta's nose had healed, her black eyes were no more, and although she looked a little pale, she was pleased to see her face in the scratched steel mirror again. They had bartered for scissors, and now all had what they laughingly called "camp cuts." Then they were told.

"Tomorrow morning the observers from Galactic Federation will arrive. You will be called to parade when we ring the bell. You will stay in your billets after exercise. You will dress smartly. You will not talk unless asked to do so. Your billet will be inspected in the morning. It must be clean and tidy. Is that understood?"

"Yes sergeant."

"I want you girls to go back home and tell your loved ones that we have done our best to look after you. Can you do that?" She was a kind woman. Jutta understood her very well.

Horatio Wu arrived with four others on a Valderian aircraft that was a troop transport, and he had to tie himself into his canvas seat because the turbulence over the mountains was savage. He was feeling sick when they landed on a patch of packed snow outside the camp. He took it in and was pleased he wasn't under lock and key there. The camp commandant greeted them, saluted and led them into a long bare shed with two tables and chairs set up and explained the procedure.

She was a colonel in the Valentinian Volunteer Army, Female Division, and wanted to get back to her veterinary practice and was hoping to get shot of Pushtak as soon as possible. The bell rang; they formed up. The wind was keen, and they stamped feet to keep warm but were ordered to stand still. Then their sergeant came along the ranks and randomly picked five at a time, and when she had twenty, she dismissed the rest. Jutta, holding her breath, was the last to be picked. The parade was dismissed, and Jutta joined the line that wound into the shed. The delegates were seeing two at a time. They were asking the same questions. It was only when they had completed the formal checklist that they allowed the inmates a voice.

"Yes, we are well treated. No, we have no complaints. Yes, we have adequate food; we have not been ill treated; we have had adequate exercise every day. We have basic but adequate accommodation."

Jutta waited, then asked to speak to Horatio Wu. He was at another table and looked up when he heard his name. She would have recognized him as Jackson's brother because of the likeness, even though Horatio was older and wearing a very smart Fleet uniform. He finished his interview and beckoned her over. He was a very good-looking man and was looking bored. She sat, and he asked her what he could do for her. She told him about Jackson and how they had met on Valderia, how she and he were fond of each other, and that Jackson had been to her home, and could he, Horatio, tell Jackson that she was alive and well and missing him like a calf missed its mother's milk? He had a robotic scribe, and she knew that all this nonsense would be recorded, and that hopefully, it would get to Jackson. He leant back in his chair and looked at her. "I can see why he wants to know about you, Jutta Vogel. You are the prettiest soldier I've met so far. What do you want me to tell him?"

She blushed. "Tell him I love him."

He smiled. "Does he feel the same?"

"I just hope that he does."

Then she was ordered away. She wondered if she had been premature. Did she really love Jackson, or was it just the physical pleasure they both enjoyed with each other? Whatever happened, from now on, she felt committed.

The other delegates, touring the battlefields, found a troop of soldiers from the Valderian infantry in a dugout camp. Their officer was dead, and they were like somnambulists, cooking food in mess tins and scooping what clean water they could salvage from the snow. They spoke neither Valderian nor Galactic and looked at the delegates with dull eyes. Their rifles were thrown down in the slush, and they were dirty and had little equipment. They were rounded up and put on a troop carrier and lifted out to headquarters. The Valderian command wanted them to be taken to their base camp, but the delegates wanted more information, so they were put into a converted school building and fed and watered. Medical staff arrived and began to ask questions. It became interesting later.

Jackson rec'd a cryptic message from his brother.

"The girl is alive and well and says she loves you, Horatio."

It wasn't much, but Jackson went to his mother and hugged her.

"Jutta says she loves me!"

"At times of stress, Jackson, young women have been known to be extravagant with their emotions. Wait until she gets back to her home and then you will really know. Poor girl, she has been torn from her family and you and is lost and alone. Send her a message and tell her that you need to hold her and want her."

"Is that all?"

"If she is the kind of girl you say she is, she will read between the lines. Have faith in Aton, Jackson. You will be together soon. Now I must talk to Crystal. She is making me a jacket covered with butterflies. The colors are wonderful!"

"Yes, mother." He left and went up to the comm room and sent the message.

He wanted to say, "I love, I love you, I love you . . ." but didn't. His mother was often a better judge of his emotional state than he was. He would wait.

Schiff, Maggda, Davvd, and Radnath had had an excellent dinner. Radnath thought he had never eaten such wonderful curry. Schiff wanted to buy Joe. Davvd wanted to get back to reality and forced them into a meeting of the minds. It was difficult.

"Professor, what would you want to do with your subjects now? Major, what have you to do to convince your superiors that you have done all you can to straighten this mishap out? Maggda, what would you like to see the Federation, Wu, and Ong foundations do now?"

"This is a hypothetical situation, isn't it, Captain?" asked Radnath.

"Not for Major Schiff, I think. Is it, Kurt?"

"Well, Davvd, I can do nothing until I see which way the wind blows from High Command. Then, I shall bend like the reed and lean. When these holos and tri-dees go out, then the Federation will no doubt do two things. Send an expert to check up on the expert, and Radnath here will be put under the lights, and no doubt you will be asked a lot of questions. High Command will meet and try to cover their tracks, as usual, and we will all have to decide what we did right or wrong.

"Coming here has taught me a great deal. You have to understand that I never saw the 'tribe' until I met them here. I paid bills, filed Radnath and Singh's reports and sent the ones they had flagged to High Command and the Foundation. Now, I can see the dilemma we all face."

"And the tribe faces, Major," said Maggda a little bitterly. "We are dealing with a group of human beings here. Real people with real personalities, however we may think of them as being no more than Neanderthals. They have their needs as we do. I feel very strongly that we have to, well, protect these people. We subjected them to terrible emotional stress, and we owe them."

"I am to blame. That is what you all feel, don't you?" said Radnath. "Singh and I never intended harm, quite the reverse. We wanted these people to realize their potential faster than waiting a million years or so. The planets they came from are not unlike this moon. With a population pressing ahead and producing individuals like Annrath, they would have reached a point where they could have an agricultural revolution within their lifetimes, not thousands of years. The planet would be productive and support a great variety of life. A cultural revolution would follow. Contact with off-planet cultures would be positive, once they were sophisticated enough to grasp it. The research was based on them realizing their own potential faster, not to have outside influences pushing them along paths they might regret later."

"We are to blame for interference too, aren't we?" asked Maggda.

"I think, Maggda, that when the virus hit the original group, we were all to blame for wrecking the original research. I transported them out of there to here. Radnath and Singh were kept in the dark. They thought they had fouled up somewhere and that Ong Wu Foundation had stepped in, or Valderia High Command. It was a question of putting these survivors onto a moon or planet where they couldn't contaminate humans. E5 was within a workable distance. I sent them on a robotic controlled ship to avoid human contact. When they were discovered, and Don had notified the authorities, then I did my best to get them back, and you hijacked that attempt."

"I am sorry, Kurt,"

"How were you to know what was happening? I didn't know. We were all trying to put things straight, one way or the other."

"They should not be moved now," said Radnath.

"They would resist any move right now," said Davvd.

"Fight like wolves to stop it," said Maggda.

"What we have left is to declare these people as either 'refugees' or 'displaced persons.' The Galactic Federation would have to act if it received a formal request. Radnath has done his research to the point where he was going to put them back into their original environment and monitor from outside anyway. Am I right, Professor?"

"Almost, Davvd. We did have other controls, but that is

nonsense now. As far as I am concerned, they could easily be left here. It makes the moon a non-sterile environment as far as humans go, but we have a case for settling them here. There is enough diversity amongst them to dispel fears of too close genetic mishaps. In any case, we would monitor them from here, I would imagine."

Maggda laughed. "Haven't we done well! We have one long-term research program wrecked; we have a whole moon, devoted to natural development, now of no further use for that; we have a tribe of people totally displaced and having to survive out here with not much to back them up; we have Galactic Federation going to be very unfriendly; and On Wu going to pull the plug on funding. Yeah, guys, I think we should all be given a medal!" She went out to get her holos and tri-dees working and Joe and Don went with her. The men sat and thought about it.

Schiff said, "I have no further use here. We have a situation out of my hands, and I will have to go back and report. It won't affect anyone, except maybe someone in High Command or a subcommittee somewhere in Ong Wu Foundation."

"Can you bear to do a piece for Maggda? She wants you and Radnath to appear as concerned parties, and it wouldn't hurt. Galactic Media has a lot of pull, and she is not silly, so you wouldn't appear in a bad light. She is working on the sympathy angle, so anyone who has been directly concerned is good for her story."

"What about you, Captain Ong?"

"My terms of employment with Fleet rule that out. As you know, I don't give interviews but will happily make statements that Fleet approve of. Maggda knows that."

"So why should I have my face on the media?"

"If you choose to say no, then we would all understand. Your uncle might not like it?"

"Why bait the bull when it is calmly grazing." said Radnath, and they all laughed.

"I think we just have to wait," said Davvd. "All our hands are

302

tied. Let Maggda do her big publicity bit, and wait. Whatever happens, I feel that we all tried to put things right, and circumstances were against us."

"May Aton smile on us," said Schiff.

Maggda was pushing Schiff into a corner. "Kurt, you have a real chance here to make things straight and to heck with your uncle. He wanted you to sort things, and you have, and can, on your terms. When he sits up there in his palace, how can he know what is going on except by hearsay? I think you should do this broadcast not just for me or Galactic, but because if you don't, no one will know that you were the meat in the sandwich. Do your thing and I think you will feel better for it."

He looked at her in her tailored denims, looking like someone working on a wrecking crew, and had to smile. "Do you know a woman called Suzanne?"

She shook her head. "Kurt, if you and Radnath get your say in first, you have the advantage. You are here, your critics are off planet, so what will the mass of the public believe?" Don't just scuttle off and hope Uncle leaves you alone."

Joe came in, and she went out with him to fix location shots.

He went to Radnath. They discussed it, and Radnath said, "I have nothing to lose, Singh has nothing to lose, and you have nothing to lose. Your position makes it very hard for your uncle to publicly blame you when he was giving the orders."

They took their places, told their story as Maggda directed, and when she replayed the footage, they had to agree that they came out of the mess smelling much sweeter.

Radnath was the "expert" who explained the nature of the research, Schiff filled in the Ong Wu background, and Davvd did a voice-over to link the segments. E5 provided a wonderful scenic backdrop, and the tribe went out hunting in the snow with their bows and spears and heavy fur coats to create a romantic interlude.

Maggda was pleased. "If that doesn't kill them what will guys? Now we have to get that packed and off to Galactic, while we make a lot of short stuff, tribal background, get some individual, personality stuff, get Annrath to provide the female, mother to be side, chart her progress . . . I have a lot of work to do."

Don and Davvd saw Schiff and Radnath off the next morning. They uplifted the holo cubes and records up to the passing freighter enroute to Mars and waited.

Maggda and Davvd sat in the rec room and had a shot of a Joe Brew while waiting for their dinner. They sat on the battered lounge, and he put his arm around her. "You did well, you know that?"

"I try, Davvd, I try."

"You think this publicity angle will work?"

"What do we have to do to put the squeeze on the Valderians? Can't send you off there with an intergalactic cruiser, and we can't threaten them. All we've got, Master of the Universe, is the truth. Simon, my devious boss, was absolutely straight about one thing. He never, ever put out anything that wasn't totally fact checkable. I think he would have said, "Cover your back," but he could never be accused of rumor and innuendo. That's why Galactic is where it is. People trust it, and let's face it, if Fleet was having doubts, I wouldn't be here, would I?"

"I'll drink to that."

"Well, we still have things to do. It will take Simon and the team a couple of days to get that mass of information edited and made to look pretty."

"What have you had Joe making when he wasn't working flat out on holos and tri-dees?"

"Oh, just a little gift for Annrath."

"You, Styxx, are a big, soft, sentimental, marshmallow. You know that? So what is it?"

"A cradle."

"A cradle."

"Yes, you know, with rockers, and you put the baby in it and rock it back and--"

"I do know what a cradle is, Maggda".

"Well, you know, I just thought she would use it and like it . . . and you *are* right, I am a big, soft, sentimental marshmallow."

"Give me a big, wet, Joe Brew kiss, and then we can go eat. You keep surprising me, Styxx. Life here with you is never dull."

"Thank you, Lord of the Universe. Compliments I like."

They went to eat.

On Valentine, the medical team assessing the health and welfare of the combatants were doing scans of the company of the infantry discovered as lost souls in the forward trenches. Strange results came up in the brain responses. All of them had tiny nano implants. Their dead officer had a Pod and a pad, tuned to a frequency that could only be used to activate the implants. The Galactic Federation made records, and sent a very stiff request to Valderia with a "Please explain." Valderia ignored the first request, so they sent another, adding that failure to answer would result in the closing down of all Valderian industry on the planet immediately and the arrest of all senior officers and officials on the planet. Valderia replied that the Federation had no right to do either. They were there quite legitimately to restore the political balance, and that was all they were doing. Galactic Federation sent a very large Fleet battleship and six cruisers to Valentine and told the senior officers that they would be taken off the planet within the next two planet cycles and sent to New Babylon for interrogation. Valderia remained silent for one cycle.

Jutta received Jackson's message with mixed feelings. He hadn't told her he loved her. She felt betrayed. She had given him her heart, and he was playing hard to get. Was that it? Or was there something that she didn't know about? She was short tempered, and the old sergeant made her stay back after parade.

"Are you sick, Lieutenant? If you are, I need to know. The way things are going 'out there,' the last thing we want here is for you to get sick. Fleet has a battleship up there which could blow us all to pieces with one missile, and if that isn't enough to keep me awake at night, you go and get sick."

"I am sorry, Sergeant. I am not sick."

"You look sick, and you act sick."

"I am depressed, not sick."

"Just sick in the head?"

"No, Sergeant, just sick in the heart."

The lady laughed and squeezed Jutta's arm. "You know that I have a daughter, just like you? Heart sick will cure itself. I can't send you to the medical center, Lieutenant. They would laugh at me. Now do you want to talk to a mother?"

The Federation had arranged an exchange of prisoners. Small groups went and came and went. The forward troops out in the mud came in first; then slowly, it came down to the petty and the ordinary and the administrative souls. Eventually Jutta's barracks were cleared, and she was put on a truck and taken to a landing pad where a Valderian troop transport took her and her companions back to the Valderian Command. Up in orbit, the sensors kept sharp eyes on the movements. They watched to see that there were no sudden buildups, no marching columns going the wrong way, no machines building barricades or bunkers. Over the battlefields the birds began to sing, and Red Jane plowed a whole large paddock in one day, and Ramona gave the big animal as much care as Jutta had done.

Captain Johann Brant was sick. He had the shakes. He had shared a hole in the snowy ground for two days and nights with his dead friend when they had all but been wiped out in an ambush. He was back at Barracks Ten and had been to the medical center to be assessed. The major looked him over, scanned him in all directions, asked him questions, gave him drugs and wanted to send him on leave, but he protested that he had nowhere to go, no family other than his friends in the barracks and that he would be all right.

She contacted "Compassion and Comfort" and spoke to Trudi.

"Suzanne is on leave. She is seeing Dr. Reismann and won't be back for days. I have Veronica free. How old is your client? Young? Not terribly young?" She gave Trudi the details.

"Send us his file, will you? I can speak to Veronica. The usual fees, yes, and I will get back to you."

Mrs. Vera Sandler was nervous. She had made an appointment to see Dr. Reismann at the Reismann Clinic to get her body assessed. She was not a young woman but had kept herself pretty trim, she thought. Her husband, that miserable bastard, had taken off with his assistant, a younger woman with long legs and a crooked smile that had captivated him. He had paid handsomely for his infidelity, which ruined the business, and Vera had piled the credits and wanted another chance on life.

The clinic had discrete offices and grey marble floors and bright plas-steel décor, and the girls wore smocks of dazzling white and, Vera Sandler thought, very little else. She had paid her "assessment" fee, which was enormous, and waited. Finally she was ushered into the doctor's rooms. One of the girls took her details, again, and led her through to the clinically clean and light "Assessment" room. The doctor wasn't a young man. He wore a white lab coat and looked very "professional," and she was nervous about that, but he was all smiles and generated warmth. He told her not to be nervous, and then Rebecca took her into a cubicle, showed her the robe and left her to undress. She stepped out, naked under the flimsy paper, feeling vulnerable.

"Please, Mrs. Sandler, could you just stand here? On this platform. It will rotate very slowly, and we will scan your contours, and that will go into the computers. Then I will examine you, and we can then see what it is we can do for you. I have to touch you, you understand, but the girls are here, so don't be nervous. I examine thirty women or more every week. Good, now we have your essential details in the records. Could you remove the robe? Rebecca will take that, thank you, Rebecca. Now could you put your hands on your head and stay like that?"

He stood to her right and looked carefully at her breasts. He had small sensors on his fingertips, and he felt her breasts, lifting them and weighing them in his hands.

"Bethany, right breast 7.5, left breast 7.00. Flex: right flex, 8.4, left 8.3."

"Nipples." He explored her nipples. "Now, do you want these a little more pert? Sharper looking? Sharper, I think, thank you, Bethany. Now stomach. You can put your hands down now."

He ran his hands down over her body. "We will tighten this up a little, Mrs. Sandler, so don't worry. Now, your pubic area. Are you happy with the hair? We do remove it if you want, on a permanent basis. Now, I am going to assess your labia." He slipped his hand between her legs, and she blushed as he gently touched her.

"Balanced lips, Bethany. You will see that it is a minor adjustment, but it will be much "neater." Now turn around please."

He ran his hands down her back and over her buttocks and down her thighs. "Good tone, just a tighten up, I think, Bethany. Now put the robe back on, please, Mrs. Sandler. Now when I asked about the pubic area, you may have doubts, so Rebecca, will you show Mrs. Sandler, please?"

Rebecca opened her smock, and her pubic area was smooth and clean and like that of a young girl.

"You may have a man who is attracted by this very youthful appearance, and most men do appreciate it. Rebecca's breasts are what yours will look like once we have completed the rebuild. Now you can see what your nipples will look like. Can you turn around, Rebecca? Now Rebecca's bottom is what yours will look like after we tuck and tighten. Will you be happy with that? Thank you, Rebecca." Now, Mrs. Sandler, you have slight spinal curvature. We will adjust that, but you have to adopt a very upright posture. Good posture gives your breasts a lift, you understand, and makes breathing easier. Do you have an exercise program? The girl at the desk can give you details. Now you can get dressed, and we will see you when you are told to come in. Do you have any questions? You can contact us if you think of any later. Thank you for using the clinic, Mrs. Sandler. We look forward to making you what you wish to be."

Suzanne came out of the cubicle and stood on the platform. Reismann looked at her. "Are you sure you need us, Suzanne? You look magnificent. Your breasts are wonderful. Just a tighten up, maybe? Can we just tuck the bottom a little to keep it the way it is? I love the way you look, Suzanne. If you want to come and work for me, then just let me know." He felt and lifted her breasts. "I wish all our clients could be made like you. Would you like to have lunch with me? I need a break." They went to Bruno's.

Captain Brant met Veronica in the square. She had on a suit of aubergine silk, beautifully tailored, a crisp, pale blue blouse, a gold medallion on a chain around her slender neck. High heeled shoes and sheer stockings of synthetic spider silk. She held out a pale blue gloved hand and said, "Veronica."

He was stunned by her incredible, clean good looks.

"Johann."

She reached for his hand.

"I need my coffee. If I don't get my fix about now I crumble. I know where to take you."

She spoke to the human waitress.

"Gretchen, my usual blend, and the same for my friend, please. And do you have those little pastries I had last week? Now, Johann, tell me about it." He talked, and the little medallion listened. "I want to take you to my apartment. Please come. It isn't far to walk."

They walked hand in hand and up the steps to the apartment beside the river. There were fresh flowers in vases and open windows, and the breeze was gently stirring the subtle floral curtains.

"Just sit there, Johann, and I will be back in a minute." She went to the bathroom and then beckoned him into the bedroom. He followed her in.

"Sit there; can you smell the flowers?"

She undressed with a delicate skill and took her suit and hung it in the wardrobe. Her underwear was very fitting and lacy, and her stockings were held by very old-fashioned garters, which she left on. She stood in her stocking feet and smiled at him.

"Get undressed and get into bed, Johann, or I will get cold. He took off his clothes and threw them on the chair, and she got into bed and turned on her stomach. "Rub my back, Johann, please. I have an old injury there, so be gentle. He rubbed her back and slipped his hand over her rounded, firm bottom. He kissed her neck, and the scent of her hair went into his nostrils, along with the drug that relaxed him and made him susceptible. She turned her back to him. "Hold my breasts, please. Just hold me and keep me warm for a little while; can you do that?" Her breasts were firm and pointed, and her nipples were small cones and perfectly shaped. "Kiss my neck, I like that. Now move your hand down . . . yes, now gently, yes, gently." He and she made love three times, and he talked to her about his experiences. He felt he could tell her anything, and they lay, warm and satiated for a short while. Then she looked at her time band and slid out of bed. "Oh, by Aton's breath, Johann, I shall be late. I have to meet my mother. You can't stay here much longer because she will want to come back here. Take a shower and leave everything clean and tidy when you leave." She went into the bathroom and emerged a little later looking fresh with her hair arranged, and then he watched her dress, and she was so methodical and tidy that she radiated calm. "Now kiss me, before I put on my lip color." They kissed, and she left quickly, waving a hand at him as the door closed. He had a quick shower, pulled the sheets back up on the bed and dressed. He wandered back to the cab rank and took a robocab back to the barracks. He felt strangely calm and yet elated.

The major in the med center smiled when she received the report from Veronica. She was wondering how Captain Brant would respond to treatment now. Veronica called the housekeeper and told her to clean the Compassion and Comfort apartment and to close the windows when she left. It was a beautiful day, and Aton smiled on everyone.

Schiff went back to Valderia. He was granted leave and didn't know what to do with it. After the third day the broadcasts began, and Simon and Maggda had cooked up a publicity storm. There he was, there was Radnath, and there were the lost souls from E7, and it was a heartwarming story. He emerged as the hero of the piece, and E5 as the only place these displaced persons could go, and despite the fact that it violated the pristine sovereignty of the moon, there was nowhere else to send them to save their lives. The scenery was exploited; the robotic drones flew and gave wonderful coverage from the air; and it made the top of the newscasts.

The troop withdrawal and the intervention of Galactic Federation on Valentine came second.

Schiff awaited the thunder and lightning, but there was a deathly hush. He didn't contact his uncle, just waited. He went shopping and bought Maria a present. Maria saw and heard of his return and asked to see him. They met in town in civilian clothes, and he greeted her with a warm kiss, and she hugged him back.

"I am so pleased to see you back here and well, and now I know what you were going through. I wish I could have done something for you."

"Maria, it wasn't that bad! I met with Davvd Ong and Professor Radnath, and I had long talks, and we had no choice but to do what we could for the so-called, Neanderthals on the moon. I didn't know, but Maggda Styxx was there with Davvd Ong, working for Galactic Media, and she set up the broadcasts; that is why she stars in them."

"She didn't give you any samples of Second Skin, did she?"

He laughed. "Shall we eat? What would you say if I asked you to come back with me to my apartment after dinner?"

"If I had enough to drink I would probably say yes. Are you going to seduce me, Kurt?"

"Would you mind if I tried?"

"That depends on how you do it. Flowers are good. Some ancient poet once said, "Candy is dandy, but liquor is quicker. Had you heard that before?"

"Let's eat. Is it still the Blue Boar, or do you have somewhere else in mind?"

"Buy me a long gin and tonic at the Blue Boar. Order me something I don't recognize, buy me wine, tell me I look wonderful, and I might go back to your shack with you."

"That sounds good to me. Now, did you know that Jutta will be back soon? She was exchanged and should be home shortly."

"We can drink to that, then!"

They idled at the Blue Boar. Maria drank three stiff gins and then a wine that made her feel a bit disorientated. He made her eat and drink a lot of water. She was feeling high but happy. They finished the meal with coffee and then took a robocab to his apartment. The autolights came on as they entered, and his music comm played cello music. She had never heard it before.

"Do you know who is playing, Maria?"

She shook her head.

"Freya Schiff. Once the most celebrated cellist on four planets. She is my mother."

She looked at him without saying anything.

"My mother, Maria. All these years I thought she was dead, and do you know what? She lives just across the city. I have had a reunion with her, and I was so taken aback, I nearly cried."

She came over to him and put her arms round him. "It must have been a shock."

"Oh, it was, but now we are reunited, I feel better. Would you like to meet her?"

"Can we go a bit slower? Can we sit for five minutes?"

"I don't mean now! When we can arrange it."

He went over to the lounge and sat beside her, kissed her and felt her warmth, and she responded in a way that surprised them both. "I do have a present for you, but I don't know if you will like it. Just follow me." He took her hand and led her to the bedroom with the flowered sheets on the bed and flowers in a tall vase on the dressing table. She hung back. "I wouldn't hurt you, Maria, you know that. Now close your eyes and tell me if I did the wrong thing."

He took the box with Second Skin underwear out of the drawer and gave it to her.

She looked at him very hard. "I suppose you will want me to model this now?"

"Not if you don't want to."

"I thought you were going to get me drunk, but now this!" She went into the bathroom, and he heard her laugh. He sat and waited while the cello played.

"Close your eyes until I tell you to look."

"I have my eyes closed." He heard her come into the room.

"Open your eyes."

She was lovely and slim, and the underwear let her skin glow through. She was still wearing her dress shoes, and she turned on her toes to give him a three hundred and sixty degree view. She had chosen the cream set, and it enhanced her natural warm skin color.

"Will you wear the blue ones next?"

"Anything you say, master." She went out and returned dressed in the blue. It had more lace and was very fetching. "You know that Jackson Wu bought Jutta underwear just like this, don't you?"

"I guessed."

"Then she took it off and went to bed with him, did you know that?"

"What are you going to do?"

"If you go and get undressed and get into bed, I will show you."

"Is that an order?"

"There are occasions, Major, when a junior officer is forced to take command when a senior officer shows he is incapable."

"I agree." He took off his clothes, and she skinned out of the underwear. He turned down the lights, and they held each other in the floral patterned bed sheets, and she took charge of him. They made love in a way which was an experience for both of them, a getting to know you, sometimes hesitant manner, but they enjoyed each other, and she held him close and whispered, "I wondered if you ever would Major."

"I wondered if you wanted me to, Lieutenant."

"Can we sleep now? I think the drink is getting to me."

It was late morning when they finally got showered and breakfasted and back to the barracks, and her commanding officer was sour.

"Don't let it happen again, Schmitt. I can always find a replacement. A tour out on Valentine wouldn't hurt you, and you might smarten up."

"Of course, sir, anything you say, sir," didn't endear herself to him.

Jutta went out from Valentine on a troop ship that bore a much happier group than had come in. She and a host of others were sent home. It was cheaper to have them housed back on Valderia than out in the wilds of Valentine. She was given compassionate leave and went to see Maria before she left the barracks.

They hugged each other, and Jutta had wet eyes.

"Maria, you don't know how much I missed you and this dusty hole of a place! Have you seen Major Schiff? I was so worried about him up on Valentine. We thought he was going to die, did you know that?"

Ah, yes, I have seen him." Jutta looked at her.

"Is that all you can say? What's happened?"

Maria pulled up her skirt.

"Second Skin! Where did you get? . . ."

"Um, Kurt and I, we have been seeing each other, and he bought me these . . ."

Jutta laughed. "And you did what Jutta Vogel did with Jackson, didn't you? You went to bed with him, you vixen!"

"Oh Jutta, it kind of happened. I did have a few gin and tonics and some wine, but I wanted to anyway. He makes me feel . . . well, he is quite a different man when . . . well, you know!"

"You love him?"

"I don't know. I felt sorry for him. I think I wanted to mother him. He makes me feel important, and he is kind, and he treats me like a lady."

Jutta laughed. "I do love you, Maria. Just fancy you and Kurt Schiff! . . ."

"I know. You don't have to make such a fuss about it. How could I say no when he buys me this underwear? It was worth putting it on just to take it off again!"

"Vixen! Now I have to go home."

"Jackson?"

"I told him I loved him, and he told me he missed me."

"Oh!"

"I must go home. I want my mother to hug me." She left and headed home. She had to smile; fancy Maria and Kurt Schiff?" It occurred to her that Maria might well end up as "Empress of Valderia." Now that *was* worth taking off her undies.

Jackson had sent a message from Belvedere to his mother asking if he could bring Jutta to see her, and his mother had told him to bring her. She was very interested in this girl.

"I wonder what she will be like, Crystal?"

Crystal smiled at her and said, "If Jackson loves her, then you will love her, Sylvia." With that kind of logic, there could be no argument.

Jackson took leave from Belvedere and took passage on a Wu starliner to Valderia and booked into the Palace. He had not told Jutta that he was coming. The city was busy. There were a lot of uniforms coming and going and some turmoil. Troops recalled from the Valentine conflict were being pushed around to barracks. The local newscasts were full of the conflict between Valderia and the Galactic Federation, with all the usual belligerent noises about the sanctity of Valderia being compromised by illegal, outside interference. Jackson wondered how his brother was doing up on Valentine. He had seen Jutta that was for sure. He bought her a jeweled heart to wear on her Maxxi dress and a potted plant for her mother and a big new leather apron for her father. He had run out of ideas without Jutta. He hired a car and programmed it for her home in Grunvald.

Jutta came home to much hugging and kissing and comment about her hair, and they fed her and let her sleep in her old bed and didn't ask about Jason, because she hadn't said a word about him. Her mother could sense that she was depressed but didn't know what to do, except be a mother. The car appeared in the bumpy driveway, and Gerhardt went to meet it. Wulf wagged his tail and licked Jackson's hand. He shook hands with Gerhardt, and then they hugged.

"I am pleased to see you, boy. Now come in. Does she know you are coming? She hasn't told us. She is very depressed about something."

The long warm kitchen, her mother and the smell of cooking, the flowers in the little vase on the white and blue tablecloth, and then there she was, with her hair looking like a mad haystack, and she was in his arms and kissing him, and her mother cried a little. It took a while, but it became very clear that he had missed her so much that he just had to come to see her and to heck with his studies and his father. They laughed at the gifts and thanked him, and he told them he didn't know what to give them without her advice, and then he gave Jutta the jeweled heart. She cried and hugged him and kissed him, and they had wine, then he asked her father if he could take her to meet his mother and father. They looked at each other.

"If that is what she wants, boy, then of course you can." They sat in the parlor.

"I have just come home, Jason. I want to feel at home for a while before the army sends me off somewhere terrible. Do you understand?"

"Would you feel better if I said that I love you and want you to marry me and to hell with waiting?"

"But your parents will go mad."

"I've thought about it. I can go on with my studies. We can live close to Belvedere. You can study with me. What would you want to do? You could do medical programming for robot surgeons."

She kissed him. "Stay here with us for a few days. Your "Jutta Palace" room is free. Give me some time to think it over. Everything is happening in a rush."

"You said you loved me."

"Give me a little time." There was a silence he couldn't fill.

"Maria, my best friend, is having an affair with Kurt Schiff."

"By Aton's breath, I hope she knows what she is doing."

"You think he treated you badly. Well, he was just doing what he had to do because his uncle was breathing down his neck. Get to know him, and he is a very kind man underneath all that bullshine. Believe me. He worried about me when I was with him on Valentine, did you know that? He was nearly killed. We were posted to the same part of the battlefield." She was very quiet.

"I was worried about you too, Jutta."

"I know." She gave him a quick kiss.

"Let's take some lunch, and we can drive round the lakes. They are beautiful. If you are a really good boy, I might let you kiss my rosebuds!"

"Is that a promise?"

"I told you, but you have to be good."

The Galactic Federation had ordered the Valderian High

Command to send representatives to a meeting on Old Earth. It was going to be held in the Arctic Temperate Zone city of New London. The old London had long succumbed to global warming and the rising of the seas a thousand years earlier. They were reluctant but had little choice. There were noises about them putting troops into battle with electrodes in their brains, and they had to find answers. Blood would be spilled, metaphorically, and both sides knew it. Horatio Wu was asked to attend as an observer. He was not happy but was under a spotlight and had nowhere to run to.

Davvd Ong and Maggda were relaxing after a long, hard day. They had made a great deal of footage of the tribe and had focused on Annrath. She was very large, and Maggda thought that she would be having the child any day. She wanted to get her into the center to be looked over by the medical robot, but Davvd didn't.

"She is under enough stress, Maggda. What with having us putting her through that meeting and greeting, winter, and the holo cameras . . . just let her rest a bit."

"What if she has the child in the middle of the night, and we can't get to see her . . . ?

"She will have the child in the middle of the night, and there are other women of her kind right there who have probably delivered more babies that you have. So how many have you delivered?"

"One hundred and twenty-three."

"I love the way you lie Styxx."

"Well, this is a woman thing, isn't it?"

"I know you care, and you know I care, so just leave it for a bit. When she goes into labor, the sensors and cameras up in the cave will let us know, and Joe and Don are watching those screens like hawks."

"I wonder what Schiff is doing. I felt sorry for him. Did you know that?"

"His High Command is going to get its backside kicked if Galactic Fed has its way."

"Maybe the whole of Valderia needs a reshuffle."

"Maybe, what are we going to drink? That seems to me to be a priority right now."

Kurt Schiff was waiting for the axe to fall. The silence from up above and his uncle's total lack of any communication was making him jumpy. He fled into Maria's warm embrace and made love to her in an excited and passionate way that frightened her a little. "Is there something I should know?"

He lay on his back, and she put her head on his chest and hugged him.

"It is all too quiet, Maria. I haven't even been given a post. No orders, no job to do. I think I am on leave, but no one has told me. My damn uncle hasn't so much as growled at me. No one has mentioned all that publicity we stirred up on E5, do you know that?"

"You came out of that like a hero, you know that?"

"Thanks to Maggda Styxx. She is a clever girl apart from looking good wearing next to nothing."

"You noticed, did you?"

"And you. You look good just wearing nothing, so who needs the underwear?"

"I do. Get me a red set."

"What will you do for me?"

"Can't give you any more than what you get now, you beast!"

"How about just once again, then?"

The comm tone sounded, and he cursed and answered it. He swore again and came back, knelt by the bed and kissed her.

"I have to go. Someone overheard me. General Voight wants to see me. He is close to the old man, so I had better find out what is going on. You stay there and take a rest."

"Are you coming back?"

"No, I think you had better get back to barracks before too long, or your beloved leader will get nasty."

She heard him go and lay back in the bed and dozed. She had a rude wakening when the robot cleaner buzzed into the room, followed by Schiff's housekeeper wielding a duster. Maria climbed out of bed naked and smiled and received a frosted look. She went, got dressed and left for work. The housekeeper sniffed. This one was young and very pretty, and she was army too. Was that a good thing or not?"

Schiff saluted and was told to sit. General Voight wasn't young, but it was hard to tell just how old he was. He was still hard and lean and grizzled.

"What do you know, Schiff?"

"Know, sir?"

"Been getting a lot of publicity from Galactic. What does that mean?"

"Had no choice, but it worked out well for all of us, I think."

"Worked out well for you. We have been getting some flack up top. Galactic Federation doesn't like us, and they are getting very heavy. The old man isn't happy, you know that?"

Schiff felt suddenly lighter and had the strange urge to laugh. "Well, sir, you and your boys have had it coming. You went off the rails and took over a dangerous research program that should have been left to die, but you got carried away with it. Now we have to explain what a few hundred or so infantry are doing with remotes in their heads and fighting for us against so-called rebels without knowing why. Poor bastards. High Command has shit on all the conventions, and now you are getting to get shat on, and it is about time. I got to be used as the scapegoat, and I had had enough of it. Radnath gets hung out to dry, and Singh, and me, but thanks to the media getting involved, we get to explain. Now it's up to you."

"You forget yourself, Schiff!"

"I don't think so. All this is going to come out when the Galactic Fed has that meeting, and you boys get asked some serious questions."

"You think so?"

"I know so. If they call me, I have to tell them the truth. Radnath will have to tell the truth. Someone will have to tell the truth about putting influenza virus on E7. That should make you feel good."

"Your uncle is going to step down."

"What?"

"Your uncle has told High Command that he is considering it. He can duck and run. We have to face an inquiry. Galactic Federation is moving towards that now. We have all been 'grounded,' Schiff. Go outside, and Fleet will turn us into stardust, we have been told."

"Can they do that?"

"We didn't answer Galactic Federation's last ultimatum with regard to Valentine. They shut the door on us. Now, they have us in their sights, and we just wait and see."

"So, let's get to the point. What do you want with me?"

"Much as I dislike you, Schiff, you are pretty well next in line to the throne. The public will love you after all this publicity. The High Command and the Governing Council would vote you in without a dissenting vote. You come across as a 'clean skin.' We get to clear our names, you get to be head of planet, and . . ."

"And you pull strings, and I get told what to think and do . . . No deal, Voight. If I am going to sit up there, then I pull the strings and no one else."

"Right now, no one is pulling anything. I was asked to sound you out. You don't want a deal, fine with us. We will come out on top anyway. We always have, Schiff, we always have! By the way, how is your mother?"

Maria slid out of bed and naked, went to the kitchen and punched "coffee" on Schiff's console. He was still sleeping. She wandered back into the bedroom and slipped in beside him and rubbed his chest, then settled down with him. He reached for her and fondled her bottom.

"What were you telling me about your mother?"

"Hmm?"

"You said your mother lives here, didn't you?"

He sat up and scratched his head.

"Yes, she does. Close. In Valhalla. Why the questions?"

"Sorry. I didn't mean to sound like that. I just wondered if you see her now."

"I try. She is still very much in demand for her playing. I hated her, you know that? I couldn't get over the fact that she just, well, abandoned me. Only child and she left me to fate and Aton's luck."

"I want to meet her."

"Are you sure?"

"You don't still hate her, do you?"

"No, I actually feel quite warm about her now. She may have been a pretty hopeless mother, but she is a remarkable woman. I have forgiven her. I understand now what drove her. I suppose she never really bonded with me. She was bonded to her cello."

"Can I meet her?"

"Only if you really want to."

"I just want to see where the little Kurt sprang from."

He laughed. "Are you making coffee?"

"Can't you smell it?"

"Make us some breakfast, and I will see if we can visit her."

The apartment smelled of roses, and Maria could smell credits, not just flowers. Taste is money, and this place reeked of it. When she met Freya Schiff she knew what Kurt had been saying. His mother was beautiful even at her age. She had a stately aristocratic air about her, but was warm enough. She gave Maria a kiss on the cheek and stood back and looked at her. Maria felt that she was blushing.

"Does he tell you that you are a lovely young woman? If he doesn't, then he should. Now, where did he find you? No, don't tell me. Army. You look like a junior officer that decorated his office, and he kept falling over you until one day he bothered to really look at you, am I right?"

Maria did blush.

"Yes, mother. I didn't realize how fond of her I was until I got wounded, and then she was the only one who bothered to care for me."

"Now, Kurt, you had very good medical care, didn't you?"

"Ah, but what Maria gave me was from the heart, mother, not from science."

"Is that what they call it these days?

"Can we change the subject, mother? Maria isn't used to this kind of verbal gamesmanship."

"Maria, I am sorry. I follow his career with some pride, but he is a difficult man, and you know that his uncle is chancellor, don't you? That is a distinct disadvantage if you want a private life, I can tell you. I was married to the brother, and it was always uncomfortable. But enough! We will have coffee, and then Kurt is going to take us out to lunch, unless his precious army wants him back there."

Jutta and Jackson went to visit the horses, and Jackson heard the story of Red Jane. Gerhardt had a sniffle, and then he laughed.

"I would have loved to see her running away with you, Jutta. She was always a great runner when she had the chance, despite her size. So now she plows the enemy's fields, you say?"

"Papa, I can't see Ramona's family as the enemy. Her father saved my leg, and they looked after me the way you and Mama do. They were in a bad way, thanks to our forces trying to kill them all, so I feel sorry for them."

"It is bad, girl. I think that when the Galactic Federation has had its share of us, there will be some drastic changes. I can't see our chancellor coming out of this smelling of roses."

"He will resist, won't he, sir. Threaten and bluster. Claim that Valderia has been illegally represented and all the usual sidesteps and shuffles?"

Gerhardt laughed. "Hear this boy, Jutta! We have a diplomat on the farm already! It sounds as though we have the makings of a planetary delegate, right here and now!" They all laughed.

"Now, Jutta," said her mother. "What are you going to do? I want to know if you are going to fly away with Jason to see his parents, or are you going to take him around the lakes sightseeing? I need to know what to cook?"

"The lakes, Mama. I am afraid his mother and father won't like me."

"My mother will love you, Jutta."

"You say that, but I am still nervous."

"Mrs. Vogel, Mama, may I say I love Jutta? Sorry, but I have to say it. I don't care if my parents disapprove. I love her, and I think she loves me, and why should we care if they don't like it? It is our lives, isn't it?"

"Oh, Jason, you are a lovely boy. Let her make her mind up. Go and see the lakes and enjoy each other's company, and let her think about it."

"Thank you, Mama. I just need a little time."

Mrs. Vogel talked to Gerhardt and wondered what life would be like for Jutta if she married young Jason. The lakes were spectacular. It didn't help Jutta from being nervous. Jackson did get to kiss her rosebuds, even if he hadn't been good.

The weather had closed in around the E5 cavern research centre. It got dark early. Snow began to drift. It was cold, and Maggda turned up the heat in the gas fire that sucked it out of the rocks a long way below. She had sent out the drones and had made holos of just the weather and the activities in the cave, and she saw that what was going on there could well herald a few more pregnancies. Annrath was blooming, but it looked like it may be a while before she went into labor. Maggda went to consult Joe, and he projected what she wanted on the screen. She went to her personal supplies and set up shop in the rec room. Davvd had been in touch with Fleet.

Communications shot back and forth. He and Don were busy. She watched some old tri-dee soaps as she worked. Time passed quickly.

"So, Lady of the Long Legs, what are you doing? It looks complicated."

"Can you guess?"

"What is it?"

"A very, very ancient skill, Ong. All women were expected to do this. It is called 'knitting.'"

"And it obviously has direct connections to one Annrath and child?"

"You bet!"

"Show me."

"You create it on these needles, and you keep making stitches until you grow a garment. You need a pattern of stitches, and Joe has a huge collection in his memory banks. Printed this one off, and I am having a go."

"There are holes in it."

"Well, the whole thing is full of holes, sort of held together with fine wool."

"Well, yes, but are those holes supposed to be there, look, there and there."

"No, but don't get critical. It isn't easy, Ong. If you are so smart, you have a go."

"All right, Maggda, I didn't mean to be mean. Why don't you get Joe to knit it? Bet he could do it."

"I know he could do it. He is wonderful, but he isn't me, is he? I want to make the baby a garment that I made. I could have bought a ton of clothes, but I didn't, and you know why, because I want her to make her own. So I am trying to make this one . . .

"And then you show her how, and she is into weaving and wool crafts, and we jump another thousand years forward."

"Sort of, weaving was a very early skill, Ong, like ancient amongst the ancient."

"And knitted baby clothes?"

"No one knows. Knitting was pretty ancient, so Joe tells me. Why not give them knitting? You gave them bows."

"Survival skill stuff."

"You want to go out there tonight without your thermal, heated undies? Knitting wins!" She put the knitting down and took the drink he had brought in for her. "What is happening, Lord of the Universe?"

"Well, sort of 'in process' might best describe it. Galactic Feds are stirring things up on Valderia. They are digging in the heels and going for, as predicted, the legal, illegal angle to buy time. Valderia is taking out troops off Valentine, but Fed has found a lot of iffy infantry out in the mud and is bringing them in. Ong Wu Foundation is pressuring Valderia to make good the infrastructure it destroyed on Valentine and is going to build it back up, but Valderia has to repay the cost. The usual stuff."

"What about us?"

"I can only guess that with winter here and now, they will just hang on until it becomes easier to inspect us. Ong Wu Foundation knows all the details now pretty well. They must think there is no point in rushing here with a team of experts until the weather improves. They can still get a lot from Don and the satellites anyway."

"Boy or girl?"

"Fifty-fifty odds. What's the prize?"

"Me on Mars?"

"You promised me that anyway!"

"Just thought you had forgotten."

"Come here and let me kiss you in a very sleazy way. I feel like it tonight."

"Key to my door?"

"You leave it open anyway."

"How come you never come in and violate me during the night?"

"You really want to know? I am getting too fond of you, Styxx, and I want to wait til Mars. I keep thinking of you in that lab coat, and it makes the waiting worthwhile. I think it beats expensive underwear, any day."

She gave him a kiss. "What has the chef knocked up for us tonight? I am hungry."

Joe had worked his wonders, though they didn't ask him what the ingredients were. If it looked good and tasted good, it was often better not to know. The snow fell. To visit the tribe one had to take the loader, and since it was basically a platform with no cover, it was a cold trip to and from. They put on as many clothes as they could. The tribe was rugged up in their heavy furs, and since they had been brought up on a planet which was cooler than E5, they didn't suffer. Their deep cave home had been very well weatherproofed. Moss and grass and mud mortar had been used to fill cracks and gaps. Inside, the fires were fed and the smoke left high up and out of the mouth. They had begun to cook food in earnest, making use of Annrath's cooking vessels. The bowls became saturated with fat and no longer wept. They were heating water to wash faces now. Annrath told Maggda that it was very close now.

"I can feel it, Maggda, my star woman friend. It kicks like a strong boy."

"Whatever it is, we will love it. Your child is like my child. It is part of my heart too, Annrath!"

"Get your star man to give you one, Maggda! You are young and strong. Get your own."

During the night it blew a blizzard, and in the early hours, Annrath's pains began, and the little bat recorded the birth. It was a girl. That morning Maggda and Davvd saw it on the screens, and Maggda recorded it and felt angry that she had not been there, but she sent it off to Simon, who would make it into an event, and millions would watch it, and Annrath would become a star in her own right.

"I want to see the baby!"

"Not until we have eaten a decent breakfast, you mad woman.

Let her rest and suckle the child, and then we can go and see it, and you can take it its gifts. I know you have some, Styxx. You are a big soft marshmallow."

She was going to tell him what Annrath had said about her having her own child but thought better of it. Knowing how soft he was too, he might have said it was worth thinking about. They braved the snow and the intense cold and went to the tribe. Annrath was on her large bed with the child under the softest skins, and she showed them the wrinkled little face and laughed as Maggda held it.

"See, star man Davvd, your woman and a child. Give her one to have and hold too."

"What is the baby's name, Annrath?"

"Maggda, Davvd. What else could we name her?"

Maggda was a little overcome.

"Come now, star woman, and let the child sleep and feed." Davvd dragged her away and onto the loader, and they went back to the warmth of the research center.

"It is a dreadful feeling, Ong."

"What is?"

"I didn't realize I had gone all maternal. My breasts ache now!"

"Is there anything I can do?"

"Apart from making me pregnant, no!"

"Go and see if Joe has finished painting that cradle. We can take that over in the morning."

She was delighted with the cradle. Joe had made flower stencils and had decorated it, and it was a little work of art. She took it to show Davvd, and he laughed. "It is wonderful!"

"I just love that hunk of plas-steel"

"I loved them when I was a kid, and my feelings haven't changed much either. They were built with love to give it back, I think."

"I think you are right, Ong."

Jutta and Jackson were in the parlor with the dog lying on the rug at their feet.

"Come and see my mother, at least. My father is always off somewhere, but Mother wants to meet you."

"Can I tell you tomorrow?"

"Tomorrow morning, and if you say you are still undecided, I have to go back to Belvedere. I am all behind with my assignments, and if my father finds out he will get angry and cut my allowance, and that would mean, Jutta Vogel, that I couldn't buy you some red Second Skin to add to your set." He went to his room early. She said she wanted to speak to her parents. He had a steaming hot shower and climbed into the feather bed and thought about her. He fell asleep and literally didn't wake until the big red rooster welcomed Aton over the mountain top.

"What is the matter, Jutta? I thought you loved the boy," growled her father.

"I do, Papa, and I wished I didn't. What I haven't told you is that he is really Jackson Wu. He is the son of Solomon Wu, and can you imagine what he would say if Jackson brought me home, a little junior officer in the Valderian Army, who comes off a farm. No, don't say it. I know that my home is as good as anyone's and that I couldn't want for better parents, I couldn't. But you see, he is expected to marry someone from his own wealthy social class. His family owns half the galaxy if the truth is known. I am not that kind of lady. He is used to girls who have their own space yacht, a dozen servants or robots, and can speak ten languages . . . I just feel totally inadequate."

Her mother sat beside her and gave her a hug.

"Jutta, my wonderful daughter! He chose you to love, not what his parents want for him, didn't he?"

"Mama, you don't understand. He is going to be a diplomat, a planetary delegate. He is going to mix with nobility from a dozen planets, and I have to be by his side and know what to do. How will I cope?"

"I would think that you would do very well, girl. Look at you.

You are smart and beautiful, and he really cares for you, we all know that. You know what I think?

"Tell me, Papa."

"Go to his home with him and meet his mother, and father, if he is there. Meeting her will soon let you know if you fit or not. If you get treated like a servant, then you'll know for sure. You are as good if not better than anyone he is likely to meet, isn't she, Mother?"

"She is wonderful."

"Go with our blessings. What do they call it in the army? Reconnoiter, isn't it?"

"I have to tell him in the morning, or he goes back to Belvedere, to the University."

"I think your father is right. Go and see how the land lies. No harm done there, is there?"

She gave them both a big kiss and went to her room.

"Well, Rachel, if she does marry a multi-billionaire, we shouldn't be short of hay for my horses."

Jackson showered and dressed and tidied his room and went down to breakfast. She was sitting at the table eating her rough grain cereal and gave him a milky wet kiss. "Yes or no, Jutta?"

"I will meet your mother."

"Oh Jutta, that is wonderful! What made you change your mind?"

"My father. He likes you, Jackson, but I can't think why. Your family is one of the wealthiest in the galaxy, which is against you from the start, and you seduced his daughter and want to take her away, yet he says, "Go and meet his mother." I think he and I are mad!"

"I love you, Jutta Vogel. We have to get back to the city today, because I can get us on the starship tomorrow. Then we go to Alpha Six and then on to Old Earth. Takes a few days . . ."

"And nights. We can just stay in bed all day . . ."

"No, there is too much to see and do on the ship. Can I use the comm? I need to make bookings."

They left after lunch. She told Maria she was going. Maria told her she had met Kurt's mother. Kurt had bought her red Second Skin for being good, whatever that meant. Jutta had a good idea.

They said their goodbyes. Jutta waved out of the window and watched the farm slip away. It was like she might be leaving there forever. They went to his suite, and she looked at it and felt a little sad. She very nearly told him she had changed her mind, but they went out to eat and gave the Blue Boar a miss. Danced at a café that had real live musicians and a tiny dance floor. He bought her one long-stemmed red rose and three gin and tonics, and after that she didn't care too much. She took off her clothes and threw them over a chair and climbed into the big bed and just lay there with her face in the pillow. He kissed her neck and her back and her bottom, and she turned over, and he kissed the rest of her up and down, and she held out her arms and said, "Just love me gently. I am feeling very fragile."

"I love you, Jutta Vogel."

"I love you, Jackson, but I wish I didn't."

"What is that supposed to mean?"

"Just make love to me and be gentle and kiss my rosebuds and don't say anything."

He didn't know what to say, but he loved her, and then she went to sleep. They had an early start. It was all splash and rush and grab the bags and onto the pad and through the customs gate and onto the shuttle with its stale air smell, strap in tight and feel sick as a dog as it went up on the scram jets and bang clang as it locked onto the starship, then down the tube and clip the boarding passes, and she felt exhausted, then they were in their suite, and she lay on the bed and looked at the painted ceiling that had people with wings flying through fluffy clouds. "I just hope I like your mother, Jackson, that's all."

He said nothing but hoped she would, or things could get complicated.

It was a Wu liner called *Moon Glow Dawn*. The food was excellent. The décor tended to be "moonish" but comfortable. She had her hair styled, and it looked wonderful. She wondered if she looked classy enough. What did multi-billionaires dress like, for Aton's sake?"

Jackson was seeing a side of her he didn't know how to react to. A side that was quiet and serious and made their sessions in the big bed strained. She still liked to romp but was quiet afterwards and spoke very little. She let him kiss her rosebuds but didn't demand it. It was as if she was someone else in a Jutta body. He hoped she would return to her original Jutta persona when they reached the estate. This Jutta was someone he didn't know at all.

On Little Lotus, the Wu family shuttle came up to carry them down, ahead of the commercial carrier. It was luxurious. The seats were real leather, the ceilings were lined with silk, and its entry into atmosphere was smooth and almost silent. She barely noticed that they were out of space and into atmosphere, and then the hydrogen engines took over, the wings extended, and they were flying across a seemingly endless ocean and over a great forest, and lower, there were gardens. Kilometers of them, streaming past under the wings, then a reverse thrust and a gentle descent and they touched down on a wide marble-tiled area with lawns extending all around and great trees covered in bright flowers, and beyond, a huge building glowing yellow in the sun. A white and gold land car appeared with a robot who loaded bags, and they sank into the white leather seats, and they slid to the house. Jutta was in a state of total disbelief. No one lived like this, no one. Not even the chancellor had a palace like this. In under a wide archway with gold lions and dragons standing guard and then to a marbled hall and great steps leading up to another level that they reached by elevator. At the end of a short hall with exotic green plants on either side and then great carved doors, there was a beautiful young woman standing there with her hands outstretched.

"Master Jackson and Miss Vogel. Welcome to the Wu household."

"Thank you, Crystal. Is my mother ready to see us?"

"She asks forgiveness, but would you like to see your rooms, Miss Vogel. I have been asked to take care of you. Your mother will see you shortly in the reception room, Master Jackson. Please come this way, Miss Vogel, or should I address you as Lieutenant? Please tell me so I won't forget." Her rooms were not too large but beautifully furnished, with silk hangings and wonderful paintings. She had a white marble bathroom with gold fittings, with huge white fluffy towels like blankets, a dressing room, enough hanging space for a barracks full of soldiers, three-dee mirrors so she could see back and front at the same time, and music from somewhere, which turned on and off as she waved her hand, a bed of gilt carved little babies with wings and gold coverings, and white rugs so deep she thought they were quicksand. Crystal followed her and told her where everything was hidden and how to use the gilded comm, and then she said, "If there is anything you want, please call me," and she pointed to the comm. "Just activate it, and I will be there. Why don't you rest for half an hour, and then Madame Wu will see you and Jackson, and we will serve tea."

"Thank you, Crystal."

"I am here to serve you, miss." and then she was gone.

Jutta took off her coat and shoes and went to the windows, which became transparent as she approached, giving her a view of the enormous gardens. As far as she could see, the manicured expanse spread, covered with flower beds and ornamental statuary, and there were gardeners tending it all, some human, she thought, but robots too. Pools with lilies and great floral trees hung over grass that looked so unreal that it was obvious that it was real, growing grass. She lay on the bed and listened to the soothing melody and suddenly was asleep.

"Did you settle her in, Crystal?"

"Yes, Sylvia,"

"What is she like?"

"Beautiful and quiet and shy."

"Let her rest a little. She probably needs a nap after that flight. I know I always do. Where is Jackson?"

"In his rooms, Sylvia."

"Buzz him and tell him I would like to talk to him before the girl comes in."

"Yes, Sylvia."

Jutta awoke, and her time band told her she had slept for nearly three quarters of an hour. She went to the bathroom and freshened up, looked at her hair and fixed that, put on some more lip color and thought about changing her dress. She slipped into the silk that Jackson had bought her at Maxxi's. She went to the mirrors, and they told her she looked a very classy girl. "I may be off the farm, but I look like a princess!"

The comm rang, and Crystal appeared and led her to the apartments of Madame Wu. It was a long walk along a wide corridor that had fossils set into the walls, mineral crystal mounted in frames, and more exotic plants that hung or stood on carved pedestals, then Crystal knocked on gilded and carved doors, and they were in the presence of Sylvia Wu. The room was all red and gold. The red carpet was thick and soft, and the walls were hung with gold silk that had wonderfully colored birds embroidered on it. There were pictures of elegant, ancient women in patterned dresses, and the furniture was white and gold with red velvet upholstery, and Jutta felt overawed, but Crystal took her hand and led her over to the lady in the large chair and introduced her.

"Sylvia, this is Jutta."

Then Jackson was beside her and holding her hand, and she gripped him so hard he knew she was a little frightened. "Mother, this is my Lieutenant, my beautiful Lieutenant."

His mother rose from the chair, and Jutta could see that she was a very beautiful older woman who was used to total control.

She smiled and held out her hands and took Jutta's cold one in her warm one and led her to a wall that opened as they approached, into a much simpler room with comfortable chairs and a low, elegant table with cups and saucers, tea pots and pastries, and silver spoons.

"Jutta, please sit down, and Crystal will serve us tea. May I say that my son didn't exaggerate when he said he had found a beautiful girl, because you are."

Jutta was a little embarrassed. Jackson sat next to her and reached for her hand.

"You know, Jutta, Jackson is smitten with you, and since you are the first girl he has ever wanted to show off to me, then I take it seriously. Don't let me upset you, please. He is my favorite son, and I want him to be happy. I may be a lonely, miserable cow at times, but that is because I lost my beautiful daughter, Su Lin, and I miss her badly. I get depressed because I don't have her here, so any young woman I meet I tend to substitute for her. If I pour out my heart to you, just ignore me. Now let's have tea. Crystal will do the work, won't you, Crystal?"

"Yes, Sylvia, of course."

"Now, tell me about your terrible time in the war. Jackson was going mad worrying about you."

"Mother, you can see why, can't you? Just the thought that she might get killed, or worse, maimed out there, was enough to give me nightmares."

"And your parents, Jutta, what about them?"

"They know I am in the army, and that is the risk I take. I have a brother in the Space Corps, and he is on active duty too. They know the risks, and they are, well, what is the word, philosophical?"

"Her parents, Mother, are just wonderful. Her father breeds these huge horses, and Jutta was working with one of them when she was captured and nearly died . . ."

"Do your parents approve of this boy?"

Jutta laughed. "My father calls him 'boy.' I have to tell you that they didn't know that he was your son because he was using

335

his college name, so they thought he was Jason West, and they didn't know that he was, well, part of the Wu family. I didn't want them to know. I am sorry. I thought that if he was, well, just an ordinary boy I was bringing home, then they wouldn't . . ."

"Judge him too harshly? I know exactly what you mean, Jutta. The Wu name has a hundred advantages but a million disadvantages; that's why he goes to Belvedere as Jason. So did they like him or not?

"I think they liked me, Mother."

"Be quiet, Jackson. I am asking Jutta. Well, did they?"

"My mother likes him, I know; my father calls him boy, and he only does that if he feels he can trust him. They were nearly drinking buddies, and he only does that with someone he really likes."

"What do they think of this trip here to meet me? They must know that this 'boy' here is in love with you enough to drag you across the galaxy and to think about marrying you, don't they?"

"Yes ma'am."

"Do you love him enough to want to marry him, Jutta?"

There was silence.

"If we get married I will have so much responsibility that I think it will kill me. I do love him, I do, but how am I going to cope with his being away and expecting me to know what I am supposed to do as the wife of a diplomat who will probably be going to all the high-powered places in the galaxy?"

"Jutta, trust me. You will be a wonderful diplomat's wife! I know it. Won't she, mother?"

"I want my tea. Crystal, pour the tea, and let's just sit a while. Jackson, this girl isn't just a pretty face. Crystal, tell us about this tea. Change the subject for us."

"This tea set is nine hundred years old. It is made from the finest bone china and was made in a country called Japan. The tea leaves come from New India from Wu plantations developed over four hundred ESYs. It is a light flavored tea and best suited without any additive, though some sweetness may be added. It is beneficial as a mild diuretic. The leaves--"

"Thank you, Crystal, enough is enough. In other words, Jutta, it will do you good and taste fine. Now, Jackson, you can say anything you like. We want to hear what you think now."

"I don't know what to think. If you won't marry me, Jutta, I suppose we will just drift apart. I love you. I don't know what I will do without you."

"May I say something? Here you both are. You need time to think, Jutta. Enjoy your time here. This boy here will wine and dine you, buy you expensive gifts and try to let you know just how much he loves you, take you to bed, probably, and become a real lover. Now I respect your views very much. You are not just some bubblehead that he has found. He has to appreciate that too.

"Now drink your tea, have some of these little pastries that I like so much, and Crystal will show you what she is making for me."

They went back to her rooms, and Jackson came and put his arms around her as she looked out onto the gardens.

"I like your mother, Jackson. She says what she thinks. I like that. I do need time to think. You have a future all planned out for you. I have no idea what mine will be. I don't know how any woman could cope with it all. At least your mother has that girl, Crystal, to talk to when your father is away so much."

"Come out here with me, just for a moment." He led her out across the wide hall and into another room filled with tri-dees. "Who is that, Jutta?"

"Crystal?"

"No. That was my sister, Su Lin."

"Crystal could be her, couldn't she? Same hair, same figure. What are you trying to say, Jackson?"

"Crystal is the very latest android our Robotic Company has developed. So human that you didn't guess she wasn't, did you? So human that she makes up for Su Lin in many ways, and my mother has difficulty separating the two. Crystal is her daughter that died and has come back to life again."

337

Jutta looked skeptical.

"But she knows she is just a machine, doesn't she?"

"Of course she knows, but she felt the loss of my sister so badly that she now can use Crystal as a substitute. She is a wonderful companion, Jutta. Tomorrow Crystal will show you my mother's exotic flowers, and you can judge for yourself. I am going into the city to buy you a couple of very expensive and quite unnecessary gifts so my mother can see I am doing my best to woo you, and you will have time to think and have some space. After dinner tonight, may I come to your room and sleep with you? I just want to have you near me, and if you say no sex, then I will understand."

"How can we sleep together without it, Wu! Once we get warm and naked, we are both hopeless."

"I want you, Jutta."

"Wait until tonight, and then I might give in. Show me this palace. I don't believe anyone could build something like this, anywhere."

"My father loves excess."

"I can see that, Jackson. I can see that."

The meeting of the High Command took place in the Chancellery, and it was not the usual dinner with drinks and rubber stamp discussion. Voight chaired the meeting. It was heavy going.

"Gentlemen, you have your briefing notes, and you know that today we have hard decisions to make. The chancellor has told us that we have to get rid of the Galactic Federation in one way or the other, and if some fool suggests we send a heavy force to attack anything, then be prepared to get eliminated. Force may have worked last century, but we are now under the eye of the media, and the whole galaxy can see us squirming. No, gentlemen, now we have to clean house, clean out the bad smell and show the Fed that we are totally on their side."

"You mean, Voight, that Valderia just puts up and shuts up, is that it? We won't crawl to the damn Federation, will we?"

"No, Gunter, we won't, but belligerence we don't want. What

we need now is what they call 'diplomacy'. Diplomacy, if you weren't aware of it, is saying one thing and meaning another. One achieves results by saying what the Feds want to hear and then quietly getting what we want, without stirring up too much of a hornet's nest."

"And how are we going to do that?"

"The chancellor is going to stand down."

"And that will achieve what?"

"You, and the rest of you, who brought human robotic infantry into that battlefield, are going to quietly resign and draw a nice big pension."

"And you, Voight?"

"I sit here and play the peacemaker. It is called being 'diplomatic'."

"Very nice for some, now let's assume, Voight, that when Federation gets here and wants scapegoats and wants to hang us all out for war crimes, they include you in the bag."

"No evidence whatsoever that I was ever party to it. You had a monopoly on it. The records will bear that out. Now, before you all start screaming at each other, listen carefully. You stand down and resign and lose all your status, which is what Federation wants to hear, but Valderia will give you a wonderful start in your new lives. We can get you out of here. Get you off planet before they want heads; it isn't that difficult. Go now, and we can get you off; hang about, and there is no choice. Fleet gets called in, and you hang."

"Our families?"

"Well taken care of, boys. We have set up an estate on Alpha Six that will suit everyone. Trust me on this."

"The chancellor?"

"We replace him. He wants to duck and run anyway."

"We replace him with . . . ?"

"Schiff. Right now he is squeaky clean. He has an excellent war record. The rest of space thinks he is some kind of eco hero for saving some of your 'Neanderthals'. He has the birth credentials. The Valderian public will love him. Governing Council will vote him in without a single dissenter. What is more important is that we can convince him that he is the hero in shining armor who alone can save the world."

"How in Aton's name can you do that?"

"I talked to him the other day and told him that we would win if he didn't play ball. He laughed at that, which is what I had hoped he would do. Virtuous and self-righteous, you see. Then when we eat humble pie, and we clean out the latrine, as he sees it, which way will he jump? He will take charge. We let him, but we will still have the casting vote. Chancellors are only as righteous as their governing councils. Now gentleman, we need action. We need a press release to send to the media. We need to get you off planet, and we need to start cleaning up the crap. Destroy what incriminating records you have and report here tomorrow at Aton's first breath. Get your robotic staff cleaned and do this without a word. You want to hang, then make a noise. Now, tell me all the reasons why you want to stay and face the music."

There was a lot of grumbling, but no real dissent.

"How can we trust you, Voight?"

"You and I have very little choice. I am the one who sits here in Federation's sights while you disappear into the void. You want to change places? You deployed that ragbag army out on Valentine, hoping no one would notice. The way things are today with every satellite and news hawk with a data bank of scientific gurus at their beck and call, did you expect to not get caught out?"

"It was supposed to be a quick campaign, Voight, you know that. Get in quick, crush the revolt, take over the industry; and Federation would have been none the wiser. You were the one for the 'quick result', or have you forgotten that?"

"Circumstances, and a determined enemy, and the weather, as Napoleon found, changes the tactical plan every time."

"And we lost the battle, Voight. Valderia never admits defeat, you know that."

"If it makes you feel happier, Gruber, call it a 'tactical withdrawal'."

"Bullshit, Voight, but that is what we are left with now, isn't it? It is going to take a big broom to clean it up, and you had better start sweeping."

They left after more discussion, went to their respective departments and figuratively, burnt the boats. Voight called the Federation representatives for a quiet meeting, which proved very fruitful, and went back to what he was doing before the dung had hit the fan, and that was withdraw troops from Valentine as fast as he could. The Federation battleship *Thor* hung off- planet and waited until the mid-watch, when it intercepted a Valderian cruiser with a party aboard who seemed surprised that they would be taken for trial before the Intergalactic Human Rights Committee on New Babylon. The chancellor announced he would be retiring. The press had a field day. The stream of men and arms from Valentine increased to a flood. Voight was complimented on his diplomacy and smiled. All he had to do now was tell Schiff he didn't stand a chance in the race for the Chancellery, and that if he didn't take it, the Governing Council would have no choice but to appoint a general in his place. He loved diplomacy, and he hadn't fired a shot.

Simon watched the sun set on Mars and sent a message to Maggda. She would not be pleased, but she was under contract. She had a lot of credits to pay off. She had given Galactic wonderful coverage from E5, which was losing its newsworthy status, but fresh fields were opening up. He marked the message "urgent."

Maggda had been to see Annrath, presented her with the cradle and a pile of toys that rattled and made nice noises, held little Maggda in her arms and thought her breasts might be leaking. It felt like it. Then she hurried back when Don had told her via her earcell that she had an urgent message. Davvd was not pleased but was philosophical.

"To be truthful, my Lady of the Long Legs, there isn't much

here for either of us now. Don and Joe are back on station. Directly after this weather clears up, Radnath and Singh will be here, together with a couple of Ong Wu Foundation observers, and we become redundant."

"Davvd, they are sending me to Valentine! The back end of the horse and nowheresville! Can you beat that?"

"So, what's the brief?"

"I, we, there is another couple going with me, get all the lowdown on what Valderia blew up, destroyed in the name of putting down a rebellion, but which had no military connections whatever. Schools and hospitals, water supplies, you name it. Boy, is that a fun assignment!"

"Could be very important to get a noncombatant point of view. You don't have axes to grind, so you can be objective. What does Simon say?"

"Why are you so smart, Ong? Pretty much what you said. We have leads to follow because they had their own press doing it too, but Galactic packs more punch, we can cover a wider audience, and we are better funded. By Aton's breath, Davvd, Valentine of all places! What do I do?"

"You do what I have to do. You take orders, go and do what you do best, and hope Simon cancels your debt. You can do it, Maggda."

She asked Joe for a drink that made her eyes water. "What about Mars, Ong?"

"Put it on hold, you beautiful girl. I didn't tell you, but I had a short, sharp message from Fleet yesterday saying I have been recalled. I have to go back to Alpha Six ASAP. Didn't want to tell you when you were mooning over the baby and Annrath. Sorry."

She went to him and they hugged each other. "Come into the rec room and hold me tight, Ong. I need it." She snuggled up against him, and she put his hand on her breast. "See, Ong, I told you I had come out in sympathy."

They left the tribe and Annrath as well as Joe and Don with very mixed feelings and caught a Wu liner to Alpha Six and parted. He stayed, and she went on to Mars and Simon, and then she and the team were away to Valentine. When she left her apartment, she spread the old white lab coat over her bed. "Don't go away. I am coming back."

Jutta and Crystal were in the huge conservatory, and Crystal was showing her the exotic plants and the orchids, the butterflies and moths, and the little lizards, and Jutta was trying to take it all in. Crystal held her hand or slipped an arm about her waist, and Jutta was confused. This wasn't a machine; this was a real living girl. She was warm and felt like flesh against her flesh, and she had such a brief speech hesitation that it seemed normal. She had heard real people with exactly the same speech patterns, and suddenly Jutta forgot and was with a friend, not a machine at all, and she felt totally at ease.

"You see this flower, Jutta? It is very rare. Sylvia imports these rare blooms from all over the galaxy, and we have botanists come here just to study them. She loves anything rare and exotic or endangered. She is like a mother to them, you see."

They entered another section where giant trees grew right to the glassed roof, and a myriad of butterflies made living flowers all around them and came down to little pools to drink and feed from the nectar pots.

"It is wonderful, Crystal, wonderful. I have never seen anything like it. It is a magical world."

"Sylvia would like to hear you say that. We walk here often, Jutta, and she confides in me about her feelings and her fears, as if I were her real daughter."

"You are like her real daughter, aren't you?"

"I try to be, but you know that I am a machine and cannot really give her a human relationship. But you, Jutta, can give her that. She wanted grandchildren so badly, and then Su Lin and Davvd Ong's parents were destroyed in a shuttle crash, so that left her alone. She is hoping her sons will give her back her family. Will you marry Jackson?"

343

Jutta was speechless for a moment. How can I tell this beautiful machine what I can't tell Jackson? "I love Jackson Wu, Crystal. I want to be with him. I would like to have his children, but I am a simple country girl at heart, and he needs someone from his own class, someone who comes from the same kind of background. He loves me now, but will he go on loving me when he begins to find out just how simple I am compared with other women? So I have doubts, and I can't really tell him, and it hurts."

Crystal put her arms about Jutta and said. "I can recognize that your feelings are mixed. I am a machine, Jutta, but I know how deeply these things can affect any human being. I was built to be sympathetic to that. Sylvia relies on me to make her feel better when she is depressed. Can I help you?"

"You have, Crystal, you have. Now, tell me where Mr. Wu has gone, or is that a secret?"

"You must ask Jackson when he comes back. I am not allowed to discuss his father without Sylvia being there. Do you understand?"

They went back to the great, sprawling house and the stables and the golf course and gallery, where a history of great art hung from the red silk-lined walls. It was all too much for Jutta, and she left Crystal and went to her room, where she felt less vulnerable. She went to the windows and looked out over that great formalized expanse and suddenly felt homesick for Grunewald. "What have I let myself in for, Mama?"

Jackson came back and asked for Jutta and found her in her room lying down on the great bed.

"What's happened? Are you sick?"

"No, Jackson, just a bit depressed."

"Here, look what I have bought for you. Open them and tell me you like them."

Jutta opened the boxes and found two nightdresses of synthetic spider silk, one white and one black, a set of Second Skin in red, and a small box with a ring that had an emerald so large that it was obscene.

"What do I say, Jackson?"

"I know how you feel. The ring is for when you want to say yes, but the rest is for now, and I just want to please you."

"I will try on the nightdresses and show you. Will that make you feel better?" She went into the dressing room and took off her clothes and slipped the black nightdress over her nakedness and came back into the room. The material reacted to warmth and changed from opaque to transparent. It shimmered, and her body showed through it but slipped away again as she moved.

"You look wonderful, Jutta. Come here and let me hold you."

She allowed him to run his hands over her and to kiss her, then she gently pushed him away. "I want to wait until tonight. I must get dressed. I want to talk to your mother. Can you tell me where your father is, Jackson? Crystal wouldn't tell me."

"I don't know for sure, but I think he is on Valentine."

She reacted strongly, "Valentine! Are you sure?"

"No, not sure, but he had to meet with some Galactic Federation people about the restoration of the industry there or some such thing, but why do you want to know?"

"Your mother never seems to see him. He is always away doing something. Does he ever come home?"

"Well, he does, but I am usually away at college, so we don't cross paths too often. He does call her every day, I do know that, but what is this leading to, Jutta?"

"If you and I get married, Jackson, will you just leave me with a robot for a friend while you do what you have to do, somewhere out there?"

"No, of course not. You would come with me and play hostess. I need you by me."

"And would we have a home somewhere? A place we could call our own with a dog and a cat and a couple of kids playing in the meadow, and maybe a cow, and nice neighbors?"

"I think so. If that is what you want, then we would have it, wouldn't we?"

She shook her head. "This is your home, but it is really like some mad palace, and your mother is like a prisoner in it. She has no friends, just a wonderful, human-like machine that is playing the part of Su Lin. I couldn't live like that, Jackson, I just couldn't. I love my humble home and my simple mother and father, and you never had that, so how would you know what it is like? Perhaps my father was right. Maybe you have had a terrible childhood and didn't know it."

"I love your mother and father too, Jutta. When I am there I feel like they are my parents too, you know that." She went to him and kissed him, then went to get dressed. "I have to talk to your mother, Jackson, alone."

Solomon Wu was touring the industrial heart of Valentine, up in the boondocks and mountain mines and oil fields and deep pits where the iron ore was blasted out, where the gas was bottled up and exported. Valentine was on the verge of great wealth; it just needed a few billion credits to get it kicked into gear. He went to hospitals that had been flattened by sonic mines and educational centers that had been destroyed because they were in the way, and he talked to the Federation team about funding, and they listened, because when Solomon Wu talked credits, everyone listened. He was putting a plan together, and Federation listened and shook their heads. He talked some more, and the Fed reps went into a huddle and spoke to head office, and then it seemed that maybe, just maybe, he could bring in some of his expert teams and work with both Valderia and Valentine, and everyone would profit.

Maggda and her team were on his heels. Getting an interview with Solomon was easy. Shutting him up was difficult. He talked about his plans from a point of view that if it was right for Wu Industries and Enterprises, then it was right for everyone, and often he was right. Maggda and her team talked to the people who had survived in bunkers, the half-starved farmers, and the Valentine press corps was there to put them onto those who could

346

tell them what happened when the Valderians met resistance, and it wasn't pretty. They were still clearing the battlefield of the dead from both sides. It was grim viewing, but Maggda was determined to be objective. Simon had trained her well. "If you can't tell the truth or check your facts, you don't work for Galactic." She knew that that wasn't spurred by righteousness so much as the deadly fear of getting involved in lawsuits. As he was often heard to say, "Cover your backs, boys and girls." Then she found a big red horse on a farm that had been part of the Valderian Army Medical Rescue team and made a wonderful human interest story out of it, then asked Simon to find a young lieutenant called Jutta Vogel. Get her, and she had both sides of the story. She missed the tribe, and she missed Ong and Joe and Don, but she and the team made the most of the reasonable luxury of the laser-pocked hotel, ate well and drank too much and made good news. When they found a whole barracks full of "Neanderthal soldiery" being examined by neuro specialists like Radnath, she had completed the whole cycle. She went to bed and wished she knew where Ong had gone.

"One week fishing with your Uncle Max, Captain, then you are out of here. I need you to do a little piece of dung smelling on Asgard. Real briefing when you get back. Have a good week." The admiral shook his hand. Sonna asked Ong if she could go with him and he said yes, but the Admiral said no . . . so he went, wondering what in the name of Aton was on Asgard to get Fleet to send him out there. It rained most of the week, but they caught good fish, ate well, slept well and drank good wine, and his uncle didn't ask him too many questions about what he had been doing with Maggda Styxx on some remote moon. Publicity had been kind to him, and he hadn't offended anyone. In the big void of space where worlds roamed, the starships came and went, and he was back at Fleet before the fish had time to freeze. He refused a drink and while he waited, looked at the very decorative Captain Sonna. She really was a lovely woman, who smiled at him a lot. She was very smart in her uniform and looked scrubbed clean and fresh. He thought her legs were like Maggda's and became aware that he was watching her too closely and that she was aware of it.

"Captain Ong, I know that I don't stand a chance with Maggda Styxx in the room. She isn't here now, is she?"

"I am sorry. I was thinking how smart and clean and lovely you look, and if that sounds like a weak line, I didn't mean it to come out like that. The old man is lucky to have you here, and you know that, I hope."

"I think he does. I envied Maggda, you know, romping off with you on E5."

"It wasn't all fun and games. She had a bit of a tough time, but she didn't complain, which for someone who had never had to rough it, was pretty commendable. She can think on her feet, and that helped a lot."

"Where is she now?"

"Valentine, you should be getting her stories soon. She is on assignment there. Her boss sent her out there to pay off debts."

"And to get her away from you?"

"I don't know about that. Ask her boss."

"Might just do that."

The admiral came in, and they sat, and he listened and felt depressed. "Here are the briefing notes. Asgard is rugged, primitive, and Jurassic, and we are only interested in it because we are going to put an advance base on there soon. There is a beacon there that directs star traffic to the next jump-off zone, as with Beebop. Now we had three Fleet personnel there and no problems, but two were killed, or rather disappeared without trace, and that left a captain, who was there doing air patrols along the coastline. Daily routine stuff and training flights for the beasts--"

"Wait a minute, what are the 'beasts'?"

"Oh, you know, they are a kind of mutation of the pterodactyl and pterosaur, big, flying reptiles. They are native to Asgard, but we have adapted them to carry a pilot--"

"I don't like the sound of that."

"Let me finish, Ong. Captain Jenna was in charge of those, and they are like pets as far as she is concerned--"

"Are we speaking about the Mary Jenna who was with me on Zendor?"

"I think she may have been, yes."

"We disliked each other."

"Tough, Ong. She is down there on her own, and you are going to try and find out who 'disappeared' her colleagues. This isn't anything personal, just business. You get down there, tell us what you can find and come back and—"

"Smell the dung?"

"One way of putting it. Read your notes, look at the tri-dees and get on your way. Nice spot down there, really. Peaceful, they tell me!"

"Until now."

"Well, yes. Get down there and sort it out. Shouldn't take you long."

Three days on the Fleet cruiser going as hard as the drive allowed, gave him time to read the notes and to make him feel despondent. It would be wonderful if he and Maggda could have at least a week on Mars together. Aton had not smiled on him lately.

Mary Jenna. A girl who had been born to love reptiles and who wasn't keen on anything much else. She was lean and mean and a good combat soldier. Could handle herself well and took no bull. She had disliked him because of his name and because he was able to make friends easily; and she didn't. They had fought together, and that was all. She had avoided him when she could, and he had never bothered to really care why. It had been a short campaign, and he and she had gone their separate ways. Asgard would have suited her. As far as he could see, the only strategic importance was that it was a beacon site, a place where starships could coordinate their next jump. His notes suggested that Fleet wanted a base there. To do what, watch the space ways? Who knows?

Asgard, a planet with just below Old Earth gravity. A lot of water. Vast oceans and two main continents. Jungle and more jungle, snow-covered mountains, and two active volcanoes. Wildlife, lots of it, all lizard-like and dinosaurs but with a mammal mixture. Old Earth, but very Old Earth. Climate? According to his pod notes, benign, but there were bad storms. He thought of Bare Head and he and Maggda, but this base was different. He was dropped off on a rocky headland overlooking a vast blue sea. There were the spikes and the spires of the beacon ahead of him, and he wandered over to what looked like an entrance; it opened as he came near. There was Mary with a stun gun in her hand and a bleak look on her face.

"Why did they send you, Ong? I was looking forward to someone I could talk to, but you?"

"Nice meeting you again, Mary. See you haven't changed much."

"What are you doing here, Ong?"

"Well, Mary, if you ask me in and give me a drink and let me sit, I might tell you. Trouble is that I don't know either."

She showed him into the underground complex, and it was as comfortable as any, with good showers and a decent bed and a rec room with comfortable chairs and gym equipment, a kitchen with a basic robotic chef, and the usual comm consoles and tri-dee screens. He found himself a drink and sat after stowing his gear in one of the bedrooms.

"Can we call a truce, Mary? I don't want to be here; you don't want me to be here; but Fleet sent me to make sure you were all right and to ask about the missing. Can we start fresh?"

"I am sorry. I have been very jumpy. Roberts and White went out to check on something strange along the coast. I had one comm call. Roberts said, 'I think we've found it,' and that was it. Nothing. I went and did a patrol and found nothing. No wreckage, nothing. So I yelled for help and have just gone out to feed the 'girls'.

Otherwise, I have kept the doors locked with the alarms active."

"And a stun gun in your hand."

"Stay alert and stay alive, Ong, you know that!"

"Show me the trace. When the fly went out of here it would have activated the trace, so it would have been tracked by the satellite, right?"

"Right, but look at it. It gets halfway along the beach above the big rock shelf, the escarpment, and then it just ends. No spiral down, no crash alarm, no sudden climb, it just ends."

"Like it runs into a hole in space."

"Something like that."

"I'd like to see exactly where it ended its trace."

"Have to wait until tomorrow. Too far to walk. Tomorrow morning I will get you kitted up, and we can fly over it on a couple of the girls. You ever flown one, Ong?"

"No, and I don't want to, but if you are there to hold my hand, Mary, I might feel better."

"Don't sweet talk me, Ong; you know what I'm like."

"And I thought you'd changed."

They ate a simple meal, courtesy of the robo chef, and had a drink of what Mary called beer but which Davvd thought was anything like that. He went back through records to see if there were any clues to account for White and Roberts going off screen but found nothing. He went to bed and slept well. It was quiet there, after all. After a quick breakfast, Mary appeared in her flying suit and kitted him up. Light helmet, goggles and thick boots, thin gloves and the spider silk suit that was light and flexible and waterproof, and she led him out to the elevator in the face of the rock and they went up. As they stepped out, he could smell decaying fish. Along a short corridor and there were the girls in their caves, which opened to the air and sea two-hundred meters above the waves. They stank. They were the ugliest creatures he had experienced for a while. Slime worms were cuddly compared to these. They were huge, grey skinned, with strong gnarled legs and huge clawed feet, long necked with a small head but a long, scythe-like beak with backward curving teeth, and an eye that was black with a bright red rim all round. Their enormous leather-like wings were folded back, and they stood in feces that would be washed away when they left the roost. They shuffled about as Mary approached and clacked their beaks. He felt a twinge of horror and fear.

"Just stay back a little, Ong, since they don't know you, and I have to get them radio linked, or they might take an arm off." She went to a console nearly hidden in the rock wall, buttoned a couple of switches, and the girls stood still.

"Okay. Now here is what you do. You take this simple controller, which is just like a kid's game controller, and it clips onto the back of their neck. One simple control stick, forward for down, back for up, left to go left, right to go right. Now the bar at the bottom is for speed. Move your finger to the right, and they flap faster; left, they slow down. These girls like to glide, so they mustn't get stressed. Each wing beat is going to shove you along very fast, so tuck in and don't fall off."

"I don't think I am going to enjoy this, Jenna."

"Ah, you big wimp, Ong. These are like little duckies compared to slime worms. Now climb up and get settled on her neck, then slip back a bit till you reach the sweet spot. You got it?"

She climbed up on the other ugly monster and settled. "All right, now I am going to take off the passive control, and when I do they will walk to the edge of the cave and fall out. They won't open wings until they get enough air speed, so don't wet yourself. They haven't crashed yet. Then they will soar and get up to a good height to see where the fish are. Now, you let them take a couple of big fish before you take control, as if you don't let them feed first they can get very ornery . . . Are you ready?"

Before the beast fell out of the cave, he was aware of a thin sliver of metal inserted into the creature's skull. The rush of free fall had him gasping, then the huge leather wings cracked open, and his stomach sank as the girl soared up and up, and he had a view of the ocean beneath him. Mary Jenna rode to his left, and he was about to yell at her when the beast dived. For one sickening moment he thought it would plunge headlong into the sea, but it flattened out, and he was covered in spray, and it had a large fish in its jaws. It glided while it gulped the fish down, and then it rose again and repeated the performance, and he could see Mary pointing to the controller, and he took over. At the first contact the creature let out a long, wailing croak and then settled. He could direct it now, and he rode it high to catch up. They flew side by side down the edge of the escarpment, and then she began to circle, and pointed down. There was nothing to see other than gray rounded rocks with the sea pounding in, slopping over animals that were also gray and looked like huge slugs. He pointed down; she shook her head and turned the beast back. They flew back to the caves, and it was exciting to have the experience of heading for a blank rock face before the 'girl' put on the brakes, rose suddenly and dropped onto the floor of the cave. The mess had gone, flushed out by high-pressure hoses, and they slipped off the backs and removed the controls. "You can land these on the rock shelf, but they wouldn't get off without a terrible struggle. They live high up in caves or on rock ledges and they only get airborne on a huge updraft. Land them in the sea, and they flap until the waves and wind gives them enough lift, but they are rock hoppers really."

"Who devised the cerebral control?"

"Some guy called Radnath, I think. Some professor who was doing that kind of research years ago. He did a good job with these. They don't have much of a brain anyway, and he was doing early control stuff. It's on the files. Fleet took these over when they pulled the plug on it. Here, they are an asset. Live for years and years, don't need much to keep them flying, self feeders, and useful. I patrol along here every day and fit in with the weather, and the girls go out and feed themselves when I take the control off, so they are no trouble. They are pretty nasty if they get angry, but I calm them down, and they have gotten used to me."

"I know Radnath."

"Hey, really? What is he like?"

"Professor-ish!"

"Am I allowed to ask where? Let me guess, E5 or E7? We heard about it."

"I have just come from there."

"Right, and you had Maggda Styxx with you romping about in Second Skin, and you hated every minute of it, right?"

"Something like that. Now, I want to change and eat, ask more questions and see more data and let the mind rove free. Something downed that fly, and when it did, it did it very, very efficiently. Went poof and left no footprints. What's your theory? You live here."

"Something snatched it. It came out of the sea and took it."

"What?"

"Plesiosaur."

"Not another damn Plesiosaur. Maggda Styxx and I were in a fly in a situation just like this, and we got taken and nearly drowned."

"I rest my case!"

"I need more evidence. A bit too simple, and without trace? I'll keep an open mind. Do you have anything here that tastes better than that so-called beer you gave me earlier? I need a drink, but that stuff is like . . . well, you know what I mean?"

"Will try. Now what do you want to eat tonight? We got a lot of fresh fish!"

That trace worried him, but he said nothing to Mary Jenna. It just didn't read right. Now if a plesiosaur had jumped the fly, it would have registered a drop and then a sideways motion and possibly carried on into the sea. It just ended in midair, which defied the comprehension. Were there plesiosaurs out there? He thought that they only existed on E5. Davvd and Mary ate in silence. He drank beer—which did taste like beer—and asked her what White and Roberts drank.

"Oh, Julie had her own stash of wine, and Sandra drank spirits. They didn't drink much. We liked coffee and left the hard stuff alone."

"Wait a minute. Are you saying that there were three women here? White and Roberts were women?"

"Yes, what else did you think?"

"I am sorry, but I assumed that there must have been a male officer here too. I don't know why."

"Didn't they tell you at your briefing?"

"No, I just had names. No sex was mentioned."

"Typically Fleet, but then, very nonsexist, you have to give them that."

"I never thought you being a woman was anything against you in combat, you know that."

"Being nice to me will get you nowhere, Ong."

"Hey, relax. I want to know where the women went, and if they are alive, get them back, don't you?"

"Sorry, Ong. I miss them, and I am jumpy. It is about a month EST since they went, and I have been sleeping badly and expecting something to come and bash the doors in. It is dark at night here!"

"What did Roberts and White do?"

"Okay, I get to look after the girls up in the rocks and read the screens and collect data, star traffic, and movements, all routine stuff. Julie was 'security'. Did all the usual boundary fence checks and set the alarms, had the radar set up and the satellite focused and watched for alien infiltration. We had a lot of animals wanting to get through the fences at one stage, but she set up the usual 'hot-wire' perimeter, and that stopped that. All very dull routine stuff. This place has been peace on earth until now."

"And Sandra?"

"Fleet communications, was responsible for direct stuff to Fleet on the coded channels. Handled anything that Fleet sent to us. She used to go outside a lot to survey the site that Fleet had mapped out for the shuttle and cruiser base, and for an 'Exploration HQ'. I think they were going to send a team down to set up a base to explore the interior a bit. We sent all the geological reports to Fleet that the satellite pulled up. You want to know something,

Ong, out there, not far from here, there is alluvial gold on the river that you can shovel up!"

He looked skeptical.

"Look at the results. All on record."

"How did Sandra get out there?"

"They took the fly or the floater. She and Julie would go out for a couple of nights sometimes, set up a secure, hot-wired campsite and do detector tests. Didn't tell Fleet everything, if you know what I mean."

"But you knew?"

"Have you tried to keep secrets from women, Ong? I wasn't that interested. I had to be here all the time because of the girls. They did a lot of walking out there, and it wasn't easy. There are creatures out there that eat you!"

"And you still think they got snatched by a plesiosaur?"

"Or something like that. There are huge creatures out in the sea with great long necks that come inshore and snatch the young sea slugs off the rocks."

"Get me a closed comm to Fleet, please, Mary. I want to send a coded top security flash just to find out what Fleet did know about this. I think they may have known, but you know how they work sometimes . . ."

"Never let the left hand know what the right is doing. Fleet instruction number one?"

"You've grown cynical, Jenna, you know that?"

"We have to survive, Ong, we have to survive."

Jutta was with Sylvia Wu. She had poured her troubles in Sylvia's lap and felt better. "I see you here, ma'am, and I worry about the future. Please don't think I am being rude, but you seem to be a kind of prisoner here. You have Crystal, but you don't seem to get out or to meet other women you can talk to, and if I marry Jackson, I can see that happening to me!" And Sylvia had to agree with her, but she pointed out that she had chosen this life. She was like an empress in her palace and knew her place. She lived her life as Solomon had decreed, and she wasn't like Jutta.

"You, you beautiful girl, have a wonderful family back on Valderia. The life they lead is simple, but you are surrounded by love, and that is what made you what you are and what Jackson loves in you.

I don't know if he can see that, but my advice is that you go back to Valderia and wait. Jackson is all fired up to marry you because he wants to have you now. At your age it is all passion and sex, but when you get a little more experienced, you will know."

"I think I do know, but Jackson doesn't, does he?"

"Go back to Valderia, do your Army work, whatever that is, and wait. If he matures in the next year, finishes his studies at Belvedere, you will find out if you are destined to join each other. Keep in touch. He can come and visit and you can come here any time you want. Just let time and Aton do its work."

That night she and Jackson made love in the great gilded bed, and the next morning she asked to go home. It was a sober parting but not without hope.

Maggda had a cryptic message from her contacts on Valderia. "Found the Lieutenant who was with the Red Horse on Valentine. What next?"

"Hold her hand and don't let her roam. Am sending a team."

Jutta went home and her family was discreet.

"Listen, girl. It is your life and much as I like your boy, you have to be really sure. Take your time. Live a little here and don't mope too much. See your friends and kick your heels up a bit. That won't hurt, now will it?"

"Anything you say, Papa."

She went to Maria, and they went out shopping together. Maria had set up home in Schiff's apartment. She had been playing, house and making everything very feminine. She shopped for kitchen gadgets and bath towels. Jutta was secretly amused.

"You are the little married woman now, Maria Schmitt!"

"Well, go ahead and laugh at me, but this is our little love nest. I have to be back at barracks, and so does he, and so do you, but when we do get time off, we come here and relax. I go to see his mother a lot, and she comes here, and it is very cozy. I like it."

"Ah, domestic bliss! Have you told your parents what you are up to?"

"You know they are the other side of the planet, and my father is busy with his business, and my mother has work at the hospital, so I call them once a week, and they don't ask questions. So, Vogel, what is with you and Jackson?"

"I was afraid you'd ask that. To tell you the truth, I don't know. He bought me lovely clothes and a ring with an emerald the size of a loaf of bread, which I gave back, and I suddenly felt trapped. I did like his mother. Straight talk and no nonsense and she knows what Jackson is like. I can't describe how they live, Maria. It is like something from a fairy story. I was standing there in my bedroom at the palace, and I suddenly had this terrible ache inside me, and it said, 'Go home, Jutta, go home,' so I did."

Poor Jackson, he was really upset, but I couldn't explain it. He just thinks that we should spend all our time in bed together."

"Has Kurt been speaking to him?" They laughed.

Her mother sent her a comm message and told her that there were people looking for her. Jutta met Galactic Media and became a reluctant star overnight. Simon thought that the reunion of Jutta with her captors and her subsequent release were worth sending her back to Valentine, so she went first class on an Ong starship and met with Romana and her doctors and Red Jane. Maggda made a sincere human interest story that was all about reconciliation and the stupidity of conflict, and it was a wonderful tearjerker. It sold so well that Simon almost weakened enough to cancel her debts to Galactic. Jutta received a payment from

Galactic that the army appropriated, but she had an exciting time. Maggda hadn't heard from Fleet or Davvd and wondered. Where the heck had he gone? She plugged on making news and worried.

Jenna was out with her girls, and Davvd was reading the records. Two freighters had contacted the beacon in the recent past. They had stopped in orbit and 'delivered supplies'. That wasn't in itself suspicious, but they had no Fleet code, just a commercial entry. He wondered if they were doing deliveries for Fleet anyway. He found a dusty service robot at the back of the complex and activated it, but it hadn't been used for a long time and had no memory of recent past events. He ordered it back into the recess and told it to charge up. He went out of the complex and into the warm air. The lighter gravity made walking easier, and he enjoyed that. In the distance he could see Mary Jenna riding a thermal above the high escarpment. He went to the hangar and landing pad areas, but the heavy plas-steel doors were locked, and he had no palm key access. He experimented with a bit of rock climbing and found it a great pleasure. He was tempted to go on and up, but he came back down and went back to a comfortable chair and read the manual for the beacon. It was the usual stock-in-trade stuff, with no surprises. It appeared the women had played it straight, and there were no dramas likely to occur. The comm chimed, and he decoded the message from Fleet.

"The beacon is a normal directional, jump-off point and has no top secret status. The projected base is necessary because the mineral wealth is being exploited in the future under an agreement between Ong Wu Developments and Fleet. Fleet leases the beacon site and an area surrounding the perimeter that is very rich in rare minerals. This would be secured by the base, and mining would take place within the near future. A token force would be housed there. Construction of the base will take place shortly. The beacon will be taken over by the garrison, and Fleet operatives taken off as soon as the base is established."

He closed the comm down and said nothing to Jenna when she appeared.

"How are the girls, Mary?"

"They are fine and love to fly. Why are you interested?"

"Just being conversational. I can see why they are of interest to you. I have never seen anything like those anywhere!"

"They stink, have disgusting habits, but they are wonderful flyers. What I like about them is that they can feed themselves, and they don't need much in the way of shelter or TLC."

"Do they like you?"

"If I said they were pleased to see me when I go up there, probably not. They have very little brains; they are like a chicken: most of the brain is in the neck. Cut their heads off and they could still operate."

"And I thought you loved them."

"One thing I do know, and that is, I respect them, Ong. They can take an arm off if they get cranky."

"Don't worry. I don't intend to get too close to them, believe me. Now, what's the story with the hangars? I wanted to see the floater and to do a little trip outside the perimeter, but you have it sealed down."

"Well, so would you if you had your friends disappeared in a hurry. Will open it up for you after we've eaten, if that is all right?"

"Fine. What is there to drink? What is on the menu?"

"Why don't you play chef and punch some buttons, and I will find you a bottle of something special. I know where it is."

He went into the kitchen area and dialed up steaks and found a salad in the boxes in the thermidor, and when he came back she had laid the table. She had opened a bottle of wine and had poured two glasses. She raised her glass. "Let's drink to getting off here, Ong. If I don't see another day on this stinking place, I shall be happy."

He drank, and then they ate the steak, and he felt suddenly very sick. He looked at her through eyes that were beginning to lack focus and staggered to the bathroom and vomited. She came after him and stood in the doorway. "Don't you like the brew, Ong?"

He was sick again, "What did you put in it, Mary?"

"You'll just go out long enough to let us head for the great galacticvoid, Ong. You will probably live."

She grabbed his arm and dragged him to his room and pushed him onto the bed. He slowly slipped into a black void, and she tied his wrists to the bed frame and his feet to the bottom, then left him. He was helpless but was beyond caring.

Roberts and White sat with Mary and drank. "Damn Ong. Why did they send Ong! Why didn't they send some dumb bastard who would have swallowed that story? I thought he would have bought it, but we didn't do the trace well enough. He smelled a rat."

"Well, Julie, what have we got to do?"

"Not much. We have the last of the gold packed up and ready to load. You disable the scanners and make the console a heap of junk so he can't scream for help until we are long gone, and we are free of this dump, and Fleet, forever."

"They won't be able to track us, will they?"

"Once we get out of orbit there is nothing to track. Now do your work, and we can get our gear together, and all we have to do is catch that freighter."

Davvd Ong came to his senses slowly. He was cold. He had no idea of the time of day. His wrists hurt, and he felt sick. He twisted about and finally, after much wriggling, freed a wrist, and then it wasn't too long before he was free. He wondered why she hadn't used the ties that would have been totally impossible to break; maybe she didn't want him to die of starvation. He discovered the wrecked consoles and didn't know where to start, but then he thought of the service robot and called it out. It had basic Galactic, so he told it to repair the console. It made noises that could have been interpreted as, "tsk, tsk" and then scanned the mess and trundled off to get spares from the stores. He left it to it and tackled the hangar door. He had found a sonic key and after a few combinations, the doors opened and there was the fly, but the floater was missing. He walked to the landing pad, and the floater was parked on the edge of the area. He assumed that Mary wasn't alone, that White and Roberts and Jenna were in something together. They had never died, he was sure of that, so what the heck was going on? He went back to the complex and drank a lot of water but still felt sick. The service robot was still working.

"The damage is not great, master, but I may have to modify to get the whole system back together."

"Not required, just give me signal power to Fleet frequencies."

"Yes, master."

"What else is down?"

"The fence has no power."

"What is the security risk?"

"Total, master. Any alien animal can now enter the complex unimpeded."

"How dangerous is it?"

"Some of the wildlife here are carnivorous, master."

"Make the fence the priority."

He had no desire to end up as a meal for some raptor roaming outside the doors. He had one stun pistol of indeterminate power and nothing else. Maybe he could stand up and shout, "Boo!"

The admiral was enjoying himself with Sonna's breasts and kissing her neck, and she leant back against him and then said, "Enough. I want to go home. You and your wife are going out to dinner tonight, and if you are late she will get cranky, you know that."

She pulled away from him and buttoned her shirt and went to the ensuite and did her hair and tidied herself before leaving. "And Arthur, have we heard from Davvd Ong?" she shouted at the door,

"No." he shouted back. What was Ong doing? He had been unable to get back to him, and the frequency was dead. Even his high-tech boys in the satellite up above him were not getting anything back from Asgard. He made a mental note to see about it in the morning. Meanwhile, get home, get changed and go out with his comfortable and personable wife. Sonna was right.

Night fell on Asgard. Ong made himself a meal and drank beer. He had some power, but the robot, Servo 10, was still making connections and rebuilding units. It had told him the fence was operating at two hundred volts, so he felt easier there. He wondered about the three women and reflected that if he had been stuck out here for two ESY's without relief, he might have gone a bit stir crazy too. He felt helpless. He went to bed early. There was silence, and he slept. He was awaked by a great crash and wondered what it was; there was another, and he turned on the bedside light. It was fed by sunlight from above, so was isolated from the damaged sections. There was noise in the complex. He cracked open the bedroom door, and there was a shape he didn't recognize. He closed the door and went back for the stun pistol by his bed. He leant against the door and listened. Something scratched against the other side; it sounded like a rough skin. He gingerly opened the door, and something was thrust into the gap. It was a sharp clawed forearm from beyond time, and he flung himself at the door and crushed it against the frame, but it pushed hard, and he was slowly pushed back. He could smell the thing's breath, and it was malodorous. He put his shoulder against the door and pushed the stun gun through the gap to where he thought the head of the thing might be and pressed the firing button. There was a roar and a lot of crashing noises. He opened the door a bit more, and something was thrashing about on the floor. He hit the stun gun button again, and it jerked and then lay still. He hit the button again and then went to find a light. He had lights at least, and there, jerking a little and trembling, was what looked like a small version of a tyrannosaurus. It had a fearsome jaw and sharp teeth

363

and clawed arms and toes. It stank. He stepped back as it began to tremble and hit it again with the stun gun, hoping the charge had had time to build up again. It slumped, and he wondered what in Aton's name he was going to do with it. He found the ties that Jenna should have used on him and secured the jaw for a start, then the front legs, and finally the feet, then took a deep breath. "Check the rest of the space, Ong. Make sure this bastard thing was the only one." He went and secured the doors. The creature had got his scent and had just shouldered the heavy doors aside. He made himself a stiff drink and went to check on the repair job to the console. It wasn't ready, but he could see that in a couple of hours, it might be. He put the stun gun on charge, and it registered that it was sucking up power, so that was something. Then he switched off the lights and went back to bed. What else could he do? It wasn't the best night's sleep he had ever had, but at least it was rest.

Daylight. The creature lay on the floor, occasionally making futile attempts to move and break the ties. It could only have got down to the complex when the fence was off. He opened the doors and attached a rope to the neck and led that outside. He went and brought the floater down and backed it into the restricted space and connected the rope up, then slowly dragged the creature out of the complex and up the slope to the open grassed area and then out beyond the perimeter fence, which he switched off to pass through. He checked the stun gun charge and zapped the creature, then cut off the ties and hurried back through the invisible barrier and switched it back on. It revived quicker than he thought possible, and it made towards him until it got zapped by the fence. It tried once more and then turned away into the undergrowth and crashed away. He checked the area for wildlife and found two creatures like rabbits with long snouts, eating the grass, and two large birds that had flown in over the defenses, but nothing he considered dangerous. No wonder Jenna was jumpy. With things like that always on the lookout for a meal, who could blame her for being cautious? He took the floater back and considered taking the fly up to reconnoiter but decided to stay close to the comm. There might well be a response from Fleet. He documented everything on his pod, made himself some coffee and went outside to enjoy it. It was a beautiful day, and Jenna's girls were circling and using the thermals along with other flying things. The sea was a blue blue, and things slid through it and occasionally breached the surface. Aton smiled. He wished Maggda was here to share it. He checked with the service robot.

"The comm is operational, master, but for Fleet frequency only."

"Thank you. Now you are to call me sir, not master. Have you recorded that?"

"Yes sir."

"Good boy! Now let's see if this thing does work." He entered the codes, and the lights danced across the screen. Then he told Fleet what had happened, and what he thought had happened and waited. It would take a day before they could answer.

Sonna picked up the hard copy of the coded message and took it in to the old man. "Captain Ong ran into trouble, sir."

He read the report and cursed quietly. "It looks like the women had planned it all, but what was the motive? Ong thinks they shipped out with a load of gold and maybe more than one. Won't know till we get down there and find out. Point is, Sonna, who would know *what* they got away with? We had no records. Anyway, those smart-ass women had better be really smart, or they are dead. Get the names out to Fleet Security and to every damn planet that they are likely to try and run to. You know, Sonna, it isn't the gold but the desertion from duty that will hang them. Desertion is the death penalty, you know."

"Yes sir."

"Now, get Ong off there. Send a cruiser and a set of replacements to man that beacon, and we can start over,"

"Yes sir."

Davvd Ong was helping the robot to finally fix the comm. It looked a bit better, the screens all worked, and the satellite links were home and hosed, so he felt better. He swept up bits of rubbish and broken circuitry and plas-steel scraps and even mopped the floor. He did a security check on the base perimeter, and rode up to look at the girls, but stopped short of riding one. They were ugly and they stank, and he left them to their own devices. He took out the fly and checked the fuel, then flew slowly over the immediate area until he located the river that he had targeted for a close-up look. It ran through a great, wide and very shallow, rocky bed, and he could see some signs of disturbance. He dropped the fly and walked over to the scrapes and kicked over a few rocks. He found three sizable nuggets under the rocks and once his eyes had accustomed to the sheen, more of the metal. He had to laugh to himself. This was more than enough motivation for desperate women to take the chance, load up and flee the Fleet. He put the nuggets into his pocket and flew back. He checked the fusion reactor, but they had stopped short of attempting to shut that down. He was thinking that maybe all three deserved to get away with it. "Fly high, Jenna, fly high and watch your back."

Maggda had a message. It read, "I am alive and well and coming back. Where are you?" She had been going stir crazy in her suite at the hotel but now felt better. Ong was alive at least. She asked Simon for leave and a replacement.

"Give me ten days, Simon, please?"

He had been looking at her stories and knew that she had about exhausted her talents there. A good journalist could now take over, and he didn't need an inspired one. He told her she could have ten days, but no more. She packed a bag and caught the next ship out to Alpha Six and then to Mars. She went to the office and Simon gave her a chaste kiss.

"You did well, Maggs, you know that?"

"No, Simon, I did brilliantly."

"Your modesty becomes you, Styxx. So how was it?"

"I felt for the folks who were all caught in the crossfire. It was bad, and Valderia has a lot to answer for, you know that."

"Well, they are, right now. The old chancellor is stepping down, and it looks like your friend Schiff will get the nod. Federation arrested four generals trying to fly the coop, and they have been accused of war crimes, which they all deny. Your friend Ong is coming back to Alpha Six after a bit of excitement on Asgard. He gets around, doesn't he? The tribe you fell in love with on E5 is getting a lot of attention--"

"What about the baby?"

"Baby?"

"You know what a baby is, Simon. I meant the child of one Annrath on E5, my friend and wise woman."

"Who has a baby called Maggda for some reason. Is that the one?"

"I could kick you sometimes, you smart—"

"I can show you some lovely footage of your namesake if you can contain yourself long enough."

She sat and watched and felt very emotional. The child stirred her up, and she wanted to reach out and hold it.

"Can I go back there and see her, Simon?"

"Pay your own fares, and you can go where you like for ten days."

"I could do a follow-up story, very personal, human interest . . ."

"No! Milked that dry, Maggda. Have to find something hot for you to go and write about now. How about Old Earth and the generals being tried for war crimes? That would suit you. Sitting in a dusty court for hours listening to a lot of old legal farts discussing what was legal and what wasn't. Sound like fun?"

"A laugh a minute, Simon. Are you really going to do that to me?"

"What would you like to do?"

"I think I shall just go home and rest. I need to talk to my potted plants. Where did you say Ong was?"

"Last heard heading for Alpha Six to be debriefed. Can't get much out of Fleet about him, you know. Something happened on Asgard, we do know that, or he wouldn't have been there, would he?"

"Hope he had the soup cans."

"What?"

"Nothing. Just being silly. I am going home."

"Take care, Ms. Styxx."

"And you, Brent."

She went to her apartment and talked to her jungle plants that had automatically been fed and watered, and they clicked back to her their cheerful little chatter.

She hung up her 'dressing gown,' and sorted her messages. There were the usual bills and of course, the offers of trips to the poles for wild sand-duning parties with young jocks and unlimited fun and games, for only a few thousand credits. There was a note to advise her of a delivery that hadn't been delivered because she wasn't there, and she got in touch with the company and told them to deliver it, if it wasn't going to cost her anything. It was after lunch when the knock came on the door, and there was a big crate. The human attendant had the robot shifters wheel it in, and she looked at it. "What is it, and where does it come from?"

"Well, miss, it just has '447' on the description. Shipped from a Barracks Ten on Valderia, if that helps."

She sat and laughed. "Uncrate it, please. This has to be the most elaborate joke . . ."

And there was 447, with a yellow ribbon round its neck with a card.

"Dear Maggda, he is impossible. I have bought him for you because you made him what he is. He says he is no longer 447, but Rex, and that he loves you." My very best wishes, Kurt Schiff."

They took the crate away, and she signed the pod screen and looked at the robot.

"Rex, are you alive and alert, you wonderful thing?"

"Alive and alert, miss."

"What happened to you?"

"I was declared unfit for duty, miss."

"If you were human I would kiss you."

"Thank you, miss."

"How did you get here?"

"Major Schiff was told he could have me at a discounted price because I was useless to the army. They didn't want me to cook, miss."

"What am I to do with you?"

"I could do a really good soufflé for you, if you have the ingredients."

"Later, Rex, later." She laughed, and Rex went into her kitchen and checked it out. Life wasn't going to be dull anymore. She had a wonderful meal that evening. Rex organized a whole set of menus, ordered food and brought her a drink, and she kept laughing because the situation was totally absurd. How could she repay Schiff, she wondered?

Davvd Ong sat and watched Sonna go about her duties and thought of her and the admiral. She caught his look.

"What am I doing here? Isn't that the next question, Captain?"

"Almost."

"Kicking my heels for a bit, that's all. I go for promotion next month, and if I get it, I shall be out of here."

"And then?"

"On duty with you somewhere?"

"I can think of worse things."

"Ah, but you have Maggda Styxx in your sights, not me."

"Who told you that?"

"She did."

"Well, it must be right!"

"How was Asgard?"

"Interesting. If you like disappearing beacon staff and flying reptiles and man-eating raptors. Laugh a minute really."

"What next, Captain?"

"Where he sends me, I guess, but I have to tell him that my next stop is Mars for a bit of R and R."

"Or a bit of M and S?"

"I could get lucky."

"Come on through. I think he is ready for us."

Debriefed, exhausted by it all, he went to his bare-assed quarters and had a stiff drink and a bare meal and then bed. He dreamt of Maggda, who had a baby in her arms and bare breasts with milk dripping from them. She refused to let it suckle, and he was angry and shouted at her, and then he woke, with sweat on his body and the bed clothes in turmoil. Next morning he rode out on a Fleet cruiser to Mars. The crew was pleasant and asked him if he thought they could hack it on Asgard. He told them it was an experience they might like to tackle if they liked lizards. He sat in with the commander, caught up with some neglected skills and watched the hyper-drive screen as the ship plummeted through no time and warp space on its run to Mars. Two nights of mess food and beer, and he began to feel human. He laughed at old jokes and watched holos of young women dancing naked on ice and Martian sand racers burning across the deserts and a documentary tour of Solomon Wu's palace and thought of Su Lin and went to his bunk. He carted his duffle bag out of the spaceport and caught a cab down through the lava tube expressway into the city and arrived at Maggda's apartment tower as the sun was setting across the red, red plains and rocks. He stood in the entrance and called her on the cell, and she laughed and told him to wait. He was nervous. Why would he be nervous? She pressed the door switch, and he was inside, and there was someone whom he recognized, and he laughed from surprise and pleasure.

"Rex? Is it really you? How in Aton's name did you get here?"

She came to greet him in the old labcoat, and he slung the bag down and reached for her, picked her up and carried her into the bedroom and lowered her onto the bed, and she smiled at him. He took off his clothes, and she flung the old coat open and held out her arms. In the kitchen, Rex was making pot roast. Somehow, it never got eaten. Aton smiled across the red sands and glittered off the plas-glass domes and the water of the lakes and the canals. They lay in the wide bed, and she reached for him. He stirred and ran his hand over her body, and then he kissed her and lay on top of her and smiled.

"What's for breakfast?" Later, as they drank their coffee, he suddenly stood and went to his bag.

"Nearly forgot. I have a little souvenir for you from Asgard."

"I thought you were the present, Ong."

"Thanks, but no."

He rolled the three nuggets onto the table.

"What is this?"

"Alluvial gold. The place is reeking of it. That's why Fleet and Ong Wu are keen to get out there. The beacon staff decamped, we think, with loads of it and went AWOL. Of course, Styxx, that is classified."

"Of course."

"I just thought you might string them together and make a really nice chunky piece of jewelry."

"You do have nice thoughts, Ong."

"What are you doing today?"

"Why, what have you planned?"

"I have to report to Fleet down in Dome Three, and then I want to talk to your Simon. While I do that, you can get the bauble made up, then we can have a really epicurean lunch, and you can drive me out into the desert in a sand hopper. I need the exercise."

"Last night wasn't enough, huh?"

"Just a warm up, Styxx. Tonight we get heavy!"

"Promises, Ong, just promises."

Fleet Agent Betty Blokk yawned and stretched and looked at her time band. She had slept in the car overnight watching the apartment block entrance and was awaiting her replacement. She hoped Maggda and Ong were having a good time. The door opened, and John slipped into the passenger seat. He had two take-out cartons of coffee, and he passed her one.

"Tell me the story, Blokk."

"About two morning cycle, a guy came by with a box and the sensors read 'explosive device,' and he went to the entrance. I went over, and he wanted to play, so I zapped him."

"And?"

"I got him carted off by local security."

"Bomb?"

"I left it in the back for you. Couldn't leave my station here, right?"

"I got a bomb in the back?"

"Looks like it. Look, I'll leave you with it; I gotta get home." She slipped out of the car and walked off down the street. He got out and shouted after her, but she crossed the street and was gone.

"Aw! . . ." He went round the back of the car and stepped back as the lid opened. There was a small black box sitting there. He gingerly reached for it, and the lid suddenly popped open and he reared back. There was an arm and a hand holding a neat black sphere labeled "BOMB," which waggled back and forth on its spring. A flag appeared from the top that said "BANG!"

"You bitch, Blokk. I am going to kill you! I swear I am going to kill you!"

Simon was taken aback to have Davvd Ong appear, but he recognized that this was a golden opportunity to get to know this man, and he wasn't disappointed. He listened, and he became aware of what Maggda and others saw in him. He had a good sense of humor, was self-deprecating and had an air of polished confidence that Simon knew came from wealth and very good breeding. So he listened and they talked.

"Maggda," said Davvd, "keeps telling me she owes you so many credits that she will be in your debt forever."

Simon laughed. "Maggda is a wealthy woman, Davvd. She can repay that little debt anytime she wants, but you don't know her. She won't pay it because she thinks that if she does, we would cancel her contract. She just uses that old debt story to get some leverage. If you really want to know, we cancelled that debt last week, but we haven't told her."

"You guys sound like Fleet!"

Maggda is one of our best assets or hadn't you noticed? What with her pre-publicity from Second Skin and her natural nose for sniffing out a good story, we need her. We aren't likely to pull the plug on her, but we play the game. No, Davvd, she is pretty secure here. I keep her guessing because she works better that way. I couldn't deny her much. Could you?"

"Nothing. Maggda gets under the skin, Simon. Like a bad rash, hard to get rid of or forget!"

They met and ate, and he admired the nuggets on a thin chain spaced between pearls.

"I love it, Davvd."

"See how I look after you, Styxx? In any case, if you get into real debt you could hock it and pay it off."

"Don't give me ideas, Ong, or I might."

"Is Rex still the master chef?"

"I think so. We eat in tonight?"

"Yeah, let's get domesticated. Remind us of E5."

"I want to see my niece."

"Get permission from the Foundation, jump a starship and go!"

"You have to come with me."

"Can't."

"Why not, you are on leave, aren't you?"

"I am awaiting a recall at any minute. We get this week together, and then I will probably get to polish up the soup cans and pack the bags."

"Could I come with you?"

"Only if you join Fleet as a special agent. Now don't look round, but you see that guy over there doing an outhouse impression? That is Agent John Banks. A Fleet heavy. He is here to make sure you don't threaten me with excessive sexual overtures or something equally destructive to a young man's health."

"They watch what we do in bed?"

"Probably."

"Get me out of here, and let's lose him in the sand. How can I concentrate tonight thinking about having a tri-dee under the bed!"

The red sands flew, and the sand hopper fled across the wastes on its huge soft tires and leapt the ridges, and it was more fun than he had had for a while, outside of the bedroom. The landscape was beautiful in its starkness, and it was a reluctant Davvd Ong who turned back as Aton plunged over the horizon. Through the airlock doors and down the lava tube and into the comfort and sterilized air of the domes. Mars had an eerie appeal, and he could see why the original settlers had fallen in love with it. It was greening up now. Algae and mosses now grew where nothing could. In another few hundred years as the terraforming took over, Mars would look green instead of red. They booked in the hopper and went back to the apartment and smiled to see the 'tail' behind them.

Rex was instructed, and they sat back with a drink, and Davvd looked at her in the fading red light. She was a lovely woman and at ease now. Her long limbs and wonderful body rested, and he thought how lucky he was to have her as a companion and bedmate. She caught his gaze and raised an eyebrow.

"Just thinking of how good you look and how much at ease I am now. Would be wonderful to just stop time and stay here like this forever, but I know it has to stop."

"Don't get maudlin. Marry me, and we can go live on E5 and start a colony of Ongs to blend with the others."

"You would get bored, I would get bored, the kids would get

bored, the tribe would sling us out, and we would be back to square one. Let's face it, Maggda, both of us need the adrenaline."

"Nice to dream. What are we going to do, Ong?"

"Aton knows. Just drift for a week and satisfy our mutual lust and then await the call of the wild."

"Things could be worse."

"Let's drink to mutual lust; at least we have that in common."

Rex was making chiming noises, so they went and ate.

Jackson Wu was despondent, but he went back to Belvedere and finished his assignments and was given a 'Pass.' He slogged along and thought of Jutta a lot. She went back to the farm and slogged along and thought of him. Depression became mutual.

Solomon went to see Horatio and found him surprisingly busy and motivated. He had discovered the hidden joys of doing something right for once. Hard work was paying off. He was now being asked for opinions he never knew he had, and it pleased him. His father and he ate together and drank together, and they spoke together.

"What do you see in the future, Horatio?"

"Well, Father, when this political duty ends, I suspect I will resign my commission and come and join you, somewhere. I don't think I can go back to Fleet."

"What do you want to do?"

"Open up new enterprises, start new projects that will push Wu along? Whatever you think I could do."

"You know that Jackson will finish at Belvedere soon, and his mother is worried about him. He fell in love with a girl on Valderia, wants to get married, but the girl is playing hard to get, and he may just rebel and not go on to diplomatic studies. She doesn't sound suitable anyway. I can see you as a planetary delegate or on the Galactic Council or even just taking over from me. I never see your mother these days. I need to spend more time at home. Think about it. Resign from Fleet, and you will be free of their beck and call, and we can work something out. It would be good if you found a proper girl to marry. You know, someone with a decent pedigree and one who likes to play the hostess and is used to high society. I know the whores you usually escort about, so what you need is a high-class woman for a change. I can tell you this, that in bed they are all the same."

"What do you want me to do?"

"Get out of Fleet. Become more socially active. Get your name in the media a bit more. Become eligible. Your mother wants grandchildren. She was betting on Jackson, but it looks like you might fill the bill."

"Am I on a fishing expedition?"

"No, if you do what I tell you. Make yourself 'eligible', and the fish will find you. New London is full of them, believe me. You need one with good looks and a pedigree, and old money wouldn't hurt. Play the field; that's what you are used to doing anyway."

"And love?"

"Don't let sentiment cloud your judgment. Love comes from familiarity in bed, Horatio. Try it and see."

Fleet accepted his resignation. It solved a few problems for them anyway. The press wondered why he was suddenly available. The women's holos called him "eligible", even though he had been, eligible all along. The fish began to swim his social stream.

Jackson had a week off and was going to see Jutta, but he went home and talked to his mother. He got nothing from her, but "wait." He was frustrated and thought of what Jutta had said about simplicity. When was he happiest? When he was with her on the family farm with the smell of the horses and the cows in the fields, a shaggy dog licking his hand, Mrs. Vogel baking wonderful bread, and her father pouring him wine and saying, "Try this, boy; it's the best we have"? He drank too much at dinner and talked to Crystal and his mother and went to his bed bemused.

He slept the sleep of the drunk and in the early hours woke and felt a warm body next to him. He reached for it and thought Jutta had miraculously appeared, and he held it and wanted to make love to her, and then the voice whispered in his ear.

"I can give you pleasure, Jackson," and he knew it was Crystal, and he felt very strange indeed.

"I can satisfy your needs, Jackson, because I am programmed to do that, if that is what you want."

He crawled out of bed and asked her to leave, and she picked up her clothing and left, still in the dark. He wondered if he had made love to the machine or not, and he just wanted Jutta. He had to have Jutta or become mad. He had the strange feeling that his mother had sent Crystal to please him, and he felt like weeping.

What had the world come to? He made up his mind that he had to speak to Jutta. It was now or never. He booked on the next starliner to Valderia and sent her a message which said, "We have to talk. Meet me at the Palace. Will contact when I am there. Love, Jackson."

Cassandra Merton-Hoy met Belle Randolph-Smith outside the Crest and went in for coffee.

"Belle, you look wonderful, darling. Are you here with your mother?"

"Yes, she is shopping. Where are you staying?"

"Here, Binkie, here. My dear, have you seen Horatio Wu? He is everywhere these days. I went to Pinky Pinkerton's the other night, and he was swanning around there."

"Pinky knows his father."

"Really, what luck! She likes to be seen, dear, does Pinky. She'll be in the holos with her arm round the man, gushing away as usual."

"Your mother, is she here?"

"No, she is at the horse sales. Daddy wanted her there, so I am off the leash. Horatio is having a dinner party here tonight with lots of top brass and the usual crowd. Are you invited?"

"Mummy sneaked me an invite."

"Then we had better tart ourselves up, dear. Who else is coming, do you know?"

"Franny Parker-Taylor is back from New India."

"What on earth was she doing there. It's a dreadful place."

"Some charity thing. You know how pious she can get. Loves to be seen in tears over some dirty child, especially when the cameras are about."

"We all know darling. We all know. My mother calls her a self-righteous bitch."

"She got some award, for 'Humanitarian Example', or something like that from Flag of Compassion."

"May Aton burn her eyes out."

"Oh. Cassie, don't be so unkind. I thought you were great chums when we were at school."

"School, Binkie, is a bit different from the great social jungle. Horatio Wu, Binkie darling, is out looking for a wife, and he would be a really, really good catch, and that is why, Binkie darling, your mother has got you an invitation, and why I, Binkie darling, will be wearing an outrageous dress that shows just about everything I own, and I know, I just know, Binkie, that you will be doing the same, in the hope you can get laid by the man tonight."

"You always were crude, Cassandra."

"No, Binkie, just thinking aloud and telling the truth. Your family has pots of money, so you won't be as keen to get to bed with him as some of us. My father has just about lost all we had. They are selling the horses now. Next, we will put the estate up for sale. Mummy told me, but in not the same words, that it was all right to be a whore if you got paid enough."

"Oh Cassie, she didn't!"

"Well, no, Binkie, but she came close. If Aton smiles on me, and I can marry Horatio Wu by hook or by crook, then I can line the toilet with credits."

"I bet he doesn't know just how vulgar you can be, Cassie."

"The only place he will find out, Binkie, is between the

sheets. If sex isn't dirty, it isn't good sex. Even you should know that!"

"I wonder sometimes, Cassandra, where you learned all this, I really do!"

"You think Mummy was an angel, Binkie?"

Horatio was charming. He could be when the need arose, but he was looking at the women like a butcher buying beef. He had no illusions about these so-called upper crust girls. They were on the market, and he was the buyer, and he was following instructions. Solomon had almost given him a set of specifications, and he had a short list. His agents had done their homework, and he looked hard at the Merton-Hoy girl. Family was of very good pedigree but was on the skids financially; however, she spoke six languages and had had a silver spoon education. The accents were right, and she had a nice controlled laugh, a low voice, and looked like a trembling virgin, even if her dress was an advertisement for a quick tumble.

Then there was the "Binkie" girl, who had been introduced as Binkie, and who tended to giggle a bit too much, but he put that down to the champagne. A pretty girl, with long legs and a dress that was a bit daring but discreet. Family had good credentials and stock in everything including Ong Wu Corporations. Daddy was a "business consultant", whatever that meant. She looked, what was the word? Sweet? But Horatio was looking for a good night. A chance to sample the merchandise.

The Frances Parker mare looked right, but she wanted the limelight and was keen to get herself tri-deed by the magazines, even though she was working hard at being a modest little girl just doing what she could for humanity. She even had the miniature flag badge for the Flag of Compassion award on her dress. She knew how to play the press.

So Horatio tossed a coin and came up with the Merton-Hoy offering, and he danced with her a lot and held her close. She was firm-fleshed and yielding and didn't flinch when he passed an exploratory hand around her backside. He had the waiter ply her with drink and talked to her and looked in her eyes when he wasn't looking at her blatant display of breasts and thigh. When they declared the evening over, and they were all saying goodbyes and wobbling out to the lined up transport, he asked her to stay back for a final drink, and she shyly accepted. Binkie scowled as she wished Cassandra goodnight and went back to Mummy and swore, discreetly, of course. Horatio took her up to his luxurious room and dimmed the lights and clinked glasses with her, Then she said she had to lie down for a little while because she felt a bit dizzy, so she climbed onto the big bed and lay on her back with her eyes closed and her legs discreetly but suggestively open and dress ridden up. She said, as he climbed up beside her, that she hoped he wasn't going to take advantage of her because she might have to tell Mummy. By daylight, she had quite a lot to tell Mummy, and Horatio had added her to his short list. She had all the skills of a good whore, and he had known a few of those. She looked good and had a good voice and underneath the veneer of high-class respectability, was as hard as Solomon when he had a deal going. He nearly expected her to ask for a bundle of credits. He made sure she would come back for another session, and she actually thanked him! As he told himself, she did have class. He thought he might give the Binkie girl a run, and he asked the agent to ask her to meet him that evening for dinner. It was terribly tiring, this social whirl, but after all, he was just doing what his father had asked him to do.

Binkie was pleased that she had received the invitation to a private dinner with Horatio Wu. She knew he had been to bed with Cassandra because Cassandra had told her she had a wonderful night. She didn't actually say she had had sexual intercourse four times, but she was a happy girl, which annoyed Binkie. She did some homework. Binkie decided that she couldn't whore as well as Cassandra, so went for the shy young lady from a genteel family who was a little overawed by Horatio Wu's family background. Her evening dress was pretty, frilly, and very feminine. She ate in a delicate way and drank carefully but relaxed when it came to the champagne, which she knew was so expensive that it just had to be appreciated. She looked a little flushed when he suggested she come up to his room for a nightcap but went anyway. She had talked to Horatio about her mother's love of exotic blooms and how she loved the gardens because she had seen them on holos. He told her about Crystal and the orchids, though he had barely seen them for years. In the room he held her and kissed her, and she told him she liked that, and when he began to explore her, she said, "I must hang up my dress. I don't want to ruin it." She climbed on the bed with him in her undies and said that she wasn't used to this, and should she undress?

He found that making love to Binkie was like teaching a Girl Scout how to tie knots, but she progressed very well and won her "efficiency" badge, so both were satisfied. She intrigued him. She wanted to be kissed and hugged a lot and explored with great tenderness, and he felt warmth towards her. She seemed so innocent and fresh that he really did wonder if she was one step from virginity.

In the morning she clung to him and covered her breasts with her hands when the curtains opened to the light of day. She was really very sweet and wouldn't let him watch her dress or shower with him, and somehow, that appealed to him. Binkie went on the short list with a four-star advantage. Horatio thought he could teach her a lot, but she already knew the manual backwards. Not being used to subtlety, he was easy game, and she smiled to herself, gave him a little girl kiss and left him bemused.

Cassandra watched her leave from the window in the dining room at breakfast and said things to herself that couldn't be repeated in polite company, but at least she was being given a second chance. Was Binkie in the same league? Only Horatio knew.

The winter is harsh, but we are warm, and we have food. We break the ice on the lake and catch fish with our spears. Annrath, my woman, and

381

Maggda the child are healthy and strong and the child grows day by day, and Annrath is pleased. Men came from the stars and spoke to us, and they have the servants Joe and Don, like Davvd did. They say we are strong and will be allowed to stay here, and that we are to be called 'Ong's Tribe,' which makes Annrath laugh. Two of the girls that came with us from the old place are with child, because Manta laid with them both, and so did Motan. We need more hunters. The little pigs we kept are large and ready to kill, but the star man said that we should let them mate, and then we will have lots of pigs that we don't have to hunt, but we like to hunt. It is the way. We make bowls, and now every hunter and the women have bowls to eat from and to cook in, and the food does not spoil so much. Annrath asked the star people if Maggda would come back, but they say they didn't know. She is away to the stars with Davvd. Life is good. The star man Radnath has been to see us, and he laughed and smiled and said he was happy for us. He is a strange man. We await the turning of the season so we can go out into the forest and the hills, and the game will return. We wait for the long sun days. The Ong tribe prospers.

Maria was arranging flowers. She had struggled all day with her C.O. and had fled to "her and Kurt's" apartment. He had been meeting with Voight and came home an angry man.

"Voight is playing politics, and I get to be between the proverbial target and the cannons."

She gave him a long kiss. "What's happened?"

"I get to be chancellor, if Voight has his way."

"But you are next in line anyway, aren't you?"

He sat and took the drink she handed him. "Yes, but of course, there are strings attached. Voight will be head of the new high command structure. The Governing Council will act the way he wants and vote me in as chancellor, but until I can find a way of actually ousting him, he will pull the political strings. Now I could do that, just let him have his way, and if you marry me, my lovely Maria, we could just play royalty. You get to be 'Countess Maria', and we dress up and look magnificent and smile a lot while those bastards ruin the planet."

"What can we do? He holds all the cards, doesn't he?"

"There has to be a way. He sent those four top officers to Old Earth for war crimes, and I came close to being involved in that debacle too. If it hadn't been for the publicity, I would have been. My uncle has gone off planet now. Voight is acting chancellor. It's one big mess, Maria."

"Come and eat. Who can you talk to? Isn't there someone who can advise you? Isn't the Chancellery full of so-called advisers?

"All paid by Voight and loyal to him. I need someone off planet, someone with clout."

"Could Solomon Wu help?"

"I don't think he would buy into that, but if we could find something that Galactic Federation could get involved in, other than this, 'robot army' fiasco . . . The trouble is, they walk a very fine line when they interfere with sovereign planet status. I don't think he would buy into that, but he might find something that would alert the Federation, and we might get some action, apart from the robot army. They walk a very fine line when they interfere with sovereign planetary status. I will just have to be as devious as Voight and find a way of removing him."

"Kurt, become the damn chancellor. Once you have that power and the planet's population behind you, you can act. It is no good nipping at heels like a terrier."

"Will you marry me?"

"I keep thinking we are."

"When I become chancellor, and you become Empress Maria, you will find the air up there very rarefied. If you thought the barracks was a backstabbing, empire-building nest of crooks, then the Chancellery makes the barracks look like a kindergarten."

"But if you were there, Kurt, with some good, handpicked people around you, you could oust Voight and his cronies. There must be some honest souls left up there!"

"You will make a good chancellor's wife!"

"I am sick of all this. Let's eat at the Boar and invite Jutta and get a little drunk."

"Let's drink to the future, Maria, and hope there is one."

Jutta went with them since Jackson wouldn't be on Valderia until the next evening, and they commiserated with each other. Jutta was at a loose end, and Maria suggested she ask if she could come back to the office and help out. Schiff had no duties and was chafing at the bit. He turned to his mother for support and help. He felt that he deserved it after all the years of being alone.

Maggda was sleeping, and he lay beside her wondering what, if any, future they had together. He could, of course, marry her, and what then? They both liked freedom, but he could see them becoming hemmed in by the Ong business empire and her feeling trapped. She was an incredible woman both in and out of bed, and he knew she wouldn't just take the role of the Ong wife, and neither would Su Lin, if she had lived. He leant on an elbow and gently suckled her breast, and she stirred and opened her eyes.

"You are impossible, you know that? I was dreaming I had a baby there."

"Would you like one?"

"What would I do with your offspring, Ong? Sorry, take no notice; it is just the hormones talking. I'll get over it. Right now we have it made. I have you, and you have me, in a manner of speaking, so let's stick to the comfort of a good sex life for the time being. By the way, is Rex making breakfast? All this extracurricular activity makes me hungry."

"What is the plan, Styxx?"

"Get out, explore, take you on guided tours, go see my parents, whom I haven't seen for ages, tell them you are another reporter working for Galactic, and they'll feel sorry for you . . . the usual 'let's do Mars' stuff."

"Your parents are going to believe that?"

"They don't get to see the holos much, so all the publicity we've stirred up will probably end up as 'I didn't know that.'

Who do you want to be? I know, Bennie Konstantis, he writes the 'Interplanetary Gossip' stuff."

"Go away, Styxx! Just tell them I work in the office, all right?"

"And I thought the Interplanetary Gossip was just right for you!"

He slapped her bare backside and crawled out of bed. "I am going to challenge Rex. Bet he can't make fresh croissants."

Jackson met Jutta in the foyer and bought her a gin and tonic, and then they went up to the suite. It was getting dark and bleakly drizzling with rain. They got into bed, and she straddled him and moved gently until he asked her to stop and just sit there. "I want to know what you would say if I told you that I would come to Valderia, even take out Valderian status. We could get married and buy a farm, and we would be close to your parents, and you would be happy."

She dismounted and lay beside him.

"Are you mad?"

"Listen to me. I can't face going on to become something I know I would hate. You couldn't live at the palace, but I could live here with you because your family is like my family. What would be wrong to buy a farm? Your father would advise us, and you know about it anyway, and I have enough credits to make it work."

"Does your father know about this?"

"No doubt mother will tell him what you two spoke about, if she hasn't already."

She hugged him. "Jackson, it sounds lovely, but what about your studies? All that time and effort gone to waste?"

"Well, no, Jutta Vogel, because once I become a citizen and have a lovely business, with a lovely wife, I would stand as a local delegate!"

"I want to talk to Mama and Papa. Now let me finish my ride Sergeant. I want to get home to my oats."

Horatio was sitting on the bed after a torrid night with Cassandra. He went and showered and dressed and bit her ear. "Get up and come down to breakfast. I have to talk to you, and our agent will be there, so shake a leg. I will see you there in a few minutes, so don't keep me waiting."

She felt like saying that she would be there when she was ready and not before, but his tone suggested there might be something important she should know, so she was showered and dressed and looking at her bleary-eyed best in ten minutes. There was a man she didn't know, and they were drinking coffee. They both stood and nodded to her as she came to the table. Coffee appeared, and she was glad of it.

"This is my agent, Teddy Bates, and he works for Wu here in New London. This is Cassandra, Teddy, and when we have had breakfast, I would like you to tell her what we have in mind." They ate, and Horatio excused himself. "Work won't wait, sorry." Tell her the story, please, Teddy."

"Now, Cassandra, let me fill you in. Wu Intergalactic Enterprises has an office here as you know. Business delegates come in and out of New London quite a lot. Wu has a service for those called the 'Meet and Greet' section. Visitors are met and then welcomed to the city. We have several girls and men to do this. Wu likes business contacts to see the city and to be entertained, and the staff does this. Wu has, for example, boxes in all the major theaters and entertainment centers. Our hosts and hostesses have apartments in the best part of the city that are maintained and paid for by Wu. You, for example, would have—" He consulted his pod.--"23A St. James Park; do you know it?"

"Oh yes, it's magnificent there."

"The girls make sure the Wu clients are, how shall I put it . . . happy. The same goes for the female clients. Now, Cassandra, you have all the right qualifications. You come from an excellent family, you are very well educated, and if you will forgive me for saying so, you look wonderful. You are used to meeting and greeting important people for your father, so it wouldn't be a chore, would it?"

"What are you saying, Teddy. Is this an 'escort' service?"

"Certainly not. If a client wants to repay you for your kindness and makes you a gift, then that is between you and the client, but I have to warn you, Cassandra, that if you asked for credits from a client, then we would have you on the skids so fast you wouldn't know what hit you. Wu has a reputation that cannot be questioned in the business world. Most of the girls give an excellent service and receive a lot of gifts, usually credits, and they benefit from that. On top of your excellent salary package, you would be a rich young woman in no time."

"You mean, don't you, Teddy, I become a high-priced whore?"

"On the contrary, Cassandra, you have to decide what you want. Whores set the price, and you won't and don't. Now to be brutally frank, although you have a five-star education, your family is about bankrupt. Your father gambled it away, and your allowance next year won't be worth enough to keep you in shoes, will it? You have no job skills, you're not trained for anything, and you don't have much to offer except your looks and your pedigree. You can become totally independent of your family and make a large sum of credits if you play your cards right. You will be living at a very desirable address, and Wu does have a clothing allowance in the package. You have to look the part, after all. Now, drink your coffee, and I will show you over to 23A St. James. It may help you to make up your mind, and while we are there, I can go through the contract. No harm looking, Cassandra, is there?"

Binkie went to the hotel in the late afternoon, and Horatio came down to greet her.

"Sorry Binkie, I have been so busy that time got away with me. What do you want to do? There is a wonderful show on at the Royalty Gardens. Would you like to see it?"

"Horatio, all the tickets were sold out in twenty-four hours, so that is out of the question."

"No, sweetheart, I have a box there that we rent all year, every year, so we will have the best seats anyway. We could have a wonderful dinner and then go there, and then, we can do what we fancy. What do you say?"

She hugged his arm. "What can I say except yes?"

"Good, now what do you want to do now? I have to work. I am sorry, but I can't escape it. If you want to go up to the room . . ."

"How long will you be?"

He shook his head. "Maybe an hour or two?"

"Oh, you go. I can amuse myself. I'll be here when you get back."

In the lobby she ran into Cassandra, who greeted her like a sister. "Binkie, darling. Are you here with Horatio? Well, come up to my room if you have to wait. I have something to tell you." She was twisting a key on her finger with a fancy plas-steel ring plate. There was a large number 23A on it.

Horatio was mildly indignant. "No, Binkie. I did not make her a whore! Teddy offered her a very well-paid job, and she obviously took it. I wasn't there. Our agent, Teddy Bates, negotiated a contract with Cassandra; she signed it and seems very happy.

"But isn't that really another way of putting her on the market?"

"I think we got Cassandra off the hook. Her family is broke; she is a wonderful girl and needs the credits. We give her an excellent salary as well as her dignity."

"Dignity?"

"We ask her to meet and greet people. We don't ask her to do anything else, and if you read the contract, Binkie, you will see for yourself. If Cassandra wants to accept gifts from visiting businessmen, then we have no control over that, have we? Now, if you come to dinner with me, and I pay for it and take you to the theater and pay for it, and you get into bed with me, does that make you a whore?"

"Do you think I am a whore, Horatio?"

"Binkie, I think you are very sweet, and I would happily give you anything you wanted, and not because you shared my bed. I think you are, well, lovely. Now, if we made love, and you asked me for five hundred credits--"

"Then I would be a whore!"

"I would seriously consider that you might be!"

"Is Teddy going to talk to me about a contract, Horatio?"

"Would you consider it?"

"Goodbye, Horatio!"

"Did you think I would? No, Binkie, I admire you too much for that and want to know you much better. Are you going to forgive me?"

"After we get back from the theater, I might."

She forgave him in bed. It never occurred to her that in some ways, she was doing almost exactly what Cassandra would be doing.

Jutta and Jackson were in the big kitchen with Mama and Papa, the dog and a jug of cider and were serious. Jackson was telling the story.

"You see, Papa, sir, I know I can't go on and spend another two whole years at the Diplomatic Institute. I might have if I hadn't met Jutta, but even if we waited, she would just be unhappy being a wife of a starched-up diplomat. So I thought, if we bought a farm here, and you advised us and helped us a bit, we could all be happy. I have enough credits to buy the valley if the truth be known, and my father wouldn't object if I was going into a sound business. I think he knows my heart isn't in the diplomacy thing, anyway. He would insist on a sound business, whatever it is, but I need your advice, sir."

"What do you think, Jutta?"

"Papa, I am afraid that if he does come here and finds he has done the wrong thing, then . . ."

Her mother was angry. "Oh, Jutta, all I hear from you these days is doom and gloom! Your boy here is bending over backwards for you, and all you do is make his life a misery. Won't go and live in a palace with him, won't live on a farm with him; what is the matter with you?"

"Boy, if you want a good place, then Muller's across the valley is coming up for sale. He has arthritis and won't get treated because he says it is Aton's will, silly old beggar, and since his wife passed away . . . Now he has room there for a wonderful vineyard and access to the river, and you could run sheep or better still, cows. We need another dairy, and there is a lovely little shop in Grunvald for ice--"

"Papa Vogel! Give the boy a chance! Why don't you take them down there in the truck, talk to old Muller, and ask some questions? I wonder what has come over you sometimes."

Muller had an old but a well kept farmhouse with all the outbuildings in good repair, and he showed them round. "What's this, Gerhardt? Your place not big enough anymore?"

"No, Muller, I"m buying up the whole valley. Going to run elephants, and they need a lot of room."

"Elephants? Are you mad?"

"They give lovely dung, Muller. One good elephant and you have enough manure for a hectare of cabbages."

Jackson was laughing; Jutta had a red face.

"Mr. Muller, my father is teasing you. My boy here and I want to get married and buy your farm so we can live close to Papa and Mama."

"Then why didn't you damn well say so, Vogel, you old fool?"

"Because it was worth it just to see your face, Henrique, that's why."

"Have you got the money, boy? I won't give it away."

"I think he may have if you don't make it too steep, Henrique. I think his father has a few credits under the mattress, somewhere."

"Well, who do I talk to, him or you?"

"Sir, would you speak for me? You know more about these things than I do."

"If you trust me to do that, boy, I shall be happy to, but you know I have to charge an agent's fee."

"Papa!"

"Well, in your case, I might just forget it. Come on Muller, let's go inside, and you can give me a drink of that awful cider you make, and we can haggle."

"Haggle, Vogel? Who said anything about haggling?"

They stood in the cobbled yard and hugged each other.

"I love you, Jackson"

"I love you, Jutta."

"We are sure about this, aren't we, Jutta?"

"It would make Mama, Papa and me happy. You will love it too because I would do things in bed with you that would make you the happiest boy in Grunvald."

"You, Jutta Vogel, are a wanton vixen sometimes."

"Sometimes I surprise even myself, Jackson."

Papa came out, shook hands with Muller, and they climbed in the old farm truck and went back up the hill.

"Well, Papa, well, what did he say? Don't keep us hanging in the air, what did he say?"

"Wait til we get home so I can tell your mother as well."

Jutta groaned. "Papa, you are killing us!"

"I liked the place, Jutta, and if he wants half the planet, I want to buy it."

"Now, boy, enough of this half the planet talk. I'll tell you when we get home."

They sat in the parlor. "How much does he want, sir?"

"He wants twenty thousand credits for it."

"Is that a fair price, sir?"

"Well, boy, it is a bit steep, but you have nothing much to spend on it. The old house is like this one, old but looked after for I don't know how many generations."

"So you told him we'd buy it?"

"No, Jutta Vogel, I did not. I told him we were going to look at another farm down the valley, and that if he wanted to sell, his price could come down a bit."

"Oh, Papa, and we were about to move in."

Her mother sighed. "Jutta, have some patience. Your father is right. Wait a couple of days, and Muller will come down a little, and if he does, you will have a really well-kept farm."

"Thank you, Mr. Vogel."

"Just make Jutta happy, boy; that's all the thanks I need,"

"I have to tell Maria and Kurt!"

"Jutta, wait. Wait until you sign the deed, girl!"

"Well, I can tell them we are thinking about it, can't I?"

"What are you going to tell the army? Haven't you got to serve another year before you can resign your commission?"

"Well, Jackson won't finish at Belvedere for a few months anyway, will you?"

"I think I can sit my final exams earlier than scheduled, if my tutor approves."

"Just bribe him, Jackson."

"Jutta Vogel!"

She clung to him and kissed him, and her mother smiled. "I think she may love you, boy."

"Now, Mama, let's plan the wedding!"

Maggda was talking to her plants. They had been brought in from Circe, a jungle moon that circled a world that was spawned from a binary system on the edge of nowhere. Her plants had cost a small fortune because they were alive in the sense that they had senses, and they grew in vast colonies on their home world and were not unlike insect-eating plants on Old Earth. Maggda loved her plants in the way that pet owners love cats or dogs. She was an intelligent and aware girl, but she was convinced that her plants understood her every word. She had observed that if she spoke loudly and harshly, they retreated. The "blooms" shrank back into the stems and closed, but if she was sweet and praised them and told them how lovely they looked that morning, they would extend and chitter away in tiny, high-pitched voices. They were listening to her praises, and when she gave them baby talk, they waved slowly and appeared to be looking at her. She had stopped short of giving them names but had come close.

"I am not sure if they like you, Ong. Don't raise your voice when you come in here, because it upsets them."

"As if I would. So now I have to take second place to a plant?"

"They are not just plants, Davvd, you can see that. They understand what I say."

"My mother had a dog that she thought could do that."

"No, seriously! They are doing a lot of research on Circe now. Simon told me. These so-called plants may well have group intelligence. They appear in large colonies, and you know that plants do communicate with each other even on Old Earth, so why not these?"

"Communicate with me, Lady of the Long Legs, and tell me where we go today?"

"First, I am going to see Simon, and then we can round up my parents and maybe eat with them."

"So we are all systems ready and go?"

"I have to see Simon. I want to know where next. I want a really good assignment, lots of allowances, and no more dead and dying for the time being."

"I think you are being a bit optimistic, Styxx. Bet you he has you off to Valderia again doing a follow-up on those brain-damaged soldiers."

"Then I quit."

"What, and go without paying off your debts? Tsk-tsk, Styxx. He would sue you!"

"Tell you what. You pay my debts off, and I can owe you. Then I can go when I like."

"How are you going to repay me?"

"I'll have to think about it. Why do you make my life complicated when I had just sorted it out?"

"All right. I will pay it off for you. No complications. Consider it done. We go to see Simon and I'll transfer the credits then and there. How about that?"

"How can I repay you?"

"Don't have to. Just being here with you in a warm bed on a cool Martian night is payment enough."

"I am not sure about this, Ong. Can I think about it a bit more?"

"Take as long as you like. Now, are we going out? If so, say goodbye to your babies."

The admiral was reading the decodes. Sonna was working at her screen.

"What is the next assignment for Ong?" she asked.

"None until he finishes his leave on Mars."

"With Maggda."

"He deserves a break."

"He could have come home with me, you know that."

"Don't I excite you enough?"

"Arthur, just lately you are about as exciting to me as a limp lettuce."

"That's unkind, Bea, after all I have done for you."

"What have you done for me lately, Arthur? Ruined two pairs of stockings, split my blouse; do I have to go on?"

"What do you want?"

"I want a well deserved hike up to major. I want to go and do a combat course. I want special weapons training, and I want to get my shuttle license upgraded. I am going stir crazy in here. Now, you hold me back, and I will make a lot of noise."

"Sounds a hell of a lot like blackmail to me."

"Yes, I thought it might. Reason being, that it is."

"I could say no."

"And I could release the tri-dee of you making love to me on your desk. A girl has to have an insurance policy, Arthur."

"I like you, Captain. You think like a real Fleet officer. I shall miss you. Now get yourself booked onto those courses and find me someone who can take over from you as soon as you can."

"Is the bra size important, or not?"

"Get out of here, Captain, before I change my mind!"
"Major, sir. Remember, I just got promoted?"
"How am I going to forget it?"

Galactic Federation had finally tightened its grip on the Governing Council of Valderia and had begun asking questions of the High Command, or those who remained. Even the local press was active, despite a ban on reporting government business. The acting chancellor came under scrutiny. He denied ever having known that they had sent "brain-damaged" infantry to fight on Valentine, but the screws were tightening every day. Galactic Media smuggled out reports and interviews despite the bans. Voight was being squeezed. The families of the generals who had been sent to trial were talking and talking. It was about "duplicity" and "treason", and Voight was feeling the heat. Those on trial were also talking and talking and were naming names. Voight was one of them.

Freya Schiff, who moved in exalted circles, having had her son tell her the story, began a campaign that moved opinion against Voight in a way that he hadn't foreseen. She knew all the Governing Council and their wives, and they listened.

Kurt Schiff had emerged from the debacle as a person who had shown his humane side by protecting the innocent from exploitation. Valderia loved war heroes. Schiff was one, and his pedigree was in no doubt. His mother was more important to him now than she had ever been. She had felt guilty and was doing her best to make up for it. Her son would get what he wanted now, and she wasn't going to abandon him. They met in the apartment over a bottle of wine after a meal.

"Now, Kurt the time has come to ask for dissolution of the entire Governing Council and High Command and to press for new elections. This is all politics from now on, my son. I suggest you take over as chancellor and demand a set of elections to 'put the planet straight.' The public is on our side; Galactic Federation would be on our side, but they can't do it. That would be interference in planetary sovereign rights, so it has to come from the inside, and you could do that. So things look better, don't they?"

"I am not sure if I am up to this."

"Well, my son, let me tell you now that you have to be, or let Voight get his way."

"Mother, you are wonderful. Nothing would have gone right if you hadn't stepped in."

Yes, Kurt, it is wonderful what playing a cello can do! Now, pretty Maria, what are you two going to do?"

"I don't know."

"Well, let me tell you. When Kurt gets what he wants, and they hold elections, and we have a new Governing Council, then I suggest you get married with as much pomp and splendor as you can raise; you get every media outlet here, and you have a public holiday and make it a day that will make all Valderia forget we were ever in the Galactic black books."

"You will become an empress, Maria. Think about it."

"I am, and I am terrified, Kurt."

"That makes two of us."

Freya finished her glass and stood up. "Get me a robocab, please, Kurt, and I will let you two get to bed."

She kissed them both and went out into the night, and they went to bed.

Simon smiled as Maggda moaned about her long-standing debt, and when Davvd said he would pay it for her, she told him not to. It was her obligation, and she would weather it. Davvd and Simon smiled behind her back.

"Two things, Maggda. I could send you back to Valderia right now, and you must know that things are hotting up there. Your friend Schiff looks like he will take the chancellor's post, Voight will get deposed, and they will hold elections. Good, solid, political news. Nice easy work, liaise with the Valderian Press office, and a lot of dirt if you dig a bit. Your friend Schiff has started a campaign to get rid of the whole rotten lot of the top dogs, and his mother is acting like a campaign manager. Freya Schiff, world celebrity cellist once married to the old chancellor's brother. Isn't that enough to get you going?

Now for a nice, human interest story. The young lieutenant who was with the big horse, Jutta Vogel? Talk is, and this is unsubstantiated, that she is going to marry young Jackson Wu, the Wu Dynasty son. How's that for a surprise? Terrific story there, all tears and tissues. Good background stuff for the women's holo mags, and what's more exciting than a wedding? 'Poor girl marries rich prince'? I can see it now. Galactic will pay your expenses, you can stay at the Palace, and we'll send three staffers to go with you. Now, Maggda, if that isn't enough to excite you, what will?"

"No bodies or mangled corpses?"

"This is all high society stuff, Maggs. I know they stab each other in the back all the time, but there isn't a lot of blood."

"What do you think, Davvd?"

"Well, it's not my business, but I think you could do a lot of good there, if you can get the story out of there without the censors screwing it up."

"Staying at the Palace in a premium suite, with expenses?"

"Promise."

"And you will send me to E5 after that to follow up on the tribe?"

"Well, maybe, but not first class, and it would be a very short trip."

She looked out of the windows, and Simon winked at Davvd. "When do I pack?"

"Well, when Davvd has to go back to Fleet. A few more days? I'll get things moving from here, and you are on your way. They sat and drank.

"Pity you can't come with me, Ong."

"Maggda Styxx, I would just be in the way, and who would want a couple of Fleet Security agents listening to us through the bedroom wall? In any case, I have the feeling that while you are doing your job on Valderia, I may be asked to do something the other side of nowhere."

"Well, while we have five minutes of domesticity, let's drink to happy days."

In the kitchen the "plants" chattered to each other and twined together as the red light faded.

Mrs. Madeline Gruber was incensed. Her husband had believed Voight and had walked into a trap and into jail, and she and the family were now literally, fighting for their lives. It was dangerous to criticize. It was impossible to publicly denounce the acting chancellor or risk being asked questions by men in dark uniforms who wore face shields. She knew it happened and had just accepted it as part of planetary security, but now that it had happened to her, she was coolly angry.

Freya Schiff had spoken to them all, and they felt that with this woman making noises that no one dared, they could get some redress. Madeline Gruber was having her leg re-created. She had always had good legs and was vain about them. When her knee was attacked by arthritis, she decided to have a total rebuild and grow another. Doing it made her walk with a stick, but as the nano surgeons built the tissues back, she was hoping that the new knee would soon be as good as the other. That took time but she was prepared to wait. Her friends discussed the future, as if there was going to be one for them after their husbands had been sentenced. They hired the most expensive lawyers this side of the galaxy and rested their hopes on the clause that might get their men off the hook, and that was that they were all acting under orders from a higher authority. It was a slippery slope, but they lived in hopes.

Davvd said goodbye to Maggda. She was wearing just her Bare Head dressing gown, and they had just enjoyed each other's warmth, sleeping in until they had to move. He held her close and told her to take care.

398

"Take care, Ong."

"Enjoy Valderia. Tell a good honest story, and you will soon be out of there."

"And where will you be?"

"If I knew that, I would be truly telepathic."

"Goodbye, Ong."

"Goodbye, Maggda."

He went back to Alpha Six and waited.

Jackson went back to Little Lotus and the palace, Crystal and his mother, and they waited for his father to come back from Old Earth. His mother hugged him and asked him, and he told her.

"I can get an early finals, and then I will graduate at the end of the year and won't have wasted my time there. I need to buy the farm, and then Jutta and I can get married, but I have to have Valderian status, which gives me temporary citizenship. Do you think Father will let me?"

"Well, Jackson, you are past legal age, so he can't really stop you, but you are going to need credits, and he could be tight about that. I suggest you wait and see how the land lies. I know that he wanted you to go on and become a high-powered diplomat, but we both knew your heart wasn't in it. Now, he tells me that Horatio has left Fleet and is doing a really good job all round and might have found a wife too. Who knows, I might get grandchildren after all!"

"I shouldn't say this, Mother, but I know Jutta would love a baby, so you won't have to wait long!"

"She is a lovely girl, Jackson, and will make a wonderful mother, I can tell that. Just keep her happy."

Horatio and Binkie were weighing each other up, and Binkie felt that even though he was bit rough round the edges, she could smooth that off. He was surprisingly kind in many ways and had made her feel warm and wanted. She still played the shy violet, wore clothes that were genteel yet full of style, blushed a little in the bedroom, kept her small privacies to herself and kept him guessing. He liked the sight of her and the smell of her, her shyness and the way she submitted, as if he might hurt her. He was aware that she was a very smart girl, and he knew that she had had two quite long lasting affairs with rich young men who had given her a gallop, but he could forget that. He wouldn't want her to know his bedroom background, but she had followed his career there from those who had reported it, so she knew more than he thought she did.

So they came together, and if she felt she was falling into the love trap, he was becoming convinced she would get his father's approval and make a good Wu wife. She spoke like a lady, had all the credentials and would fit into the lifestyle like a key into a well-oiled lock. He took her to meet his father, who was still in town. His father looked at her and smiled at her and thought his son had got a bargain. Binkie's parents were delighted. She had done well. Not every day one could get a daughter married to one of the Wu's. They were looking forward to some share of the overflow. It was all now just a matter of putting the wheels in motion, and it was all going to happen.

Maggda arrived, booked into her hotel, spent money and saw her team, then began to sift the newscasts and the noise from the public and the Chancellery. She tried to get an interview with Acting Chancellor Voight, but he denied access, and an official in a very smart uniform came and told her to go home. She went to see Freya Schiff and did a wonderful "mother of the next chancellor" interview with all the background, and then she spoke to the man. Kurt played along like he had rehearsed every line. She and her team interviewed the dissident wives and families of the suspect generals, and Mrs. Gruber was a natural. She walked with a stick, looked distraught and had the sympathy of the crowd. Her favorite expression--"betrayed"-- became the headline for the holo. Her team interviewed Jutta Vogel, who was beautifully pink and blushed at the mention of marriage to Jackson Wu but didn't deny it. She went into the women's holo mags and tri-dees as the face of the future. The dirt continued to get dug up. The local Valderian Press, suppressed for years, confided with Maggda and Galactic.

The Governing Council attempted to suppress the newscasts, and a crowd threw stones at the gates of the offices. The security police were not doing very well at keeping protesting crowds off the streets. They often felt sympathetic. The army was put on alert in case of civil riots. Freya Schiff was questioned and laughed at them.

"If you want a civil war, arrest me.!"

Kurt and Maria went to the barracks every morning. Maria put a request to her C.O. for Jutta to come in and help, and her miserable boss agreed. He just had to see the Jutta Vogel who was going to become the wife of a billionaire. Maria and Jutta now had company and loved it. Both felt they now had a purpose in life. They gossiped about weddings. Jutta already had her dress. It was going to be the traditional one that she had worn for Jackson. Jackson's father was a bit tough but asked about the business prospect and wanted to come and see it for himself, but he put half a million credits into Jackson's account just to see the project started. He asked Sylvia about Jutta, and then he asked Crystal, who couldn't lie, and he was satisfied. Of course the girl was a lovely country girl with simple tastes, but then, so was Sylvia when he first met her. It wouldn't hurt to have a Wu engaging in some worthwhile business activity on Valderia, and if Jackson had to take Valderian status, who cared? Business was business.

General Voight was unhappy. His makeshift High Command was threatening rebellion.

"Why should we trust you, Voight? Everything points to you selling the boys down a black hole. It wasn't just coincidence that

401

Federation had a cruiser sitting there in orbit waiting to snatch them, was it?"

"Is that what you think, Goethe?"

"And all those promises about the families. What about those?"

"Listen to me, all of you. Federation has us in a corner, and the damn media is stirring up the dirt all round. With the Schiff woman running a hate campaign and squealing all the time, we have to think, not fight amongst ourselves."

"Can't we just disappear her?"

"Oh yes, a brilliant idea, Donant. That would be very helpful for public opinion. Those days are long gone, and you know it. Lay a finger on her, and we would probably have an army revolt as well."

"So, smart-ass 'diplomat', you tell us."

"We pour cold water on it. We get Schiff in to take over as acting chancellor until we can get it ratified through the council. We all step down and ask the Galactic Federation to help supervise elections through the army for a new high command."

"Isn't that what they want?"

"Federation won't be able to do it because it contravenes the planetary sovereignty of Valderia, so they will allow us to do it. We can virtually put in who we want, as we have always done, but publicity-wise, we are bending over backwards to please them. You step down, I step down, Schiff gets the hot seat, and we regroup. We have to keep the army sweet. Get the rank and file off our side, and we will have a rebellion. That is what the Schiff woman and her followers want. Schiff himself is keeping a low profile and letting momma do it. Can't have his name dragged through the mud, can she?"

"How are we going to do all this?"

"We need a very public occasion. We need a ceremony of some sort, prior to the full-on installation of a new chancellor."

"Schilling, you have the floor."

"A big parade out the front of the Chancellery. We install Schiff with pomp and ceremony, and we announce that we are all stepping down to make way for the new head of planet to set up his new advisers and all that. We stand up, and all vow to serve the new man, should we get chosen by the delegates—"

"Right! Full-on public view, advise the press to do the whole thing on holos, lots of color, lots of pretty soldiers all marching past, lots of flags and regimental banners, brass bands and drums, and Schiff taking the salute."

"Very good PR, Schilling."

"And we have enough good men to choose from when the public thinks we have done exactly what they wanted."

"That sounds to me like diplomacy, Schilling."

"My father used to call it smoke and mirrors."

"How do we vote, gentlemen? Are we for it or against it? Good, now let the staff know when and where and get the gold paint out. We are going to need a lot of it. Who handles Ceremonial these days?"

On Old Earth, the Galactic War Crimes Commission had decided that the defense offered by the generals' lawyers of "acting under orders from a higher authority" wasn't going to work. Since they were all on the board of the High Command, they were all complicit. It was absurd to suggest that they worked in secrecy, especially since their judgments involved the army at every level. The next move, according to the Galactic Federation, was for all of the High Command to be called to answer for their actions, or lack of them. These four would be the test case, and after that, the whole crew would be questioned very closely. When Mrs. Gruber heard the news, she began to get very coldly calculating. "Damn Voight!" She planned a revenge that would end her torment.

Muller sold the farm for eighteen thousand credits, threw in the stock and went off to his long-suffering daughter. Gerhardt did a survey and then called in the tradesmen, and they modernized the bathroom from a stone slab and a tub to something Jutta could be proud of. Jackson went back to Belvedere and paid his fees and sat his early finals, and was rewarded with an honors pass. He put that down to the stability of his relationship with Jutta, the Wu endowment of a million credits to Belvedere, and the hope for the future. He now knew where he was heading.

Horatio took Binkie to Little Lotus and showed her off to his mother, who thought the girl had promise because she knew most of the artists whose works hung in the palace gallery and identified the tea set by its vintage and maker. She went with Crystal and inspected the exotic blooms and identified their planetary origins to nearly ninety-three percent accuracy. She and Crystal seemed to be joined at the hip. Binkie, lovely, quiet, and shy Binkie, was a great help.

Solomon thought that a big wedding was in order. Five hundred guests, maybe? He left the arrangements to Sylvia and Crystal, who never forgot anything. Binkie, lovely, shy Binkie, pretty Binkie, was already calculating to the last credit how much she could screw out of Horatio after the wedding. Lovely Binkie, who had Horatio totally captivated, knew exactly what button to push next.

Maggda and her team worked and worked, and she made sure that everything she sent was verifiable. The news of the huge parade and the enthroning, albeit a stopgap measure, of Kurt Schiff, was wonderful. She had more details than she knew what to do with. There seemed to be a lot of gold paint being put on railings and statues, lots of troops rehearsing salutes, and armed vehicles covered in flowers going around. There was a burgeoning air of excitement building up. Maggda and her team were even allowed to speak to the "average citizen" in the street. That was one of the biggest breakthroughs.

Jutta and her father were in the kitchen of the Muller farmhouse when Wulf barked, and there on the doorstep was a man whom Jutta thought may have been dead. It was Corporal Heinz.

"Oh Heinz, you brave man, I didn't know what had happened to you! Are you all right?"

"Well, ma'am, I am now. That mine made me deaf, and they fitted me with new ears so I can hear again, but I have been invalided out. I wondered what happened to you when Jane took off with you."

"Come inside and meet my father, and we can have a drink and talk. You have no idea how pleased I am to see you."

As Mr. Vogel pointed out, she and Jackson would need a responsible hand on the farm, and if they could find Webber, the old team would be back in harness. Heinz made mention of the horses, and Gerhardt co-opted him. They drank to a rosy future.

Maggda was exhausted. She sat in the bar of the Palace with her crew and began to get quite drunk. They had all worked themselves to a standstill. They had worked wonders, and there was nothing they had left uncovered. They had spoken to shy soldiers back from the Valentine front, who were selected to speak, but who seemed quite genuine. If they were worried about their families should they say the wrong thing, then they didn't show it. Maggda missed Davvd Ong very badly, and it wasn't just in the bedroom. Ong got under the skin, and she knew it.

Kurt, Maria and Freya sat in the small apartment and drank good wine and talked. They had tried to cover all the angles, and if no one trusted General Voight, then they had to take the chance. Maria was nervous. How could she be an empress?

Freya comforted her. "You will be the best empress Valderia ever had, and you know why? Because you will have risen from the people, from the army, from the grass roots, my dear. Nothing could be better training than that."

Maria and Jutta thought about it. "Both of us, Maria, are probably the luckiest women in the whole of Valderia right now. Two little simpletons, marrying two of the most important and rich men on this planet. Can you sleep at night? Because I can't." And then they laughed.

"Who needs sleep, you vixen!"

"When are you and Kurt getting married, do you know?"

"It's a kind of government decision. Things have to settle down first, and then I suppose we will have to go through all the pomp and ceremony, with two thousand guests and brass bands, and me hoping I don't make mistakes or falling over the train. I wish we could just go on as we are."

"I think that Jackson is hoping we can have a simple ceremony here and then go to Little Lotus and have a kind of reception there. His brother, Horatio, is going to marry some girl he picked up on Old Earth, so being the older brother, he gets the precedence."

"Picked up?"

"Well, Jackson says, that his father told him to get into society, find a woman and get married!"

"Wonder what she is like?"

"High class, used to wealth, highly educated, probably speaks six or seven languages, that sort of thing. Jackson told me that Horatio would have a list of things to look for and check off!"

"Like Jackson did with you, you mean?"

"Well, Jackson had a short list. Took one look at my rosebuds and said, 'Marry me!'"

"You make me laugh, Jutta Vogel."

"Come and see what the bathroom looks like now. Sylvia Wu can have her palace; I'll settle for this."

Major Sonna was covered in dirt and face paint and exhausted. She and the rest of the advanced weapon training group were in a "jungle", and things kept reaching out to trap them. Their heavy laser weapons were hard to aim and fire, and she had been "killed" at least three times. The sergeant instructor was scathing.

"Listen, girlies, this isn't a game. Of course the weapon is heavy; of course it catches on every vine and branch; of course you are tired. You want to fall down and sleep? You get two minutes before the creeper comes out of the forest floor and strangles you. So keep going, stay alert and stay alive."

She struggled on, and when they reached "Safety", she and the others collapsed in a heap.

"Now, girls, you need toughening up. You will carry that weapon at all times from now on, until it feels like a magic wand. Get used to every nut and bolt on it because it will save your life. It should feel like another part of your arm. If I see any of you without that weapon after today, you will be off this course, is that understood? Now get off your fat backsides and turn around, because we are going back in there. Let's go, fairies!"

Davvd Ong was shown into the admiral's offices by a young female lieutenant who was a little shy but immensely decorative. "He will see you soon, sir."

"May I ask what happened to Captain Sonna?"

"She was promoted, sir, and has gone on a few courses, I understand."

The admiral told him to sit and offered him a drink. He accepted, which surprised the old man. "You usually refuse, Ong. What's brought about the change?"

"I think I may be getting domesticated. Spend time with Styxx, and you want to settle down."

"I would think she was *very* unsettling, Captain, but I mustn't get personal."

"I wouldn't be offended. May I ask what prompted Sonna to leave you?"

"You make it sound as though we were married. All right, we were very close, but she wanted promotion and a change of pace, and she has gone on to get back into Fleet Active Service, like you."

"So what Aton forsaken planet are you going to push me off to now?"

Have you heard of Circe?"

"Yes."

"Then you must be one of about five people who has. What do you know?"

"Well, not much. Jungle and hot and dense. Exotic plants that Maggda says are telepathic because she has a little set of them in her kitchen, and they talk to her. That is what she tells me. Apart from that, I know nothing."

"Go through to the other office, and Lieutenant Bridger will show you some holos. Fleet wants to put a base there because there is going to be a lot of exploration taking place. They will need some Fleet presence because the talk is that there is a multitude of rare elements, oil, and all the usual resources, and it becomes strategic if that is the case. The satellites say there is. The Galactic Federation has given permission for Ong Wu Industries to survey it and then take out mining leases, if the place looks worth it."

"So why do I have to go there?"

"I want you to accompany the first construction crew. Just act like a watch dog. You have a good nose. We are dropping in the usual accommodations. Mostly robotic staff, of course, who will set up, and then when they have finished, we put in a security team to literally 'hold the fort' until we can get the specialists there. All very routine, Captain."

"Why do I find that phrase worrisome, sir? Why do you need a watchdog?"

"The original survey team had five members working out of an orbiter pod. Two went missing, and there was no trace of them. The company recalled the three. Talk was that they just got lost. The jungle there is very dense with strange electronic disturbances to communications. The tracers the personnel were wearing when they went missing just stopped functioning. There was no further trace of them. Satellites showed nothing. The jungle swallowed them up, in a manner of speaking. Just take a few good men and . . .

"Smell the dung, sir?"

"Something like that, but nothing immediately. Where is the Styxx girl now?"

"On Valderia, working hard and paying off her debts to Galactic."

"Well, look hard at those holos that Bridger will show you, check out the notes, and you can take a bit of leave if you want. Go and sweet talk Maggda Styxx. She will probably appreciate it. Federation is getting tough with Valderia, we understand."

"Yes sir."

"Get those holos under your belt, and then you can go. That will be all, Captain."

"Thank you, sir."

Jutta and Jackson were in the parlor.

"I will have to be back for Horatio's wedding, you know that. You and I will be there as husband and wife, which will be nice. It will be a huge affair, but we can enjoy it as a once in a lifetime spectacle, and my father and mother will be happy."

"I wonder what she is like, this 'Binkie' girl?"

"Well, Jutta Vogel, soon to be Jutta Wu, I would guess very beautiful and highly polished and smart. I think she saw Horatio coming, stuck out a foot, and he fell for her."

"Just like I did with you?"

"Very amusing, Vogel. Have we done everything for our ceremony, or not?"

"Mother and I have tried to think of everything. It is a pity your parents can't be here."

"Maybe better if they just see us in the holo's, because when my father goes anywhere, it is like a travelling circus. He has so many staff and security around that we would need another five Palace Hotels just for them. Better if we can get married the way we met. Just a simple ceremony, with lots of lust!"

"Did you get the confirmation of the temporary citizenship?"

"On my pod record. When they saw "Wu," they asked no more. I don't think the hundred credits I gave the clerk was a hindrance either."

"Are you joking? You didn't bribe a government official, did you?"

"No, I just wanted to see your pretty pink face get pinker."

"Don't joke about things like that, Jackson. We could end up in real trouble. We want to be trouble free from now on. I just want us to have our farm and be happy and live a nice simple life. Your brother can have all the honors and the noise and the publicity."

"And Maria and Schiff?"

"Poor Maria. She is going frantic. She doesn't think she can cope with it all. The same way I felt in your parents' palace. They are going to get married after this naming of the new chancellor thing, but it won't be for a while. She says maybe longer than she thought. When Kurt gets named, there will be a huge parade and all the pomp, bands and fifty-one gun salutes, and everything. She will be in the front row of guests out in the forecourt with Mrs. Schiff and a crowd of other important people. She just wants it all over and done with."

"I know just how she feels."

"I have resigned my commission."

"Did they accept it?"

"When I told them I was marrying you and gave the C.O. five hundred credits, there was no problem."

"Very funny. Now let's get back to your place. I am hoping your mother will have finished the guest list and cooked something good for lunch."

Bea Sonna was exhausted and trying to stay awake on the simulator, which gave a three-dimensional and real speed approach to a mystery planet. Getting there was easy; getting down there was no picnic. She was not allowed to just let it go on automatic but had to pilot it down.

"Now, Major, you get into a situation where the panel goes on you, you get to fly it down by the seat of your pants. No other way. Now, you will have all the warning lights, so try not to burn up this time. This is the second shuttle you've destroyed this week, plus you and all your crew. So concentrate. You keep wanting to extend the wings too soon, and that is a bad move. Be cool, Major, and just get the feel of it. Now we are going to start afresh. Drop off the cruiser, and away you go. Trying to bring it down with wings extended at a thousand kilometers an hour won't work. You got that now?"

She sighed and tried to stay alert. She wondered why she had left the cozy clutches of the admiral in favor of this, but at least the simulator didn't want to put its control yoke down her blouse. "Concentrate, Bea, concentrate, and you can have a rest."

On Valderia, in uptown Valhalla, they were setting up the forecourt for the ceremony. Barricades and chairs and podiums on the front steps, lots of gilding, a bandstand and a saluting dais, and snipers' posts set up on the roof between the ancient statues. The Security Force was rounding up known criminals and sending them off to work in the fields on the basis that grappling with a cabbage left little time to think about crime.

Freya Schiif had been allocated a seat close to the front of the guest area, and she had managed to swindle Maria a seat next to her. The bride to be was still incognito as far as Ceremonial knew. It was going to be a large crowd. Maggda and her team had holo cameras and overheads all set up, and she was going to join the guests. There was a press section behind the seats that would contain the families of those generals who had been sent to trial. The army would stage a huge march past, the air arm would fly past at two thousand kilometers an hour just to make its presence felt and deafen everyone. There was an abundance of flowers in tubs and banners and bunting, and everything had been scrubbed clean and then scrubbed again. It would all come together in the morning, if Aton smiled.

At her parent's house, Jutta dressed in her pretty, traditional dress and turned in front of the mirror and thought dreamy thoughts. Up in the small room above the stables, Jackson dressed in the clothes of a Valderian gentleman farmer and grinned at himself. The guests appeared, and the celebrant arrived in his yellow robe with his gold circle on his brow, and they gathered around the "Circle of Aton" laid out with yellow and white flowers. The girl who had taken their holos shot at the Blue Boar was there with cameras and recording equipment and loving it. Jutta and her father and mother came out of the house and walked to the spot facing the sun in front of the celebrant, held hands and looked down. Then Jackson was called, and he came and took Jutta's hand with her mother and father on either side, and they swore the oaths and vowed to love and respect, and Jackson vowed to take her and care for her for all their lives. Then they closed their eyes and faced the sun and were told, "Aton smiles upon you." Jutta's mother was in tears, Maria and Kurt were laughing and feeling very emotional, and Wulf barked.

They had a huge meal at long tables, and after everyone had kissed them both and said goodbyes, they went with their father in the old farm truck to their farmhouse, and Gerhardt went to a shed and brought out a puppy to guard them and their home. It scampered about and established its territory by peeing on the door post. It was a little Wulf.

Later, in the big bed, they just held each other and listened to the silence, then slept until the gift of the red rooster and hens from Heinz woke them. They had begun a new life. Jackson had never felt so complete and content.

The parades began at ten cycle and got off to a roar of engines and a multitude of crashing boots, brass bands blaring, and flashing swords and bayonets. They sat in the gilded chairs, and the generals gathered, looking polished and creased with medals flashing in the sun, and then Kurt appeared in a dress uniform, but with no medals and hatless. He stood beside

General Voight, who had mounted the podium, and waited. There was a hush.

Next to Maggda, Mrs. Gruber shifted her walking stick, and as Voight cleared his throat, she raised it and pressed the firing button on the concealed laser and shot him through the chest and again through the head, and he fell back. The sniper on the roof shot Mrs. Gruber through the chest, and Maggda dived for the cobbles as panic took over. She was covered with blood and just lay there. When in doubt, freeze.

It wasn't the best ceremony she had ever attended, but it was news on a very big scale. Her recording devices and the cameras were still floating or hovering, getting it all as the security forces fanned out, the vehicles pulled away, and the stunned crowd was on the verge of an indecisive panic when the voice of Kurt Schiff boomed across the vast forecourt. He told them who he was and that he was now the chancellor. He told them to go quietly and do as Security asked them. He told them to act like true Valderians and not be afraid. He asked them to accept him as their new planetary ruler, and said that he would take them and Valderia to a new era that would bring them honor.

It was masterly, and it had the desired effect. He told them he would speak to them at twelve cycle and that they could trust him to tell them the truth. Freya Schiff was in tears with pride, and she and Maria hugged each other. The crowd dispersed, and Maggda picked herself up as the corpse of Mrs. Gruber was taken away. It was a time of change for Valderia and all of them. Maggda just wanted to rest and have Davvd Ong reach out for her and make her feel safe, but he was the other side of the galaxy and lost to her.

Davvd Ong rode the Fleet battleship *Royal Crane* to the binary system and dropped down to the base on Circe. Everything steamed and smelled of rotting vegetation and blossoms and fecund growth. He stood there in the clearing next to the raw and ragged new buildings being slung together by the robotic construction crew when from the chaos came a figure he knew well.

"Captain Ong, I presume? Welcome to Ceres," and she laughed.

It was Major Sonna.

THE END

Lightning Source UK Ltd.
Milton Keynes UK
UKOW051145281211

184445UK00001B/299/P